Praise for *The Last Ember*

"A banquet of everything I crave: history, conspiracy, secrets, action, adventure. Strap yourself in and hold on for some heart-throbbing, throat-grabbing, pedal-to-the-metal pacing. Levin captivates the reader with both plausibility and imagination. *The Last Ember* is a prize to be savored. A superb debut from a talent that bears watching."

—Steve Berry, author of *The Charlemagne Pursuit* and *The Amber Room*

"One of the most capaciously learned of this new breed of hero makes his appearance in Daniel Levin's debut...[Levin] brings the Roman ruins gruesomely to life...[H]e seems to know the Eternal City's every nook and cranny.... It's not giving away the plot to report that [Jonathan] Marcus survives his adventures without resorting to gadgets or guns. Let's hope Levin brings him back to teach us, once again, the benefits of a classical education."

—*Los Angeles Times*

"Levin is an excellent writer and even better researcher...*The Last Ember* is a terrific achievement for a debut novelist." —*Providence Journal*

"In his fast-paced, erudite, and original debut, Daniel Levin reveals a vivid world where archaeological, legal, and religious secrets swirl together into a thrilling nexus. Its rich texture and global cast of characters ignite genuine suspense and intrigue."

—Matthew Pearl, author of *The Dante Club*

"*Da Vinci Code* addicts will enjoy Levin's debut, a dense, complicated novel of religious suspense . . . [a] fevered pace." —*Publishers Weekly*

"Cracks the code of solid storytelling...An attorney, Levin's bachelor's degree was in Roman and Greek civilizations. He does what many textbooks can't—make these eras feel as vibrant and as fresh as they were in reality."   —*South Florida Sun-Sentinel*

"What a glorious journey from the tumultuous world of today's Middle East to the imperial world of Roman antiquity and then back. With a flair for detail, drama, and elegant prose, Daniel Levin keeps us transfixed by his page-turning tale of deception, politics, history, and life."
                                                        —Alan Dershowitz

"Levin's religious and archaeological thriller has all the elements needed to appeal to *Da Vinci Code* fans: long-buried secrets, hidden puzzles based on ancient religious texts, and a race around the Mediterranean. With its strong Roman atmosphere, this dramatic and complex debut novel will please fans of both European crime fiction and religious thrillers."   —*Booklist*

"Daniel Levin's novel, written with pathos and conviction, represents a much-needed literary protest against modern and ancient revisionism."
                                                        —Elie Wiesel

"A smart, sophisticated thriller that entertains as it educates. *The Last Ember* is engrossing. Levin knows his stuff and it shows—to the reader's great pleasure. Fans of *The Da Vinci Code* will devour it happily."
             —Christopher Reich, author of *Rules of Deceptions* and *Rules of Vengeance*

"A stellar debut. ... *The Last Ember* shines."   —*The Globe and Mail*

"As Levin's own excitement for the subject builds, it comes out in his characters and in his descriptions; propelling his story forward and creating needed tension...*The Last Ember* is a sophisticated debut that will have readers asking for more."

—*Deseret News*

"The Indiana Jones 'spirit' lives again in Daniel Levin's new book, *The Last Ember*... A must read for anyone who desires a greater understanding of the role of archeology to Christians and Jews alike."

—Examiner.com

"An exciting debut."

—*Deadly Pleasures*

"Following in the footsteps of such authors as Dan Brown and Katherine Neville, Levin gives an ancient history and religion tutorial while weaving a thrilling plot. Readers who enjoy artifact-seeking books with behind-the-scenes tours of real sites will be captivated."

—*Library Journal*

PALAZZO DI GIUSTIZIA

VATICAN CITY

PIAZZA NAVONA

© 2009 Meighan Cavanaugh

Rome

THE GREAT SYNAGOGUE

ARCH OF TITUS

PONTE ROTTO

COLOSSEUM

The Last Ember

DANIEL LEVIN

RIVERHEAD BOOKS

New York

RIVERHEAD BOOKS
Published by the Penguin Group
Penguin Group (USA) Inc.
375 Hudson Street, New York, New York 10014, USA
Penguin Group (Canada), 90 Eglinton Avenue East, Suite 700, Toronto, Ontario M4P 2Y3, Canada
(a division of Pearson Penguin Canada Inc.)
Penguin Books Ltd., 80 Strand, London WC2R 0RL, England
Penguin Group Ireland, 25 St. Stephen's Green, Dublin 2, Ireland (a division of Penguin Books Ltd.)
Penguin Group (Australia), 250 Camberwell Road, Camberwell, Victoria 3124, Australia
(a division of Pearson Australia Group Pty. Ltd.)
Penguin Books India Pvt. Ltd., 11 Community Centre, Panchsheel Park, New Delhi—110 017, India
Penguin Group (NZ), 67 Apollo Drive, Rosedale, North Shore 0632, New Zealand
(a division of Pearson New Zealand Ltd.)
Penguin Books (South Africa) (Pty.) Ltd., 24 Sturdee Avenue, Rosebank, Johannesburg 2196,
South Africa

Penguin Books Ltd., Registered Offices: 80 Strand, London WC2R 0RL, England

This is a work of fiction. Names, characters, places, and incidents either are the product of the author's imagination or used fictitiously and any resemblance to actual persons, living or dead, business establishments, events, or locales is entirely coincidental. The publisher does not have any control over and does not assume any responsibility for author or third-party websites or their content.

Copyright © 2009 Daniel Levin
Cover design © 2009 Roberto de Vicq de Cumptich
Cover photograph of the Colosseum © Walter Meayers Edwards / Getty Images
Book design by Nicole LaRoche
Map by Meighan Cavanaugh

The author gratefully acknowledges the permission to reprint the following images:

Photographs of the sketches of Giuseppe Valadier on page 69 (drawing of an arch of the Colosseum) and 379 (architectural sketch of the Colosseum). Reprinted with permission of Professor Elisa Debenetti.

Reproduction of the Forma Urbis on page 14. Reprinted with permission of the Stanford Digital Forma Urbis Romae Project.

Photograph of the Arch of Titus relief on page 371. Used with permission of Beth Hatefutsoth, the Nahum Goldmann Museum of the Jewish Diaspora, Tel Aviv.

First Riverhead hardcover edition: August 2009
First Riverhead trade paperback edition: May 2010
Riverhead trade paperback ISBN: 978-1-59448-460-5

The Library of Congress has catalogued the Riverhead hardcover edition as follows:

Levin, Daniel, date.
The last ember / Daniel Levin.
    p.   cm
ISBN 978-1-59448-872-6
1. Antiquities—Fiction.   2. Treasure troves—Fiction.   3. Rome (Italy)—Fiction.   I. Title.
PS3612.E92373L37   2009   2009017118
813'.6—dc22

PRINTED IN THE UNITED STATES OF AMERICA

10   9   8   7   6   5

For my mother, storyteller

All references to ancient texts in this novel are real, as is the Waqf Authority—a secretive Islamic land trust that has administered the Temple Mount in Jerusalem since 1187 A.D.

Historians are forgers.

—*The Life of Flavius Josephus,*
first century A.D.

12:15 A.M. Fiumicino Airport. Rome

W hy have I been flown here?" Jonathan Marcus asked the chauffeur, raising his voice over the winter rain.

The downpour of a Roman *burrasca* pounded the hood of a black Maserati Quattroporte sedan. The chauffeur's shirt was soaked, his stomach blousing out like a sack of grain.

"The partner is expecting you, *Signore,*" he said, taking Jonathan's carry-on and opening the back door.

Water streamed down Jonathan's suit pants and gathered on his Ferragamo shoes, but he seemed not to notice. He pointed at Fiumicino's runway lights.

"Underneath the runway where my plane just landed was once the largest sea harbor in imperial Rome. The *Portus,* it was called. Two-thousand-year-old Roman ships are still under there!"

The chauffeur nodded politely. He laid Jonathan's briefcase in the trunk and, when he closed it, was surprised to see the tall young man still beside the open door, elbows on the roof, the wet folds of his white dress shirt clinging to his athletic shoulders. He was staring at the runway.

Jonathan Marcus had returned to Rome, a young corporate lawyer in a navy chalk stripe suit and a loosened Hermès tie, but just ten minutes back on *terra antiqua* and memories from his doctoral work in classics beckoned to him from the stones.

"Signore?" The chauffeur gently pointed to the door.

Jonathan ducked into the car's immaculate leather backseat. In the finished-wood console, a freshly brewed cappuccino steamed in a bone china coffee cup bearing the firm's dignified logo, DULLING AND PIERCE LLP. He was reminded of the firm's mania for formality, and although his jacket was still sopping, he slipped his arms through its sleeves and buttoned it.

"Still not exactly presentable," he said softly, raking back the soaked, brown hair from his brow. Stubble accented the strong angles of his attractive face, darkening his boyish looks.

A digital clock in the center of the console displayed the time in a cobalt blue glow: 00:17 a.m.

Long day, Jonathan thought.

Only twelve hours before, Jonathan was sitting at his desk on the forty-first floor of Dulling's headquarters in midtown Manhattan, another solitary night of document review before him, when the intra-office mail cart delivered a travel itinerary with the word UR-GENT stamped across it like a red sash.

The details were few, listing only the departure time of an Alitalia flight out of Kennedy Airport in three hours and his seat number in first class. This exceeded even Dulling and Pierce's legendary standards for client secrecy. A partner's recent toast at a firm dinner now sounded like an ominous oracle. "With your background in classics, Marcus, antiquities dealers all over the world will want you on their lawsuits, won't they?"

Last month, Jonathan's representation of Dulling client and Roman antiquities dealer Andre Cavetti catapulted him into the spotlight of the antiquities world. The Italian government had brought a lawsuit in a U.S. District Court in Manhattan, alleging that Mr. Cavetti's gallery on Madison Avenue displayed a twenty-inch-high nude bronze statue illegally excavated from the ancient town of Morgantina on the Sicilian coast. Jonathan's cross-examination of the Italian government's expert, Dr. Phillip von Bothmer, curator of Greek and Roman antiquities at the Metropolitan Museum of Art, left the Italians' case a smoldering ruin.

"And the ancient town of Morgantina, Dr. von Bothmer, the site of my client's alleged excavation, when was that town destroyed?"

"Beginning of the second century B.C." Dr. von Bothmer spoke *reprovingly, as though Jonathan had not been listening to his hours of testimony. "Morgantina foolishly backed Carthage against Rome in the Second Punic War. The strata of archaeological dirt is black soot, which indicates that everything in Morgantina was laid to waste at that time. Total destruction."*

"Total destruction," Jonathan repeated. He paused, approaching *the small sculpture sitting on display in front of the witness box.*

"Tell me, Doctor, are you a breast man?" Jonathan said.

A juror laughed out loud, then unsuccessfully disguised it as a cough.

"I'm sorry?" Dr. von Bothmer said.

"Breasts, Doctor." Jonathan cupped his own chest a few inches *beyond his shirt. "Aren't the statue's breasts a little small for you?"*

The lawyer from the Italian embassy exploded from his chair. "This is badgering, Your Honor!" The gallery came alive with laughter. At the Dulling table, the supervising partner collapsed his bald head into his hands.

"The depiction of breasts of Roman women, Your Honor, is a helpful metric to determine the date of a relic's origin: Whether the breasts are una manus *or* duae manus, *Latin terms for one handful or two."* He spoke as though explaining the dullest of courtroom *technicalities. "The expert's theory that this statue is pre–first century would require a more voluptuous representation, exhibiting a*

pagan influence. These slender breasts betray a Christian influence more fitting of a later artifact from, say, Byzantium."

The District Court judge flipped up her reading glasses, turning to the witness.

"Is that true, Dr. von Bothmer?"

For the first time, the witness appeared uneasy.

"Pagan imagery of a voluptuous Venus was replaced by a tamer Christian portrayal after the first century. So"—he cleared his throat—"perhaps . . ."

"Perhaps," Jonathan repeated, walking toward the jury. "Then how is it that a statue with a Christianized bust could come from Morgantina? According to your own testimony, Morgantina had been nothing but ashes for two hundred years before Christianity's rise."

Dr. von Bothmer shifted, a nervous glance at the Italian counsel's table.

"Let me withdraw that question, Your Honor," Jonathan said after a moment, allowing the professor off the ropes to get him squarely in the jaw.

Jonathan used the same respectful tone but now without the smile. "Doctor, didn't your own museum just return the Euphronios Krater to the Italian Cultural Ministry, having learned it was illegally excavated? Isn't it possible that by offering your testimony here today—a testimony even you know to be academically tenuous—the Met hopes to avoid a renewed interest by the Italian embassy in other items in the museum's collection?"

Dr. von Bothmer opened his mouth to speak, but no sound came out.

Jonathan walked back to the defense table. "Cognoscere mentem, cognoscere hominem," he said, just loud enough for Dr. von Bothmer to hear. "Know the motive, know the man."

*S*ignore," the chauffeur said.

The Maserati had stopped in Piazza Navona in downtown Rome. The chauffeur let the engine idle.

Jonathan leaned forward. "I haven't received any information where to go."

The chauffeur said nothing, only pointed to the floodlit Baroque façade of a sixteenth-century palazzo at the far end of the piazza.

A line from Jonathan's graduate work in Latin literature came back to him. *"Ducunt volentem Fata, nolentem trahunt,"* he murmured.

His eyes met the chauffeur's in the rearview mirror when, to Jonathan's amazement, the chauffeur translated the phrase from Seneca.

"'Follow the fates,'" the chauffeur said, "'for they will drag you anyway.'"

2

*A*fter midnight in an abandoned warehouse along the Roman shipping docks of Civitavecchia, Comandante Jacopo Profeta removed a snub-nosed Tanfoglio combat pistol from its holster. As commander of the Italian Cultural Heritage Protection, or Tutela del Patrimonio Culturale, the world's most sophisticated antiquities crimes investigation unit, Profeta knew artifact raids had grown increasingly dangerous. He had more than 250 officers in eleven regions to assist investigations, ranging from staking out a deadly excavation site in Pompeii to conducting tonight's raid of a portside warehouse in search of illicit antiquities.

"The Taliban used the opium trade to finance their activities," Comandante Profeta often reminded his officers, "but terrorists have discovered a new source of revenue: antiquities. These men are not archaeologists. They are murderers."

Profeta's flashlight cut the warehouse's blackness. The rank scent of fermented olive oil mingled with the stench of sewage and rust. Weeds had reclaimed the warehouse's overgrown floor. He caught a glimpse of himself in a shattered windowpane. With receding silvery hair cropped close to his skull, gold spectacles framing his lumbering brown eyes, and a gray beard in need of a trim, Profeta resembled a strong but aging sailor too long at sea.

"Watch yourself, Profeta," he said. "Not as young as you used to be."

Lieutenant Rufio, a recent transfer from Palermo's antiquities division and Profeta's new *primo tenente*, first lieutenant, turned on a ground spotlight, flooding the warehouse in a low purple illumination.

"What are they trying to hide?" he asked, taking in the size of the room. "The Trevi Fountain?"

"*Comandante,*" the shaken voice of the squad's youngest recruit, Lieutenant Brandisi, interrupted, "there's something on the ground."

In the center of the room, an ancient marble column lay across the floor. The column had been crudely ripped from an ancient ruin and its base was still attached to a section of *pepperino*, a volcanic stone on which the column had stood. It resembled a stone tree trunk pulled out of the ground with the roots still attached.

As Profeta and his officers approached the column, a cloying woodsy scent of pine pitch and cinnamon filled the air.

The marble column had been sawed lengthwise, the top portion removed to reveal the column's hollow interior. A mournful silence came over Profeta's men as the contents of the column became visible.

The preserved corpse of a naked beautiful woman lay suspended in a yellow pool of herbal oils, her pearl-tone flesh as flexible and lithe as at the moment of death.

Profeta's men stared at the corpse as though it might move. In the viscous fluid, her open blue eyes and flushed cheeks preserved the colors of life. Her mouth was partly open. Her hair was rolled meticulously into two spiral volutes, large tight curls that resembled the scrolls of an Ionic capital, a hairstyle popular among ancient Roman noblewomen. Four long strands of sutures fanned up her torso from her narrow waist to her breasts. If those gashes had once ripped her open, they would have been deathblows even today.

Profeta walked slowly around the corpse. The source of a fleeting rancid smell became apparent. The woman's left leg had been propped up, and her kneecap broke through the surface of the pool. Decomposition had attacked with the force of an animal, eroding the flesh down to the bone. The sinew around it had decomposed to a gangrenous black seaweed. Above the liquid, a horsefly gnawed at the black cartilage. Out of respect, one of the officers waved it away.

Beneath the liquid's surface, her supple white skin was as pristine as a fossil preserved in amber. Profeta knew of ancient Rome's embalming techniques of using honeyed cinnamon, wood tar, and smoldered cedar oil, which Pliny the Elder called *cedrium*, to keep microbes at bay, but this level of preservation from the ancient world seemed impossible.

A small circular tattoo of Latin and Greek words encircled the corpse's navel in a deep burgundy script.

"Phere nīkē umbilicus orbis terrarum," Profeta said, reading the tattoo aloud. "Victory in the navel of the world," he translated.

"What kind of sick hoax is this, *Comandante*?" Lieutenant Rufio asked.

But Profeta did not hear him. He leaned over the corpse, searching for a smallpox vaccine scar below the right shoulder, or dental work on her small, uneven teeth, or signs of having worn footwear on her calloused feet—any indication of modernity. There was none.

"Rufio," Comandante Profeta said, "get a coroner in here."

3

Outside the golden cupola of the Dome of the Rock in the Old City of Jerusalem, four men on a scaffold wore stolen restoration jumpsuits with "UNESCO" printed across the back. Their forged and laminated identification tags bore the seal of the Jordanian Hashemite Cultural Ministry, which gave them permission to restore the shrine's exterior medieval blue tiles. But restoration was not their intent. Their muffled drills whirled through the marble latticework around a second-story window to access the sanctuary below. They worked with the well-rehearsed efficiency of bank robbers burrowing into a vault.

"Sheikh Salah ad-Din, we have removed the window," said Ahmed Hassan, a talented young bomb maker.

Salah ad-Din did not acknowledge the boy, keeping his gaze on three laptop computers fixed to the base of the scaffolding. He ran his hand over the black stubble that carpeted his head. His copper complexion, thin straight nose, and light chrome-colored eyes made him appear more European than Arab. His meticulously clean-shaven face and wired spectacles gave him a thoughtful, academic air, as if he might have been a young faculty member at Nazir or Gaza University. He did not resemble a man whom Interpol had hunted for years and who was known in the organization's files only by his nom de guerre, Salah ad-Din, the name of the twelfth-century Islamic warrior who defended Jerusalem from the Crusaders.

Grid images of the Dome's interior octagonal structure rotated on the laptop screens. To Salah ad-Din, the Dome of the Rock's perfect mathematical proportions were far more important than the shrine's religious significance. Those proportions had determined the length of rope required for his team to rappel inside.

With military focus, Salah ad-Din checked the black digital chronograph on his arm: 1:13 a.m. "We must enter immediately," he said. "Come, Professor."

"We are not ready yet," replied Professor Gustavo Cianari, a balding little man. He nervously removed his glasses, which revealed eyes as beady and squinting as a nocturnal animal's. "The passage in Josephus does not reveal the artifact's location, only that it was moved through a Hidden Gate."

"Which is why I rescued you from your academic dungeon in Rome," Salah ad-Din said. "You are perhaps the only living scholar in the world who could have deciphered the hidden gates' location from the tattoo on that woman."

"*That woman* was the last princess of Jerusalem," Professor Cianari said, offended by his employer's disrespectful tone. "She chose death in the Colosseum, rather than reveal the meaning of *umbilicus orbis terrarum*. 'The Navel of the World.' You saw her level of royal preservation."

"And as of ten minutes ago, so have the carabinieri. Your Italian police just discovered our research facility in Rome. We must find the artifact *tonight*." Salah ad-Din stepped toward the small man. "Think of it, Professor. An artifact for which Titus conquered all of Jerusalem, but still failed to bring back to Rome."

Reluctantly, the professor followed Salah ad-Din up the scaffolding and through the spade-shaped hole where the arabesque window had been. Now inside the shrine, they stood on an interior ledge forty feet above the sanctuary floor. The professor's trepidation gave way to awe at the grandeur of the Dome of the Rock's interior. The vast octagonal sanctuary resembled an orientalized Saint Peter's Basilica, a cavernous pavilion of inlaid marble walls and decoration funded by centuries of Arab conquest. Rays of moonlight checkered through latticework windows and converged on the gilded shrine's most precious treasure: the Foundation Stone, or Al-Sakhra, which was the natural summit of the Temple Mount—a large promontory of bedrock that stretched thirty square feet inside a protective fence and was further secured by the red crossbeams of motion detectors hovering above it.

Cianari's archaeology students in Rome never ceased to be astonished that the enclosed floor of bedrock was more precious than the gold dome above it. "The world's largest encased jewel," Professor Cianari called the thirty-square-foot stone. It was the most sacred ground on earth to three religions: the very spot described in Genesis where, according to Christianity and Judaism, the patriarch Abraham bound his son Isaac at the sacrificial altar and where one thousand years later Solomon would build the Holy of Holies of the First Temple. A rectangular depression in the center of the rock is said to have been the resting place of the Ark of the Covenant before the Babylonian sack of Jerusalem in 586 B.C. And, according to Islamic tradition, Muhammad ascended to heaven from this rock, and the faithful still view the embedded hoofprint of El Burak, the horse that transported him.

"There, 'The Navel of the World,'" Salah ad-Din said, pointing at a hole in the southern end of the rock. "When the Roman troops breached the Temple walls in A.D. 70, the priest moved the artifact through there into a tunnel beneath the stone." He spoke as though seeking a fugitive who had escaped only hours before.

"Unfortunately, whatever lies beneath the Foundation Stone is inaccessible," the professor said, secretly relieved that this man's obsessive quest might finally come to an end. "The motion detectors prevent any access to the stone from the ground."

"From the ground, Professor," Salah ad-Din said, "but not from above."

Ahmed assisted Salah ad-Din to slip his legs through a Velcro harness and secured a high-tensile-strength rope through a belay device.

"You intend to rappel *through* the stone?" Professor Cianari said.

As his answer, Salah ad-Din stepped off the ledge and descended through the sanctuary's dim air as though climbing down the rungs of moonlight. The professor watched, in horror and fascination, as Salah ad-Din floated through the center of the Dome, moving forty feet downward and ultimately through the aperture in the Foundation Stone—easily avoiding the flickering red lasers that protected the sacred rock's perimeter. From the ledge the professor could hear the harness jangle as Salah ad-Din touched down inside the crypt beneath the stone.

The professor heard the sound of imams approaching the outer doors of the sanctuary. The empty harness returned to the ledge. Two men brusquely grabbed him, shoved his stout legs into the harness, and lowered him after the sheikh. As the professor descended, he noticed, to his amazement, that the Foundation Stone's surface was more textured than he ever imagined. Crevices in the ancient surface undulated like frozen storm waves, as if making visual the ancient Judeo-Christian tradition that from this single stone, the entire earth expanded in all directions.

And Cianari now regretted that it was he who had led Salah ad-Din here, to the exact center of the world. *Umbilicus Orbis Terrarum.*

Professor Cianari tightened his grip on the harness, moving through the opening of the stone. Beneath this sacred rock, unborn souls were said to gather, and the sudden sound of whispers chilled him to the core.

He disappeared through the hole in the Foundation Stone and his breathing shortened, as though somehow knowing he was forever parting with the world above him.

4

Jonathan stepped out of the sedan into Piazza Navona. The tourists, caricaturists, and performers who gave the piazza its life during the day were long asleep, the outdoor tables stacked and chained for the night. The bristles of a street-cleaning *spazzatrice* hissed past.

He walked across the floodlit palazzo and soon recognized the baroque façade of Dulling's Rome office. He had seen it in an article of *Architectural Digest*, displayed in the firm's lobby in New York. The firm took pride in the palazzo's sixteenth-century design by a wealthy papal family, and its five ornate floors, which had been the scene of numerous banquets for popes and Roman nobility throughout the centuries.

The palazzo's giant doors were as tall as a drawbridge, and two feet thick, of iron-studded oak. Jonathan lifted the knocker, an angry wolf's head sinking its fangs into a circle of brass, but before it dropped, the massive doors began to shutter and creak, opening slowly.

Jonathan walked into the palazzo's column-lined courtyard, the gravel's crunch echoing with his every step. The only trace of modernity was overhead, and understated: The red light of a surveillance camera blinked beneath a sculpted marble angel perched above an archway. The lens trained on Jonathan as he moved across the courtyard.

The latest-model BlackBerry rattled in a holster on his waist. A text message prompt appeared on the color screen.

To: Jonathan Marcus
From: Bruce Tatton (Managing Partner Europe)

He clicked the message.

Upstairs. Conference Room.

Jonathan remembered how the ancient historian Suetonius described Roman generals transmitting their battle plans to their field officers by hiding them inside clusters of grapes. The firm's partners sent their marching orders via BlackBerry. *More the world changes,* Jonathan thought, *more it stays the same.*

At the end of the courtyard's northern colonnade, a grand oak door had been left ajar.

He climbed a marble staircase, and on the second floor, a hallway lined with sculptured niches led to a *salone* refitted as an executive conference room.

Beneath a crystal chandelier, Bruce Tatton leaned over a deeply polished oak table, his knuckles flat on it, as though he were braving a gust of wind. He was a solidly built, middle-aged American, with a full head of expensively cut gray hair carefully combed back, and thick black eyebrows. His black satin bow tie and the matching moiré silk suspenders under his dinner jacket suggested he had been pulled out of an important affair to put out a fire at the office.

At Tatton's side was Andrew Mildren, a Dulling and Pierce associate formerly of the London office. Mildren was seated at the table, looking as obedient as a terrier. He was wearing a smart gray pinstripe suit and a massive Windsor knot of navy satin. Mildren was a few years senior to Jonathan and was gunning for partner. In every law firm, one associate makes an art of defending the devil. Mildren's inspired defense of a firearm manufacturer (safety-latch malfunctions) had recently persuaded a London High Court to dismiss the case with prejudice. A great victory for the Dulling London office and the European firearms market. Rumor was that it earned Mildren an additional six-figure bonus—in sterling.

In front of the conference table, in a glass display case, lay two ancient marble fragments. They were large, each three feet across, and fit together like an oversized jigsaw puzzle. Bruce Tatton hauled the coattails of his dinner jacket to one side and rounded the conference table toward Jonathan.

"You were the bloody Rome Prize winner in classics, Marcus," Tatton began without preamble, pointing accusingly at the marble fragments.

"Recognize them?" With a certain violence, he unknotted his bow tie so that it dangled from his neck.

Jonathan approached the ancient stone fragments, his eyes not leaving them.

"They're fragments of the *Forma Urbis Romae*," he said.

"Meaning what?" Mildren snapped.

"'The Form of the City of Rome' is the literal translation from Latin. It was an enormous stone map of Rome carved in the late second century A.D. that spanned more than a hundred feet in diameter." Jonathan moved his hand above the marble engravings. "You can still see the street markings of ancient Rome. These curved concentric markings were an arena of some kind."

"One hundred feet in diameter?" Mildren said. "Bloody huge map."

"It was," Jonathan said. "Covered an entire building wall in the Roman Forum. Most early scholars thought the size was a myth, an exaggeration, until the Renaissance, when pieces of the map slowly began to resurface, found among building materials in the garden patios of Roman nobility and stairway decorations inside the loggia of Saint Peter's."

"Your expertise in classics, Marcus, has become"—Tatton lifted his eyes to the ceiling mural—"*relevant* to our client who owns this artifact. Can you recognize which part of Rome these fragments depict?"

"It must have been a large amphitheater of some kind, most likely the Colosseum. These rectangular grooves inside the lines must be the gates."

Mildren slid a thick folder across the conference table. It stopped abruptly under Jonathan's hand.

"That is the *fascicolo*, or case file, for those fragments."

"What case?" Jonathan said. "I haven't received any information."

"Our client anonymously loaned these two fragments to the

Capitoline Museum," Tatton explained as though setting the rules of an athletic match. "The Italian Cultural Ministry alleges they were stolen from the Italian state archives in Rome decades ago. The ministry's expert witness is a UN official who claims to have seen these fragments last year, stamped with the very words that strike fear into the heart of every antiquity collector, 'Archivio di Stato,' meaning from the state archives."

"Where did he see these fragments?"

"*She*," Tatton said. "She claims to have seen these fragments while investigating an illegal excavation in Jerusalem near the Temple Mount."

"Their witness saw *these* fragments exactly?" Jonathan asked. "The Forma Urbis shattered into thousands of pieces when the Goths sacked Rome in A.D. 455 and scattered them across the ancient world. Scholars discover new fragments every decade or so."

"The UN official identified an inscription on the underside of the fragments," Tatton said.

Jonathan crouched and looked up through the display case's glass bottom. Three Latin words were carved roughly into the underside of the stone.

"'*Tropaeum Josepho Illumina,*'" he read aloud, his voice sounding cramped under the display case.

"Can you translate it?"

"*Tropae* means 'monument' or 'trophy.'" He recalled the origins of the word, how ancient soldiers staked the ground where a battle would "trope," or turn in their favor. "*Illumina* means 'revealed,'" he continued, "or, literally, 'brought to light.' The inscription is broken off there at the end, but it was probably *illuminatum*, meaning 'revealed,' as in, 'A monument revealed to . . .'"

"To whom?" Tatton said, folding his arms expectantly.

"Josephus," Jonathan said, standing back up. "A monument to Josephus revealed."

"You did your graduate work on Flavius Josephus, I'm told," Tatton said. "At the American Academy in Rome."

"Years ago. The research wasn't worth very much, I'm afraid."

"Worth the cost of a first-class plane ticket from New York, wasn't it?" Mildren said brittlely. "Take your jacket?"

Jonathan gladly removed his damp suit jacket, but Mildren did not take it. Rather he motioned vaguely toward an upholstered chair at the conference table. Jonathan stepped forward but could not bring himself to put the wet jacket on the antique fabric. He tucked it under his arm instead.

Tatton picked up a manila file on the conference table and read aloud. "Rhodes scholarship in first-century Roman literature and a pre-doctoral Rome Prize for your thesis on the ancient historian Flavius Josephus." Tatton looked up. "Indulge me if I have a question or two."

Jonathan pointed to the fragment. "I'm not even certain this inscription refers to Flavius Josephus," he said. "We have only a partial name on this inscription, and, besides, the fragment here mentions a *monument*. The historian Flavius Josephus wasn't very popular in the ancient world. A monument in his name would have been unlikely."

"Why?" Mildren asked.

"Few ancient authors have been as vilified as Flavius Josephus," Jonathan answered. "He was a Jewish general who defended Jerusalem, but once captured by the Romans, later handed over information to help them breach Jerusalem's city walls. It didn't help his historical reputation that Emperor Vespasian, to thank him, awarded him Roman citizenship after the war. His historical account of Rome's siege of Jerusalem became an instant best seller in the Roman world. The age-old question is, was his eyewitness account from the perspective of a political realist or a murderous traitor? His credibility is questionable."

"Then Josephus has something in common with the UN official who says she saw these fragments," Mildren said. "Her credibility is questionable, too. She claims to have seen the identifying stamp, 'Archivio di Stato,' on this part of the fragment." Mildren pointed at the smooth end of the marble slab. "On our fragments, no stamp," he said proudly.

"But that portion has been sanded smooth," Jonathan answered, pointing to the side of broken marble stone. "Artifacts are often altered to escape museum identification. It's like a quick paint job on a stolen car." Jonathan inspected it even more closely. "Looks as though someone even tried to artificially age that section with chemicals. Proper archaeological testing—"

"Will not take place," Tatton cut him off. "Mysteries of the ancient world do not concern us here. Archaeology may dig up the truth at all costs, but legal discovery does not. Our client's version of history is the only one we seek to advance. That presents us with a single question: How to discredit this UN official's testimony by showing these artifacts were not the ones she allegedly saw in Jerusalem?"

"Why didn't her UN team recover these fragments in Jerusalem?"

"Because she couldn't," Tatton said. "She claims to have found the fragments inside"—he waved his hand dismissively—"a *hidden* research facility of some kind. But when she brought UN investigators back to the site, it was an empty cavern. No trace of artifacts anywhere. Even her UN colleague who stayed behind was no longer there."

"Well, *some* of him was still there," Mildren said. "The UN investigators found a piece of the chap's brain on the floor. All that was left of him." Mildren's tone was upbeat. "That'll work very well."

"Excuse me?" Jonathan said.

"Mildren means from a legal perspective, of course," Tatton said. "Her colleague was killed on the site, the trauma of which"—Tatton shrugged innocently—"we will argue has altered her recollection. Truth is, her restoration efforts are respected as among the best in the UN, but administrators describe her as impulsive and overzealous." Tatton picked up a yellow-bordered magazine and tossed it onto the table's center. "See for yourself."

It was a *National Geographic*, an issue dedicated to a remote dig site in Sri Lanka, but the cover photograph was more befitting of a glossy fashion magazine. A woman's tan, fine-boned face framed by wet curtains of ash blond hair, a semiautomatic rifle slung across her bronze shoulder. Jonathan stared not at the image but at the caption: "Dr. Emili Travia: The Angel of Artifacts."

"Across the world of antiquities conservation," Tatton said with contempt, "her nickname was instantly born."

"Marcus, you all right?" Mildren said. "You're white as a ghost."

But Jonathan's mind was elsewhere. He was picturing Emili at the academy seven years ago, where she was a Rome Prize winner in preservation, her elbows resting on the floor of her preservationist's studio beside an open bottle of wine, her eyes squinted in laughter as she demonstrated to Jonathan how to scrub an ancient mosaic Roman tile covered with two-thousand-year-old dust.

"Yes," Jonathan said, the shock so palpable he could taste it in his throat. "Fine."

"Marcus, I want you to assist our efforts to cripple Dr. Travia on cross-examination tomorrow," Tatton said. "What you bring is background knowledge, historical expertise. Look over these artifacts and prepare a memo attacking her testimony from every historical angle. I don't want any surprises."

"Tomorrow?"

"You'll have ample time to prepare," Tatton said. He pulled back his sleeve to check a wristwatch laden with more gold than an ancient funereal bracelet. "Seven hours. We'll meet you at the Palazzo di Giustizia a little before nine."

"And do change your suit," Mildren said. "Looks like you slept in a washing machine."

Tatton grabbed his overcoat and stood in the doorway. "It must feel a bit strange for you now, being back in Rome after all this time. A five-star hotel like the Exedra will be a bit different from those graduate student days, no?"

"Like a different life, sir."

"Perfect." Tatton flashed a smile, but it was one Jonathan could not quite decipher. *"Roma, non basta una vita,"* Tatton said. For Rome, one lifetime is not enough.

5

Comandante Profeta stepped back from the corpse in the abandoned warehouse, taking in the high-technology equipment of the operation. Flat plasma screens were strewn across the floor, their polymer liners bashed in. Computer server towers lay on their side, one with a fresh bullet hole through the CD drive.

Someone knew we were coming.

"Old manuscript pages over here!" called out Lieutenant Brandisi. "Dozens of them, *Comandante!*"

Profeta crossed the room to find a pile of loose parchments on the floor. They looked centuries old. He picked up one of the pages from the pile and then another.

"Flavius Josephus," Profeta said.

"Who?"

"The first-century historian who chronicled the Roman siege of Jerusalem," Profeta answered, pointing at an illustrated title folio page. "These parchments were torn from Renaissance manuscripts of Flavius Josephus. Someone here was smuggling—"

Profeta stopped suddenly.

"*Comandante?*" Lieutenant Brandisi said.

"*Queste sono pagine che scottano,*" Profeta said. These pages are hot.

"As in stolen?" Brandisi asked.

"No, their temperature," Profeta said, putting his palm to the center of the parchment. The area was so darkened and brittle it might have caught flame. "There's a heat source in the pile," Profeta said, alarm rising in his voice.

Profeta's concern caught the attention of every officer in the room. Throughout his long career, the *comandante* displayed an eerie intuition during his raids to recover stolen antiquities. In a recent documentary, *Fugitive Masterpieces*, Profeta's team had given up searching a fish-packing plant when, to the documentarian's delight, Profeta stabbed one of the fish with a pen, revealing a shipment of glistening Byzantine glass smuggled in the bellies of frozen carp. The episode's title was a play on Profeta's insight and his surname: Il Profeta, the Prophet. His gray beard reinforced the image of Old Testament wisdom, but "the Prophet" was a nickname Profeta never used and never liked. Whether it was superstition or a fear of blasphemy that made him bristle at the nickname was unclear. "No one is a prophet in his own lifetime," Profeta often said. The illicit antiquities trade was growing dangerous enough without tempting fate.

Profeta knelt in the pile. He felt the heat intensify as he sifted through the parchments. He dug more rapidly, sweeping the pages to the side until he uncovered the orange, luminescent coils of an old space heater housed in a dented steel box.

"A heater!" Lieutenant Brandisi said, relieved. "They left a space heater on."

Profeta examined the device. It was old and low-grade with a rusted grate and no thermostat. Beneath the heater, two tubes filled with clear liquid were duct-taped to the basement floor. A dark trail of liquid led to the walls, which glistened as with condensation. Small curls of smoke wisped off the floor closest to the heater.

Profeta leaned closer to the substance and bristled at its sharp, acidic scent.

"Everyone out of the room," he said evenly. He recognized the peroxide-based explosive, triacetone triperoxide, a gelatinous substance that he knew was responsible for new airline regulations prohibiting liquids in excess of three ounces. A few hundred grams of the gel could produce hundreds of liters of gas in a fraction of a second. The walls were coated with it.

"But the body—" Brandisi said.

"Go," Profeta interrupted, straining to keep his voice calm. "These walls are coated with explosives."

The officers scrambled out of the warehouse. Making sure he was the last one out, Profeta looked back and saw the column.

All this evidence will be destroyed.

He ran back toward the column and plunged his hand into the thick yellow liquid. He worked to lift the puttylike flesh of the corpse's hand above the surface and pressed her fingers on the back of a manuscript page, making five ocher-colored fingerprints. A thick lock of her hair was floating freely, and Profeta grabbed it. He raced through the warehouse's darkness and out the door, dodging through the dock's obstacle course of barnacled propellers and rotted wooden dinghies. Twenty years before, his kneecap had been shattered by a tomb robber's shovel, and his sprint still resembled an awkward sideways gallop.

Profeta saw his team racing in front of him toward six unmarked carabinieri cars that secured the perimeter of the dock. The cars were decrepit on the outside, but beneath their weathered frames, they were outfitted with bullet-repellent windows, Kevlar-coated tires, and a modified Italian engine designed to outrun even the newest German commercial roadsters. The officers inside them were completely unaware of the imminent explosion.

He hoped they were parked far enough away.

The waves of an incoming storm jostled the tugboats noisily against the docks, their oversized tire bumpers squeaking against the wood pilings. The noise made his own shouts inaudible.

"Get back!" he screamed, flailing his arms above his head. "Get—"

The dock beneath him shuddered, and Profeta dove over a low concrete street blockade as a blast of ovenlike heat pressed him against the dock's damp wood. The windows of the moored tugboats shattered. Bricks rained on the police cars like cannon shot. A small rusted propeller impaled a plank inches from Profeta's arm.

After a moment, Profeta lifted his head; gray ash clouds billowed out of the warehouse as rain sizzled on the dock's charred wood planks. Dizzy from the smoke and unable to hear a sound, Profeta saw the red beacon lights of a cruise ship pull into a distant pier. A few feet in front of him lay a dead egret, blackened from the explosion. He willed himself to stay conscious, although he drifted, seeing the egrets of his youth, flying over the sun-bleached docks of Salerno. Slowly his hearing returned and he did not welcome the intrusion. The inevitable chaos of shouting officers and screeching tires surrounded him.

6

Jonathan sat alone in the firm's conference room. He put down the legal file and stood up to stretch his legs, walking toward the two ancient fragments inside their glass case.

"Emili," Jonathan said softly. "What did you get yourself into?"

Jonathan carefully inspected the inscription along the fragments' bottom. TROPAEUM JOSEPHO ILLUMINA. Other than the peculiar Latin, nothing was out of the ordinary. If the word *illumina* was the full word, it was mistakenly conjugated in the Latin imperative, but it wouldn't be the last time that street graffiti would be grammatically incorrect.

Tatton's voice echoed in his mind. *Mysteries of the ancient world do not concern us here.*

Jonathan grabbed his coat, stood up from the table, and walked to the panel of light dimmers beside the door.

Get some sleep, Jon, he thought, scaling down the lights. The conference room was dark, except for a low halogen light hanging above the display case. The beam of light spread over the stone map making its gray marble nearly white where the ray was strongest. The light then spilled onto the floor through the glass bottom of the case, except for directly beneath the fragment, where a large shadow traced the contours of the stone.

Something caught Jonathan's eye, and he crouched beside the case, inspecting not the fragments but the shadow beneath them. In the midst of the shadow, some of the halogen's light appeared to break through to the floor, casting various lines. Jonathan stood up, and looking at the top of the map noticed that the concentric curves depicting the Colosseum allowed light to pass through the entire half-foot of marble to the floor.

Jonathan ducked again. The light illuminated vaguely formed Latin letters inside the stone's shadow as though through a small projector.

He suddenly felt a long-dormant scholarly exhilaration, like what he had experienced during his graduate school days when after weeks of research a tattered papyrus became legible.

Jonathan now understood the words of the inscription, *Tropaeum illumina*. The imperative form. A command to "light," as in "to shine light on the stone." The grammar on the underside of the fragment was not an accident. It was an instruction. *Shine light on the stone.*

He pushed the display case, wheeling it a few inches until it rested directly beneath the ceiling's halogen light. With astonishing clarity, the light projected an uneven row of Latin letters illuminated against the stone's shadow.

ERROR TITI

"Titus's mistake," Jonathan translated. He grabbed a pen and scribbled on an Alitalia napkin from his jacket pocket. "A steganographic message," Jonathan said, referring to the ancient art of invisible writing.

He backed out of the room and hurried down a corridor lined with museum-quality Piranesi engravings. Jonathan could hear Mildren's voice on a phone call and saw that one of the office doors was ajar. He knocked on the door and pushed it open. Mildren sat at his desk, speaking into a wireless headset. It was nearly two a.m. and Jonathan guessed it was the New York office on the other end, six hours behind European time. *Does this guy ever sleep?* Jonathan thought, waiting in the threshold.

"I'll ring you back," Mildren said, removing the small headset from his ear. "Yes?"

"Have we had an expert look at those fragments?" Jonathan asked.

"You're the expert," Mildren replied, leaning back in his office chair, arms crossed on his chest. "No others. Client's instructions."

"Because I think there is some kind of . . ." Jonathan paused. "Some kind of message engraved inside the stone." He pointed toward the corridor. "I can show you if you'd—"

"Inside the stone," Mildren said flatly. "A message inside the stone."

"Carved inside, yes," Jonathan said, handing Mildren the crumpled napkin where he drew a messy three-dimensional image of the marble fragment. "The top of the fragment depicts a location in Rome, just like other fragments of the Forma Urbis. But the carving of the Colosseum's arena is deeper than it appears, allowing light to pass through the marble. On the reverse side someone chiseled cracks, which look natural, but really they filter light in the shape of letters. The halogen's beam above the glass case projected onto the floor the words *Error Titi*, 'Titus's mistake.'"

"Titus's mistake?" Mildren sat upright. "What the hell does that mean?"

"I think it's a historical reference to a Roman emperor. According to ancient historians, Emperor Titus supposedly said on his deathbed: 'I have made one mistake.'"

"What bloody mistake?" Mildren asked, losing his patience.

"One of the great unanswered questions of the ancient world," Jonathan said with a shrug. "Before he was emperor, Titus led the Roman conquest of Jerusalem. Some historians say the mistake refers to his entering the Holy of Holies in the Temple, where no mortal was permitted."

"Sounds a bit paranoid, no?"

"It would have, except when Titus later ascended the throne, an entire bustling Roman city was swallowed in ash."

"You mean Pompeii?"

"Right, and Titus's magicians told him it was the vengeance of the God of Israel to choose Pompeii, a city named for the only other Roman emperor to enter the Temple's inner sanctum in Jerusalem."

"The only mistake I see here, Marcus, is that you're spending billable hours on this. Whatever you saw was just coincidence, a reflection, or maybe—"

"A message intended to escape the Roman censors," Jonathan interrupted. "It could be ancient steganography at its finest."

"Stenography? What's a court reporter got to do with this?"

"That's *steno*graphy, from the Greek *steno*, narrow, and *grapho*, writing, meaning 'shorthand.' Steganography is different. It's an ancient form of encryption. Letters buried under blank wax, or smuggled inside the belly of a hare. *Steganos* means a concealed note, as in hidden writing. A steganographic message isn't simply encrypted, you don't even know it's there."

"Concealed writing, right." Mildren's tone was even, as though to draw Jonathan out further. "An encrypted message."

"Except that encryption gives you privacy, but someone still knows you're sending a message, like Caesar sending encoded letters to his generals or the Internet scattering your credit card number until it reaches the vendor. Steganography offers not only privacy, but secrecy, obscuring that you have sent any message at all. Whether it's a nineteenth-century British spy disguising enemy artillery positions in butterfly-wing drawings or a twenty-first-century Iraqi insurgent embedding an MP3 file within written text, the technique is the same. Ancient espionage differed only by method."

"Ancient espionage," Mildren repeated in a monotone.

"I know it sounds a little crazy—"

"A *little* crazy!" Mildren's voice escalated to a shout. "We are in the middle of a hearing and you're dreaming up some kind of ancient spy plot! I mean, Jon, you're talking about ancient Rome here, not the Cold War."

"Hundreds of years before Rome, Herodotus described the Greeks' tattooing secret messages on the scalp beneath the hair of slaves. They wrote invisibly with urine, wax, and cipher codes to hide—"

"The only thing hidden, Marcus, is your point."

"My point is that if the prosecution sees this message, it could support Emili's—Dr. Travia's allegations. It might explain why these fragments were stolen and researched somewhere in Jerusalem. Someone from the ancient world left a message here, and I think I know who it was."

"Not unless the fragment is signed, which it bloody isn't."

"But it may be," Jonathan said. "The Latin inscription on the underside of the fragment."

"A monument revealed to Josephus," Mildren said. "You're the one who translated it."

"Not *to* Josephus, but *by* Josephus. The Latin would be spelled the same way in both cases. This hidden inscription might have been carved *by* Josephus himself."

"Let's just hope your legal arguments are more consistent. Why would Josephus have to leave secret messages? You said an hour ago that he was Titus's chum, and every researcher agrees with that."

"Not *every researcher*," Jonathan said, his tone gathering conviction. "At the academy I researched the possibility that Josephus was not a traitor to Jerusalem, but surrendered to the Romans to become a—"

"Spy?" Mildren cut him off.

"Yes," Jonathan nodded. "A spy from Jerusalem planted in the Roman court."

Mildren rose from his desk. "Let me give you some advice, Marcus. I'll keep it simple. No hidden messages here, nothing backward, inside out, upside down, okay? Here it is: This conversation never happened."

"Which conversation?"

"This one, the one we're having right now. You were never in my office, and you most certainly did not discover any Bible code–type messages under the artifacts on trial. No rays of light. Am I understood?"

"We should at least notify Tatton. He said no surprises at trial." Jonathan pointed at the crumpled napkin. "*That* is a surprise."

"No, *that* is a napkin," Mildren said. "And whatever you've scribbled on it, *that* is your imagination. Only surprise here would be if anyone at the Italian Cultural Ministry were to notice."

"They would need only a flashlight," Jonathan said.

"A flashlight," Mildren said, his voice revealing how much stress he was under.

"That's right."

"A flashlight will help them detect the grammatical irregularity of the Latin verb, a flashlight will help them read these imperceptible cracks like a cereal box decoder ring? Is that what a flashlight will help them do? Because I think you are greatly overestimating those bureaucrats at the Italian Cultural Ministry, not to mention *underestimating* your capacity to make their case for them!" He paused, wiping his receding hairline. "For God's sake, man." His tone broke and Jonathan could see how much Mildren had riding on this case. "Know when to stop *digging*. You're not a damn graduate student anymore."

"Our case is vulnerable here," Jonathan said, picking up the napkin. "That's the only reason I'm mentioning it. If the prosecution finds out—"

"Then don't repeat this to another soul," Mildren said, reshuffling some papers on his desk. "Unless you can prove those cracks are meaningless graffiti—a bored monk, a medieval prankster—or just a coincidence. Enough monkeys at a typewriter and one of them will write *Hamlet*, that kind of thing."

"But what if the truth—"

"The truth is not your client!" Mildren yelled. "The backbone of our case is that there is nothing unusual about these artifacts, remember?" Mildren pointed at the napkin in Jonathan's hand. "And you come to me with *this*!" His eyes would not have been wider had Jonathan brought something radioactive into his office. "I mean, what do you really think you've stumbled across here?" Exhaustion replaced the anger in his voice. "Some kind of ancient truth that only you can salvage? You're not Ben-Hur, Jon. You're a lawyer."

Mildren stood up and walked Jonathan to the door. "I'll tell Tatton he can reach you back at the hotel. You don't need to do any more research. What you need is sleep."

It was nearly dawn by the time Jonathan arrived at the Hotel Exedra. He walked across its white palatial lobby, staring through sections of the Lucite floor that displayed the ruins of late Roman baths, or *exedra*, still beneath the designer hotel. Jonathan entered his suite to find his briefcase delivered and his one extra suit pressed and hanging in the bedroom closet. The suite's veranda continued the ancient bath theme, and steam rolled off the vanishing edge of a private outdoor heated pool.

Jonathan stepped through the sliding glass doors onto the veranda overlooking Rome. He smelled the poplars of the piazza below mix with the street salt and wet cobblestone. The scent of winter in Rome. Street vendors were already setting up their stalls for the day's fruit market. A streak of orange pastel sliced the ash-dark sky.

In four hours the firm's sedan would return to pick him up for the hearing. He needed to finish the memo and get some rest. He needed to put the past behind him, to forgive himself for his mistake seven years earlier. But memories kept resurfacing: of sneaking beneath an eighteenth-century Roman villa into the catacombs below, of the sudden collapse of the tomb walls, of watching an academy fellow disappear in a gray cloud of earth. And it was his fault. All of it. The academy's disciplinary committee rescinded Jonathan's Rome Prize and threw him out. Exiled like Philoctetes by the Greeks, Jonathan soon discovered that news of the tragedy had spread through the closed world of university classics departments. A faculty position at Columbia was now out of the question. Even community colleges wouldn't offer him a job. Within two months, Jonathan went from being a Rome Prize fellow to tagging amphorae in the storeroom of Sotheby's back in New York to make rent.

He stepped back into the suite and picked up the half-finished memo from where he had left it on the coffee table. He settled into the couch and kept the glass door to the balcony open, hoping the cold air would keep him awake as he reviewed the file. But within minutes he was asleep, the briefs resting on his chest, the breeze rousing nothing but a sweeping sash of curtain.

7

Beneath the Dome of the Rock's Foundation Stone, Salah ad-Din and Professor Cianari crouched inside a cavern that had the quality of a forgotten crypt beneath a cathedral altar. Overhead, the underside of the bedrock roofed the cavern in a low, gentle curve.

The air was damp with a faint smell of mildewing prayer carpets. Through the hole above, Salah ad-Din heard two imams from the Waqf Authority noisily opening the shrine's doors to make their security rounds.

Right on schedule, Salah ad-Din thought, glancing at his chronograph's green digital glow.

Salah ad-Din had instructed Professor Cianari to remain nearly motionless, knowing that any noise beneath the stone would echo through the Dome. Only Salah ad-Din's fingers moved, turning the worn pages of a small leather book he consulted with the same care someone would a religious text. He had never shown the professor the contents of the book and the front cover bore only a single calligraphed Arabic word, مقباس, for which the professor's careful, scholarly translation left him only puzzled further. The word meant "a dwindling flame" or, more precisely, "an ember." The professor knew better than to inquire.

"The Grand Mufti Haj Amin al-Husseini led the Waqf for years on this Mount," Salah ad-Din whispered, "and yet the imams have forsaken his research."

The professor knew the regard Salah ad-Din held for the book's mysterious research, so he refrained from telling him that its author, Haj Amin al-Husseini, the grand mufti of the Jerusalem Waqf in the 1930s, used his close friendship with Adolf Hitler to pillage archives throughout Nazi-occupied Europe to research his eccentric archaeological theories. From what the professor could see, the book's illustrations appeared scattered and unprofessional, but on every page burned the obsessive focus for which the grand mufti was notorious.

"One hour until *fajr,* Sheikh," Ahmed said. He had rappelled down swiftly behind the professor and now unloaded a green cloth army bag from his shoulder. Though barely a teenager, Ahmed Hassan possessed a talent with explosives that surpassed the abilities of any professional bomb maker in Gaza.

"There must be a tunnel beneath this floor," Salah ad-Din said to Professor Cianari. "During the Roman siege, the high priest escaped through an underground channel that was used to drain the blood from the Temple altar." Salah ad-Din turned abruptly to Professor Cianari. "What were the altar's measurements above the stone?"

The professor checked his notes. "The altar was five *tephachim* high," he said, using the biblical measurement. "That corresponds to five handsbreadths above the stone."

Salah ad-Din walked across the floor, counting his paces until he found a seam in the stone.

"Here," Salah ad-Din gestured to Ahmed. "The tunnel begins here."

Ahmed removed an aerosol can of nitromethane-based foam from the bag.

"No," Salah ad-Din said. "The imams will hear the blast."

Ahmed's quick, intelligent eyes registered. He assembled a narrow-barreled machine with six long pipes bound together.

"What is that?" the professor asked.

"A pressurized helium piston," Salah ad-Din said. "A single blast blows loose a square foot of concrete."

A silent jackhammer, the professor thought. He should not have been surprised, considering Salah ad-Din's other gadgetry: satellite phones, acoustic ranging devices to create digital maps of underground passages, not to mention helicopter transport. But far more imposing than his resources was his intelligence. Professor Cianari had heard the young man speak without an accent in half a dozen languages, not even including his countless dialects of Arabic. He translated obscure Greek and Latin texts without assistance and could recite them from memory, having seen them just once.

Ahmed lifted the machine to his shoulder, targeting its nozzle to the floor. Unlike the sound of a jackhammer, the blast was singular, an air gun's release—*phht*—followed by the crack of broken marble. The stone floor was instantly eggshelled and with the single tap of Salah ad-Din's foot the stone shattered inward. Strangely, the fragments made no sound as they fell into what seemed a bottomless cavern below. *It's hollow beneath the floor.* A dank wind breezed upward from the opening like the breath of a living being.

Salah ad-Din shined his flashlight into the opening. Carved stone stairs descended to a platform.

Salah ad-Din climbed through the hole, and the professor followed. They reached a narrow stone bridge that seemed to hover above a vast black cavern.

For Salah ad-Din, it was only fitting that as he neared the end of the text's research, this humid subterranean chamber would remind him of its beginning: the dark cinder-block basement of his childhood home in Beirut, where—against his mother's wishes—his grandfather first showed him the moldy parchments from which he translated ancient Greek into Arabic for the young boy.

He read to his grandson the battle scenes of the Roman siege of the Temple Mount, bringing the first century alive in the squalor of their basement. He painted the scene of Jerusalem under siege in A.D. 70: thousands of Roman legionnaires, spearmen, and smoking fires and wooden catapults all pitched around Jerusalem's city walls. Salah ad-Din remembered his grandfather's crooked finger stabbing a thick vellum manuscript folio of Flavius Josephus. *The Roman general, Titus, did not conquer Jerusalem for political reasons,* he reminded him after every reading. *He conquered Jerusalem because he was afraid. His magicians said there was a power inside Jerusalem's Temple stronger than he, one he had to defeat.* Once, Salah ad-Din had fallen asleep on his grandfather's lap and awakened to find his grandfather not reading, but sadly shaking his head. "Titus's mistake," the old man said, running his hands over the page. Only years later did Salah ad-Din understand that his grandfather's remorse was not for the Roman emperor's failure, but for his own.

After his grandfather died, Salah ad-Din often revisited the mildewed cardboard boxes, piecing together the old man's incoherent narratives, both ancient and modern. Yellowed newspaper photographs struck the now teenaged Salah ad-Din with the exhilaration of learning the truth of a fairy tale: clippings of his grandfather with high-ranking German officers in Berchtesgaden, an Italian front-page photograph with Mussolini grandly showing his grandfather a Roman ruin. "Famous," he remembered his grandfather wheezing as he pointed to the caption of his youthful photograph: The Grand Mufti of Jerusalem.

Salah ad-Din slowly learned why his mother had moved them from Cairo to Damascus, Baghdad, and now Beirut. Her father had been convicted by a Yugoslavian military tribunal for war crimes for recruiting nearly twenty thousand Muslims to the SS. His grandfather's scribbled notes revealed that agents from the Israeli secret service were looking for him. Most of the writing was incoherent, and it was difficult to distinguish between actual news and the recollection of a disjointed nightmare.

But at the bottom of the last cardboard box, beneath pages of scribbled notes, lay a small leather-bound notebook jammed with quotes from Josephus and directions to various locations, such as the attic of a Parisian mosque and a storage room in the Baghdad Archaeological Museum. Each location returned Salah ad-Din to a different story his grandfather had recounted, ranting with his back hunched against the basement's cinder block, pulling at a scraggly white beard thin as torn cotton. *The research was seeking an artifact,* Salah ad-Din came to realize. *Something not even the Greek or Roman military could capture.* Salah ad-Din blamed himself for not believing him then. The small book proved everything his grandfather had told him. It was the cipher to his soul.

Now, years later, Salah ad-Din stood beside Professor Cianari, surveying the subterranean cavern they had just discovered. His conquest was more imminent than ever.

"The Temple Mount was surrounded by fifty thousand Roman soldiers," he said, turning to the professor, "and the priest escaped through here, along this aqueduct."

His flashlight revealed a narrow stone aqueduct stretching into the darkness. It appeared to float across the dark chasm that lay on either side.

"And he took with him the one artifact that brought down a Roman emperor."

8

Rome's morning traffic crawled across the Ponte Palatino, and Jonathan raced up the marble steps of the Palazzo di Giustizia, taking two steps in each stride. The building's vast neoclassical façade stretched like a civic temple along the Tiber's bank, longer than two United States Supreme Court buildings laid end to end.

In the interior loggia of the courthouse, Jonathan gave up his passport and stepped through a metal detector. Fifteen-foot statues of famous Roman lawyers from Cicero to nineteenth-century Italian lawmakers adorned marble hallways vaulting upward higher than a cathedral's.

At the end of one cavernous hallway, Jonathan saw a cluster of people filing into a courtroom. The last of the group was a young woman with blond hair tied in a loose bun. She wore a gray wool pantsuit, a cream silk blouse beneath her cutaway jacket, and stylish black-framed glasses. Her professional, slim-fitting suit was a far cry from the oversized cable-knit sweaters she wore at the American Academy, but Jonathan knew at once it was Dottoressa Emili Travia.

As though feeling his gaze, Emili glanced down the corridor. Jonathan stopped, separated by much more than the expanse of marble between them. From her unyielding glare, Jonathan knew his role as a lawyer in this trial was not a secret. Neither of them said a word. She held the stare, as if she were trying to sift through his past, searching for the clue that would reveal the gradual decline in his ethics that had allowed him to take this case. Even from a distance, Jonathan could see her lightly bite her bottom lip, which she always did when she was thinking. They were full lips, accented by her narrow chin and delicate features. Her beauty was more striking, more daunting than he remembered. Without a change in her expression, she turned around and walked through the courtroom door.

The courtroom was as grand as Jonathan had imagined. Pilasters separated triple-height Palladian windows overlooking Rome. The one modern amenity was a bullet-repellent glass witness case, which Jonathan supposed was installed for use in Mafia trials. The original dark wood witness stand, which would be used in this morning's hearing, sat near the bench.

The Dulling and Pierce table was in front of the courtroom's gallery rail, where Tatton was already seated at the table's end. Beside him, Mildren was writing furiously on a legal pad, transcribing Jonathan's memo for Tatton's cross-examination. On the other side of the courtroom, beside their table, the lawyers for the Italian Cultural

Ministry had set up an easel with large poster-board photographs of the various inscriptions on the Forma Urbis fragments. Behind the polished walnut helm between them sat a small Italian magistrate with dated brown plastic glasses and thinning dark hair, like iron filings, on his head. Despite the ornate woodwork of his throne, he resembled an overwhelmed bookkeeper.

A legal assistant handed Jonathan a black gown like a judge's robe, and a white doily cravat, a *fiocco*, for Jonathan to wear around his neck. It resembled something from a sketch of the seventeenth-century British House of Lords, and by the time Jonathan was done fidgeting with the *fiocco*, it looked like a lobster bib.

"That's the Cultural Ministry's lawyer, Maurizio Fiorello," Mildren said as Jonathan sat down at the counsel's table. He pointed to a short man with windswept gray hair who was in the process of donning his lawyer's robe over a rumpled suit and knit tie.

"That's Fiorello?" Jonathan said. Maurizio Fiorello was renowned in art-recovery circles for his ability to wrest art and antiquities from private collections and museums. From his reputation, Jonathan expected a more imposing courtroom presence. Then again, perhaps Fiorello's ordinary appearance was a deliberate contrast to the aristocratic elegance of Tatton, and a reminder to the Italian magistrate of what the country's antiquities squads were up against. The rivalry between Fiorello and Tatton went beyond appearance. Fiorello once called the Dulling partner the "American consigliere to the organized illicit relic trade."

"*Silenzio!*" a bailiff called out, and with the sound of a hand bell, the hearing was called to order. Without introduction, the magistrate picked up the papers before him. "Article Forty-four of the 1939 Italian patrimony law, prohibiting the unauthorized removal of historic objects from the Italian Republic. The Cultural Ministry has alleged that artifacts in the defendant's collection belong to the State Archives. Is that correct, Signore Fiorello?"

"That is correct, *Magistrato*." Fiorello stood up, reviewing some final notes in his hands. He stepped toward the center of the courtroom and placed the notes down on a wooden lectern in front of the magistrate.

"May I proceed to call our first witness to testify?"

The magistrate nodded, leaning back in his chair.

At the sound of her name, Emili rose from her seat beside Fiorello and settled into the *banco dei testimoni*. She removed her glasses and folded her hands. She looked composed and professional. Jonathan envisioned the last time he saw Emili alone. She was sitting on the edge of his single cot at the academy, naked from the waist up, smiling as she read him a stanza of Ovid's erotic poetry in Latin.

Jonathan held the bridge of his nose, taking scattered notes, trying to proceed as rationally as he could. "I can't believe this," he murmured.

"Me neither," Mildren snickered. "Bloody lucky testimony isn't weighted by sex appeal, right?"

"Would you please state your name and title?" Fiorello said.

"Dr. Emili Travia," she answered. "Deputy director of the International Centre for Conservation in Rome."

Fiorello's direct examination of Dr. Travia developed a rhythm of question and answer, establishing her expertise—her Ph.D. at La Sapienza, her receipt of the Rome Prize, awarded to only one Italian biannually by the American Academy in Rome—her rise through the International Centre's administrative ranks, from staff assistant to deputy director.

Fiorello stepped away from the lectern, his line of questions turning to the events surrounding her team's preservationist efforts in Jerusalem. He asked Dr. Travia to explain her team's work on the ground to survey the Temple Mount.

"In 2007 my team of preservationists from Rome arrived in Jeru-

salem to respond to allegations of archaeological destruction beneath the Temple Mount by the Waqf Authority."

"The Waqf Authority?" Fiorello said.

"From Al Waqf, or literally 'the preserve,' the Waqf is a religious
land trust that has administered the Temple Mount in Jerusalem
since 1187. Our office heard reports of unauthorized excavation,
and our initial investigation discovered mounds of rubble in the
olive groves of the Kidron Valley at the foot of the Temple Mount."
Emili recounted how her team moved through the heap, picking
out shards of biblical-era pottery and shattered Crusader amulets,
like stunned medics surveying a smoldering battlefield with no survivors. "A local monastery confirmed that bulldozers had been
dumping rubble in the middle of the night."

"And you contacted the Waqf Authority?"

"Yes. And as we expected, we received no response."

"You expected your preservation efforts to be ignored?" Fiorello
feigned surprise.

"The Waqf Authority has been as vigilant against non-Muslims
visiting certain areas of the Mount as the Manchu priests in imperial
China once were in preventing the entrance of mortals to the Forbidden City. If we were to inspect beneath the Mount, Dr. Lebag
and I knew it would have to be without permission."

"Dr. Sharif Lebag was part of your delegation?" Fiorello now
approached the witness on the stand in the same way he was beginning to approach the heart of her testimony. He touched the railing
as though offering his support, preparing her to broach the topic of
her murdered colleague.

"Dr. Lebag had been in Jerusalem for a few months." Emili swallowed. "His spoken Arabic and traditional Islamic observance were
helpful to recruit informants. A shopkeeper in the Old City's Muslim Quarter told him of a possible illicit excavation near his stall in
the spice market. Men with drills and pickaxes were using a previ-

ously abandoned rusted door located opposite his stall. Dr. Lebag and I visited the spice market and inspected the door. It looked abandoned for centuries, except for one detail."

"Which was?"

"The rusted iron handle had silicon sensors to authenticate fingerprint recognition."

"*Magistrato!*" Tatton objected. "This is all fascinating background, but this case is about an artifact. Is there any relevance—"

"*Magistrato,* I am demonstrating the worth of these fragments by the extravagant efforts to hide them."

The *magistrato* nodded, permitting the inquiry.

Fiorello resumed. "If this *abandoned* door required fingerprint authentication, presumably you could not enter?"

"No, but we obtained a map of Jerusalem indicating an ancient underground street that ran beneath the spice market and directly beneath the door. The next morning we entered the market." As Emili spoke she could picture the events in her mind. "Dr. Sharif Lebag and I dressed as tourists, carrying in tattered backpacks our lithium flashlights, climbing rope, and spades. Sharif's contact, the shopkeeper, allowed us to remove the stone drain beneath the table in his stall. The ancient street was a considerable distance below us and we roped down to it. Enormous columns supported modern Jerusalem above. Our flashlight beams could barely reach the ceiling."

"And that's where you saw these fragments?"

"Not at first. At the end of the street there was a cavern converted into a room reinforced with steel beams. The room contained high-tech archaeological equipment, including a humidity-controlled glass case for original scrolls and parchments. Digitized images of Renaissance Greek and Latin manuscript pages papered the cavern walls with labels documenting the folio year."

"Did the labels identify the source of the text?"

"Yes. All the pages included passages, copied by scribes, from the works of Flavius Josephus. In the center of the room, a group of marble fragments lay on a glass table beneath a fiber-optic lamp. Both Sharif and I recognized the artifact at once. Fragments of the Forma Urbis"—she pointed at the photograph of the artifacts on the easel—"*those* fragments of the Forma Urbis."

"There were identifying markings?" Fiorello said.

"Yes," Emili said. "'Archivio di Stato.'"

"Roman State Archives," Fiorello mused. "And you saw another inscription on the fragments?"

"Sharif—Dr. Lebag, I'm sorry—identified the inscription running along the underside."

"Which was?"

"The same inscription present on these fragments. '*Tropaeum Josepho Illumina.*'"

"And then what happened, Dr. Travia?"

"From the market above us, there was the sound of a gunshot. A single blast. Through the street grate overhead, we could see the spice market was in chaos. Sharif and I returned to where we had roped in, and, using the pulley we'd fixed to the drain, he belayed me back up to the market stall." Emili swallowed, willing herself to stay calm. "I climbed out of the drain, and saw the shopkeeper's legs, just as he had been, sitting at the table. I climbed out from under the table and"—Emili paused, and then continued—"saw him seated, folded over the table, eyes wide open." Emili closed her eyes, picturing the image, how the blood from the middle of his forehead streamed down into the yellow mound of ground mustard. Emili looked up at Fiorello. "That is the last I remember before being knocked unconscious."

"When did you wake up?"

"An hour later. In a Catholic hospital outside the Damascus Gate. I had suffered a severe concussion, and the attending nun would not

THE LAST EMBER   43

let me leave until an official from the Israel Antiquities Authority signed me out. No one had heard from Dr. Lebag. Immediately, we returned to the Muslim Quarter in search of him."

"You returned to the stall?"

"Yes, but there was no trace of the dead vendor or his table. The stall where Sharif and I descended was empty. Neighboring shop-keepers insisted it had been empty for days. I showed the official the rusted door but the silicon sensors were gone. In fact, the door now hung slightly off its hinges and you could step right through." Emili remembered the muscles in her legs tightening as she opened the door and hurried down a long flight of steep stone steps. Fueled by a headlong rush of fear, she ran into the cavern they had entered only hours before. She remembered the shrill echo from screaming Sharif's name.

"And what did you find, Dr. Travia?"

"The room was empty. The long steel tables were gone, so were the copies of manuscripts papering the walls. No cabinets. No marble fragments. It was all gone; the room was completely stripped—" Emili stopped. She remembered seeing a gruesome broom stroke of blood, thick on the floor like a brush of red paint. The street grate in the ceiling high above allowed in enough light to see a small, dice-sized fragment resembling a piece of white marble on the floor.

"There was a small fragment," she said, remembering the shard glistening at her feet as if it had been cleaned with a pink protective resin. Moved by a force outside herself, she picked it up and held it in her hand. Turning the piece over, she saw a tuft of black hair. She felt a stab of shock and then convulsive dry heaves seized her. Her legs gave way and she fell to the floor.

"The UN investigation," Emili said, breaking her silence, "concluded it was from Sharif's skull, the back of his head and brain, carried away by the exit of a single bullet."

9

The headquarters of the carabinieri's Cultural Heritage Guard once housed an ecclesiastical college in the early 1700s, but the late-baroque building was now known to the officers of this elite unit as "the Command." The morning sun slanted into the dim conference room on the sixth floor, and the lieutenants watched Comandante Profeta step into the blue blaze of a projector's light. His hand was bandaged—cut by a flying wood plank in last night's blast. The officers sat silently around the table, their uniforms still darkened from ash.

Profeta massaged his shoulder. The paramedics had brought him to the hospital and, throughout the night, doctors X-rayed him up and down like a Greek *kouros* of questionable provenance. Nothing broken, but the physicians protested his departure, wanting to prod him further. Profeta ignored them and returned to the Command at dawn. He knew they were running out of time.

The lab had not yet returned any information about the corpse. Because of much-needed emotional release, the lieutenants created their own mythology surrounding the discovery. "The Princess of the Pier," Profeta overheard them call her. The junior officers created a betting pool, wagering on her age pending laboratory results.

A first slide appeared on the screen: an oversized photograph of the female corpse submerged inside the viscous fluid of the ancient column. Taken from the foot of the sarcophagus, the crisp digital image made the woman's naked figure even more lifelike.

"Late last night, beside an unused commercial dock in Civitavecchia, our team discovered this victim, female, age estimates range in the late thirties, and the cause of death appears to be lacerations sustained across her torso. The perpetrators disguised the homicide as an ancient burial: a perfect imitation of a Corinthian maiden."

"Corinthian maiden?" Brandisi asked.

"An ancient practice in which conquerors marched women prisoners of war back to their city and literally buried them inside columns. They were called Corinthian maidens."

"Barbaric," another officer said.

"It's no coincidence that the flutes of Corinthian columns today still imitate the folds of the togas of women once buried inside them," the *comandante* said, "or that our Ionic capitals emulate the hairstyle of first-century women." Profeta knew how much of classical architecture bore hidden cultic secrets. Universities trimmed their buildings with moldings of eggs, darts, and claws, not realizing that any ancient Roman would recognize those symbols as the trappings of pagan sacrifice.

"Could this have been a cult murder?" one of the officers asked. "An initiation rite gone too far?"

"Could be," Profeta said. "Someone studied the ancient practice carefully, right down to the emollients used in ancient Rome. The hoax appears better researched than any I have seen. Next slide, please."

Profeta nodded toward the back of the room. The next slide displayed ornately illustrated parchment pages lying scattered on the warehouse floor.

"We found dozens of these pages. They are from manuscripts hundreds of years old. Most would have been quite valuable, particularly this fifteenth-century page"—Profeta touched the screen with his pointer—"except someone made them virtually worthless." The slide changed, displaying a close-up of a manuscript's text. Inked bracket markings and circled letters dotted the parchment's ornate script. "Someone marked up the texts, conducting research of some kind. Has anyone noticed what all these pages have in common?"

Even under pressure, the *comandante* never missed an opportunity to impart a historical context to improve his officers' investigative skills. He offered a continuing education in ancient history so rigorous that his lessons became renowned across Interpol's antiquities units.

Profeta stepped to the side of the projector's screen and, on the dry-erase board behind him, wrote in big block letters.

FLAVIUS JOSEPHUS, A.D. 30 TO A.D. 100

"Flavius Josephus," Profeta said, pointing up at the illustrated manuscripts on the screen. "Notice how the first letter on each page is decorated with a small portrait of a city in flames, depicting the smoldering turrets of Jerusalem's city walls after the Roman siege. It was Flavius Josephus who wrote the defining eyewitness account of the Roman conquest of Jerusalem, known as *Bellum Iudacium*, or *The Jewish War*. It became an instant best seller in the ancient world, recopied by scribes throughout the ages. By the Renaissance, Josephus's histories were the most widely read texts in the Western world after the Bible. The manuscript pages we found in the warehouse"—Profeta pointed at the screen—"were each torn out of priceless editions of Josephus, ranging from medieval manuscripts to Renaissance folios. All from different scribes, different centuries, and different languages, but they are all translations of the same first-century historian. It's as if they were comparing versions transcribed across the centuries to find something inside the text."

Profeta paused a moment, surveying the room.

"And if our targets are researching the ancient historian Flavius Josephus . . ."

The officers knew the commandant's method well enough to chorus, "Then so must we."

Profeta turned his attention back to the manuscripts on the screen. "What else do we know of this ancient author?"

"*Sorcio!*" Brandisi said, inviting much-needed laughter into the room. *Rat*, a term unique to the organized crime families that the carabinieri battled in the rougher patches of Torre del Greco, outside Naples.

"A turncoat." Profeta nodded. "That's the popular view. Josephus's swift rise from prisoner of war to Roman citizen suggests a deal greased during his capture. Even more mysterious are the circumstances of Josephus's surrender described in this manuscript page on the screen."

"You mean when all the other soldiers in Josephus's battalion chose suicide over capture?" asked Brandisi.

"Precisely," said Profeta. "Imagine that Josephus was a general, leading his troops to stop the Roman advance toward Jerusalem. But when Roman forces outflanked his platoon, Josephus and his men were surrounded. The men under his command threatened to kill him if he surrendered. So Josephus suggested a mass suicide pact: pick lots to determine who would kill the next man and the one after, and so on." Profeta pointed at the slide, running his laser pointer beneath each line, translating the text as he read:

"*Murder me,*" *Flavius Josephus said,* "*but let us first draw lots and kill each other in turn. Whoever draws the first lot shall be dispatched by number two, and so on down the whole line as luck decides . . .*" *Without hesitation each man offered his throat for the next man to cut. But Josephus—shall we*

put it down to divine providence or just to luck?—was left
alive. . . .

"And here lies the heart of the mystery of Flavius Josephus," Profeta said. "How was he left the last man alive?"

"Reminds me of the Josephus problem in computer science," said Profeta's technology director, Lieutenant Lori Copia, a woman at the long table's far side.

"The Josephus problem?" Profeta asked.

"A security dilemma in computer database protection. Most firewalls are built to secure a digital perimeter by eliminating unauthorized codes. The Josephus problem arises when an unauthorized code detects the firewall's pattern of elimination, and can avoid being eliminated each time."

Profeta grinned. "The modern term goes to the center of the historical controversy of Josephus. How did Josephus keep drawing the right lots? The original Josephus problem."

The projector's screen whirred upward, and the room's dimmers gently returned the lights to normal.

"Speaking of technology, Copia, any information from the smashed computers at the warehouse?"

"Still searching, *Comandante.* We managed to retrieve only one of the computers before the explosion. It had an Arabic keyboard. We are running ninhydrin tests for prints."

"Hard drives?"

"There are a few intact sections of the hard drive. Likelihood of recovering anything is slim."

"Next, Brandisi. Have we found any activity along the pier near the warehouse? Witnesses?"

"Not a soul, *Comandante.* Last reported activity on the pier was a preservation project months ago. A third-century Roman watchtower, a small circular structure adjacent to the warehouse."

"Next, Rufio, forensics?" Profeta said, but then paused a moment and turned back to Brandisi.

"On second thought, get a list of everyone involved in that preservation project, Brandisi. Donors, staff members." Profeta turned to Rufio. "Forensics?"

"We found some burnt municipal identification tags," Rufio said.

"Manufactured or stolen identification tags?" Profeta asked.

"Too early to tell," Rufio said. "The blast gave them a pretty good scrub, *Comandante*."

"The men running that safe house were professionals," Profeta said, returning to the dry-erase board and tapping it with the back of his marker. "And whoever was running that operation was not interested in academic history. They were studying Josephus for a very practical purpose."

The meeting broke, and Profeta's ranking first lieutenant, Alessandro Rufio, left the Command, pulling hard on a hand-rolled cigarette as he walked across Piazza di Sant'Ignazio.

Rufio was a tall, rangy young man with fair skin and red curly hair that announced his Sicilian heritage like a flag. Like many Sicilians, his light features owed to the Normans' eleventh-century conquest of Sicily, but here in Rome he was more conspicuous. He walked rapidly now down side streets, turning frequently to ensure no one trailed him from the Command. He scanned each alleyway for a pay phone. His instructions were always to use a pay phone. He knew the reason better than anyone: the carabinieri's random surveillance of cellular phones to monitor organized crime was vastly underreported.

He turned off Via del Corso into a small alleyway, not three feet wide. The pay phone's proximity to the morning scooter traffic was intentional: the unmuffled blare would make any carabinieri-model listening device useless within the booth.

His instructions were to dial collect, using the foreign prefix provided him. The number was Egyptian, most likely Cairo, but of course he knew it was merely a switchboard. He stood nervously in the half-booth, his short breaths frosting the metal of the receiver. The tone brayed irregularly before steadying, and then grew silent as the number routed elsewhere. A sudden click interrupted the tones. Someone had answered.

"You blew up the warehouse," Rufio said furiously, incautious about his volume. "I was still in there."

10

Maurizio Fiorello returned to the lectern, where he began his direct examination. *"Magistrato*, it has taken generations for these fragments of the Forma Urbis to cycle through the black markets of the Arab world and western Europe before recently resurfacing in the Capitoline Museum on anonymous loan. Dulling and Pierce will offer a provenance for this artifact as shopworn and fabricated as any other unscrupulous dealer would do. Their briefs will try to convince you that this artifact slumbered safely in an anonymous Geneva estate or in a private French collection *coincidentally* having left Italy just before our antiquities law came into effect in 1902. But this time you must not believe them, *Magistrato*. These fragments of the Forma Urbis, at last, have returned home to Rome. Unlike the brave UN official, Dr. Sharif Lebag, they survived their voyage across violent waters of the illicit antiquities trade. We must not allow them to chance that sort of trip again."

As Fiorello sat down, the magistrate leaned forward in his chair, taking some brief notes. Emili surveyed the courtroom from the witness stand. Lifting her head, she noticed in the upper level of the gallery an old man sitting alone. He sat in the last row of the balcony wearing a shabby brown coat and tweed cap. He was barely visible as he watched the courtroom proceedings below.

From the bench, the magistrate nodded to Bruce Tatton. Tatton pushed himself to his feet to begin his cross-examination. He allowed the silence to settle as he approached the witness.

"These custodians of the Temple Mount, the 'Waqf Authority,' is it? For how many years has this Islamic trust administered the Temple Mount?"

"As I said, since the Muslim conquest of Jerusalem in 1187. Salah ad-Din's defeat of Richard the Lionheart."

"And you said you did *not* have their permission to enter the cavern you discovered." Tatton paced. "Is that correct?"

"We attempted to contact—"

"It's a yes-or-no question, *Dottoressa*."

"We received no formal permission from the Waqf."

"So you were trespassing, then?"

"Objection, *Magistrato*!" Fiorello said. "Is any of this *relevant* to Dr. Travia's identification of this fragment?"

"Very relevant, *Magistrato*. This witness violated countless jurisdictional laws by crossing beneath the Temple Mount. According to the UN, the Temple Mount may lie in the heart of Jerusalem, but it remains under Jordanian administration. By crossing from East Jerusalem into the subterranean chambers of the Temple Mount, the witness flagrantly disregarded international law. Her behavior presents issues regarding her credibility."

"*Proceda*," the Magistrate said. Proceed.

"Dr. Travia, you have accused the Waqf Authority of illegally excavating beneath the Temple Mount. Is that correct?"

"Yes."

"And that this room you discovered somehow relates to those excavations?"

"We saw topographical maps displaying various strata of the Temple Mount's archaeological layers."

"How then do you explain the presence of Forma Urbis fragments? We should expect a marble carving of ancient Jerusalem, not Rome."

"I am merely reporting what I observed." Emili breathed out, frustrated. "And what I observed were those two exact fragments," she said, pointing at the easel's photograph in the center of the courtroom. Fiorello nodded, satisfied with the dramatic effect. "I saw them in perfect lighting, under an examination lamp, lying there."

"For how long?"

"I'm sorry?"

"For how long were you in this subterranean room?"

"I gave all the details to the UN officials investigating Dr. Lebag's death."

"Ah, yes," Tatton said. "Right." From the Dulling table, he lifted up materials from the internal UN investigation tabbed in a thick binder.

"By your own calculations, *Dottoressa*"—Tatton took a little tour around the witness stand—"*less* than four minutes and then"— Tatton's voice lowered as he was quite close to her—"BAM!" he shouted. Everyone in the courtroom jumped.

"Sudden, wasn't it? The gunshot that ended your examination?"

Emili said nothing, her eyes staring, as if through Tatton.

"One single gunshot, then chaos in the marketplace, the souk, which was above you. The UN investigation of Dr. Lebag's death suggested that the murder of the shopkeeper was retaliation for assisting you. Whoever killed him, and later Dr. Lebag, did so to retrieve the items in the cavern you claim to have seen. Is that your belief?"

"Yes." Emili stiffened. "I believe word got out that the shopkeeper assisted us."

"And you're sure you saw *these* fragments of the Forma Urbis? There are so many fragments of this ancient map still at large." Tatton approached the witness box, his tone flat. "Isn't it true that there are many fragments of the Forma Urbis that would have looked"— here he protracted each syllable for emphasis—"just"—he paused— "like"—and paused again—"these?"

"But the inscriptions on the fragments," Emili replied from the stand. "They are identical to what I saw in Jerusalem."

Jonathan leaned forward in his seat, a subconscious, protective reflex, as if she were his own witness. Emili had misstepped. She should not have used the word *identical*.

"*Identical?*" Tatton said, leaning on the word, as though the world depended on it. "But it is *not* identical, even by your own admission, is it, *Dottoressa*? The piece you described bore an inscription." Tatton theatrically looked down at his folder. "'Archivio di Stato,' did it not? This piece has no such inscription."

Fiorello shot out of his seat, trying to save his witness.

"*Magistrato*, we have entered expert testimony that the sanded portion along the fragment's reverse side is recent and intentional. Is this sophistry necessary?"

Emili shifted in the witness box, her first sign of unease.

"Entirely necessary, *Magistrato*." Tatton's baritone was pleasant, almost friendly. "Forgive me for being simpleminded, but I am suggesting the witness has confused these artifacts with similar ones. It is, indeed, a strange enough thing to think of a fragment of an ancient map of Rome beneath Jerusalem to begin with, and now, not to have physical proof of it?"

The magistrate nodded, signaling that it was an acceptable line of inquiry.

Tatton raised his hands, as though he were willing to demur. But Jonathan knew this was a show of false grace. He had already won the point in the magistrate's mind.

"One last line of questioning, Dr. Travia." Tatton moved closer, in the arc of a circling shark deciding where to inflict the deepest wound. "Tomorrow is the World Heritage Committee meeting here in Rome, yes?"

From this question alone, Jonathan knew a bad moment awaited Emili.

"Yes," Emili said, looking to Fiorello.

Fiorello nodded, indicating that her candor was good strategy.

"And you have submitted a proposal before the committee to investigate alleged illegal excavating beneath the Temple Mount?"

"I have requested permission from the committee to send archaeological inspectors beneath the Temple Mount, given the facts that we gathered in Jerusalem."

"But what facts are there?" Tatton said. "You don't have a single piece of evidence of the Waqf's archaeological destruction—" Tatton stopped suddenly, looking at her directly. "Except perhaps one?"

"If you're suggesting I'm using this incident to—"

"I'm not suggesting anything," Tatton said with great deliberation. "I intend to tell you directly." Tatton leaned against the witness rail as though giving advice. "Sometimes what we yearn for is not the truth, but the mystery of something bigger." His voice increased in volume. "A larger conspiracy on which to blame our own tragic mistakes. The fact is these pieces are not the ones you saw in Jerusalem, are they?" His avuncular manner faded as he pressed on.

"One of our colleagues, a former Rome Prize winner like yourself, has researched these fragments and concluded that, for all we know, fifty or a hundred pieces of this ancient map could be mistaken for these two. He shared with us that there are hundreds of pieces scattered across museums all over the world."

Emili's gaze moved slowly to Jonathan. Her look of disgust was so casual, so immediate, that it startled him. After a moment, her glare returned to Tatton, saying nothing. Fiorello had warned her. She must not lose her composure.

"Not one piece of evidence of illegal excavation." Tatton frowned, his disappointment visibly pretended. "So you crafted a grand theory, didn't you? A theory that our client somehow obtained a stolen artifact from those who killed your colleague." He walked back toward his seat. "But there is no conspiracy here. No great alliance of illicit antiquities cartels."

He leaned over, resting his knuckles on the table. "There was only a decision." He was silent for a long moment. Jonathan knew he was preparing to deliver his deathblow. "A decision made by you to trespass beneath the Temple Mount, and it cost the life of an innocent shopkeeper and a UN official who was also your friend. And now, in order to forgive yourself, your emotions have created—"

"I am not being emotional, Mr. Tatton," Emili interrupted calmly. "I have explained the facts as best I can reconstruct them." Her tone took a sharp edge.

Fiorello raised his hands above his table, signaling her to back down. He sensed her rising frustration. *Do not fall into the trap he is setting,* his gesture warned.

"You *are* being emotional," Tatton replied. "*So emotional* that you've made up a *theory* that some lost meaning lies beneath this fragment's surface." His expression was now deadly serious, watching her suspiciously, "All to vindicate *your own* emotions!"

"Emotions?" Emili said, simmering. "What I have told you are facts!" But by now, her pitch was too loud for the decorum of the courtroom, proving exactly the point Tatton set out to make from the start. "And no, I have not made up a *theory*. Someone on my team is dead, and there is nothing theoretical about that!" Her shrill voice echoed against the courtroom's back wall. The magistrate banged a gavel. Fiorello exhaled audibly at the UN table.

"Decorum, *Dottoressa*," the magistrate whispered to her in a gentle rebuke, but understanding the pain that Tatton had managed expertly, with devastating subtlety, to expose.

"No further questions, *Magistrato*," Tatton said.

11

Walking deeper beneath the Temple Mount, Salah ad-Din and Cianari stood on the narrow stone aqueduct with the darkness of an abyss on either side. A thin trickle of water moved down the trough.

"An aqueduct," the professor said, touching the water. "Just as described in biblical texts. An aqueduct used in the daily purification and sacrificial duties carried out by the priests on the altar."

At the end of the aqueduct bridge, the ground widened to a tunnel lined with ancient columns the size of redwood trees.

"These columns are older than the Second Temple built by Herod," the professor said. "Look at the Assyrian design and the rough, chipped trowel markings." The professor turned around, the glint of excited disbelief in his eyes. "They are from the *First* Temple built by Solomon, dating to the eighth century B.C. Herod must have used these pillars to support the foundation of the Second Temple, which was built overhead." He knew the find of these columns alone was career-making. There were notoriously few archaeological remains from the Solomonic era, especially after the Israel Museum's only relic from the First Temple, an ivory pomegranate-shaped top of a scepter, was deemed to have a forged Aramaic inscription. Professor Cianari knew the Waqf had used the lack of evidence to challenge that there even *was* a biblical temple.

In front of them, huge sections of stone rubble lay on either side of the tunnel, allowing only a small passageway between.

"These stones are from the Assyrian siege of the First Temple in 715 B.C.," Professor Cianari said, his voice straining as he lifted himself over a large column lying across the corridor. Clumsily, he rolled over the column, dropping the large sketches he carried in his arms. He marveled at the massive stones lining the corridor and tried to match up his surroundings to the hypothetical sketches of what archaeologists suggested lay beneath the Temple Mount. His colleagues still debated whether these secret passages even *existed*, and here he was walking through them. At a moment like this Cianari remembered why he journeyed to Jerusalem. Without permits or a budget, Salah ad-Din's secret excavations beneath Rome and Jerusalem allowed the professor to defy the Roman archaeological superintendent's bureaucracy that had relegated him to a library as if to a prison.

Beyond the stones, the subterranean tunnel came to an abrupt end in a high dirt-packed wall.

Cianari consulted a parchment map and then looked up at the wall. "This tunnel collapsed in the earthquake of 1202, blocking the entrance to the Royal Cavern."

"The Royal Cavern," Salah ad-Din said. "You will be the first archaeologist to confirm its existence."

"The cavern has been forgotten for a thousand years," the professor said, exhilarated. "Josephus described an enormous subterranean cavern beneath the Temple Mount used as a quarry of limestone to build the entire Temple. It supposedly stretches one thousand feet in diameter."

Salah ad-Din motioned for Ahmed to move in front of them. With the full swing of a metal pickax, Ahmed stabbed the wall, removing a large divot of dirt. He swung again and more packed dirt crumbled off the wall.

"It could take weeks to excavate through this wall," Cianari said. "The cavern must be filled with thousands of years of rubble."

"Again," Salah ad-Din said.

Ahmed kept swinging at the wall, his arms moving like a flywheel as he hurled one blow after another, making little progress. He stopped only to catch his breath.

"Again!" Salah ad-Din yelled.

The young man swung the pick again and the metal stuck in the wall as if it had penetrated. He struggled to remove the implement, and when he did, the small hole in the wall beamed a bright ray of white light through the tunnel.

"We are one hundred feet underground," Cianari whispered. "What is that?"

"Again!" Salah ad-Din said.

Ahmed swung the pick at the wall, each stab revealing another fleck of intense brightness, shooting through the tunnel like tiny sunbeams. The professor squinted, moving closer, trying to peer through the holes into the radiance on the other side.

"What in God's name is behind there?"

12

The hearing adjourned, but Jonathan remained in his seat at the Dulling lawyers' table. Without so much as a word, Tatton glided out of the courtroom and Mildren dutifully carried his briefcase behind him.

The courtroom emptied and Jonathan sat alone, staring at the witness stand as though, with enough concentration, he could undo what Tatton had just done.

The leather-padded door at the back of the courtroom swung open. Jonathan turned and watched Emili walk toward the front of the courtroom. She passed through the gallery rail in silence and grabbed a folder she had left near the witness stand. She turned around without looking at him and walked back down the courtroom's aisle.

"Emili," Jonathan said.

She stopped and turned around slowly. The expression on her face brought another snapshot of their past back to Jonathan. It was in the Piazza di Spagna seven years ago at semi-dusk, and Emili was sitting for a local sketch artist. She agreed to it only because of the three drinks they had just had during a boring cocktail lecture at the French Academy. The artist, reading glasses on the tip of his nose, was hard at work, his broad strokes grazing the sketchpad. Suddenly big drops of rain began to fall. The artist hurried to collapse his easel and handed them the unfinished drawing, Emili's face partly drawn as though floating on the sketch paper. The picture captured something hauntingly beautiful in its incompleteness. Her blond hair drawn in gray lines above a small, beautifully arched brow, and light sad eyes hovering in the gray of the sketch. "Oh, I look so sad," Emili said, laughing in the rain. She called after the artist, a playful tone of challenge. "It looks nothing like me!" she said.

And now years later, almost eerily, her sad gaze captured precisely the expression the artist had drawn.

"I'm sorry," Jonathan said. "I didn't know Tatton was going to say any of that."

She walked toward him, saying nothing. Her lips parted, as though she had begun to speak and decided against it. She glowered at him, and standing close Jonathan remembered her green-gold eyes—the patina of ancient bronze, he always thought. But they were not that color now. Now they had darkened with her mood.

"Sorry?" she said, watching him carefully. "You think I hadn't heard that you represented the Sicilian antiquities pirate Andre Cavetti? Or how you brilliantly defended a Greek sarcophagus so it could be used as a fountain in some Las Vegas hot spot? You think I didn't know you became a lawyer defending the people from whom we protected these artifacts? You think I didn't know you went from gamekeeper to poacher?"

Jonathan said nothing for a moment. "Emili, it's been seven years. You're making some assumptions that—"

"Assumptions?" She pointed to the artifact in the center of the room. "Whoever sold your client this piece may have shot Sharif. *Sharif*, Jon. He was your friend." She walked toward him, her air of professionalism disappearing. "Tell me," she said, "what broke you? Was it the tunnel's collapse? Getting suspended from the academy? Working at the Met after being a Rome Prize winner? Or was it having to take the job in the back room at Sotheby's to help pay for law school?" She took another step toward him, securing her ground. "I can still faintly see the graduate student you once were, Jon, buried like a ruin under that expensive suit." Another step. "And maybe with enough excavation someone could make sense of how Gianpaolo's death buried the heroic part of you with him."

"Heroes are for myths!" Jonathan said more loudly than he would have liked. "This is reality, and you're still talking about heroes? My job isn't about myths or heroism. It's about the law."

"This case is about something more, Jon. There is something about those fragments."

"Emili, ancient secrets were an intriguing diversion in grad school, but—"

"Someone murdered Sharif for those fragments. Your friend. If that doesn't take your head out of your legal briefs, nothing will."

In her eyes Jonathan saw a passion that he recognized vaguely, but now it struck him as wild and unfamiliar. "I'm sorry, Emili, this case is not about villains or ancient messages. It's a legal case. I hope one day you understand. *Tempus ignoscit.*" Time forgives.

"Time doesn't forgive," Emili said. "It doesn't even allow a person to forgive himself." She walked down the courtroom's aisle and turned around just before leaving the chamber. "You, more than anyone, should know that."

She stepped through the courtroom door and it swung shut behind her.

Alone now in the courtroom, Jonathan ran both hands through his hair.

"Okay," he breathed, "that did not go well."

He walked back toward the gallery rail, where an easel displayed the location of the Colosseum gate depicted on the two Forma Urbis fragments. The fragments fit along the Colosseum's southern rim, completing the arena's oval shape like missing puzzle pieces.

An archaeological notation was penciled above the gate: *Porta Sanavivaria.*

"That was the gate for gladiators," Jonathan murmured. Gladiators and the prisoners of war forced to fight them entered the arena through the Porta Sanavivaria, the Gate of Life. If killed, their bodies were dragged with hooks through the Porta Libertinensis, the Gate of Death, located on the arena's other side.

These fragments of the Forma Urbis depict a gladiators' gate.

The doors of the courtroom flung open again, startling Jonathan.

"What's taking you so long?" Mildren stomped toward the gallery rail. "Tatton is waiting for you in the car."

13

Outside the Palazzo di Giustizia, Emili carried her files down the courthouse steps. She started across the Ponte Sant'Angelo, walking by the ten oversized angels overseen by Bernini and between the unlicensed sidewalk vendors. She stopped midway across the bridge and stared into the Tiber. Its water surged from the winter rain, rolling beneath the bridge like a giant gray tarp in the wind.

"Souvenir?"

A souvenir vendor tapped Emili on the shoulder and she turned around. Rows of miniature statues of saints sat in tidy rows on a small concessionaire's display hanging from his neck. He was a middle-aged man with a gray Edwardian mustache and torn wool gloves.

"Souvenir?" he repeated.

"*No, grazie,*" Emili said politely.

"*Souvenir?*" the man said to her again, raising his arms thick with dangling rosary beads. The man was tired and the crowd's current jostled his small cardboard drawer, knocking the statues over like an earthquake in a tiny museum. Vendors usually swarmed only tourists, yet this man would not leave her alone. Emili knew her light coloring and nearly accentless English often gave local vendors reason to mistake her as a foreigner. She finally turned around to give the man a euro, when she noticed that the souvenir salesman was holding a note in his hand. It was a sheet of paper folded in fourths. Written on it in hurried script was her name.

"*Un souvenir per te,*" he said. *A souvenir for you.* He handed her the note and Emili tore it open.

There were two words.

Il Ghetto. The Ghetto.

Emili looked up, scanning the crowd along the bridge.

"Who gave you this?" Emili said. The tone of her Italian was harsh.

"*Prego?*"

"This note, who gave you this note?" Emili showed the souvenir vendor a fifty-euro bill.

The souvenir man smiled and shook his head. He was not interested in her money.

Emili stared at the note. She had received anonymous tips before. There was even a dedicated hotline at her office to receive correspondence from antiquities dealers or illegal excavators with a sudden conscience. But she did not have time for a goose chase.

Even so, she understood the note's possibility and walked over the bridge toward the note's destination: *Il Ghetto.*

In Italian, the word *ghetto* has a more historical meaning than in English, originating from the word for "metal factory," or *geto*; in

the fifteenth century, a Venetian church official had confined all of
that city's Jews to live in the foundry district. Within fifty years the
Vatican borrowed the practice and the term, and Pope Paul IV de-
creed that all Roman Jews were to live within four flood-ridden city
blocks along the Tiber.

The Ghetto was not far, and within minutes Emili was wandering its sooted labyrinth of winding streets. Walls of ancient Hadri-
anic brick supported sagging sixteenth-century town houses. From
the narrow slivers of sky above the alleyways, Emili caught glimpses
of the Great Synagogue of Rome. Its aluminum cupola glinted even
in the overcast skies, its grand marble shoulders with Ionic pilasters
on each side stretched a city block. It rose into view along the Tiber
like a Turkish-style cathedral.

Outside the synagogue, an old man leaned against a high wrought-
iron fence. Emili recognized him at once: the old man she had seen
in the courtroom's balcony. He wore the same dusty blazer that was
two sizes too big, and his wispy hair fanned out like white threads in
the wind. Cataracts had misted over his bright eyes, but the intensity
of his gaze sparkled with an energy that defied his age. A small cy-
lindrical green canvas bag hung from his shoulder by a thin strap. It
held a small oxygen tank, but the tubing wrapped tightly around the
canister indicated its infrequent use.

He extended his right hand to introduce himself, and Emili realized it had only two fingers extending below the knuckle. The
smooth brown nubs pressed in her palm in a terrifyingly straight
line, suggesting the single slash of a blade.

His grip greeted hers with unexpected strength. "I am Mosè
Orvieti."

The name was familiar to Emili. "The archivist?" She knew of
Signore Orvieti from her Holocaust restitution work at the UN, but
she had never met him. Few had. Fabled for his efforts to recover

manuscripts and lost artifacts belonging to the Jewish Ghetto of Rome, Mosè Orvieti had been a young archivist in the Great Synagogue during the German occupation of Rome in 1943.

Emili knew of Orvieti's past. She read his personal testimony in one Holocaust restitution case recounting the liquidation of the Ghetto. He described how, on October 13, 1943, 2,091 people, including his wife and all of his children, were deported from Rome's Collegio Militare train station to Auschwitz. Of those 2,091, Orvieti was one of sixteen people to return.

"You received my note?" he said.

"You know every souvenir vendor in Rome?" Emili said lightly.

"The ones in Piazza San Pietro," Orvieti said. "All of them are from the Ghetto. It's still the law."

"The law?"

"In 1555, the pontificate of Paul IV gave only Jews licenses to sell Catholic souvenirs in Saint Peter's Square, as the task was beneath Christian dignity. The licenses are now quite valuable, having been passed down from one generation of Roman Jews to the next."

"Why did you send for me?" Emili said.

"Last year, during your work in Jerusalem, you said you saw manuscript pages of Flavius Josephus."

A declarative statement, Emili noticed. The first time someone had not said *allegedly* or *even if* regarding her experience in Jerusalem.

"Yes."

"With your permission," Orvieti said, "I'd like to show you the archives where they came from."

Emili followed Orvieti past three heavily armed Roman policemen who patrolled the perimeter of the synagogue. A fourth was on break, leaning against the steel-caged window of his carabinieri jeep, smoking a cigarette. Emili knew their twenty-four-hour shifts had been an unfortunate precaution since 1982, when masked Palestinian gunmen opened fire on Jewish children exiting services.

Orvieti unlocked a Dutch oak door along the synagogue's side and closed the door behind Emili, dropping a thick metal bar across its inside, as though fortifying a battlement.

The archivist and Emili stepped into the sanctuary. Its ceiling mural vaulted to a height of more than one hundred feet, with rainbow colors around a gilt skylight. They moved almost ceremoniously down the aisle, walking up five marble steps to the sanctuary's bimah, an elevated platform supporting a velvet-curtained ark. Dwarfed by the double-height curtains, Orvieti unlocked a small pine door beside the ark, and Emili followed him into a narrow stairwell with curved walls of reinforced concrete.

The tight curve of steps upward to the synagogue's cupola resembled the stairs of a lighthouse, and Orvieti's legs moved with unexpected vigor, stopping only occasionally with labored breaths, as though waiting impatiently for his aged body to catch up to the rest of him. He ignored the small oxygen tank that hung from his shoulder. The curved walls displayed pieces of ancient tombs with Hebrew inscriptions and even medieval symbols of the zodiac. From her work at the International Centre for Conservation, Emili knew that the belfry contained the world's finest trove of medieval folio commentary on the Old Testament, even after the 1943 looting by German professors of the Einsatzstab, an elite Nazi SS regiment that pilfered rare Jewish manuscripts and documents from countless archives throughout occupied Europe. To this day, the treasures of the synagogue's archive were too valuable to appear in any public catalog.

The archive's door was heavy oak with cast-iron fittings. In contrast, a technologically advanced black security keypad was embedded in the stucco wall by its side. Orvieti punched a seven-digit code, and the door's steel bolt clicked open with a timid electronic beep. Three stories of caged books came into view, their thin balconies connected by corkscrew staircases inside the cupola.

And people think the Vatican secret archives have an exclusive access policy, Emili thought.

"I was eighteen years old when the Josephus manuscript pages were stolen," Orvieti began. "I was assisting the senior archivist." Orvieti's eyes were red and damp. He walked over to the narrow stained-glass window, his face suddenly older in the amber light, a mass of lined crevasses and bony angles.

"A man came with two German officers. It was the day of the Ghetto's ransom."

Emili understood immediately what Orvieti meant. In September 1943, during the Nazi occupation of Rome, the Obersturmbannführer, Herbert Kappler, demanded 110 pounds of solid gold within thirty-six hours from the Jews living in the Ghetto.

"The lines to donate stretched from the sanctuary's door around the block. Men and women donated their wedding rings, family brooches, and other heirlooms. Some local priests lined up as well, donating their gold at great peril to their own lives. Yet we were still a few pounds short. Since many of the medieval folios were gilded in precious casings, I was sent back up to the library to strip the gold buckles and plated bindings from the library's medieval texts."

Orvieti gestured to a distant point in the belfry, as though someone were still standing there. "That's where I saw him. He was dressed in exotic garb. An Islamic mullah, I could tell from his square black beard and Eastern fez. He was a small man, perhaps not even five feet tall. He wore sunglasses even inside the archive. He paced along the shelves as though he were visiting royalty, draping his hands across the book bindings. I knew he was a man of importance, flanked on either side by German soldiers and young professors from Berlin, who were fluent in Latin, Hebrew, and Greek. He supervised the Nazi officers as they searched up and down the stacks."

Orvieti could still hear the man's German with a guttural Middle Eastern accent.

"He brought the Einsatzstab here?" Emili said.

Orvieti nodded.

"Years later," he said, "investigators from a Yugoslavian military tribunal came here to the archives. They told me the Islamic mullah was Haj Amin al-Husseini, grand mufti of Jerusalem from 1926 to 1939. He had been convicted in abstentia for war crimes and they were searching all leads to find him."

"'The Führer Mufti,' he was called," Emili said. She knew of the mufti's notoriety as the highest-ranking Islamic cleric in British-mandate Jerusalem in the 1930s. The mufti received permission to use Gestapo forces to ransack archives throughout occupied Europe. He searched for manuscripts and artifacts relating to Jerusalem with an obsession that rivaled Himmler's search for Atlantis.

Emili knew that the grand mufti's deep anti-Semitism had become indelible in the Arab world. During her restoration work of a Byzantine church in Gaza in 2000, Emili was surprised to learn that Sheikh al-Husseini's Arabic translation of *Mein Kampf* was still the sixth-best seller in the Palestinian-controlled territories. She had never heard of an archivist or a librarian who had seen the mufti and survived.

"He demanded that I bring him the archive's oldest Josephus manuscripts and lay them on a table, which I did. The German professors began searching through them for particular pages and ripping them out. But the mufti was searching for something else, demanding to see all of the archive's sketches of the Colosseum." Orvieti could still hear the small man's fit of outrage. "Each time he found a folio of architectural sketches that was not what he was looking for, he ripped it to shreds, repeating the words, 'I will not make Titus's mistake,' as if it were a kind of mantra." Orvieti walked to a large book of sketches lying on a table in the center of the room. The leather cover was cracked like driftwood, and in profile it resembled a bound stack of dried leaves. He carefully turned the brittle pages until he arrived at a certain sketch. "I believe he was looking for this."

The drawing depicted the Colosseum from the exterior, one of its arches crumbling and overgrown with brush, as it was in the nineteenth century. "It is a drawing from Napoleon's archaeological excavations of the Colosseum in 1809," he said.

"I wouldn't call what Napoleon did to Rome *archaeology*," Emili said, controlling her preservationist's ire. "During his occupation of Rome, that man's archaeological excavations did more damage to Rome's ruins than his cannons did."

Delicately, almost reverently, Emili held the drawing above the desk lamp, illuminating the parchment's thick weave. Humidity had damaged the center of the sketch, but the rest was in good condition.

"I found this during a renovation years after the war, hidden inside one of the sanctuary's wooden pews. Only then did I remember that the previous archivist once said that a member of Napoleon's excavation team bequeathed his drawings to the archive. It was the papal architect, Giuseppe Valadier."

"The *architetto camerale*?" Emili knew that Giuseppe Valadier, as papal architect, had completed dozens of archaeological restorations in the early 1800s. "Why wouldn't he leave all his sketches to the Vatican?"

"I think he found something during his excavation of the Colosseum," Orvieti said. "Something he wanted to keep from Napoleon, and even from the Church. Something important enough to bring the Mufti from Jerusalem two centuries later looking for it."

"But after all these years"—Orvieti shrugged—"I don't know which arch is drawn here."

Emili inspected the drawing. "Just a minute," she said. "Look at the top, above the keystone. What do you see written there, *Signore?*"

"Nothing," Orvieti said.

"*Exactly.* This arch, *Signore,* has no number. Nearly all of the eighty arches of the Colosseum were numbered." Emili recalled her recent preservation work inside the arena. "But not the gladiator gates used by prisoners sent to their death. If we could search beneath—"

"I'm sorry, Dottoressa Travia," Orvieti interrupted her, lifting his hand, "but I gave up searching long ago. To understand the drawing's full meaning, the previous archivist claimed one must"—he paused—"believe." Orvieti averted his eyes ashamedly. "He said one must still believe."

"In what?" Emili asked.

"The splitting of the Red Sea," Orvieti responded without hesitating. "And that is the reason I want someone else to have this sketch, Dottoressa Travia. I am afraid I no longer qualify."

Walking back across the Ponte Palatino to Trastevere, Dr. Emili Travia returned to her office in the renovated seventeenth-century convent that housed the International Centre for Conservation. She sat at her desk beneath a small brick-domed ceiling that was once a granary roof. The late-morning sun sifted through a high window, illuminating photographs of preservation projects tacked above her UN-issued Formica desk: A ninth-century Buddhist temple damaged in the 2004 tsunami. A Shiite mosque in downtown Baghdad. She tried not to think about the morning's trial, but the *Herald Tribune* article she had stared at all night still sat in front of her.

TWO YEARS LATER, FRAGMENT OF FORMA URBIS
RESURFACES IN ROME. UN OFFICIAL TO TESTIFY

Rome. Representatives of the Italian Cultural
Ministry are expected in court today to dispute
the provenance of two Forma Urbis fragments
on loan to the Capitoline Museum from an un-
named source. The Ministry asserts the fragments should be returned to Rome. . . .

A museum display, Emili thought. Over the last two years she had
researched the black markets in London and the auction houses of
Shanghai, trying to locate these pieces of the Forma Urbis that she
believed were responsible for Sharif's death. And they turned up in
a museum. Emili massaged her temples in exhaustion.

"Dottoressa Travia?"

Emili was startled by a voice in the doorway. Dr. Jacqueline
Olivier, the director general of the International Centre, carried
a thin black briefcase and a black-and-tan-checkered coat over
her arm. As usual, she arrived at the UN offices after a breakfast
meeting and was neatly turned out in a double-breasted suit and
French-knotted scarf, her charcoal-colored hair cut to feathered
perfection. With her fine aristocratic features and quiet air of Parisian nobility, Director Olivier was the very personification of the
prestigious organization that conserved priceless monuments of
civilization. In contrast, Emili had loose strands of blond hair strewn
across her exhausted face. She sat up abruptly, embarrassed to
have such an elegant and accomplished figure discover her lost in
reflection.

But in the director's eyes there was not the least bit of judgment,
only concern.

"I heard about your testimony today," she said.

"I know your thoughts on the strength of our evidence, Director."

"Or the lack of it," Director Olivier said, stopping her. "Emili, I know what this artifact means to you, especially with the World Heritage Committee meeting this week. You hoped this artifact would rescue your efforts to show illicit excavations beneath Jerusalem."

"They confirm what Dr. Lebag and I saw."

Olivier leaned against the doorway, tucking her gloves into the front pocket of her overcoat. "But are we *really* to believe that someone began a riot in the Muslim Quarter of Jerusalem to stop your investigation? That to protect their research they were willing to take Sharif's life?"

Emili answered quietly. "They were willing to take many more lives than Sharif's. He was just the only one down there."

Olivier offered her a consoling smile, an expression meant to soothe. Instead, it so clearly revealed her own administrator's agenda of wanting to let this go, of wanting the office staff to move on, that it had just the opposite effect. It emboldened Emili. The political expediency that made the director want to believe Sharif's death was accidental had fostered exactly the kind of revision of history that Emili, as a preservationist, was trained to guard against.

"Emili, I wish I could convince you to stay for the World Heritage Committee opening ceremony tomorrow."

"Not unless you allow me to present our findings about the illegal excavations beneath the Temple Mount at the plenary conference. Otherwise, I'll be returning to Jerusalem this evening."

"On the World Food Programme charter, I suppose?" the director stepped out of her office, wagging her finger maternally. "You're deputy director now, Dr. Travia. You should start traveling like one."

The director's footsteps faded down the hallway, and Emili stood up. She unhooked her herringbone overcoat from the back of the door, tightened her scarf, and carefully picked up the Napoleonic sketch Orvieti had entrusted to her. If answers about those fragments of the Forma Urbis lay in the Colosseum, she would find them.

14

Comandante Profeta, followed by Lieutenant Rufio, swiped his access card outside the Command's computer forensic laboratory and stepped through its glass doors. The preserved ceiling of the laboratory reflected the building's original purpose as a Jesuit college, and domed frescoes vaulted over tables of confiscated computer servers from the midnight raid. The computers were dissected; their exposed wires resembled electronic open-heart surgery.

"We salvaged a digital image, *Comandante*," Lieutenant Copia said proudly. She handed Profeta a computer printout. "Came from the one LCD monitor we removed before the explosion."

"But you said there was a bullet hole directly through the screen," Profeta said.

"Correct," Copia responded, "but the bullet through this screen short-circuited the LCD display, burning the last image onto the screen's hyper-compressed pixels." The technician pointed at the printout in Profeta's hands. "That was the last picture on the screen."

The image was a black-and-white sketch, prismed in shards as though the sketch had been photocopied behind a sheet of shattered glass. The imprint of a bullet hole lay at the center of the image.

"These are Forma Urbis fragments," Profeta said. "Looks like they are assembling pieces of the ancient map to reconstruct an image of the Colosseum."

"*Comandante!*" Brandisi said. He charged into the room, holding clenched pages in his right hand, as he would a torch. "I have information about the restoration project adjacent to the dockside warehouse in Civitavecchia."

"The restoration project?" Profeta said.

"Yes, you said to research the restoration effort of a small Roman ruin located on the same dock as the warehouse we raided last night. As expected, the restoration was sponsored by the Cultural Ministry of Civitavecchia and the local tourist bureau, but there was a private donor. A Saudi-based cultural heritage fund called the al-Quds fund." Brandisi looked down at the wrinkled pages in front of him. "A UNESCO-subsidized fund incorporated in Morocco in 1998 to 'preserve the Islamic cultural heritage of Jerusalem.'"

"Jerusalem?" Profeta said. "What does Jerusalem have to do with a ruin on an abandoned pier twenty minutes outside Rome?"

"Could be a cultural-exchange project," Rufio said, referring to the pairing of foreign preservation projects for reciprocal donations. "Helps with publicity. It's probably nothing unusual."

"I searched for other local restoration projects with contributions from this same fund, and I found one. It's a restoration project for a ruin downtown."

"Where?" Profeta asked, his eyes shifting to the printout of the shattered screen depicting the Forma Urbis.

"Just outside the Piazza del Colosseo."

"Along the northeastern gate of the Colosseum, along the Via del Colosseo?" Profeta asked.

Brandisi glanced again at the wrinkled pages in front of him. "Yes," he said, stunned. "A restoration of the gladiatorial barracks, just outside that area of the Colosseum. How did you know?"

Profeta pointed at the shattered image. "It's the location of the gate on these fragments of the Forma Urbis." Profeta turned to Rufio. "Rufio, I want four squad cars surrounding the Colosseum. These antiquity thieves could be beneath the ruin even as we speak."

"*Comandante*, are you sure about this?" Rufio said, his cheek twitching. But he knew Profeta had not heard the voice that haunted him since he had hung up the pay phone in the alleyway only an hour before.

"If they discover the excavations near the Colosseum, you realize the measures Salah ad-Din will have to take," the hushed voice had said.

"But there are hundreds of tourists in the piazza around the Colosseum!" Rufio protested. "It's not some abandoned commercial pier you can just blow—"

But by then, the line was dead. A recorded operator's voice had interrupted Rufio in rapid Arabic, presumably asking the caller to try again.

15

Tatton and Mildren returned to the firm like a triumphal procession victorious in battle. Jonathan walked behind them, seeing the palazzo's façade glisten in a sudden burst of winter sun, much like his future career at Dulling. Seven years ago, he would have burned with excitement at the discovery of hidden writing inside a piece of the Forma Urbis and probably presented a scholarly paper on the concealed letters. Now Mildren's suggestion about taking a power sander to their underside made terrifying sense.

Tatton's voice echoed in his mind. *Mysteries of the ancient world do not concern us, Marcus.* And he could hear Emili's counterpoint as if to answer, *"Sharif knew these fragments meant something more, Jon. It's why he stayed behind."*

In the courtyard, the palazzo's arched stables were outfitted with sleek glass walls for the partners' indoor parking. Now, during the workday, it resembled a luxury Italian car dealership of vintage Ferraris and Alfa Romeo roadsters.

Jonathan was somewhere in the middle of the courtyard when he realized he simply could not let it go. *Titus's mistake.* The ancient spy craft was too obvious for him to ignore. If an inscription about Emperor Titus lay inside the gladiators' gate, a message carved *inside* a fragment of the Forma Urbis would have been the most durable way to signal someone to retrieve it, even centuries later.

"Damn it," he said, turning away from Dulling's palazzo. *The Colosseum is not far from here,* Jonathan thought. *In this weather it probably won't be packed with tour groups.*

He walked at a determined clip, as though the firm's eyes were still on him. He suspected the research he was about to do could come dangerously close to betraying attorney-client confidentiality, and he could not afford to leave a trail. He turned off the Piazza della Repubblica into a narrow alley, past a small Renaissance niche that housed a statue of the Virgin Mary and fresh flowers supplied daily by the local faithful.

The wind had picked up considerably, nearly pushing him across Piazza Venezia. *The reason the message* Error Titi *was carved inside those fragments of the Forma Urbis was to identify a gladiators' gate in the*

Colosseum. Jonathan shook his head, as though trying to snap himself out of the notion. But an adrenaline rush well known to classicists rose within him, a sense of imminent discovery as palpable as the freezing gusts whipping at the tails of his suit jacket.

From the precipitous height of the Vittorio Emanuele Monument, the top of the Forum's ruins came into sharper focus.

The Roman Forum, the open-air archaeological park located in the center of downtown Rome, lay sixty feet below the traffic-clogged streets on either side. On a summer day, its ancient pavement would be packed with barking tour guides and screaming children. But on a cold winter afternoon beneath gathering clouds, the foggy, slumbering ruins looked more desolate than ever.

To Jonathan's trained eye, the strewn pillars and marble debris were silent ghosts of the bustling marketplaces and ancient office buildings that once stood in this downtown of the Roman Empire. For Jonathan, the whistle of the wind was a haunting reminder of how quickly civilizations fade.

Jonathan jogged down the stairs through the entrance gate. Touching down on the Via Sacra's original Roman pavement, he felt the uneven texture of the ancient road through the soles of his still-soaked Ferragamos.

It began to drizzle again, but Jonathan pressed forward, stretching his long legs with each stride, his shoulders thrust forward as he walked through the ruins, passing the Arch of Septimus Severus, the burned masonry of an ancient notary public's office, the onionskin marble of temple columns. Jonathan's pace quickened, his anticipation growing more intense as the Colosseum loomed into view.

He entered the Piazza del Colosseo, a vast expanse of cobblestone that even on this winter afternoon was packed with tour guides shouting in different languages over the calls of souvenir hucksters with arms full of Colosseum paperweights. Locals dressed in gladiatorial garb stood in front of the outer arches, knocking tin swords against their plastic chest shields to solicit pictures for two euros apiece.

Even from across the piazza, the Colosseum's massive pilasters of limestone and travertine dwarfed the souvenir tables. An orange mist of late-morning sun hung low around the Colosseum's four stories of classical stone archways.

"Marcus Aurelius!" A voice nearly startled Jonathan out of his skin. The meat of a hand struck Jonathan, a friendly back slap, with enormous force.

Jonathan recognized the voice immediately. Chandler Manning. Jonathan had not seen him in years. He was much the same as Jonathan remembered him from the library at the American Academy: a small, paunchy frame; disheveled hair over his ears; a partially untucked dress shirt beneath a wrinkled blue blazer. Chandler had lost weight, but not enough.

"Look who's returned!" Chandler said, throwing up his stubby arms. He was shorter than Jonathan had remembered. In his right hand Chandler held an extended pointer with a purple feather glued to the top for the benefit of a small group of tourists trailing behind him. For a moment he jogged to keep pace with Jonathan's long strides, tripping over the Forum's uneven stones.

Jonathan stopped and extended a hand. Chandler playfully batted it away, offering a clubby male hug.

"Hullo, Chands," Jonathan said.

When Jonathan was a graduate student at the Academy, Chandler Manning was the librarian. Chandler spoke with a vaguely British accent, with his jaw thrust forward. He was American, but from his many years abroad and facility with languages, he had abandoned his native inflection for a foreign air that would make few guess his childhood origins were a small mining town in northwestern Oregon.

"Ladies and gentlemen"—Chandler turned to the semicircle of people on his tour and spoke to them effortlessly in German—"this is an honor, really. The former Rome Prize winner who dazzled us all."

They nodded enthusiastically, as if Jonathan were an unexpected monument not on their itinerary. One of the tourists took a picture of him.

"Seven years it's been, Aurelius?" It was a Chandler affectation, nicknaming the world around him to make it instantly his own. Marcus Aurelius, Roman emperor A.D. 161–180. "I still remember you running around this Forum," he said, leaning in with a close, nostalgic smile. "Could date the stones of this place to the year, couldn't you?"

"That's overstating things, Chands," Jonathan said politely. "How are the ancient cults treating you these days?"

"Not ancient cults, Jon, it's the modern ones I've been up to." He handed Jonathan a card. It looked vaguely occult with green designs resembling crop circles. Jonathan glanced down at the card. It said, "Roman Kaballah: Eternal Knowledge in the Eternal City."

"Need anything at all while you're here, Aurelius, you call that number, or just show up. I'm around."

Jonathan looked up from the card. *"Kaballah?* You're not serious, Chandler."

Chandler shrugged. "Commercial mysticism and some entrepreneurial savvy go a long way these days. Bought some dead occultist's library just off the Campo dei Fiori for a song. Place is just magic. Up to two lectures per evening. Even have a girl at the receptionist desk taking credit cards."

Not that this surprised Jonathan. He remembered how Chandler could captivate entire tables of scholars over drinks at the local pub by the American Academy, the Thermopolium. Showing off his photographic memory for a pretty Italian bartender, he would combine

codices by Benedictine monks with Egyptian astrology to produce a
theory that the sphinx was *really* a representation of Saint Paul. It
was nonsense, of course, but the only offensive part to Jonathan was
how the party tricks masked Chandler's remarkable ability to synthe-
size endless material spreading across centuries and recall details at
a moment's notice.

"Sounds like you've found your calling, Chandler."

"And you?" Chandler leaned in rather close, his eyes wide open.
He flashed a deadly serious face. "Your exit was the stuff of ancient
myth." Chandler stood back, as though to give space to the grandi-
osity of the statement. *"Myth,"* he repeated. "I mean, after the tragedy in the catacombs that night, it's like there was *damnatio memoriae*
about you," he said, referring to ancient Rome's political tradition
of blotting out inscriptions and defacing statues to erase the memory of previous emperors. "Remember how the academy keeps
portraits of former Rome Prize winners above that little wooden
bar off the villa's salon? Well, they even took yours down. *Nerve,* I
tell you."

"Listen, Chandler"—Jonathan's eyes caught the long line for
the Colosseum—"I'm in a terrible rush, but it's good to see you.
Really."

Jonathan edged away, a tight-lipped smile, holding up Chandler's
card as though intending to use it.

Chandler moved his pointer in Jonathan's direction, holding it
like a tilted foil. "One more thing."

He tapped Jonathan's chest with his pointer, an air of playful
menace. He turned to the members of the tour group, again in German. "Did I mention that Marcus here was not just a scholar but
an excellent swordsman?" He switched back to English. "Division I
saber fencing champion for Columbia, was it?"

"City College of New York."

"Even better. Those uptown snobs can't handle anything other than a foil anyway."

Jonathan looked over Chandler's shoulder. "Chandler, really, I—"

"Come, Jon, one point for old time's sake." Chandler took another pocket pointer out of his jacket, pulled it to full extension, and handed it to Jonathan.

Chandler bent his knees in the classic pose of a fencing advance, jiggling the purple feather in front of Jonathan.

"Next time"—Jonathan imitated a smile—"I'm afraid I'm just too—"

Jonathan stepped to the left to make his way politely around him, but Chandler stepped to the left, one foot in front of the other. With a one-two beat, he scraped Jonathan's pointer with his own, tap-tap, egging him on. *This is ridiculous,* Jonathan thought, and if he weren't in such a rush, Jonathan would have waited out his showmanship, but tourists were starting to gather, and this was becoming a spectacle. Reluctantly Jonathan raised the extendable pointer, holding it loosely enough to lead Chandler to lunge, and when Chandler did, Jonathan deftly rapped Chandler's knuckles from below. As though on a string, Chandler's pointer flew into the air and landed flat in Jonathan's palm. Turning around, Jonathan straight-thrusted the pointer with such force into Chandler's breast that it collapsed to its pocket size, giving the German tourists such a perfect illusion of impalement that their eyes went around their tour guide's body to see if the pointer had exited the other side.

Chandler reddened, embarrassed, but after a moment he laughed. "Always were one up on me, weren't you?" He threw an arm out, smiling, as he walked off, motioning for his tour group to follow. "That's a point for you, Aurelius, but I'll take the match!"

16

In a carabinieri trailer parked outside the Piazza del Colosseo, Profeta and Rufio spread out an aerial map of the Colosseum across a small folding table. The area's senior patrol officer crouched beneath the trailer's fluorescent tube light pointing at the map as he briefed them.

"The cameras outside the Colosseum show the excavation team here, inside the gladiatorial school on the other side of Via del Colosseo." The officer grew more uncomfortable as he spoke, his eyes not leaving the map. His patrolling officers were at fault for not checking the excavation team's permits. They should have investigated any work conducted within such proximity to the Colosseum.

"These men worked in the ruins for two weeks in broad daylight thirty meters from the Colosseum? Without a single permit?" Profeta asked in an even tone, careful to restrain his anger. *So much for the tighter security that Roman municipal forces promised for the city's most popular attractions in the wake of the London bombings.* It was only a few years ago, in 2002, that the carabinieri discovered large quantities of a cyanide-based compound in utility tunnels beneath Via Veneto near local water-supply points. Profeta shuddered to think what an efficient group of thugs could accomplish with access to the ancient tunnels that sprawled beneath the Colosseum.

"The men were in range of the Colosseum's exterior surveillance cameras," the officer said. "We're running the tapes to see if any officers spoke to them."

"What cameras?" Rufio asked brusquely.

"Vandal-surveillance cameras," Profeta answered. "The Cultural Ministry installed surveillance cameras around Rome's most significant ruins to prevent graffiti." Profeta knew the cameras had caused controversy among the older Roman locals who were wary of local government since the fascist overrun a half-century before. But Profeta had submitted a powerful letter of support to the Cultural Ministry. *The Vandals sacked Rome once before,* he said, referring to the fifth-century sack of Rome. *They must not do it again.*

"Are you sure the *municipio* has no record of any work done in this area?" Rufio said, controlling his anxiety. "The archaeological superintendent said no equipment or vehicles have been stolen."

"These were professionals," Profeta said. "They constructed their own scaffolding and brought their own equipment."

At the back of the trailer's door, Brandisi appeared. "The staffers from the archaeological superintendent's office have opened up the gates to the gladiatorial barracks."

"Lieutenant Rufio," Profeta said, "go ahead with the staffers in the ruins and search for any remnants of illegal excavation."

Despite the bracing wind, Rufio was sweating as he crossed the street from the Colosseum to the ancient gladiator barracks, which were now an excavated semicircular ruin of moss-covered brick. Rufio knew the ruin was largely ignored because of its location in the literal shadow of the Colosseum's eastern wall, but its small arena where the gladiators trained before their matches was one of Rome's most well preserved open-air excavations.

At the gate leading down to the steps of the ruin, Rufio saw two staffers from the archaeological superintendent's office, Rome's municipal bureaucracy of archaeologists and engineers charged to protect the city's archaeology from modern dangers, ranging from illegal excavations to proposed metro tunnels. The department was notorious for its bribery, but as Rufio approached the two middle-aged staffers, a heavyset woman with a clipboard and a balding man in a pince-nez, he cursed his luck that it appeared the only two in-corruptible staffers in the entire ministry had come to join his inspection.

Disregarding the *comandante*'s instructions, Rufio directed the inspectors to stay at the gate while he went into the ruin alone. His authoritative body language and harsh tone convincingly suggested that this precaution was for their own benefit, but in reality it was for his: All traces of illegal excavation must be erased.

He walked down the steps into the ruin and touched down on the damp moss, steaming. *Why had no one told him of those vandal cameras?* Within days, a junior officer would be tasked to watch all of the previous month's footage only to see none other than Lieutenant Rufio himself standing beside the ruin, surveying the men's excavation last week, preventing any other police disturbance.

Rufio walked through the sunken arches of the gladiatorial bar-racks. Noisy, traffic-jammed streets rose twenty feet above the ruin's ancient pavement on which he stood. He was grateful for the morn-ing's earlier downpour, which washed away any footprints.

As expected, Salah ad-Din's men did not tell Rufio what they were looking for. Nor did Rufio care. The men received their access to the ruins of the gladiator barracks without police molestation, and Rufio received twenty thousand euros in a briefcase on the seat at a café table beside the ruin's eastern fence.

Now, as Rufio finished walking through the ruin, he breathed deeply. There were no traces of any work.

Rufio exited the ruin, ignoring the two inspectors who still awaited him by the gate. He crossed the Via del Colosseo, walked briskly past a row of cafés, and turned into a narrow and foul-smelling medieval alleyway. In the middle of the alley was another pay phone.

The receiver shook against his ear as he nervously rolled an-other cigarette and licked the paper shut. Pulling drags between the seemingly countless rings, he finally heard the beep of an answering machine.

"No one will discover the other excavation sites," Rufio's voice quavered. "No further measures are necessary. I repeat: No further measures are necessary."

Rufio returned to the ruins of the gladiatorial barracks. He was dismayed to find Profeta and Brandisi walking among its ancient arches.

"No evidence of illegal excavation here, *Comandante!*" Rufio called out, hurrying down the steps after them.

Profeta nodded. "Not here in the ruins, no," he said. He pointed at the concrete wall that ran around the perimeter of the ruin. "But I fear they used this excavation site as access to the Colosseum."

"Access?" Brandisi asked. He pointed at the cars whizzing past along the Via del Colosseo, the four-lane street that curved around the Colosseum. "But the Via del Colosseo is between the Colosseum and this ruin, *Comandante.*"

"Only above the ground, Lieutenant," Profeta said. "In antiquity, an underground tunnel linked these barracks for the gladiators to have access to the arena."

Profeta walked along the perimeter of the ruin, continuing to inspect the slanted wall that buttressed the streets above them. He approached a weather-beaten door with a rusted bolt brace across it, secured by a padlock. The padlock was so corroded that Profeta could not even lift it. He kneeled in the moss and looked at its bottom. Beneath its brown, rusted skin was a hidden lock with a glistening titanium base.

"Get this door open *now*," Profeta said.

17

J onathan moved through the tourist line outside the Colosseum, zigzagging through a cattle pen of rope lines inside the ruin's outer vault. The sweatered ticket staff was stationed like a row of bank tellers inside a long window, issuing tickets, audio phones, and brochures, talking over the loud ratcheting clicks of the turnstiles.

"One adult please, with audio phones," Jonathan said politely to the woman behind the ticket window. The audio phones would make it less conspicuous that he was wandering around without a tour group. Nearly ten thousand tourists each day visited the Colosseum, making it Italy's most popular tourist attraction. Jonathan knew this number of visitors was only a fraction of the sixty thousand Romans who packed the stadium to watch gladiatorial battles in antiquity.

He stepped through the turnstile and entered the enormous expanse of the Colosseum's interior, which resembled an oval stone crater rimmed with hundreds of archways carved in its walls. Any classicist could not help but admire the Colosseum as a model of urban survival. Earthquakes damaged the amphitheater in 442 and 508, and in 1349 it was converted into a fortress.

Jonathan tilted his head back, taking in the vastness of its elliptical shape, six acres. On the top row, he could see the indentations in the stone that marked where a vast *velarium*, or linen awning, would unravel over the immense crowd. *The world's first retractable stadium roof.* Jonathan's eyes scanned the complexity of the Colosseum's architecture, its system of stairways cascading between seating levels with eighty arches per floor. Numbers carved above the arches revealed a modern system of crowd control. At the Colosseum's center, the excavated arena floor revealed an underground maze of ancient brick-lined passages four stories deep below. Jonathan could make out ancient metal hinges still in the brick, where systems of rollers and pulleys and counterweights hoisted gladiators and animals up through trapdoors to the arena floor. Few people realized just how technologically advanced the Colosseum was.

Jackdaws darted between the brush of the dark archways. It was impossible to comprehend the ancient chaos of the Colosseum—the stench of the dead beasts and the volume of human slaughter in the arena. The violent history of the Colosseum made it a very real political symbol still. Every time a death sentence is overturned somewhere in the world, the local government of Rome, as part of a "Cities for Life" program, illuminates a large thumb on the Colosseum's façade, referring to the ancient emperors' gesture to spare a gladiator's life.

Jonathan entered a small glass-enclosed museum shop and bought a small map of the ruins and a souvenir penlight with *I survived the Colosseum* written in glitter around it. He tested the penlight, knowing that daylight might not be sufficient where he was going. Tour groups moved around the arena as steadily as watch hands, and Jonathan joined one.

"Hail Caesar!" an Australian guide proclaimed. "Those who are about to die in the Colosseum greet you!'" Never mind, Jonathan thought, that the Flavian amphitheater was not called "the Colosseum" until the sixth century A.D. It was a common historical blunder, and during the movie *Gladiator*, he groaned every time Russell Crowe called the stadium "the Colosseum," a name not imagined until hundreds of years after Rome's fall.

Jonathan drifted away from the tour, walking around the iron fence that surrounded the arena. His eyes scanned the arches' high architraves, noting the Roman numerals above each one.

Jonathan stopped in front of an arch with no number above it. The map identified it as the *Porta Sanavivaria*, where gladiators entered the arena. A thin rusted chain across its opening indicated that it was off-limits to tourists. He knew the hypogeum, the labyrinth of passageways beneath the Colosseum, was not excavated until the nineteenth century, leaving it mostly intact. The sealed-off subterranean compartments owed their survival to their having been forgotten—proving the old preservationist's proverb that Emili had taught him years before. *Quae amissa salva.* Lost things are safe.

Jonathan stepped over the chain into the dark apse. He twisted the shaft of the penlight and it illuminated a medieval stairwell leading downward. Ghostly white roots spread across the stairwell's aperture, and he parted them as casually as if they were a beaded curtain. A sour, clammy breath washed over him as he descended, the stairs growing steeper toward the bottom. He reached an underground brick passage. The floor was slick, and he pressed his palms against both walls for support as he moved deeper into the corridor. The daylight from the stairwell dimmed to a distant greenish glow, reflecting the walls' coat of algae. Jonathan turned up the collar of his suit; the damp air was ten degrees cooler down here. At roughly fifteen feet below street level, his arguments to Mildren were fast losing their clarity, and Jonathan began to question himself. *What did it mean, a monument to Josephus? Almost no one who saw these corridors survived. Why would these passageways bear a monument at all?*

At the end of the corridor, the walls were so thick with moss and purple roots that they resembled coral reefs. Jonathan knew that much of the plant life beneath the Colosseum was indigenous to Africa and Asia Minor. In antiquity, seeds had fallen off the coats of the tigers and lions brought to Rome for combat in the Colosseum.

Over the centuries since, hundreds of species of plant life had taken root here in the labyrinth and flourished up through the sewer grates.

Not yet turning the corridor's bend, he noted crude excavation work on the walls all around him. A hatchet job, he knew immediately. The broad gashes of ax marks and electric sanders were hallmarks of illegal excavations. The walls were brutalized for as far as he could see.

At the end of the corridor, Jonathan could see a faint light growing stronger. It was a flashlight's beam moving up and down, scanning the walls. He quickly walked away from the light, ducking under the corridor's low, jagged ceiling.

He made a wrong turn and the corridor's features looked different from how they did a moment ago. Jonathan shut off his penlight, not wanting to give away his location. He hid inside a niche and stood very still, swallowing his breaths. Illicit excavators were known to kill.

The sound of rapid footsteps on the dirt-packed floor grew louder. As though sensing Jonathan's presence, they stopped suddenly. Jonathan remained plastered against the rock wall. The white shaft of light moved closer, shining into each niche in search of an intruder.

Jonathan pressed further against the wall until, in sudden terror, he realized the wall's jagged surface had pressed a button on his audio headset. The loud sound of a mellifluous French voice emerged from the dangling electronic device around his neck and filled the tunnel. *"Bienvenue au Colisée . . ."*

The light moved sharply toward him and Jonathan rushed into the darkness, using his hands to feel along the walls. The flashlight grew stronger behind him, and as he picked up the pace, his hands could no longer anticipate the corridor's sharp turns. Now running, he slammed the top of his head into the ceiling, and piercing threads pulsed down his neck as though he had swallowed the pain. He keeled in silent agony, holding his head and feeling the dampness of the blood above his hairline. A flashlight's beam trained on him and observed him doubled over against the wall. He squinted into the beam.

"Wait!" He was breathless, hands out in front, temporarily blinded.

Against all expectations, he recognized the voice behind the flashlight's beam. Around the rim of light, and beneath an open overcoat, Jonathan could make out the same gray suit she had worn in court that morning.

"Let me guess," Emili Travia said. "You're down here for legal research."

18

Inside the Temple Mount's aqueduct, Ahmed hacked through the wall, each stroke flooding the tunnel with more light. The professor stepped in front of Salah ad-Din, dazzled. The hole grew larger and the professor had a nearly religious experience, staring into an infinite light with the dry, dusty breeze of a canyon on his face. But as his eyes adjusted and the image became clearer, the vision stunned him into a horrified silence.

The tunnel wall gave way to a cavern as large as an indoor stadium. Blazing white klieg lights hung from iron girders, illuminating what appeared to be a massive construction site. The tunnel's opening was six stories from the cavern's floor, and the volume of activity below resembled a small metropolis. Bulldozers rolled along the floor of the hollowed-out cavern. Dozens of men in kaffiyehs pushed wheelbarrows brimming with piles of ashlar block, potsherds, and broken glass. A pulley system raised and lowered buckets of pottery from crude wooden platforms that swung along the cavern walls.

On the cavern floor, a man in a glass operator's cage worked a massive machine with a bucket shovel the size of a car. The professor could barely contain his fury as he watched it plow into the cavern wall. Thousands of pieces of broken Roman-era glass glimmered in the piles of crushed stones. The machine backed up from the wall, followed by a continuous popping sound of terra-cotta vases and other artifacts crushed within its jaws.

Looking up, the professor could discern that the cavern's ceiling was as jagged as natural bedrock, presumably the underside of the Temple Mount's natural contours. He knew that one hundred feet above them, people of many faiths gathered for quiet devotion in the Western Wall plaza, the al-Aqsa Mosque, or in the Sisters of Zion Convent, unaware of this destruction beneath one of the most exalted places on earth.

"I had heard rumors of illegal excavations beneath the Temple Mount," Cianari said, "but I never imagined something like this." Only now did it make sense to the professor why the Waqf Authority denied access for UN investigators, citing their jurisdiction from Ottoman times to administer the Temple Mount without regard to Israeli sovereignty or to the Christian patriarchies around it.

"This is all your destruction, isn't it?" The professor's small face reddened with fury.

"Excavation is the word I prefer," Salah ad-Din replied.

"Your men have been here for months," the professor said angrily. He pointed where countless axes had cleaved into the limestone. "Why did you need me to find where the tunnel from the Temple entered into this cavern?"

"The priests moved the artifact across an aqueduct's bridge that once spanned the walls of this cavern," Salah ad-Din said in a factual tone. "And to find the end of a bridge that no longer exists—"

"—you must find where the bridge began," the professor said resignedly.

"And now we have," Salah ad-Din said, motioning to where the tunnel's precipice led to the cavern's bright air. "We must now only find where this tunnel continues on the other side of the cavern."

A motorized, aluminum scaffolding lowered Salah ad-Din and the professor fifty feet to the cavern floor. Despite the scaffolding's electric operation, it took nearly a half-minute to reach the floor.

"You cannot even be certain there was once a bridge between these walls!" the professor said loudly over the electric saws and bulldozer engines.

Walking now across the cavern floor, Salah ad-Din pointed to a wooden sawhorse table in front of him.

"Yes, I can," he said.

When the professor saw the table's contents he became oblivious to the sound of the generators, the shouted Arabic between workmen, the smell of their hashish mingling with the diesel and asphalt.

Across the table, an illustrated eleventh-century map depicted the ruins of an arched Roman aqueduct that once spanned the cavern walls.

"This is an original Crusader-era map of the Temple Mount. I thought *none* still existed," Cianari said. "Where did you find this?"

Salah ad-Din said nothing, a sign that the professor had touched on a topic too sacred for him to trespass. Even now, Salah ad-Din remembered the instructions about how to recover this map that his grandfather had feared was lost.

"In the Assyrian wing of the Baghdad Museum, maps—" he man-
aged to say through a hacking cough in the basement of their Beirut
hovel. The mufti spoke only a few words at a time then, suffer-
ing from pulmonary disease in his last years. "A map of the Temple
Mount."

Salah ad-Din waited twenty years to retrieve it. Not until 2003,
during the confusion of the American invasion of Iraq, did he see his
opportunity. He recalled entering the bombed-out Baghdad Museum
disguised as a member of a UN preservation team, his adrenaline
raging as he stood on the verge of recovering the crates that con-
tained his grandfather's life work. A skinny American soldier es-
corted him, trudging a few steps behind, nearly buckling under the
weight of his gear. Salah ad-Din walked through the destroyed gal-
leries without the slightest concern for the shattered Babylonian
vases and display cases overturned by the recent looting. He remem-
bered entering the storage room and seeing the black Turkish scimi-
tar, the insignia of the Mufti's SS Handschar Division, on a forgotten
wooden crate in the corner. Salah ad-Din felt a moment of redemp-
tion greater than any religion could offer him.

"I should radio this in," the young American soldier nervously
said of their discovery, fumbling for his walkie-talkie, but before he
pressed down on the push-to-talk button, Salah ad-Din had un-
clipped the holster of the young soldier's sidearm, removed the Army-
issued Beretta, and now tilted the barrel into the boy's collarbone
beneath his flak jacket.

"No you shouldn't," Salah ad-Din said, and shot the soldier
through the chest.

The high priest's path of escape continued there." Salah ad-Din
pointed to the far wall. "That is where he hid the one treasure Titus
sought."

"Why should I help you find where the tunnel continues? So you can finish stripping the Mount of all Judeo-Christian artifacts, too?" Cianari's voice shook with emotion. He watched a bulldozer collide with one of the cavern walls. "I am an archaeologist. Not a butcher."

"Precisely the reason I chose you," Salah ad-Din said calmly. He pointed at the deep gashes in the cavern's far wall. "You can tell we've had little success."

"Get me out of here," Cianari grunted.

"To leave now, Professor," Salah ad-Din said, "is to ignore the priceless opportunity of this search."

"An opportunity to rape sacred strata that date to our patriarchs?"

"An opportunity to save them," Salah ad-Din said. "It is only in the absence of your expertise"—he motioned to the giant tractor below—"that less *delicate* means have been necessary."

19

The lock is titanium graphite, *Comandante*," Brandisi said. "The officers don't have the right equipment to clip the lock."

"Stand back," Profeta ordered. The officers stepped behind him and Profeta switched off the safety of his Tanfoglio. Steadying the pistol with both hands, he fired at the door. The hollow blast echoed through the ruin, sending stray cats scurrying. The lock spun and fell, and the door jolted open.

Inside the tunnel, natural light illuminated the high-tech excavation equipment against the walls.

Profeta walked up to an umbrella-sized chrome device.

"It's a helium piston," he said, impressed by the quality of equipment. "It pneumatically pushes out stone with rapid bursts of air rather than a jackhammer's metal bit."

"To drill beneath the piazza without any noise," Brandisi said.

Profeta nodded. "We must move quickly. They may know we're here."

That's what I'm afraid of, Rufio thought.

Profeta's flashlight cut through the brown dust. The faint noises of the Piazza del Colosseo drifted through the storm drains above them.

"This tunnel connects the gladiatorial barracks to the service passages beneath the Colosseum," Profeta said.

Rufio's eyes darted nervously, his face drenched with sweat.

"Are you okay, Rufio?" Profeta asked.

"Of course, *Comandante!*" Rufio said, his nerves constraining his breath.

He took the lead to project an air of confidence. But he knew better than anyone the danger they faced. The men responsible for this excavation would not hesitate to detonate the entire tunnel with them inside.

The sounds of the piazza above faded, and only the sound of their own footsteps echoed in the tunnel. Profeta examined the excavated walls.

"It's as if the digging here was done by Jekyll and Hyde," Profeta said.

"Jekyll? You know who is responsible already?" Brandisi said in amazement. *Nothing got past Il Profeta.*

"An English expression," Profeta said. "There were two personalities at work here in this excavation. Over here"—Profeta's flashlight scanned the pile of stacked rubble, sharply cracked bricks, and split stone—"the work is methodical, by someone with scholarly

training, as though these pieces are to be removed for further study."
He moved his flashlight to another pile of rubble. "And here, the
digging is as brutal as taking a chain saw to a fresco."

A high iron gate stood in the middle of the corridor ahead. It was
slightly lower than the ceiling of arched brick.

With an athleticism that surprised Rufio, Profeta grabbed its
wrought iron and pressed his shoes on its rusted cross bar, his beard
brushing the top of the gate as he lifted his other leg over and landed
on the other side. Brandisi followed. Rufio lagged behind, frantically moving his flashlight's beam down each corridor. He tried repeatedly to grab the fence's crossbar but missed.

"Rufio, you're sure you are okay?" Brandisi asked from the other
side of the gate.

"Nothing is the matter!" Rufio snapped. "And don't ask me again.
That is an order, Sottotenenente." Second Lieutenant. After a few
more attempts, Rufio managed to climb over.

When they caught up with the comandante, they found him
crouched in the corridor, his right hand raised to quiet their approach.

"Do you hear that?" Profeta whispered.

Brandisi nodded. The echo of two voices reverberated down the
corridor. The three of them drew their guns.

What *on earth* are you doing down here, Jonathan?" Emili demanded.

Jonathan stood up, still winded. "I should ask you the same thing."

Emili took a step back. "Answer me, Jon."

Jonathan noticed she had moved farther away.

"Wait, you don't think I'm—"

"Part of this? Why else would you be down here?"

"Because I saw"—Jonathan stopped himself. "It's all just conjecture, really." He pulled from his pocket the torn Alitalia napkin where he had scribbled the fragment's inscription in reverse. He held out the crumpled tissue. "Here," he said.

Emili stared at the napkin under her flashlight.

"There was a message inside the stones," Jonathan said.

"Inside?"

"The word *illumina* is imperative," Jonathan said, "as in commanding an observer to *shine* a light onto the fragment. So I did. I shined a light onto the artifact's face, and"—he halted for a moment—"some letters appeared in the fragment's shadow. A steganographic message. '*Error Titi.*'"

"A message inside the stone, *of course*," Emili said, tilting her head back, eyes closed. "That explains the bright lamps Sharif and I saw hovering over the fragments in Jerusalem."

"You don't know there's a connection," Jonathan said. "This excavation could just be *tombaroli*, some greedy thugs searching for artifacts."

Emili wiped away a small grove of mushrooms, revealing a wall carving of gladiatorial combat. "If these were *tombaroli*, Jon, this relief would have been cut out, boxed, and shipped to a London auction house by now. This excavation is different. They are not mercenaries. They are looking for something down here. A piece of information."

"Emili, even if that's true, no, *especially* if that's true, we need to report this illegal excavation immediately."

"Report it?" Emili said. "They'll rope off these corridors for weeks. I'm not leaving."

"Emili, please, the carabinieri will—"

Emili lifted her hand. The seven years of distance again crept between them. Her look hardened and she turned up her overcoat's collar against the chill. She started down the corridor. "Good luck, Jon."

"You can't even get to the end of these tunnels from here," Jonathan called out behind her. During his doctoral work, he had toured the Colosseum's underground with archaeologists, comparing the labyrinth ruins with ancient descriptions. "These passages stretch for a quarter-mile. You need someone who's been down here before!" She continued walking. "Wait," Jonathan said, shaking his head. He hurried toward her.

She turned around and stared at him, smiling.

"What?" Jonathan said. "What is it?"

"I hate to think what these tunnels are going to do to those expensive shoes."

Jonathan and Emili followed the corridor, snaking deeper underground. Bats swung overhead in the darkness. Emili's flashlight revealed a fresh gash in the wall two feet in diameter.

"These walls have been hacked to pieces." She shook her head, disgusted at the brutality. "They used power sanders and electric saw blades. *Idioti*."

The passageway widened and began to slope upward.

"We must be close to the gladiators' gate," Jonathan said. "The ground here is on a slant. Ancient sources describe gladiators entering the arena up a ramp."

He pointed to iron hooks on the walls. "This must be the *spoliarium*."

"The *spoliarium*?" Emili said.

"These hooks were for gladiator carcasses, to drain their blood," Jonathan said. "It was a profitable commodity. It was bottled and sold in the Roman Forum as a virility drink."

Emili stepped past him. "Ancient Rome's Viagra."

Through a low archway, the tunnel opened to a chamber that looked quarried out of solid rock. The air was thick with dust; tufts of moss clung to the ceiling. Along the eastern wall of the chamber, a small stone parapet answered for a bench. Rows of grooved notches lined the walls, and Jonathan ran his hand across the names written above them.

"What are all these notches?"

"Victories," Jonathan said solemnly. "Many prisoners fought for their freedom. Every notch was another victory inside the arena."

The notches were eerie remnants of humanity. Jonathan knew that for prisoners of Roman conquest, these were their last rites.

An etching above the archway read, in deeply stenciled letters, *"Damnato ad Gladium."*

"Condemned to the gladiators," Emili translated.

"An ancient punishment reserved for war captives and traitors. 'Condemned to the gladiators' meant they faced trained gladiators with little or no armor. These prisoners fed ancient Rome's insatiable desire for bloody spectacle."

Along the walls, ancient graffiti was etched in different scripts.

"All these inscriptions are in different languages," Jonathan said, his eyes moving across the wall. "Syriac, Aramaic, Greek, Latin. These are languages from the Gallic provinces conquered by the Roman army: Parthia, Gaul, Judea. This must be where prisoners and slaves waited before combat in the arena." He turned to Emili. "We're standing in the death row of ancient Rome."

An air of tragedy seemed to linger in the chamber. The inscriptions were so well preserved that both of them felt like intruders.

"Just imagine soldiers dragging the prisoners of war from this room and hurling them before a crowd of sixty thousand bloodthirsty Romans."

Jonathan looked at the wall, his finger tracing the names. At one point, he stopped. "Look at this carved name. *Aliterius Actoris.*"

"Aliterius the Actor," Emili said.

"That must refer to the stage actor Aliterius mentioned repeatedly in Josephus's historical account."

"Talk about a bad theater review," Emili said. "What's his name doing down here?"

"Aliterius was a favorite performer of Emperor Nero and used his political connections to influence decisions," Jonathan said. "Later emperors, however, were *not* in his fan club."

"Apparently," Emili said.

Jonathan moved down the wall. "And this name, Clemens." He turned to Emili. "He was a Roman consul executed for treason." Jonathan stood in front of the next name. "Epaphroditus, a publisher of politically provocative works. He, too, was executed in the last days of Titus's reign." Jonathan read another name. "*Beronike.*"

"As in *the* Berenice? The daughter of the last king of Jerusalem who became Emperor Titus's mistress?"

"Certainly possible. Many historical sources say Titus abruptly ended his relationship with Berenice. Public opinion rejected her because Titus brought her as a war prize from Jerusalem, and only then fell in love with her. Racine even wrote a tragic opera about the ill-fated love between Berenice and Titus. She may have been executed here in the Colosseum with the others." Jonathan stepped back from the wall. "The inscriptions all look contemporaneous, and written in the same script."

"What do these names have in common?"

Jonathan stared at the wall.

"Spies," he said after a moment. "They were all suspected spies in Titus's palace."

"Spies? You're joking."

"Take Aliterius," Jonathan said, "the actor who used his political connections with Nero."

"Using celebrity clout for political purposes doesn't make someone a spy," Emili said. "Or your Department of Homeland Security would have arrested half of Hollywood already."

"Fair enough," Jonathan agreed. "But there's no record of this supposedly famous actor in *any* Roman sources other than in Josephus's writings. And the word *aliterius* literally means 'other,' as in 'alias'—or as they say in espionage operations, a 'workname.' Many historians think Aliterius was not an actor onstage, but in the theater of intelligence. He was executed shortly before Titus's death."

"And Berenice?" Emili asked. "You're suggesting Titus suspected his own mistress of being a spy?"

"It would explain her sudden disappearance from the Roman history books, wouldn't it?" Jonathan said. "Josephus repeatedly compliments Berenice, for her *paedia*. In the ancient world it meant 'applied knowledge,' as in encyclo*pedia*. But he probably wasn't just saying she was smart. Some historians suspect that the term meant 'strategy,' or even 'espionage.' In Homer, Odysseus is described as having *paedia* when he returns to Ithaca in disguise."

Jonathan moved farther down the wall and stopped suddenly. "But I'm not even sure suspected espionage is the *real* connection among all these people."

"Then what was?"

"Not what but who."

Jonathan moved closer to the last name on the wall, which was etched in a larger font. "Joseph ben Matthias," he said slowly, staring at the inscription. "They all had him in common."

"Joseph ben Matthias? I have never heard of him."

"Yes, you have, but only by the Romanized name he took after he was freed as a prisoner of war from Jerusalem. Joseph added the Roman suffix '*-us*' when he became a Roman citizen. This man," Jonathan pointed at the wall, "was Flavius Josephus."

"You're saying *Josephus* knew everyone in this room?"

Jonathan walked back to the other end of the carved rock wall. "Aliterius secured private audiences for Josephus with Emperor Nero before Rome's war with Jerusalem." He stepped down the wall as if it were a blackboard. "Berenice did the same, giving Josephus access to Titus and his social circle."

"And Clemens?"

"The lawyer who defended Josephus against allegations of spying on Rome."

"And Epaphroditus?"

"His publisher. Josephus even dedicated his last book to him."

"But why would Titus have killed all those in his court who knew Josephus, *unless*—" She stopped and turned to him slowly. "Your graduate work, Jon," she said. "I remember your research on Flavius Josephus—you suggested he was a spy in Titus's palace."

"Emili"—Jonathan raised his hands—"I never proved it. Every scholar to study Josephus in the last five hundred years concluded he *was* a traitor to Jerusalem and loyal to Titus."

"Every scholar except you. Back then you didn't care if your thesis contradicted five hundred years of Josephus scholarship. You kept us all riveted—Sharif, Gianpaolo, and me—sharing your research at the Thermopolium."

The Thermopolium. Just hearing the name brought Jonathan back to the local bar near the academy. He could see the four of them sitting at a corner table beneath a nineteenth-century portrait of a battle-dressed Garibaldi and drinking the bar's more controversial tribute to his 1859 rebellion against Vatican rule, a cocktail of tomato juice and vodka, still known as "Pope's Blood."

Jonathan remembered Sharif pointing at the pages of Jonathan's doctoral thesis that lay on the knotted-wood table. "This is the theory you've been keeping from us?" he said. "This is the idea you've been guarding like the walls of Ilium?"

"Have you any idea what you're suggesting?" Gianpaolo asked in his heavy Italian accent. "Josephus is known to everyone as the greatest traitor of the ancient world."

"And you're suggesting it's all a front," Emili said, leaning forward, her tone less skeptical than the others'. "An intelligence operation so successful, scholars remain in the dark even to this day."

"Jon, historians for nearly a thousand years have viewed Josephus's defection to the Romans as an open-and-shut case," Sharif added.

"And it is," Jonathan agreed. "Unless he was running an espionage network inside Rome after Jerusalem's fall, for which the role of sycophantic court historian was the perfect cover."

"Let me get this straight," Sharif said. "You're saying Josephus wrote flattering histories of Titus as a front to operate in Rome as a double agent? Isn't that a little far-fetched?"

"It would be, except Josephus's autobiography supports it. He isn't new to the espionage game. Josephus used the unusual Greek word kataskopos to describe himself in his writing. It means 'diplomat,' but it also means 'spy.'"

"But your theory has a problem," Gianpaolo argued. "How do you explain Josephus's capture by the Romans?"

"You're not suggesting he arranged that," Sharif said, putting down his glass of tomato juice. He had mentioned his religious restrictions to the bartender only once, and the elderly man provided him nonalcoholic versions without Sharif's ever having to ask again. "That operation would have taken years to plan."

"And it did. It's all recorded in Josephus's writings . . . if you know how to read them. Remember that before Jerusalem declared an open rebellion against Roman rule, Josephus argued that the Temple would have no chance of surviving a siege by the Roman army. Why, then, after Jerusalem declared war, did Josephus suddenly volunteer to command troops in northern Israel directly in the path of General Vespasian's troops? Sounds inconsistent, doesn't it? He had no military experience whatsoever. His men would not stand a chance against Rome."

"So you're saying he was vying to get taken prisoner before the Romans reached Jerusalem?" Emili said.

"Exactly, and he had a strategy to do it. Only, it didn't go quite as planned. Once Josephus and his troops arrived in northern Israel, he convinced the local council of elders of the Galilee to authorize the locals to plunder the Roman governor's summer home for supplies.

Josephus knew the plundering would bait Vespasian's troops, bringing the Romans to their doorstep. So he told the elders to wait for his signal before authorizing the locals to plunder. Josephus needed time to ride out far enough in front of his troops so that he would be surrounded by the Romans alone.

"So what went wrong?" Gianpaolo asked hurriedly.

"The locals got greedy and, tempted by the supplies, sacked the governor's house before Josephus's signaled. Josephus panicked, and ordered all looting to stop immediately. He tried to prevent news of the premature plundering from reaching Vespasian, but it was too late, the bait was cast. Vespasian's troops came thundering toward them and surrounded Josephus along with his men. In a scene dramatized countless times over the ages, Josephus's men chose death in a cave in Galilee rather than capture. But Josephus, in a decision that chills most historians, turned himself over to the Romans."

"If you're right," Emili said, "imagine his guilt, watching his men kill themselves one by one. By the time the Romans recovered Josephus in that cave, he must have been literally covered in the blood of their mass suicide."

"That's right, the operation was nearly blown at the start. But as planned, Josephus was still imprisoned and eventually recruited to become a personal translator to General Vespasian and his son, Titus. At that moment, the heart of his mission took effect. He had earned a position of trust that no military conquest could buy. He was inside the Roman tent, knowing the precise movements of the Roman siege of Jerusalem. In a way, Josephus was merely proving his favorite proverb, used in Book Five of The Jewish War. *'Those who shine in physical combat can accomplish as much by intelligence.' And remember the Greek word he used for intelligence, Sharif. Yperisia doesn't mean 'brains,' it means 'espionage.' It's the very word used today in Greece's intelligence service."*

"But if it was all a setup to get Josephus inside the Roman war machine," Sharif asked, "why not attempt to save Jerusalem?"

"Because her destruction was a fait accompli," Jonathan said. "With fifty thousand Roman legionnaires surrounding the Temple walls, Josephus knew the city would be razed. But what if there was something else he could protect? A piece of information that, at all costs, he must transmit to future generations. Information that—to some extent—was just as precious as Herod's Temple itself."

"Then he must put it in a document he knows will survive," Emili said.

"A flattering history of the Roman emperor, for example," Gianpaolo suggested.

"Bingo," Jonathan said. "Josephus knew Titus obsessed over erasing any version of the past inconsistent with his own. So he knew he had to secretly communicate a truth through a flattering historical account of the emperor."

Jonathan sat back. "Flavius Josephus may have been Jerusalem's most successful operative until the Mossad."

Jonathan?" Emili said inside the Colosseum's tunnel. She shone her flashlight at him. "Are you okay?"

"Yes," Jonathan said, reorienting himself. He wiped the tunnel's dripping water from his lapel and tie. The damp air beneath the Colosseum seemed colder than it had been a moment before.

"At the academy you called it the greatest intelligence operation of the ancient world," Emili marveled. Her flashlight trained back to the wall, following each name as though decoding an Egyptian hieroglyph. "And all of these people may have been part of it. A spy network revolving around an ancient historian *inside* Titus's palace."

"I never proved the theory."

"These names could prove it for you, Jon." She turned to him. "Although, if Titus discovered Josephus and killed anyone who helped him—and it seems that's exactly what he did—then why isn't Josephus's mission common historical knowledge?"

"Well, that was the genius of Josephus's plan," Jonathan said. "By the time Titus discovered him, Josephus had already penned countless pages of history lionizing the emperor. Titus could never publicize Josephus's betrayal without calling into question the truth of his historical accounts."

"So he turned Titus's obsession with history against him."

"Right, and whatever information he might have smuggled into the text, he knew the emperor would protect for all time." Jonathan stopped, catching himself. "But like I said, it was just a *theory*. My research never should have gone as far as it did. Even if Josephus's treason was all a setup, my theory never established a *motive*. Why create an espionage network *after* Jerusalem had fallen? The Temple was already burned, Jerusalem was a plundered ruin. What was left to save?"

"Something powerful enough to make a man like Josephus forsake his reputation for all time," Emili said, gesturing at the walls around her. "Something to make an actor risk his fame, a publisher his legacy, and a mistress the comforts of palace life—all under the nose of the Roman *frumentarii,* the most ruthless secret police in the ancient world. Whatever it was they saved was more important than we can possibly imagine."

Emili crossed to the far side of the cavern and lifted a black tarpaulin off the wall. "Take a look at this. This excavation happened only a few days ago."

Jonathan could smell the freshly excavated dirt. He pulled the tarp back as cautiously as stripping back the bandage of a wound.

Jonathan and Emili stared at an ancient relief chiseled directly into the wall's stone. It was the carving of a tree with seven branches, framed by white uneven stones. In place of some tiles, there was shaved animal bone. Not the quality of polychrome mosaic tiles for an aristocrat's portico, but remarkable for being created by prisoners trapped in the Colosseum.

"It's exquisite," Emili said.

With her preservationist's eye, Emili could detect that the surface had been recently damaged with a highly concentrated acidic compound. "Some of these tiles were dissolved with nitric acid."

Jonathan leaned in. "Below the relief, there's an inscription in a mix of ancient Hebraic script and Latin."

$$\text{ソ ヤ} \textit{ID ARBOR JIX} \\ \textit{DOMVS AVREA}$$

"'*Ohr Arbor Kodesh*,'" he read aloud, using the rudimentary Hebrew vocabulary learned from his work with ancient texts. "*Ohr* means 'light.'"

"*Arbor*, of course, is 'tree,'" Emili said, translating the Latin.

"And *Kodesh*, the other Hebrew word, means 'sacred.'"

"A sacred tree of light," Emili said.

"It's cultic imagery. Trees were pagan references. Why would someone pay homage to a pagan image in Hebraic script? The war prisoners from Jerusalem were monotheistic, not pagan."

Jonathan moved his finger across the second line of inscription. "*Domus aurea* means 'golden house.'"

"As in Nero's Golden Palace here in Rome?" Emili said. From her preservation work on the Oppian Hill, Emili had worked extensively in Nero's sprawling golden palace. She often quoted the ancient architect Fabilius, who had called the structure "greedy for the impossible." The Roman populace despised the palace's excesses, forcing subsequent emperors to build over the palace within five years of Nero's death, which inadvertently preserved it until its re-discovery in the Renaissance.

Jonathan noticed carvings of birds surrounding the inscription of the words *domus aurea*.

"Those are owls," Jonathan said. "Wherever this inscription refers to, it must be a place to protect something, like a vault of some kind."

"And you get that from a couple of owls?" Emili said.

"In the ancient world, owls symbolized protection. Our idea of owls as wise comes from an ancient association with an owl's ability to see danger from afar. Roman armies used owls as a symbol on their armaments. Ancient Greece stamped owls on their money. Although it's another pagan insignia at odds with these prisoners' dedication to Jerusalem, the idea here of protecting something is unmistakable."

Emili reached into her satchel and removed a thin, black digital camera, only slightly larger than a credit card.

"Is this a picture point?" Jonathan asked, teasing.

Emili held the device a few feet from the wall and snapped a picture.

"I'm documenting these illegal excavations."

She crossed to the other side of the room and was photographing the other walls when she noticed a carpet of steam rolling out of a low arch on the far wall of the room. Jonathan walked over and crouched beside her. Both of them noted the rank bacterial scent of the steam.

"Must be a sewage leak through there," Jonathan said, pointing through the archway.

"No," Emili said. "It's a mix of methane and sulfur that gathers in Roman ruins when pollutants sink into the soil. We call it dragon breath."

"Pleasant," Jonathan said.

"There is one other issue," Emili said. "The methane is highly combustible. In tight passageways, even a spark can ignite the air. There's little oxygen, so the explosion lasts only a second or two, but long enough to kill every rodent or human around."

Emili stepped through the arch and waded through a low carpet of steam. She swept her flashlight's beam side to side until she found the source of the steam. A large shattered pipe lay misaligned on the floor, exhaling a hot vapor like smoke around a fat cigar.

"The steam pipe cracked," Jonathan said over its hiss.

"Not by itself," Emili said, and pointed at a gash in the pipe where its steel skin was peeled back like a tin can. In the middle of the corridor, the steam heated the methane, creating a bluish flame that hovered a few inches above the tunnel floor.

Emili began to cough. "The methane is mixing with the steam," she said, hands on her knees. "Jon, this corridor is going to explode."

22

Beneath the Colosseum, Profeta, Rufio, and Brandisi faced a choice: Three *fornici*, or passages, led in separate directions into the darkness.

Rufio stood beside Profeta, his every breath tightening as his anxiety grew. He saw no explosives inside the corridor—yet.

"Perhaps we should turn around," he suggested.

"The noise came from one of these passageways," Profeta said. "Each of us will take one. If you hear anything, radio it in immediately."

"I'll take this one," Rufio said, pointing at the corridor leading toward the arena.

"Okay, Brandisi, take the middle. I'll take the far left." They separated, moving slowly down different corridors, guns drawn.

Now alone, Rufio leaned against the wall, no longer disguising the need to catch his breath. The magnitude of these excavations enraged him, not because of their destruction, but because they would certainly trigger a departmental investigation. Over the last week, he had gone to great lengths to conceal their excavation, once even intercepting a merchant's complaint to the tourist bureau that one of Salah ad-Din's work trucks was obstructing his café from the Colosseum's tourist line. He should have known these men would betray him. *At least the illicit excavators south of Naples honored their deals with the carabinieri,* he thought, scanning the tunnel walls for explosives. As the corridor narrowed, his smoker's lungs worked harder for air. Like a scuba diver with little oxygen remaining and yet compelled to descend deeper, Rufio moved forward, feeling the darkness thicken around him.

He saw a flashlight strobe the wall.

Rufio switched off the safety of his nine-millimeter Glock. He knew that killing the first *tombarolo* in his path would raise him above suspicion in any departmental investigation. He brought his elbows to eye level to steady his aim.

Jonathan and Emili hurriedly backtracked around the corridors' tight turns. A dark stretch of tunnel opened up and they ran. The sound of a tour group above filtered down from the tourist deck. "The tourists," Emili said, horrified. "We've got to evacuate the Colosseum."

"*Ferma!*" Rufio screamed. *Freeze!* He was standing thirty feet behind them.

Jonathan and Emili scraped to a stop and ducked into a niche, their backs flat against the stone. The man was only yards away, his trembling beam of light growing larger as he approached.

"*Chi diavolo sei?*" Rufio yelled. Who the hell are you? Jonathan and Emili could see the man inspecting each niche with his flashlight.

"That's the staircase I came down," Emili whispered, pointing across the corridor.

Emili moved silently into the darkness and made it to the stairwell. Jonathan began to follow when Rufio illuminated the corridor. He darted back into the niche, and was now separated from Emili by the corridor's thick cloud of dust floating in the beam of Rufio's flashlight.

"Go!" Jonathan whispered to the other side. "I will meet you up there!"

Emili shook her head. "But how will you—"

"Just go!" Jonathan said. Emili disappeared up the steps into the darkness.

Rufio swung his flashlight side to side across the corridor, and Jonathan could now make out the man as he moved down the hallway, the red sash trim of his blue uniform pants, the white leather holster of his gun, and his officer's visor cap worn low. *A carabinieri officer,* Jonathan thought, relieved.

"*Agente,*" Jonathan said in Italian, stepping into the corridor.

"*Chi sei tu!*" Rufio yelled. He wheeled his flashlight toward Jonathan and, in his other hand, aimed his pistol at point-blank range. In the backlight of the harsh beam Jonathan could see in Rufio's bloodshot eyes an animal-like fury, a man no longer in control. His gun bobbled so wildly Jonathan thought it might go off by accident.

"I can explain," Jonathan said quietly in Italian, raising his hands. He motioned toward faint daylight of the stairwell. "But it's not safe down here."

"This was not part of our deal," Rufio yelled, waving his gun in the air. "None of this was!"

Jonathan stood frozen in the gray spill light of the storm drain above him, feeling its draft of fresh air. He kept his arms half up, elbows bent. *Deal? What deal?* Jonathan noticed the man shook uncontrollably.

"I don't know what you're—" Jonathan said.

"Get on your knees!" Rufio straightened his arm, holding the gun.

Jonathan lowered himself, dropping one knee and then the other. "There isn't time," Jonathan said.

"They discovered the warehouse!" Rufio screamed. "Tell Salah ad-Din it's over."

"Warehouse?" Jonathan said, sensing a fury in the cop that was more personal than professional. "You have me mistaken for—"

But Rufio's foot interrupted Jonathan, crushing into his stomach. Jonathan doubled over and Rufio bent down, taunting him. "Where I come from in Sicily, there are *rules*," Rufio said, landing another kick into the small of Jonathan's back. Jonathan fell over, for a moment wondering if the blow had cracked his spine. He struggled to his knees. "But Salah ad-Din plays by his own rules, doesn't he?" The officer punctuated the question with a swift stroke to Jonathan's rib cage that was so hard it actually lifted him an inch off the ground. Rufio grabbed Jonathan's hair, nestling the shaft of his gun under his jaw. "Well, I have rules, too," Rufio said. "And you tell him this isn't Jerusalem; this is *Rome*."

"I don't know what you're talking about," Jonathan wheezed. "Or who . . . Salah ad-Din—"

"Stop," Rufio yelled, *"lying!"* and yanked Jonathan's head further back.

"I came from"—Jonathan gasped for air—"the tourist decks."

As though trying to make sense of the last of that statement, Rufio blinked rapidly, realizing he had confessed to a random man.

In the gray light, Jonathan saw that Rufio's hands grew even more tremulous.

The two-way function of Rufio's mobile phone began to crackle, picking up reception from the street grate above them. An officer's frantic voice came through, but was too choppy to make out. Rufio dragged Jonathan to his feet, not removing the gun from his neck, and walked him under the grate. "Alessandro!" Rufio's two-way radio blared to life with Brandisi's panicked tone. "Get out of there! The bomb squad said the tunnel is filled with methane!"

Rufio grabbed the radio, but dropped his flashlight, its beam rolling on the dirt like a distant headlight. He lowered his gun, crouching to pick up the light. Jonathan seized the opportunity and bolted into the darkness. Almost instantly, he felt the force of the officer's clumsy tackle from behind. Both men hit the ground, rolling. Jonathan slammed Rufio's arm against the dirt-packed floor and his pistol fell out of his hand. Jonathan swiped it into the darkness.

Rufio reached for a small Taser gun on his belt. A blue filament of light flashed, but Jonathan pushed it downward into Rufio's shirt. The officer's torso convulsed, his chest flying upward in the strained arc of defibrillation. His tight grip on Jonathan's shirt faded as he collapsed, suddenly limp, arms splayed on the floor.

Jonathan stumbled up to his feet and ran through the corridor, feeling a stinging pain in his left hand. He noticed that he had cut himself across his knuckles, but he did not remember how.

In the corridor, Rufio made it to his knees, driving his palms into his eye sockets from the headache after the Taser's shock.

Jonathan dashed into the open-air maze of service passages that once supported the arena floor. From this part of the Colosseum's basement, he could see the sun flashing through the tight brick passages. Jonathan stared upward, trying to find a way out. He could hear the clicking of the exit turnstiles above him, a tour being given in Russian. A child having a tantrum. Never had Jonathan craved the twenty-first century more.

Ahead of him, Jonathan saw a multilevel scaffolding that supported a partial reconstruction of the arena floor. He heaved himself upward to scale it, his hands gripping its metal pipes one after the other. Steep aluminum stairs connected the transoms of the scaffold, and Jonathan sprinted up them toward the tourist decks. A breeze of fresh air off the Palatine Hill confirmed that he was finally aboveground. He emerged in the center of the arena, squinting as his eyes adjusted to the sky's bright gauzy overcast. He walked along the highest plank of the scaffolding toward the arena's low railing, where a tourist group stood on the other side, fortunately with their backs to him. Jonathan stood for a moment to catch his breath.

Suddenly, a hand reached up from below and grabbed his ankle, then yanked him downward with such force that Jonathan hit the scaffold's wooden plank, stomach first. He shook his whole body to free his leg, struggling to stay on the plank with one knee. It was an unrelenting force, like Hades himself pulling Jonathan back into the underworld.

Jonathan looked down, and he saw a carabinieri uniform covered in dirt, a face contorted in pain, eyes still blood-red from the tunnel's fumes. Rufio had chased Jonathan up the scaffolding.

"*Fermati ades—*" Rufio began, but did not finish.

The muffled noise of a distant cannon blasted somewhere below. Its rumble grew louder as the reverberation took on a physical force, violently shaking the metal piping of the scaffold. The sound ripened into a deafening blast as one of the arches beneath the arena spit a wide tongue of fire that quickly extinguished itself in a geyser of smoke.

The gift shop's glass wall shattered, ending the crowd's terrified silence like a starting pistol. *"Irt!"* a German guide shrieked. *Earthquake!* Families that moments before had obediently moved around the arena circumference now clawed each other out of the way. Parents carried bawling children under both arms as they stampeded toward the turnstiles.

Jonathan saw that Rufio had lost his grip and fallen backward onto a lower wooden plank of the scaffold, where he lay unconscious in the smoke. Instinctively, Jonathan climbed back down the piping, lifted Rufio's arm over his shoulder, and walked him up the steep flight of stairs to the top planks. Jonathan folded Rufio over the arena railing like a rag, the officer's arms dangling in front, and then swung his own legs over and climbed onto the modern herringbone brick of the tourist deck.

"Jonathan!" Emili ran against the crowds, spotting him.

The shock of the last few minutes left Jonathan's mind scattered, and he just stared straight ahead.

"You're right," he said, dazed. "It looks like dragon breath."

23

Lieutenant Rufio was found inside the Colosseum?" Profeta asked, rushing past a wedge of carabinieri cars, their blue lights flashing silently outside the turnstiles. The ruin had been closed for thirty minutes now. Police tape barricaded the surrounding piazza, from the Arch of Constantine across the Via Sacra. Uniformed police officers streamed through the turnstiles. Firefighters already filled the inner corridors of the Colosseum to inspect the tourist walkways and the open areas beneath the arena floor.

Profeta stepped inside the Colosseum's glass-enclosed ticket office. Rufio sat on a small refrigerator leaning against an espresso machine. A medic applied some salve and gauze over a cut along his temple.

"Alessandro," Comandante Profeta said, placing a hand on Rufio's shoulder. "We thought we'd lost you."

"Just a few bruises, *Comandante*," Rufio said.

"You have a description?"

"Male, early thirties, over two meters. He was wearing a suit."

"A suit?"

"A dark suit and cravat," Rufio said. "I chased him up the scaffolding to the tourist deck."

One of the supervising guards motioned to a back room, "*Comandante*, the surveillance tapes are ready."

Profeta walked past a wall of charging audio phones and entered the security office. Six security guards were playing back the dotty images of the surveillance cameras. They huddled over the security desk's small blue screens, viewing various camera angles of the Colosseum's interior. The room had become an on-site triage post for the Colosseum's security staff. Profeta stood in the back, peering at the screens through the leaves of a fern atop a file cabinet.

Profeta spoke from the back of the room. "Freeze that frame." He stepped forward. "Rewind just a bit, right there."

The young guard working the console pressed a button and the image rapidly moved backward. The frozen frame was a gritty black-and-white image, but clear enough to make out the features of a young woman wearing a fitted herringbone coat. The image showed her breaking from the crowd and disappearing into a dark arch.

"Rewind the tape again, please," Profeta said. The woman glanced to both sides before darting into the arch.

"Again, please," Profeta said. "Slow it down." The woman moved slower this time. "Which arch is that?"

The guard zoomed in above the arch. "No number, *Comandante*," the guard said. "That arch has no number."

"As soon as the smoke clears, I want a team down there," Profeta said. He pointed at the screen. "And send a forensics team to search for her remains."

Within minutes, police tape hung between the rock walls of the arch beside the tourist deck, and Profeta climbed down the steep stone stairs into the brick maze beneath the Colosseum. Harsh white lights illuminated the corridor, and large fans cleared the area of smoke. The smell of burned clay was overpowering.

"This is where he attacked me, *Comandante*," Rufio said, pointing to the floor. "I was coming down the corridor."

Profeta said nothing, feeling his way along the burned fresco wall. He crouched, studying the broken section of piping along one wall. It was always a criticism of the *comandante* that he dedicated himself to menial tasks when lower-ranking officers were willing to conduct physical inspections of a crime scene.

Profeta knelt and leaned down, his spectacles nearly touching the charred section of pipe.

"No wonder you couldn't breathe, Lieutenant," Profeta said. "You were breathing almost pure gas."

"*Comandante,*" Brandisi said from the stairwell, "one of the guards just identified the woman on the surveillance camera."

Profeta hurried back upstairs to the security room behind the ticket counter. Among the uniformed officers sat a young Colosseum guard. He stared mournfully at the screen, his index finger touching the glass.

"Dr. Emili Travia," the guard said when he saw Profeta and the others. "A preservationist from ICCROM."

"ICCROM?" Rufio said.

"The International Centre for Conservation in Rome," the guard said, staring blankly at a wall of charging audio phones. "Her staff has been assisting the preparation for the World Heritage Committee opening ceremony tomorrow."

24

Jonathan and Emili walked in the shadows of a side street off the Campo dei Fiori, a section of Rome built up in the Middle Ages. Its narrow cobbled streets were now home to bohemian art galleries and bars. The festivities from the night before had left empty beer bottles and cigarette butts scattered across the cobbles.

At one pub, a crowd squeezed in front of a television mounted above a bar. On the screen, a reporter was broadcasting live from the Colosseum, news vans gathering behind her. The broadcaster recounted the unexplained explosion beneath the ruin, interviewing a young British tourist who had been in the Colosseum at the time and was still nursing a nosebleed. Amateur digital footage caught the smoke-filled stampede. Early indications, the broadcaster announced, indicated a steam pipe accident. Municipal authorities were investigating.

"Accident?" Emili said, offended. "They planned that explosion!"

"They must have been excavating under the Colosseum for weeks to uncover that inscription," Jonathan said distantly.

"And to destroy it," Emili said.

They passed some carabinieri officers sharing a cigarette break with leather-clad teenagers. As they walked by, Jonathan pulled down a newly purchased Roma soccer cap over his face.

"We need to get to the American embassy on Via Veneto," he said. "Right now."

"And tell them what, exactly? That you've found an illegal excavation while trying to solve a first-century riddle? Or that you assaulted a uniformed police officer, nearly killing him?"

"Assaulted? He attacked me! I told you, that officer was involved in the excavation. He nearly killed me."

Emili looked unsurprised. "Nearly all illegal excavations in this country are the product of municipal corruption, Jon." She remembered her first ICCROM fieldwork in the hills of Capri where an entire town had been bribed to permit an illegal excavation in the town square. "Besides, I'm sure that officer will have a different recollection of what happened. Whenever he regains consciousness, that is."

"He mistook me for one of the *tombaroli*," Jonathan said, trying to beat the ash off his soiled suit jacket. "He was going on about some man, Salah ad-Din, something about—"

Emili stopped walking. "What did he say? Tell me the words exactly."

"I can't give you a transcript, Emili. The guy was using my torso as a soccer ball."

"He said that name, Salah ad-Din?"

"Yes. And that I should give him a message that this isn't Jerusalem, that there are different rules here."

Emili began to walk again, taking the information in.

"Do you know who that man is?" Jonathan asked.

"Salah ad-Din? No one does. Not his true identity, at least. The name is a pseudonym. Our informants in Jerusalem have said he is running a large illegal excavation beneath the Temple Mount. We cross-checked the name with Interpol, and they have been tracking him for two years, attributing excavations beneath Istanbul and Calabria to his operation. Interpol doesn't have a single picture of him. Not even a sample voice recognition."

"The American embassy can help," Jonathan said.

"Like they helped you seven years ago?" Emili asked. "Go to the authorities again and you'll have ruined another career."

Jonathan knew she was right. Dulling and Pierce feared publicity like an infectious disease. Not to mention that the man who attacked him beneath the Colosseum *was* the authorities.

"Emili," Jonathan said, "even if you're right that illegal excavations a thousand miles apart are connected—and I'm not saying they are—you don't know what this man, Salah ad-Din, is looking for."

"No, I don't. But whatever it is, it's been sought for hundreds of years."

"How do you know that?"

From her dusty satchel, Emili removed an oversized souvenir guide, *Rome Past and Present,* a thin book of transparent sheets illustrating modern Rome superimposed upon the ancient.

"A guidebook?" Jonathan said, raising an eyebrow. "This man is excavating for what he can find in a guidebook?"

"Open it."

Emili had protectively wedged the sketch Orvieti had given her between two transparent sheets. Jonathan removed the nineteenth-century sketch of the Colosseum and carefully held it up to the late-morning sunlight. "This arch has no number," Jonathan said. "That's how you knew where to go beneath that arch of the Colosseum."

"It was done by a member of Napoleon's excavation team at the Colosseum in 1809, Giuseppe Valadier. He never told Napoleon or the Church about this sketch, and instead, secretly bequeathed it elsewhere."

"And you think he found the inscription we just saw?"

"Yes, and somehow knew it was important enough for those prisoners to carve moments before their death."

"Emili, there's no way to prove that."

"That's because we don't know the meaning of the inscription. It could tell us what he was protecting," Emili said.

"Who's *he?*"

"Josephus. It all comes back to the same question you tackled back at the academy. Could there have been a mission important enough for him to go undercover for a lifetime? That message you saw carved inside the Forma Urbis, *Titus's mistake,* suggests there was. A deception in Titus's court so important that members of Rome's aristocracy—Berenice, Aliterius, Epaphroditus, and Josephus himself—gave their lives to protect it. We don't know what Titus's mistake was. Not yet. But there's a band of thugs massacring ruins beneath the Colosseum and Temple Mount to find out."

They walked in silence for a moment. Jonathan's mind flashed to the academy library years before. He could hear Sharif Lebag's voice as if he were still sitting beside him. *History is written in fire, Jon.* Jonathan remembered Sharif's energy, how his hands hovered above the Latin text of tawny parchments to uncover their hidden meaning, as though feeling for something still warm. *And to keep it aflame,* he would add, smiling, *we just need one ember.*

"I never should have taken the research so far," Jonathan said, shaking his head.

"You did the best you could," Emili said. "What did Euripides say in *Heraclidae?* 'Leave no stone unturned.'"

Jonathan stopped walking. "That play was a tragedy, Emili."

"You sure?"

"Yes, everybody dies."

"Okay, I forgot that," she said, turning around. "So look at it this way, the stones are already turned. Your research from the academy—"

"Was just a *theory*. That was graduate school. This is real. That explosion was real, that carabinieri officer was very, *very* real. Even if that wall reveals what those prisoners died for, we probably couldn't interpret it. Cults in imperial Rome did not even worship trees by the first century. The Mithraic cults focused on animals." Jonathan was silent a moment. "Either way, the relief should have reflected a monotheistic heritage, not pagan iconography. It will take time to decipher."

"Time I don't have," Emili said. "The World Heritage Committee convenes *tomorrow*. To petition the committee for an emergency inspection beneath the Temple Mount, I need facts, detailed allegations as to why Salah ad-Din and his men are excavating. I don't need the carabinieri, Jon. To decipher that inscription, I need an expert on early mysticism."

"An expert on early mysticism? Where in the world would you find—" Jonathan stopped, interrupted by his own thought. He pulled a business card from the inside pocket of his dusty suit jacket. "Chandler Manning."

"The librarian from the academy?"

"The former librarian. He's still in Rome, working on some kind of . . . business. Lectures on ancient mysticism."

He handed Chandler's card to Emili. "I just saw him an hour ago. He gave me this."

Emili examined the business card—"Kabbalah: Eternal Knowledge in the Eternal City."

"This is your expert? Chandler Manning?"

"He used to give regular presentations on first-century mysticism and the occult."

"At the corner bar, Jon."

"The guy is frighteningly smart. He knows more about ancient mysticism than anyone. And the list of people to help you isn't long right now."

"Oh, all right," Emili said.

"If he can't make sense of what we saw beneath the Colosseum, if he says those carvings are just coincidence, then I drop this," Jonathan said. "I pretend I was never beneath the Colosseum. I go back to my life. Got it?"

"Contratto," Emili said.

Jonathan knew her meaning at once: *It's a deal.*

She gazed at his gray suit, the pants blackened with splotches of ash and dirt.

"But first I think you should clean up," she said, tugging at the torn material dangling from his jacket's kerchief pocket. "Unless this is your version of business casual."

25

Beneath the Temple Mount, Professor Cianari studied the Crusades-era map, barely able to concentrate over the din. *I'm used to researching in a library,* he thought, guilt-ridden, *not in a demolition site.* The depth of the cavern and its solid limestone must have made the electric saws and bulldozer engines inaudible to all those above the ground. Cianari watched a middle-aged man apply an electric sander to a small wall drawing of two trumpets, a precise depiction of the priestly instruments of Herod's Temple. Horrified, the professor stood helpless as the sander touched the stone, the ancient red paint leaping off in tiny flecks.

They intend to destroy all the archaeology that supports the Judeo-Christian history of the Temple Mount.

Professor Cianari closed his eyes and rubbed his face.

And I have helped them.

He thought again of going to the carabinieri in Rome or the authorities in Jerusalem, despite the recent consequences for Cianari's colleague, Dr. Tik Aran, an archaeologist who assisted Salah ad-Din in Turkey. Two weeks after Dr. Aran finally refused to dig any further beneath Hagia Sophia in Istanbul, his body was found washed up along the downtown bank of the Bosphorus.

"No one has ever been closer, Professor," Salah ad-Din said over the noise. "I financed your excavations from the wells of Avignon to the ruins beneath the Colosseum, all to find this artifact." He pointed to the far wall across the cavern. "We need only to follow the path of the aqueduct to reach it."

"There are two hundred feet between these cavern walls," the professor said. "There are dozens of possibilities regarding where the aqueduct's course would line up."

"Not if we can extrapolate the natural slope of the aqueduct's bridge," Salah ad-Din replied.

"Project its slope across the cavern?" the professor objected. "That would take a week of fieldwork."

"Not with our technology."

Salah ad-Din motioned up to Ahmed, who still stood at the edge of the tunnel opening where they had entered the cavern. He positioned equipment that resembled a surveyor's prism atop a yellow tripod. A four-pronged blue laser emanated from the perched device, unifying into a single braid that reached across the entire cavern like a tightrope. It settled on a precise spot on the far wall.

"And there it is, the other half of the aqueduct," Salah ad-Din said. "Through there, the priest escaped with the object that Titus would have traded all the loot from the Second Temple to obtain."

Salah ad-Din relayed a message in Arabic into a headset.

A bulldozer moved toward the wall, its blackened pneumatic pipes resembling the muscle sinew of a beast capable of terrible destruction.

"You cannot use that machine to plow through the wall," Cianari said, white-faced, realizing how close Salah ad-Din was at last. "You might damage the artifact!" he shouted over the gurgle of the bull-dozer's diesel engine.

Salah ad-Din's gaze met the professor's. He could see that his control over the old man was unraveling. Salah ad-Din motioned to the bulldozer operator. The engine lowered to a rumble.

"It is sacred," the professor said.

"Sacred?" Salah ad-Din answered in an even tone, but with fright-ening intensity. "I have come to you with archaeological research from excavations spanning four countries and sixty years, and you answer me with a child's myth? I showed you inscriptions lost for thousands of years beneath the Colosseum." He stood very close, and the professor smelled the raw tobacco on his breath. "Emperor Titus began this search," Salah ad-Din said. "And I will finish it."

"I cannot allow you to destroy what a courageous few in ancient Rome gave their lives to protect." The professor straightened as he spoke, as though remembering the ancient heroism inspired a sud-den courage within him. "Titus came to Jerusalem to defeat a god. And like him, you don't just seek this artifact, do you? You seek the power of erasing it. I am too much a part of Jerusalem's ruins to help you destroy them."

"You are a part of these ruins, aren't you?" Salah ad-Din said, his gray eyes shining in the cavern's klieg light. He turned around and nodded to Ahmed, who had climbed down from the tunnel's edge. Nonchalantly, Ahmed reached beneath his slack belt and retrieved an Albanian nine-millimeter pistol, its snag-free, hammerless frame allowing for a motion so swift that the professor did not react before the skinny boy fired two rounds directly into the professor's forehead.

Cianari managed a rapid blink as his body swayed. Then his lifeless frame smacked into the dry dirt of the cavern face-first, the blood seeping through the bullet's exit wound into the professor's white hair, like lamb's wool soaking up thick red dye.

Salah ad-Din stepped over the crumpled body.

"Bury him in the walls," he said.

26

T his is it," Jonathan said. "Ten and a half Via dell'Orso."

"Ten and a half?" Emili asked.

They approached a narrow, shabby stone building with a wooden door closed with a loop of string. "Kaballah," said a sign in kitschy medieval font hanging from a nail above a broken buzzer.

"Are you sure about this?" Emili said. "I mean, *Chandler*?"

"The guy knows more about ancient mysticism than anyone."

"And he's bottled that information for sale," Emili said.

"Be polite, okay? He'll answer our questions."

They entered a musty foyer with a flight of worn steps. Emili removed her overcoat, and a long-sleeve silk blouse revealed her trim waist and rounded breastline. Her hair was still pinned, but loose blond strands gathered at her neck. Jonathan's thoughts strayed and he moved quickly toward the stairs to refocus.

"I'll go first," he said, clearing his throat.

The stairwell led to a frosted-glass door, which was jammed open with a doorstop. They entered a lavender-scented room that resembled a posh lounge at a hip boutique hotel: white orchids and plush velvet chairs beneath exposed wooden rafters. French doors opened into a larger room with seats arranged classroom style.

The receptionist was a pretty, young brunette with a small nose ring and a tattoo of some mystical Egyptian symbol on her clavicle. Bookcases lined the walls with texts on mysticism, along with Kaballah candles and Kaballah water for sale. Red strings were stuffed in a glass jar on the receptionist's desk. The label read, "Six Euros Each, Good for Eight Wearings."

Nearby, a fragrant orange candle burned in its own puddle. A sign beneath it read: "'Some only want to . . . see the garment of the Torah . . . not what lies beneath.' Zohar Chadash, *Tikkunim* II 93b."

And below that: "Visa Eurocard Accepted."

The receptionist went in search of Chandler, and Jonathan scanned the books on magnetism, the philosopher's stone, numerology. The books themselves were a reflection of Chandler, a man who could recite from memory entire passages of medieval mysticism. It didn't take much imagination to predict Chandler would wind up in this lobby with this receptionist and that credit card machine. Years ago, it had been bar stools at the local pub, where his winding theories from the Arizal to Johannes Trithemius riveted all who would listen. The only difference now was that the seats had an admission fee.

"Our hero and heroine have surfaced at last," said a cheerful voice from behind them. Chandler clumsily made his way across the lecture room, his arms open, as though Jonathan and Emili had been recovered from sea.

He looked at Emili. "If it isn't the Angel of Artifacts herself," he said. "I've been following your adventurings."

"Good to see you, Chandler." She smiled warily.

"Perfect timing. Don't have another class until noon. Come."

They walked through the classroom to a dusty old library reminiscent of a funeral parlor foyer. Stained glass bathed the room in amber light. Inside a set of small glass cases along the wall, waterlogged manuscripts were covered in mysterious symbols. It was as though Chandler's encyclopedic mind of the occult had been laid out as a visual encyclopedia before them.

"Impressive, isn't it?" Chandler said.

Jonathan and Emili spread to opposite sides of the room.

"I bought this place from an eccentric purveyor of you-know-what." Chandler scrunched his nose as though it were too distasteful to say. "I've left the library intact."

"Purveyor of what?" Emili said nervously, glancing at Jonathan as though Chandler were talking about illicit drugs.

"Why, a purveyor of the occult, Kabbalah, gnosticism, you name it, baby." Chandler sat behind a mahogany desk, cleaning his glasses with the end of his shirt.

"The old man spent a lifetime gathering obscure and out-of-print texts on neo-Platonism, alchemy, Nostradamus, the whole nine." He sprang out of his chair and walked up to Jonathan, pointing through the glass. "Just look at these. Books on Gematria, Rosicrucian manifestos, even the Shimmush Tehilim, for the magical use of the Psalms." He pointed at an ancient-looking, torn leather binding with a medieval bronze clasp intact. "That's a tenth-century copy of the Zohar, brought to Italy in A.D. 917 from Babylonia."

Jonathan leaned in, and so did Chandler. Both their faces were close against the glass, and Chandler whispered, "If it wasn't damaged by the Venetian flood of 1583, it'd be worth more than a Ferrari."

"What are these?" Emili wandered over to the library's other side.

"Ancient Egyptian rites. Those documents describe the measurements of the pyramids, as documented in 1864. Did you know that their original height of one hundred forty-eight and a half meters, multiplied by ten with nine zeros, gives you the distance between the earth and the sun?" Chandler collapsed into his chair, pleased with himself. "It's all true."

"And, according to Umberto Eco's measurements, take one of those public telephone booths out there in the piazza and multiply it by its width and then by ten to the fifth, and you get the circumference of the earth," Jonathan said.

Emili laughed.

"You've become a tougher crowd, Aurelius," Chandler said.

Emili handed Chandler her digital camera and pointed at the viewfinder screen. "Jon and I could use your help, Chandler. We just found this inscription."

"A sacred tree of light," Chandler translated aloud. "It's remarkable," he exhaled. "Where did you see this?"

"Beneath the Colosseum," Jonathan said. "In the hypogeum."

"You went *beneath* the Colosseum?" Chandler said, not attempting to disguise his envy. He wagged his finger at Jonathan. "I knew the great Marcus was out of retirement. I could see it in your eyes."

"Someone worked hard to draw attention to that location beneath the Colosseum," Jonathan said, removing the crumpled Alitalia napkin from his jacket pocket. "I found this message carved inside a fragment of the Forma Urbis. Its meaning seems well within your area of . . . um"—Jonathan looked around the room suspiciously—"*expertise.*"

"Titus's mistake?" Chandler said, leaning forward. He stared at the napkin, and after a moment his gaze slowly rose to meet Jonathan's. All his glibness was gone. He seemed more comfortable when spinning theories he knew were of his own invention, as though playing the odds at a casino table where he knew the money was fake. But as he studied the inscription, his expression turned to panic, as though someone whispered into his ear that the chips were real.

"Aurelius." Chandler lifted his eyes from the digital camera, his tone suddenly tenuous. "You have come to me with very serious business."

27

"Comandante Profeta, we are arriving at the International Centre for Conservation in Rome," Lieutenant Brandisi said, clapping his cell phone shut in the front seat of the carabinieri sedan. He turned around to face Profeta in the back. "The center's director, Jacqueline Olivier, is waiting for you in her office."

Profeta crossed the central courtyard of the International Centre for Conservation and checked his firearm before stepping through a UN-issued metal detector. A tall guard with a blue helmet in full UN regalia tagged his firearm and gave Profeta a perforated card to reclaim it. Although the International Centre for Conservation was a separate subsidiary of UNESCO, Profeta knew various United Nations sovereignty rules applied to the building, such as no local police firearms permitted inside.

The halls bustled with staffers answering mobile phones in doz-ens of languages. A mounted flat-panel television displayed live news reporting on the Colosseum blast.

Profeta studied the walls, which were lined with the center's in-ternational tributes, plaques, and awards. He stopped abruptly to read one of them.

Award for Conservation and Protection of Cultural Property in Regions of Conflict, to Dr. Emili Travia, December 2004, Paris.

"This seems like a prestigious award, Brandisi," he said admiringly.

"It is, and most deserved," Director Olivier added, standing be-hind them in the hall. She extended her hand to Profeta and then to Brandisi. "I am Jacqueline Olivier, the director of the International Centre for Conservation in Rome." Director Olivier pointed at the plaque. "Dr. Travia is my deputy director. We are all quite proud of her conservation efforts in regions of conflict, from Baghdad to Je-rusalem to Bosnia. She takes her role quite seriously."

"Appears to be the case," Profeta said.

"This way, *Comandante*," Olivier said. She escorted them down the hall and into her corner office, which was appointed with to-kens of appreciation from international preservation sites. On the windowsill sat a small Buddha head, an African ceremonial knife, a Nepalese mask. In the distance lay a sweeping view of the Aventine Hill.

"Lieutenant Brandisi and I have come regarding the explosion beneath the Colosseum."

"The World Heritage Committee meeting opens at the Colos-seum tomorrow, and the heating pipes choose now to burst." She smiled, but Profeta could see the strain in her eyes.

"I'm afraid one of your staffers, Dr. Emili Travia, was quite near the blast."

"She is all right?" the director said, her smile disappearing instantly.

"We can't be certain. She was last seen on the surveillance cameras descending beneath the Colosseum minutes before the explosion."

"It must be a mistake. Someone else," the director spoke with the false assurance of someone in shock.

"A Colosseum staff member identified her. We have teams searching the rubble—" Profeta stopped himself. "They are searching as we speak."

The director said nothing, loosening the fashionable silk scarf around her neck, her gaze drifting out the window.

"Has there been any unusual activity by Dr. Travia, any professional matters that may help our investigation?"

"A hearing began this morning regarding some fragments of the Forma Urbis that Dr. Travia's team discovered beneath Jerusalem last year. Our office lost a colleague on that mission. The hearing has taken its toll on us all, I'm afraid."

"Fragments of the Forma Urbis?" Profeta asked, watching the director's face.

"Yes," she said. "Two fragments covering the area of the Colosseum. They turned up on display at the Capitoline on anonymous loan. The Cultural Ministry used Dottoressa Travia's testimony to disprove the lender's bogus provenance." The director opened a file folder and handed Profeta a newspaper clipping. His eyes glanced across the subheading, "Two Years Later, Fragment of Forma Urbis Resurfaces in Rome. UN Official to Testify."

Profeta's eyes froze as he glanced at the photograph in the margin. The fragments Dr. Travia claimed to have discovered in Jerusalem portrayed the same section of the Colosseum that was pictured on the computer monitor his team recovered from their warehouse raid the night before.

"Director," Profeta said, leaning forward as though on the verge of a significant discovery, "I'll need to see all the information you have regarding Dr. Travia's work in Jerusalem."

28

"Sacred Tree of Light," Chandler exhaled, still wide-eyed. He was now engaged in his most nervous habit: dismantling paper clips and using them to jimmy the tumblers of a rusty padlock that he used as a paperweight. He sat at his desk, his fingers working with uncanny ease, stroking the tip of the paper clip back and forth across the lock's pins. No sooner would the lock spring open than he would snap it shut, beginning the procedure all over again.

"This inscription is a *tsurat ha-hidah*," Chandler said.

"A what?" Emili said.

"A *tsurat ha-hidah*, literally translated from ancient Aramaic as 'emblem riddle.' They were popular in antiquity," he said. "Very sophisticated, multilinguistic phrases, in this case Latin and Hebrew, would interact with amuletic symbols. The illustrations in these riddles were known as an ήδηθ, or an *embalo*, the Greek word from which we get the word 'emblem.' It's classic tradecraft of the ancient world."

"In other words," Jonathan said to Emili, "it's a message intended only for those who could understand it."

"That's right, Marcus," Chandler said, turning to Emili. "Spymaster of the ancient world, this one. The rest of the academy was basking in ancient heroic poetry, but not Marcus. He holed himself up in the academy library, searching for ancient spies under every parchment."

"The phrase 'Titus's mistake' could refer to any of the names we saw inscribed in the Colosseum," Jonathan suggested. "Many of the people listed were likely executed as traitors: Berenice, Clemens, Epaphroditus."

"It's true that Titus didn't want to take any chances," Chandler said, his eyes returning to Jonathan. "But I think his mistake is bigger than that. I think he's talking about the spies' *motivation* for their espionage."

"Which you think is divulged in the relief?" Emili asked.

"Yes. Remember, none of these people were optimistic about their chances of leaving that arena alive. This relief might have been a message, an emblem riddle, intended for the descendants of the captives from Jerusalem. That's why some words are written in Hebraic text. Just look at what all the names you saw have in common," Chandler said. "They're all connected to Jerusalem. Berenice was a daughter of the king of Judaea, Clemens was executed for treason by sending messages to Jerusalem, Aliterius is described as a Jewish stage satirist, Epaphroditus published provocative histories of Rome's war against Jerusalem."

"Then why would their last drawing reference a pagan image, a sacred tree of light?" Jonathan asked. "Sacred trees were a part of the pagan pantheon, not the monotheism of Jerusalem."

"But are you really sure that this image is a reference to *pagan* tree worship?" There was mischief in Chandler's eyes. "Or is this reference merely a disguise?"

"What do you mean?" Emili demanded.

"Yes, worshipping trees was a pagan ritual," Chandler continued.

"The earliest religious practice was mainly comprised of tree worship. These prebiblical cults appear to have worshipped the tree as a female life-giving force, a Mother Earth of some sort, often depicted as a seven-branched tree with breasts on Sumerian amulets from the Bronze Age."

"But those were pagan cults," Emili said. "Monotheism abandoned those images completely."

"Completely? I'm not so sure," Chandler countered. "Ancient monotheism included motifs of tree worship in their earliest stories to win converts. Think about it. Gilgamesh seeks a sacred vine, the divine Sitar seeks the plant of life in the underworld. How about a tree from which we may not eat? Keep away from the tree? Don't go near *that* tree in the garden." A smile played across Chandler's lips. "Sounds familiar, doesn't it?"

"Genesis," Emili said.

"It is no accident that the Holy Book practically opens in a garden," Chandler said. "Why is there a tree that we must keep away from, that cannot *feed* us? It is early monotheism's rebuke against tree worship and all those who find eating from it *nourishing*. In fact, some biblical scholars argue that our expulsion from the Garden of Eden is a story that reveals our difficult departure from the easy idol worship of fertility cults and tree worship to a more difficult and abstract spirituality that we actually had to work at. Remember, outside the garden, Adam and Eve must now till the spiritual soil."

Chandler stood up to reach for a text on the wall behind him.

"Of course, biblical texts still give us hints of tree worship. There is a bush that does not burn, isn't there? Leaves that do not wither?" He smiled. "The road from polytheism to monotheism was not as smooth as most biblical scholars admit."

"But what does this have to do with a tree from Jerusalem?" Emili asked impatiently.

"This inscription," Chandler said, "is protecting a sacred object of Jerusalem."

"It says 'tree,'" Emili said.

"But it means something far more powerful," Chandler said. "Think back to the earliest monotheists. As their mysticism matured, their worship of a life-giving tree became more *metaphysical*. Rather than shaping idolatrous images of clay trees with seven branches, early monotheists slightly altered the image to resemble a *lamp* with seven branches."

Chandler reached for the thick Bible to his right, and began reading from the Book of Exodus: "And you shall fashion a menorah beaten out of the same piece of pure gold. Six branches emerging from its sides." Chandler leaned back in his chair as though his point had been made. "The relief beneath the Colosseum is a direct reference to the menorah of the Temple's inner sanctuary, known as the *mishkan*, or in English, 'tabernacle,' from the Latin *tabernaculum*, meaning a tent or a small sacred place, from which we still get the word 'tavern.' Bet you never knew your local bar shared its etymological roots with the world's most sacred room—"

"Wait a minute," Jonathan stopped him. "You're saying this riddle is a veiled reference to monotheism's most ancient symbol, the *menorah*?"

"Think about it, Jon," Emili said. "It has been a tribute of faith throughout the ages, whether etched in the stones of Masada or carved on the concentration camp walls of Majdanek. Why should those prisoners from Jerusalem, condemned to die in the Colosseum, have been any different?"

"Well," Chandler said, "there is one way in which their drawing was different."

"How?" Emili said.

"I don't think they were referencing just the symbol." Chandler stood up. "I think they were describing the sacred lamp itself, the one fashioned by King Herod in eight feet of solid gold that remained lit in the inner sanctum of the Temple of Jerusalem. I think one of those prisoners is trying to tell you where he put it."

29

"The menorah," Emili said flatly. "The one from Herod's Temple in Jerusalem. You can't be serious."

"It's one of the only artifacts of the ancient world for which the historical account of its journey is more interesting than the popular mythology that surrounds it," Chandler said.

"Didn't the Romans melt it down?" Emili asked. As a preservationist, Emili knew the story of the menorah had been repeated throughout the ages. "We know that gold prices in Syria halved because of all the gold the Romans pillaged from the Temple in Jerusalem in A.D. 70."

"Other vessels of Herod's Temple were melted down to finance the construction of the Colosseum, but not the menorah," Chandler said. "The menorah was more valuable as a symbol of conquest than it was as bullion. Emperor Vespasian even built a new structure in the Roman Forum to display the menorah as the centerpiece of his war treasures. It remained there for four hundred years, until A.D. 455, when the Vandals sacked Rome and stole the menorah, shipping it to Carthage. The Vandals displayed the menorah as a symbol that Carthage was the only nation in a thousand years to breach the walls of Rome."

"Rome has her revenge, though," Jonathan added, turning to Emili. "Sixty years later, in A.D. 515, the Roman general Belisarius sailed for Carthage to get even. He left Carthage in ruins and plundered North Africa, returning to Rome with its treasures. The Roman historian Procopius reported that the Romans carried the menorah shoulder high once again through the streets of Rome."

"So the menorah returned to Rome early in the sixth century, then?" Emili asked.

"Not for long," Chandler answered. "Remember, in A.D. 515 Rome is now a Christian empire with the seat of power in Constantinople. General Belisarius travels to Constantinople and presents the menorah to the court of the Byzantine emperor Justinian. But here there is a historical oddity. Emperor Justinian, it turns out, is superstitious. Every city that possessed the sacred lamp has been left in ruins: Jerusalem, Rome, Carthage. Will he bring the same destruction upon Constantinople? So Justinian arranges for the menorah to be shipped to a Christian church in Jerusalem."

"So the menorah returned to Jerusalem, then?" Emili said, with a tinge of exasperation.

"It's not even there for fifty years before it was probably moved," Jonathan said. "The Persians sacked Jerusalem in A.D. 614, but according to many historical texts, Christian priests were able to smuggle the menorah back to Constantinople. That is corroborated by various seventh-century texts describing this odd-shaped lamp being displayed inside the domed palace of the *heptalychnos* for festivals. In fact, historical sources account for the menorah being in the Byzantine palace until Constantinople was looted in 1204."

"The year of the Fourth Crusade," Chandler added. "The pope charged the crusaders to take Jerusalem, but the Holy City was too well fortified, so they inexplicably made a sharp left turn and headed east for Constantinople. The crusaders sacked and burned

Constantinople and presumably took the menorah with them back to Rome."

"Are you guys done?" Emili asked.

"Yes," Chandler and Jonathan answered simultaneously.

"So it's possible that the Catholic Church has it?"

"You certainly wouldn't be the first to suggest it," Chandler said. "In 2002, a delegation from the state of Israel traveled to the Vatican and formally petitioned the Church to return the menorah stolen by the first-century Roman legionnaires, or at least provide relevant information from the Vatican secret archives pertaining to its current whereabouts. The result was that they signed a diplomatic agreement, and the Israeli delegation returned to Tel Aviv with a permanent loan of priceless Jewish manuscripts confiscated by the Church during the persecution of the Roman Jewish community in the fourteenth and fifteenth centuries. But no menorah. In fact, the Vatican's explicit condition for the loan was that no answer would be given regarding Israel's original request and the Israeli government would permit no further formal inquiries to the Vatican on the topic of the menorah."

"But if this trail ends with the Church, then why is someone excavating beneath the Colosseum to learn the menorah's whereabouts from first-century prisoners?"

"Ah. Now, here's where it gets a little complicated," Chandler said.

"*Here's* where it gets complicated?" Emili looked at Jonathan plaintively. Jonathan shrugged.

"Look at the procession portrayed on the Arch of Titus," Chandler said, scrambling to his bookshelves like a hound trailing a scent. He pulled down a poster-sized collection of nineteenth-century archaeological sketches, turning them frantically until reaching the Arch of Titus. He pointed at the southern bas-relief inside the arch. "What do you see?"

Emili's eyes took in the graphic scene, the slaves from Jerusalem under the whip of Roman taskmasters. "Roman soldiers carrying Titus's prized possession, the Tabernacle menorah, back to Rome."

"*The* Tabernacle menorah?" Chandler said. "Look more closely. Are you sure?"

"Yes," Emili said. "That's the menorah from Herod's Temple."

"Wait," Jonathan said. He leaned over Emili's shoulder, his eyes focusing on the base of the menorah carved in the arch. "Look at the base of the menorah," he said. "It doesn't match up with the biblical dimensions. It's not all from one piece of gold. And look at these images on it: an eagle bearing a wreath in its beak." Jonathan looked up at Chandler. "That was the Roman imperial symbol. And here"—Jonathan pointed at the lower hexagonal base—"it's the image of a sea monster of some kind. Or a dragon."

"A dragon," Chandler confirmed, "which we all know is a *pagan* symbol that made it impossible for this to have been the *original* menorah. And scholars have long puzzled over why Josephus's detailed passages about the pillage of the Temple do not tell us about the capture of the sacred menorah." Chandler sat back down, clasping his hands together. "Perhaps that's because Josephus is telling us that the menorah was not captured at all."

"You're saying the Romans stole a fake, then," Emili said. "That the menorah on the Arch of Titus is a copy?"

"That's exactly what I'm saying. Talmudic sources indicate the branches of the golden lamp were not necessarily curved, as illustrated on the Arch of Titus's relief, but rather straight and diagonal—an inaccuracy that may have lived on in nearly all subsequent renditions of the relic. Moreover, the menorah on the arch isn't *tall* enough. The priest tending the flame had to ascend three large steps to light its lamps."

Emili leaned forward, her eyes riveted on Chandler. "So all the conquerors who fought for this relic for a thousand years—Titus, who sacked Jerusalem, the Vandals, who sacked Rome, the Byzantines, who sacked Carthage, the Crusaders, who sacked Constantinople— all made the same error?"

Chandler nodded as he picked up the lock on his desk. "The menorah stolen from Jerusalem two thousand years ago wasn't the original in the first place," he said. "*That*, my friends, was Titus's mistake." At that, the rusted padlock popped open.

30

Sitting in the conference room adjacent to the UN director's office, Profeta lowered into his lap the UN investigation report of Dr. Sharif Lebag's death in Jerusalem the previous year. Profeta finished reading and stood up from the vinyl conference room chair.

"So two years ago UNESCO summoned Dr. Travia's team to investigate reports of illegal excavation beneath the Temple Mount. She stumbled into a research laboratory beneath Jerusalem where— to her amazement—fragments of Forma Urbis were being closely examined with sophisticated equipment. Various manuscript pages of Josephus papered the walls, but she never learned why."

Olivier replied with a dignified nod.

"And now the same fragments of the Forma Urbis have resurfaced, here in Rome. The Cultural Ministry is happy to use her testimony to debunk the artifact's provenance, but she has a different motivation altogether—to unlock the archaeological mystery of these pieces."

"*If* there is a mystery, *Comandante*."

"An illicit excavation discovered beneath the Colosseum at the exact location etched on these fragments? Sounds like a mystery to me, Director." Profeta paced, thinking. "Dr. Olivier, are you familiar with the al-Quds fund?"

"Yes, of course. Al-Quds is the Arabic name for Jerusalem. The fund supports cultural projects in the Old City."

"What sort of cultural projects?"

"Mainly the administration of the Temple Mount's two religious shrines, the al-Aqsa Mosque and the Dome of the Rock. Although the Mount is a World Heritage Site, the financial support by al-Quds allows the administering Islamic trust known as the Waqf Authority to operate without funds from our organization, an arrangement that presents its share of problems, I assure you."

"Because your organization holds no supervisory role over the site?"

"Precisely," the director said. "The Waqf has denied all UN attempts to investigate alleged construction beneath the Temple Mount for a decade."

"Including Dr. Travia's requests?"

The director nodded. "At this point, the Waqf regime just cites precedent. Non-Muslims have been denied access beneath the Mount for more than one hundred fifty years.

"As usual, though, Dr. Travia has been persistent. Last year she lobbied the General Assembly to suspend cultural moneys to the Waqf until all unauthorized excavation and construction stops beneath the Temple Mount, but the motion was easily defeated by the Arab nations voting as a bloc. Since Dr. Lebag's death, she has tried to persuade the World Heritage Committee to open a full investigation of their activities."

"She was scheduled to present at the conference tomorrow?" Profeta wrote again in his notepad. The director waited to answer, respectfully observing his investigator's method.

"No, she is not scheduled to present. Her evidence was insufficient to make a case for intervention on the Temple Mount."

"Isn't that a decision for the World Heritage Committee to make?" Profeta looked up.

"We can only use the committee's time to address a few sites across the world, *Comandante*. Our office's teams in China and Malaysia have concrete evidence of irreparable damage to Buddhist shrines. Because of the Waqf's lack of cooperation in Jerusalem, Dr. Travia's research failed to identify even a single illegal excavation beneath the Mount. Indeed, it makes Dr. Lebag's loss all the more painful."

"The remains of Dr. Lebag," he said. "They were found?"

"There was a sample of skull tissue from the crime scene. Two weeks later in Gaza"—the director lapsed into a solemn silence—"his body was found burned beyond recognition."

"DNA?"

The director nodded. "I worked with the local authorities' investigation directly."

Profeta detected a wound still open. Dr. Travia was not the only one who felt responsible for Dr. Lebag's death.

Regaining her composure, the director slipped back into character. "*Comandante*, as soon as our office hears from Dr. Travia we will notify your department immediately."

"Of course, and thank you, Director." Profeta stood up to leave. "One more question, Director."

"Please, *Comandante*."

"If an illicit excavation is burrowing beneath the Temple Mount, as Dr. Travia suggests, what help to them is a fragment of the Forma Urbis? Why research an ancient map of *Rome*?"

"That is precisely the question Dr. Travia hopes to answer."

Brandisi appeared in the doorway. "*Comandante*, I have interviewed the lawyer from this morning's trial, Maurizio Fiorello. The Forma Urbis fragments were loaned to the museum anonymously. The anonymous donors are being represented by"—Brandisi looked at the spiral notepad in his hand—"Dulling and Pierce."

"Tell them to expect us," Profeta said.

31

E mili looked out the window, dazed.

"That's why Salah ad-Din is digging here," she said. "Because there is information in Rome that he cannot find beneath the Mount. Jon, you have no idea how"—she searched for the English word—"*vast* all this is."

"Vast?" Chandler asked eagerly.

"When Sharif and I were in Jerusalem, his informants told us that Salah ad-Din was searching for a relic. It would make perfect sense that it's the menorah. If war prisoners from Jerusalem hid the menorah, and left messages in Rome about its location, Salah ad-Din's team would have to dig here first to learn where it was."

"Emili, have you any idea the kind of operation it would have taken to have accomplished what Chandler is suggesting? Eight feet of solid gold smuggled out of the Temple Mount on the eve of Jerusalem's destruction? None of the names we saw beneath the Colosseum had the kind of access it would have taken to smuggle the menorah out from under Titus's siege. Berenice infiltrated the court too late, seducing Titus after the destruction. Clemens, Aliterius, and Epaphroditus never left Rome during the conflict. None of them knew the exact moment of Titus's invasion of the Temple's Holy of Holies."

"Except Josephus," Emili rebutted. "You said yourself he was inside General Titus's tent. He could have used Roman military information to learn perimeter weaknesses in their siege, all to smuggle out the one treasure sought by countless empires before Rome. It makes perfect sense of your theory, Jon. After the war, Josephus developed a network to hide the menorah in Jerusalem, and with that line beneath the Colosseum may have been trying to tell someone where."

"There must be another message in the Domus Aurea," Chandler said, his eyes returning to the inscription in the digital camera's view finder. "The inscription beneath the Colosseum singled out Nero's buried palace for a reason. We can get maps of that ruin from the academy library."

"*The academy library?*" Jonathan threw his hands up. "Okay, that about does it for me. This isn't graduate school!" He grabbed his dust-covered suit jacket from the chair.

"Seven years ago, you spent day and night researching Josephus to find out why he would have forsaken his reputation for all of time," Emili said. "Down there in the Colosseum, we may have finally found the answer, and you are going to walk away?"

Jonathan put his coat under his arm. "In case you've forgotten, I already ruined one career seven years ago. I don't intend to do it again." His BlackBerry rattled, and he looked down. It was a message from Mildren, marked "Urgent."

Thirty minutes. Meeting in Tatton's office.

"What is it?" Emili said.

"The firm. A meeting."

"A meeting?" Chandler looked at Jonathan incredulously. "We're talking about the most precious war treasure of the Roman world, and you're talking about a meeting?"

"I am not going to jeopardize my entire career at the firm on the basis of some hunch. They may need me at the meeting," Jonathan said, heading toward the library's door. He looked at his watch. "It's eleven-thirty a.m. I have been in Rome for less than twelve hours. I spent this morning in court as a lawyer and, in the hour since then, have narrowly escaped an *explosion* in the Colosseum and had to duck down side alleys to avoid the police. That's quite enough for one day." He turned to Emili. "Go to the carabinieri. They can help you sort this out."

"Like they helped you seven years ago?" Emili shot back. "They blamed you for Gianpaolo's accident the minute they got you in that office. And you shouldered the blame without a single protest."

Her directness stunned Jonathan. He remembered sitting in a small interrogation room inside the embassy's compound on the Via Veneto hours after the catacomb collapsed. A nameless, plain-clothed American officer and an equally mysterious Italian counter-part drilled him with questions, their polite tone alternating with fits of rage alleging the accident had been his fault. He remembered feeling removed from his body, a spectator to his own silence. At dawn, the men escorted him to the academy, where his room was already packed up, his luggage waiting for him by the front gate. If only Emili knew why he accepted the academy's terms forbidding him to speak with her before leaving. It was to protect her from being banished, just as he was.

"Okay, easy now," Chandler said, sensing the depth of the accu-sation. He stepped between them. "The ol' barrister just needs some time to think about this—"

"What I need is some kind of *evidence*," Jonathan said, running a hand through his hair. "I mean, for God's sake, I'm a lawyer now."

"That's your own fault," Emili said.

Jonathan turned toward the door.

Emili stood on the other side of the room, not looking at him. The seven years had crept between them again, and Jonathan felt the permanence of what he was leaving behind.

"I won't go to the carabinieri," Jonathan said, "but I just can't be a part of this. Not anymore."

"C'mon, Jon," Chandler said. "You can't possibly turn back. This is your Rubicon, man."

The Rubicon. It was vintage Chandler. For any student of classics, the Rubicon was more than a river that served as a border for the ancient Roman Empire. Along its banks, in 44 B.C., Julius Caesar gathered his troops, and as in any heroic legend, faced his inner torment about whether to submit to the law or defy it. *Chandler's right,* Jonathan thought. Not going to the meeting meant forging across his own Rubicon into a territory beyond his self-interest. He had only to throw his coat back on the armrest of the chair and help her. It was the heroic thing to do.

"You're right, Chandler. This is my Rubicon," Jonathan said, imagining himself, like Caesar, a general atop his horse with thousands of infantrymen waiting for him to sound the charge. But Jonathan knew there would be no charge. He pictured himself pulling his horse back from the water's edge and, to the disappointment of countless troops, retreating without a word.

"Good luck to both of you," he said, and closed the door behind him.

32

At the Hotel Exedra, Jonathan changed into the only other suit he had brought to Rome: a gray worsted-wool suit that he kept as a spare in his office closet in New York and that he luckily grabbed before his flight. He did not have time to shower, but the suit, his combed hair, and two overlapping Band-Aids on his left hand restored his physical appearance. He dabbed on some cheap aftershave he had gotten from a street kiosk along Via Pasquino, around the corner from the firm.

Returning to the calm of Dulling and Pierce's palazzo had a hallucinatory quality, the aging secretaries at their baroque desks, the Italian businessmen smoking outside negotiating rooms along the palazzo's second floor. One attorney directed two aristocratic-looking Italian women in large-brimmed hats, both carrying lapdogs, to a conference room. Jonathan recognized trusts and estates clients when he saw them, no matter the country.

On the landing of the palazzo's staircase stood a statue of a young Hercules cleaning the stables of King Augeas. Jonathan thought back to his first years at Dulling and Pierce, when during months of document review he had to purge every memo from the desktops, laptops, and mobile devices of executive clients who had been indicted for every white-collar crime imaginable. *A young hero cleaning the mythical stables.* Jonathan, too, had cleaned the shit of the gods.

On the top floor of the palazzo, Jonathan stood in front of the closed double doors of Tatton's office. He was about to knock when he noticed his black shoes were caked with a layer of thick gray mud from beneath the Colosseum. He slipped into the bathroom, wiped the shoes clean, and caught his reflection in the mirror. A perfect facsimile of the lawyer he was seven hours ago, now wearing a pressed gray suit, spread white collar, and navy silk tie. The only hint of the last few hours was a cut just below his hairline, and he covered it with a forelock. Jonathan stared at the mirror, and in his exhaustion his mind drifted back to the first time he had met Bruce Tatton, six years ago. Jonathan's academic career had recently collapsed and he was working at an auction house, cataloging antiquities that had been sold the evening before.

"If not for you, our client would have a fake cupid sitting on his mantel," were the first words Bruce Tatton ever said to him.

Jonathan recognized the man from the auction the night before. He had sat among the well-dressed dealers and collectors, known to the staff as the "glossy posse." Jonathan remembered him in the first row, bidding on a marble statue of Cupid while the large flat-screen monitor converted each bid to dollars, euros, yen, Swiss francs.

From Jonathan's view backstage he had noticed the statuette's back hair locks were braided, a style unknown in antiquity. Lot 102, Jonathan knew instantly, was a fake. Jonathan remembered making eye contact with the bidder and mouthing a single word: "No."

Perhaps it had been thirty years of reading the faces of jurors and judges that allowed Tatton to react instantaneously. His paddle froze midway past his chest and then lowered into his lap.

Now, the morning after the auction, the man stood before Jonathan in Sotheby's storage room, looking out of place in his immaculate suit.

"The executive offices are upstairs," Jonathan said, walking over to a building directory on the wall. "This is the storage room. You must be in the wrong place."

"Wrong place?" Tatton leaned against a wooden crate. "Top of your class at the City College of New York and fencing finalist at the

Division I Nationals in Albany. Rhodes in Latin literature in 1999. Rome Prize in 2001. And here you are, dusting off ancient marbles like a stock boy to make the rent on an illegal sublet above a gyro shop on the Lower East Side." Tatton glanced around the stockroom. *"Not the career trajectory I would have expected."*

Tucking his clipboard under his arm, Jonathan glared. *"You'll excuse me. I have a noon auction to prepare for."*

Tatton handed Jonathan his card. *"Our law firm represents high-net-worth collectors of antiquities."* Tatton turned around and began walking out, his silhouette framed by the loading bay's daylight. He looked around the storage room. *"It's not me who's in the wrong place, Jonathan. It's you."*

You use a whole bloody bottle of aftershave, Marcus?" Jonathan's mind reeled back to the present. Mildren's head poked through the bathroom doorway, files in both of his arms. "What's taking you so long? In Tatton's office. *Now.*"

Tatton's office had the cavernous quality of a gilded ballroom. Its sheer square footage dwarfed even the large French baroque carved-oak desk that could have belonged to Napoleon. A domed Renaissance mural of pink clouds and raining angels exuded a convenient atmosphere of infallibility. Tatton paced on the lavishly restored burled walnut planks and spoke quietly into the phone as if comforting the bereaved.

Mildren slumped into a green velvet chair and Tatton acknowledged them both, nodding ominously.

"Cultural Heritage Guard," Tatton said, his hand over the receiver as he hung up. Mildren sat there silent, pen poised over a writing pad. He knew his master's habit of adding information in his own time. "A meeting," Tatton said to Jonathan directly, as though he required special instruction. "It shouldn't take long."

"Cultural Heritage Guard?" Jonathan asked.

"The Tutela del Patrimonio Culturale," Mildren responded, writing on his legal pad already jammed with notes. "A carabinieri unit."

"The antiquity squad, isn't it?" Jonathan disguised the strain in his voice.

"Indeed," Tatton said. "The *comandante* himself is on his way here."

"To the office?"

"Usually what 'here' means, old boy," Mildren said. "In the place you're standing."

A flashing red light accompanied the discreet beep from the phone on Tatton's desk. Outside the window, Jonathan watched the gates open as a police car crawled slowly through like an invading force.

"Did he mention anything else?" Jonathan knew he was asking too many questions, and hurried with an explanation. "Because I've found some research that—"

"That I'm sure is quite useful, yes." Tatton cut him off, centering the small clock on his desk to the millimeter. "Your instructions are to say nothing."

The carabinieri car parked diagonally across from the firm's doors. Jonathan watched a bearded man in an overcoat get out of the car. A younger officer stepped out of the car and remained in the piazza. Jonathan recognized his lanky frame and high hairline of matted red curls. The officer was still applying a cold pack to his right elbow. A hollow beat of Jonathan's heart struck like a pounded fist. It was the man who attacked him just two hours ago beneath the Colosseum.

In a strange fragmentation of time, Jonathan watched Tatton stand up, nod into his phone, and say, *"Mandali su."* Send them up.

"They gave no reason for coming?" Jonathan managed to ask

Mildren, but his voice must have been louder than he thought, because Tatton answered from behind his desk.

"Of course not," Tatton said, wiping imaginary dust from his desk. "What did the Greeks say? Surprise is worth a hundred men?"

Profeta walked through the corridors of the Dulling and Pierce palazzo escorted by the firm's public relations staffer, a petite Italian man in a charcoal suit and skinny black tie whose natural posture leaned slightly forward, resembling a courteous bow. He smiled nervously, explaining the palazzo's history and architecture as they walked, curious why the *comandante* of the carabinieri's most elite unit demanded to speak with the office's most senior partner.

"Built in 1660, the palazzo housed Innocent the Tenth's family—"

"His mistress," Profeta said as they walked.

"I'm sorry?"

"This palazzo was built in 1650 by Innocent the Tenth for his reputed mistress, Olimpia Maidalchini."

"We don't normally give that part of the history," the public relations staffer said. Another nervous smile.

"Of course not," Profeta said.

With the formality of a palace courtier, the public relations officer rapped gently on the oversized double doors of Tatton's office and then opened them. Profeta waited a few feet behind.

"*Comandante,*" Tatton said. "An honor, truly. Now, when was the last time you and I had the pleasure?"

"The Ara Pacis restoration," Profeta said.

"Ah, yes," Tatton said, politely unclear as to his meaning. "How could I forget?"

Comandante Profeta had become a vocal critic of heavy corporate fund-raising for local restoration projects. At the Ara Pacis restoration—sponsored mainly by Dulling and Pierce corporate clients—the *comandante*'s quip about the postmodern architecture for the altar's new museum revealed far more than an architectural critique. "The new museum's iron-and-glass cage pays homage not only to modernism but also its financial sponsors," *La Repubblica* had quoted Profeta as saying. "It even looks like a petrol station."

Tatton gestured for the *comandante* to sit in the oversized chair across from him. He gestured to Mildren and Jonathan. "*Comandante*, my associate, Andrew Mildren, and our visiting colleague from New York, Jonathan Marcus."

Jonathan nodded in greeting, squeezing the bridge of his nose between his thumb and forefinger as though massaging a migraine, making only the briefest of eye contact as he shook the *comandante*'s hand. Jonathan returned to his seat, gazing through the window at Lieutenant Rufio, who still stood beside the carabinieri car. The officer was no longer the desparate man Jonathan had encountered in the tunnels beneath the Colosseum. He was taller than Jonathan remembered, and his posture bore a disciplined grace.

Tatton sat down, his head bowing respectfully. "Now, *Comandante*," he said, his tone businesslike, "how is it that we may help you?"

A secretary came in with tiny cups of espresso and placed them between the *comandante* and Tatton. It became clear to Jonathan that—incredibly—the carabinieri was not here to arrest him.

"Late last night we raided an abandoned warehouse in the port of Civitavecchia. It appeared to be a safe house for the trafficking of illicit antiquities. The site contained high-tech equipment and crates of torn manuscript pages."

"Intriguing, *Comandante*." Tatton's tone was guarded. "But I'm not certain how we can assist you."

Profeta removed a piece of paper from the manila folder under his arm. He pushed it slowly across Tatton's desk. "Our technology team recovered this image from the hard drives. Forgive the bullet hole in the center. It seems someone wanted to dispose of their research abruptly."

From where Jonathan sat he could make out a sketch of the fragments of the Forma Urbis under a plate of shattered glass.

"Does the image look familiar to you?"

"You're in a law firm, not a classics department," Tatton said. He handed the page back to Profeta. "I'm sorry it doesn't."

"They're fragments of the Forma Urbis," Profeta said. "Your client's fragments of the Forma Urbis," he added, as though helping him along amiably.

"*Comandante*," Tatton said, leaning back slowly, his head raised, neck outstretched like a noble animal in sense of danger. His tone was still civil, but his indignance now more thinly veiled. "You're not suggesting—"

"That your client was somehow involved in the operation we raided last night?" Profeta waited a moment. "Unclear. The operation was not interested in selling antiquities here in Rome."

"Not interested in selling?" Mildren said, the thought offending him. "What for, then?"

"Research," Profeta said ominously.

"Or another smuggling operation." Tatton smiled. "Palimpsests and manuscripts are doing quite well at auction these days."

"The pages were marked up with notes, devaluing them considerably. Moreover, each page was a different scribe's version of the work of the first-century historian Flavius Josephus."

"Josephus?" Jonathan repeated aloud, although he did not mean to.

"Yes," Profeta said. "If the pages had been intact manuscripts, they would be some of the oldest complete Greek texts of Josephus's *Jewish War*. The pages spanned editions over the course of centuries."

The *comandante* slid an enlarged photograph of an old manuscript page across the desk.

"Here is a photocopied sample of the manuscript pages we discovered."

Tatton did not bother to look at it. He chose rather to gaze at Profeta.

Jonathan leaned over to see the text of the manuscript on the desk. He meant to stay silent, but his adrenaline was now working against him. "May I see it?"

"Of course," Tatton said with a frosty smile. "All here to help the *comandante*'s investigation as much as possible, aren't we?"

Jonathan looked at the text and recognized the narrative immediately. An excerpt from Josephus's account of Titus's final charge into the Temple's Holy of Holies. *"And Caesar led his staff inside the Temple,"* Jonathan translated to himself, *"and viewed the Holy Place of the Sanctuary with its furnishings. The soldiers were spurred on by expectation of loot, seeing that everything outside was of gold. But one person ran in before them."* The last phrase jumped out at him and he repeated the words, *"One person ran in before them."*

"There you are," Jonathan whispered as though spotting a fugitive who might overhear.

"There who is?" Mildren whispered back.

But Jonathan did not hear Mildren or anything else. The room around him disappeared. *Josephus managed to get inside,* Jonathan thought, *inside the innermost chamber of the Temple before Titus.* As though catching a glimpse of a suspect on a crowded street, Jonathan leaned further over the text, peering closer, as though for a better look. He scanned the manuscript page, feverishly translating it on the legal pad resting on his lap. There was the illusion that he was taking notes of the meeting, but in Jonathan's mind he was not in a law office at all but back at the academy library, creeping up behind one of history's great unanswered questions. *Great scholars have the hunter's will,* Sharif once told him, laughing.

Jonathan felt a tingling of anticipation as he moved down the manuscript's page. *Something was revealed here.* A line so important, someone scoured archives through centuries of Josephus manuscripts, ripping priceless pages to find it. As Jonathan read, the realization struck him with so much force, he spoke aloud.

"There's an additional line here," Jonathan whispered.

"What?" Mildren said.

"In the text here," Jonathan answered quietly, pointing at the parchment page, "there's a line that's not in later editions of Josephus." Seven years earlier, at the academy, Jonathan had spent weeks on end reading entire tracts of Josephus's writings. "I've never seen it."

"Just shut up," Mildren muttered.

Jonathan stared at the line, and as the answer came over him, it was not like a crashing wave, but a gradual tide. No moment of Eureka, but more like a reminder of something he knew all along. In graduate school, Jonathan imagined the setting in which he would arrive at this moment. This law office and the suit he was wearing could not have been further from his prediction.

It was all there, Jonathan thought, just as he imagined it would be, *all in a single line of text.* A single line that revealed the breadth of a conspiracy beyond the imagination of even a scholar intimate with the intrigues of Rome. One line torn from countless manuscripts because it revealed how a man—in a single moment—dedicated his life to a lie so great that historians would believe it for millennia. Jonathan touched the line, chilled by the vast conspiracy brimming beneath the text. He drew his finger across the words, and as he did, translated them slowly, reliving the moment of the creation of a double agent so effective he not only infiltrated an enemy camp, he also wrote its history.

> *During the Roman siege of the Temple, he escaped through a hidden gate carrying an ember.*

"That's how he did it," Jonathan exhaled, speaking to the page. "Josephus used a hidden gate."

"Is it your stomach, man?" Mildren mumbled. "You're all doubled over there."

Jonathan sat up, realizing he was so hunched over his face nearly touched the page. "I'm fine, thanks."

"Jonathan," Tatton said loudly, repeating his name. "You're the former graduate student in classics. Am I wrong?"

"Wrong about?"

"That this is all a bit *academic*?" Tatton squinted with disdain at the word. "The *comandante*'s precious resources spent cooking up all these connections?"

If Jonathan had been unsure about the answer, Tatton's glower supplied it.

"Academic. Yes," Jonathan said. "Very."

"There you have it, *Comandante*," Tatton said, clasping his hands prayerfully, "straight from a former Rome Prize winner at the American Academy in Rome. This is all a bit academic for us barristers. Devaluing priceless manuscripts may lack good sense, *Comandante*, but it is not evidence of a crime."

Lieutenant Rufio, having left his post at the car, now stepped through the door and handed the *comandante* a second folder. He nodded politely to Tatton, pardoning his interruption. Jonathan kept his gaze down, studying the claw feet of his velvet chair rather than make eye contact. After a moment, Jonathan lifted his eyes, catching a glimpse of Rufio—the paragon of loyalty, the faithful servant. Even Jonathan doubted the possibility of his betrayal, though he could still picture the lieutenant's fury beneath the Colosseum, as he waved his gun wildly, shouting, *"In Sicily there are rules!"* And yet now his façade was convincing.

"No, but I'm afraid this is evidence of a crime," Profeta said, leaning across the desk to hand Tatton a photograph.

Tatton stared at the photograph, marshaling the strength not to display surprise before an inquisitor—a technique he had trained countless clients to master. His only visible response was a mournful shake of his head as he slid the photograph back across his desk. The image stopped in front of Jonathan, and he could not believe Tatton had not so much as winced.

The photograph displayed a dead woman, her body ashen in the flashbulb's light, floating in an amber liquid inside a marble column. Jonathan leaned over and studied the tattoo around her navel, reaching for his BlackBerry inconspicuously beneath the lip of the desk. *Phere Nike Umbilicus Orbis Terrarum.* "Victory through the Navel of the World," Jonathan said softly. "It must be the Hidden Gate's location."

Jonathan subtly raised his BlackBerry above the desk and, using its camera function, snapped a photograph of the dead woman's image. He coughed to cover the digital shutter-click.

"A grievous matter, *Comandante*," Tatton said, but it was clear his civility was reaching its boiling point. "You managed to identify the victim?"

"The perpetrators detonated the warehouse before we could recover the corpse," Profeta said. "These men will destroy evidence of their research at any cost. They are not interested in history or culture. There will be other explosions."

"Other explosions?" Jonathan interrupted.

"Yes," Profeta said, gathering his materials on Tatton's desk. "We believe these men are responsible for the explosion beneath the Colosseum only two hours ago."

"Will you excuse me a moment?" Jonathan said, rising. *More explosions.* His nerves could not continue in this mood of crisis. *I have to stop Emili.* He walked leisurely toward the door, past the lieutenant. He could feel the lieutenant's eyes on his back, as though he had recognized him.

"What happened to your hand?" Rufio said in rapid Italian, as Jonathan stepped past.

"I'm sorry?" Jonathan responded in English, trying to distance himself from the person beneath the Colosseum who spoke fluent Italian.

"Your hand. What happened to it?" Rufio pointed at Jonathan's knuckles.

"Paper cut," Jonathan said, immediately regretting it. He tucked his hand into his pocket and stepped into the hall, closing the door behind him. As though in slow motion, he walked down the hall and passed the document copy room's immaculate supply of sharpened pencils and rows of staplers. He waited for the brass cage elevator to rise slowly, and with each ratcheting click of its gears he imagined Lieutenant Rufio swinging open the door to arrest him.

He stepped into the elevator, and just before its accordion brass doors shut, he thought for a fleeting moment that he had managed the slimmest of escapes when the sound of a slamming door burst out from the hallway.

"Fermati!" Jonathan heard someone shout, and then came the sound of shoes galloping down the marble corridor. A figure was tearing toward him in long strides. *The officer recognized me,* Jonathan thought. For a moment, Jonathan considered his options. *I have to get out of here and stop Emili.* He rapidly pressed the door-close button. But at the last moment, an arm jammed into the elevator and its accordion brass doors sprang back.

"Yes?" Jonathan said, tilting his head innocently. His heart pounded so hard he was certain it moved his lapel.

The door widened and to his surprise it was not Rufio who stood there, but Mildren.

"Marcus," he said, winded, "you are to tell no one, do you hear me?"

"Tell no one what?"

"About what you bloody told me in my office this morning." Mildren looked shaken. "If you so much as hint to *anyone* that these fragments bear some kind of *stupid* message, you might as well buy your own plane ticket home. Am I understood?"

Jonathan stared at him, saying nothing.

"Am I understood?" Mildren said, panicked veins sprouting in his neck.

"Completely," Jonathan said.

The elevator doors closed between them, and the cage reached the courtyard. Passing the guardhouse, Jonathan slowed his stride, waving nonchalantly to the guard, who offered to call a taxi.

"Thank you, but I prefer to walk," Jonathan said.

He moved through the crowd in Piazza Navona, unsure of what was more shocking to him: the solution to a mystery of the ancient world or his desire now to ignore it. *Bury it and move on,* said the young lawyer in him. Get back to New York. What did Emili call it? *Reburial.* When preservationists accidentally uncover archaeological sites they cannot afford to maintain.

Except he couldn't ignore it. Only after he realized the unconscious quickening of his legs did he realize why. Years before, Jonathan spent countless nights in the academy library, searching for the one element his Josephus theory lacked: a motive. A reason important enough for the ancient historian to forsake his reputation for all time. And now, after a single day back in Rome, a great mystery of the ancient world practically solved itself for him.

Jonathan shook his head, realizing he had been right all those years ago. Josephus's capture by Roman troops *was* carefully arranged, as was his rise within the Roman ranks—all to know the precise moment of Titus's siege of the Temple Sanctuary so he could smuggle the Tabernacle menorah to safety.

"Cognoscere mentem, cognoscere hominem," Jonathan said aloud, remembering the legal phrase he had used in court only weeks before. *Know the motive, know the man.*

33

Jonathan turned off the piazza into a narrow alley, jogging now. He moved down another cobbled street, and then hurried up an old set of marble steps. He could not afford to leave a trail.

Once he reached Via Arenula, he got in a cab and the driver turned around. Lost in his own thoughts, Jonathan had forgotten to give him instructions. After a moment, Jonathan spoke words he never expected to utter in Italian again.

"The American Academy in Rome, please."

The taxi crossed the Tiber into Trastevere, winding up the Janiculum Hill beneath a thick canopy of umbrella pines. Since the nineteenth century, the academy's villa had sat atop a steeply sloped hill overlooking all of Rome.

Jonathan stepped out of the cab beneath the San Pancrazio, a restored Renaissance arch near the top of the hill. He walked down the slope of a hedge-lined street and approached the front iron gate of the academy's villa. Jonathan could smell the academy's gardens; he remembered the chef's oregano patch.

Even after all these years, the same gatekeeper sat in the sentry box. Kossi, originally from Togo, was listening to the cheers of a soccer game on a small radio, just as Jonathan remembered him. It was only appropriate that Kossi worked at the academy. He was not an ordinary security guard, but someone with a deep love and knowledge of the ancient world. Kossi had been a graduate student in classics at a small university just outside Ghana until a rebellion decimated the university and a good part of his left cheek. After long nights of research, Jonathan used to walk down to the academy's guard gate, and over espresso at dawn trade Latin phrases from the great works of the ancient world.

Hoping the guard had not forgotten him, Jonathan approached the gate.

"Ventis maria omnia vecti, oramus," Jonathan said. A line from the *Aeneid.* Across a storm-tossed sea, we beseech you for help.

The scar along Kossi's jaw wrinkled as he grinned in disbelief.

"Jonathan Marcus?"

Kossi had grayed at the temples, but his brochure-quality West African smile was radiant as ever. Kossi knew the context of Jonathan's citation immediately. Aeneas's troops begging Dido to welcome them on her shores. The security guard replied in Latin, giving Jonathan the very next line from the ancient classic, something most Ivy League Latin professors could not do.

"Solvite corde metum." Then free your heart from fear.

The gate clicked open. Kossi clutched Jonathan's shoulder paternally. In one sense, Jonathan hoped not to find Kossi still in the sentry's box, that his abilities would have allowed for him to find a teaching position in Europe, but here he was seven years later, a copy of Catullus's Latin poetry in his hand, and the distant cheers of a soccer game in the background.

"You're a lawyer now, I've heard." There was pride in Kossi's tone, but also something forlorn.

"Kossi, is there anyone in the Church?" *The Church.* The fellows' nickname for the vaulted library inside the academy. "It's urgent."

Kossi shook his head. *"Riposo."*

Jonathan looked at his watch. It was one p.m. The Italian afternoon break, the *riposo*, had not even occurred to him. It really had been a long time since he was in Italy.

"I'm afraid I don't have a couple hours to spare, Kossi. It's . . . it's for a meeting."

"For a lawyers' meeting?"

Jonathan nodded. "It's complicated."

"Glad to see things haven't changed." Kossi gestured up the marble stairs. "I'll meet you at the door."

The American Academy spared no expense. Financed personally by Andrew Carnegie, John Rockefeller, and William Vanderbilt, the main villa was designed by McKim, Mead and White, whose other modest projects included the Metropolitan Museum of Art and New York City's old Pennsylvania Station. The central villa housed thirty of America's most talented scholars and artists to spend a year or two immersing themselves in the classical traditions Rome offered.

Jonathan entered the academy's interior loggia, still admiring its ivy-covered pilasters and salmon stucco walls. The empty *cortile*, or interior courtyard, was like a ghost town, the wind whistling through its columned cloister. He remembered the courtyard in the summer, grappa picnic lunches for the fellows. Jonathan had been certain he would never step through these gates again.

Along one side of the courtyard, large French windows opened into the academy's great room, now lit only by three spots of a billiards lamp above a cloaked pool table. Jonathan remembered how the academy fellows socialized there. In his mind he could still hear their banter about the ancient world over the crack of the cue ball. Jonathan had stepped into not only the sleeping courtyard, but his past.

"Hurry with your damn shot, Sharif!" Gianpaolo said over the pool table. "Xerxes crossed the Hellespont on his bridge of ships faster!"

The visiting fellow from the Egyptian Academy, Sharif Lebag, measured out an angle to the cue ball. "If I am Xerxes, then you are the Spartans, GP." Sharif struck the ball, a long shot, sinking it with backspin. "And this, sir"—not eyeing the ball, but looking straight at Gianpaolo—"is your Thermopylae."

He sank the shot with some English. Applause from the couch.

"You sure about that, Sharif?" a younger version of Jonathan said from a club chair he was sharing with Emili.

"Sure of what?"

"That you'd prefer Xerxes' side. After all, ten years later, Spartans annihilate Mardonius and the entire Persian army."

Sharif pointed the cue at him with a playful, accusing gesture. "Point, Marcus," referring to their weekly fencing at the Foro Italico, the sports center in downtown Rome.

"Sharif, you've forgotten the most important lesson of the ancient world," Emili said. Anticipatory laughter from the fellows.

"Which is?"

"History is unpredictable."

Walking along the loggia, Jonathan saw into the adjacent room, where the academy's disciplinary committee ended his career in academia. Jonathan could see himself, still with a bandage above his left eye from the accident, sitting in the room between the Steinway and the ivory-inlaid grandfather clock. In front of him, four professors took the collective aim of a firing squad. Never, since its founding in 1894, had the academy spent so much political capital with Rome's authorities to keep one of its own out of legal trouble.

"Gianpaolo is dead because of you, Marcus!"

Professor Rulen slammed his fist on a mahogany table. Rulen's rich voice and distinguished bearing were the embodiment of the aca-

*demic establishment. He wore a bow tie and thick white sideburns
that seemed to spring from a nineteenth-century daguerreotype.*

*"Bringing two other doctoral students with you to sneak sixty feet
beneath Rome into an unexcavated catacomb? You rappelled in
through a manhole!" Professor Rulen was one of four professors on
one side of the table, each of them sitting in a banquet chair with
carved armrests. "If the Italians had their way, you'd be in a Roman
prison right now!"*

Suddenly the room was empty again. The antique bureaus glistened in the gray light through the window. On the wall, there were small portraits of the former Rome Prize winners. Chandler was right. Jonathan's picture had been taken down, just as unpopular emperors were erased from monuments. *Damnatio memoriae.*

Jonathan followed Kossi through a large door with a small brass plaque, BIBLIOTECA. The library's dusty smell of parchments and the sherry-paneled walls released an academic scent Jonathan had nearly forgotten: the rustic, sauna-coal scent of oak and leather binding. Along the bookcases, gold script defined the categories: ancient engravings, Roman topography, and paleography. Most of the library's shelved books would be considered rare books anywhere else, seventeenth-century copies of Ovid, calf-bound copies of Vitruvius. Only the thirty annual Rome Prize winners and library staff had access here. Trust was not an issue.

Crosshatched daylight from the villa's garden filtered into the reading room, illuminating a row of bronze busts of legendary archaeologists from the turn of the last century, such as Wooley and Carter, who discovered entire underground cities with no more technology than ancient maps and a bullwhip.

Kossi flicked a switch and flat, Popsicle-sized lights in brass casings flickered to life along the bookcases.

"Welcome back," Kossi said, and closed the door behind him.

Jonathan walked rapidly down the reading room's central aisle. "Emili! Are you still here?"

He saw large maps of subterranean Rome spread across one of the tables. There were long stretches of penciled notes written in Italian cursive in an open notebook. It was her handwriting.

"Emili?" he called out. No answer.

They're gone, he thought.

Contemplating his next step, Jonathan collapsed in a chair. He stared out the library's louvered window. There was a bocce court with overgrown grass, and Jonathan remembered how Sharif would trounce him and Emili, throwing the ball with a bit of spin to curve it around a piece of third-century stone sticking out of the ground.

Behind the bocce court, he saw a faint yellow light inside the Casa Rustica, a seventeenth-century farmhouse lying at the back of the grounds of the academy. *The Casa Rustica,* Jonathan thought. *Of course.* The obscurity of the old house, nestled in the shadow of the Aurelian Wall, had made it a popular spot for hidden gatherings for centuries. In 1611, local townsmen gathered there to honor one of their own, Galileo Galilei, for his recent *strumento,* or telescope.

Jonathan ran across the academy's manicured lawn between the library and the Casa Rustica. The rain had broken and the trees were still wet and bougainvillea petals lay plastered to the stucco steps. Jonathan knew that since the 1920s the Casa's interior had been used by the academy's fellows as an archaeological research archive for digs throughout Rome.

As he drew closer, he saw that the Casa Rustica's windows were frosted, completing its uncanny resemblance to a gingerbread house. Along its stone walkway, two sets of muddied footprints came sharply into view.

34

Lieutenant Rufio waited for Comandante Profeta in the law firm's courtyard. He leaned against the idling carabinieri sedan, taking a last drag of a cigarette before extinguishing it in the gravel. Rufio walked toward the partners' vintage Italian cars nestled in the palazzo's old carriage stables and stared at a 1964 Ferrari 250 LM, feeling like a poor child shivering in the cold outside the window of a warm, glorious toy shop.

What have they done to deserve these? he asked himself, spitting flecks of tobacco that remained on his tongue. As a boy in Sicily, he worked in his father's mechanics shop. *None of these aristocratici would ever appreciate the meaning of Enzo Ferrari's prancing black horse insignia the way I do.*

One day I will be able to afford this.

But until then, Rufio knew the police would continue risking their lives to make arrests, and the lawyers would be the ones to profit with their high-priced defenses.

Crime does pay, Rufio thought, *if you're the lawyer.*

A second carabinieri car rolled into the palazzo, and Lieutenant Brandisi stepped out of the passenger seat, walking briskly toward Rufio.

"The *comandante* is speaking with the partner?"

"They're not playing *scacchi*," Rufio said dismissively, his eyes not leaving the Ferrari's candy-apple-red finish.

"There has been a sighting of the woman, Dr. Emili Travia," Brandisi said. "She may be alive."

"Where?" Rufio said, lighting another cigarette.

"Just outside the American Academy in Rome," Brandisi said. "We circulated her surveillance photo, and some officers stationed on the Janiculum Hill just called it in." He turned toward the palazzo entrance. "I'll tell Comandante Profeta."

"No," Rufio said, grabbing his arm. "I'll go."

"But the *comandante* told me to say if—"

"The *comandante* has many things on his mind. Do you know what the *comandante* looks for in making promotions?" Rufio pointed at Brandisi's inferior brass rank of his lapel. "*Delegazione.* To *delegate* an investigation before bothering him with details."

Brandisi pursed his lips, as though comprehending a great secret.

"Most likely a false sighting, anyway," Rufio said. "You wait for the *comandante.* I'll check it out alone."

35

Jonathan knocked on the Casa Rustica's barn-sized doors, and the gentle pressure pushed them inward.

"Hello?" he said loudly, stepping inside.

Photographs of archaeological fellows dating back seventy years lined the walls, along with their personal keepsakes, giving the interior of the farmhouse a museumlike, antiquated feel. A black-and-white 1928 photograph of the New York Yankees hung above a long oak table. A massive mahogany bureau with sliding drawers for maps and nineteenth-century archaeological surveys lined the entire back wall.

A filament light blazed above the oak table, illuminating old sub-terranean maps of the Domus Aurea that lay beside two small paper cups of espresso and a half-eaten slice of pizza that lay on wax paper. Jonathan put a hand over the cups. *They were cold.*

"Is anyone here?" Jonathan called out, moving quickly among the high wooden bookcases containing ancient pottery. He pictured the smoke of the Colosseum's explosion. *These men will not stop,* Jonathan heard Profeta's words in his head.

There was only silence.

"Emili!" he yelled.

A sudden, creaking sound came from the wooden planks of the casa's loft, which was outfitted with more bookcases.

"Being a bit loud, aren't you?" Emili stood on a ladder and calmly handed Jonathan a dozen maps. "Put these on the table there," she said, not at all surprised that he was standing there. "Some of us have work to do."

She followed him, setting two arms' worth of books on the table.

"I know how he did it," Jonathan said. "How Josephus smuggled the menorah out of the Mount while surrounded by fifty thousand Roman troops."

"One hour ago, you rejected the idea as . . . as *conjecture,* was the legal term you used, I believe."

"Not anymore," Jonathan said. "I just saw a passage in the text."

"In Josephus?"

Jonathan nodded. "Last night, the carabinieri raided a warehouse containing single pages of manuscripts from Flavius Josephus. Someone spent years finding those rare manuscripts and ripping out those pages, and I think I know why."

A loud crash came from within the stacks. Then Chandler's voice, "I'm fine! It's okay!"

Chandler climbed down from the second-story shelving, also

with an arm full of books. He looked at Emili as though she had just won a bet.

"Okay, you were right," he said. He walked toward the pizza, took a bite, and turned to Jonathan, chewing. "She said you'd be back within the hour."

Jonathan pointed at the reading table, where a brittle manuscript lay bound with an old silk red ribbon like a long-forgotten Christmas gift. "Is that a copy of Josephus?"

"The oldest Latin edition of Josephus in the library," Chandler said with a hint of pride. "A 1689 folio. Just brought it over from the library." Chandler pulled the ribbon loose, and up went a puff of dust.

The folio resembled a large tattered dictionary and Chandler rested the book on a thick Styrofoam stand. Jonathan reached for it.

"Here, use the pegs," Chandler reminded him. The librarians always required fellows to use wooden pegs to turn the pages because the oil secreted by hands is the primary cause of document decomposition.

Jonathan carefully turned the pages. "Here," he said. "Josephus is describing how the Roman soldiers stormed the outer walls of the city of Jerusalem and made it into the Temple's inner courtyards." Jonathan put the peg just above the line and began to translate. "The soldiers stormed into the Holy of Holies with the expectation of treasure. But someone . . ." Jonathan stopped reading.

"What is it?" Chandler said, anxious for the plot to thicken. "Someone what?"

"Someone ran in before them," Jonathan said, staring at the line. He looked up at them. "Someone got inside the innermost chamber of the Temple before Titus and his men. If there was anyone who could have betrayed Titus and smuggled out the menorah, it would have been at this moment."

"But Titus's men had surrounded the Holy of Holies," Emili said. "You can't stuff an eight-foot lamp of solid gold under your priestly vestments and hope no one notices."

"Exactly," Jonathan said, scanning down each page, his finger hovering over the text, searching a few lines down. "Which was why all the Josephus pages in the warehouse contained an *additional line* of text right here." Jonathan removed a pen to write on a scrap piece of paper.

"Pencils, please," Chandler muttered, and handed Jonathan a short pencil from his pocket. Jonathan recalled the rule shared by all rare-parchment collections the world over. No permanent ink allowed on the tables.

Jonathan wrote the line in the original Greek text and then translated it.

"And he escaped through a hidden gate carrying an ember."

"A hidden gate?" Chandler said.

"Yes." Jonathan stood up. "It was most likely a tunnel or . . ."

But Emili didn't hear the end of Jonathan's explanation. She stared at him, realizing this moment of redemption was not for Flavius Josephus alone. Jonathan was pacing around the table, and as he spoke she saw the passion she thought was gone forever flash in his eyes. He gestured wildly, becoming a spontaneous advocate not only for Josephus, but for himself.

". . . and so the priests escaped through a hidden gate, carrying a fire of some kind," Jonathan concluded, "saving not merely the menorah but more importantly—"

"Its flame," Chandler said.

"What flame?" Emili said, suddenly lost.

"The *flame*, Emili. The seventh flame, to be exact," Chandler said, "on the menorah's westernmost branch."

Emili looked surprised. "I didn't know it had a special significance."

"A very special significance," Chandler said. "The Bible is explicit in the books of Exodus and Leviticus 'to kindle the lamp continually,' calling the flame 'an eternal decree for your generations.' This was the eternal flame, burning since Moses dedicated the original tabernacle after the exodus from Egypt. The light was like a witness to Israel's covenant with God, an undying flame transferred to Solomon's Temple, hidden during the Babylonian sack of the sixth century, passed on to Ezra's Temple in the fifth century, and so on. It was the symbol of the eternal promise that Abraham's descendants would number 'like the stars of heaven and—'"

"Sands on the seashore?" Emili said.

Chandler and Jonathan looked surprised. "Sunday school," she said with a shrug.

"Right," Chandler said. "It was a promise made shortly after Abraham proved his complete faith in God by passing his final test."

"What test?"

"The sacrifice of Isaac," Jonathan said. "You know the story, God commands Abraham to offer his son as a sacrifice, only to have an angel restrain his arm at the last possible moment."

"And while three of the world's great religions have varying interpretations—whether it's the Islamic tradition's substitution of Ishmael for Isaac or the Christian emphasis on a father's sacrifice as a prefiguring for their redemption—all three religions agree that Abraham earns a divine oath at that moment, an oath embodied in the eternal flame carried by Moses through the desert. It's why Kabbalists to this day refer to the menorah's perpetual light as 'Isaac's fire.'"

"And, of course, it's no coincidence that the Bible's topographical descriptions suggest that the precise spot where Isaac was bound to the altar stood not only on the Temple Mount in Jerusalem, but at the very place where the menorah's flame burned inside the Solomonic Temple one thousand years later."

"But why would other empires care about the flame?"

"Well, if you were them, wouldn't you?" Chandler laughed. "Imagine that the year is 1290 B.C., and the Hebrews leave Egypt as a ragtag group of slaves, but suddenly they're winning unexpected military victories against larger and better-equipped armies across the desert. By the time they settle Jerusalem a few hundred years later and Solomon fortifies his Temple to protect the flame, the once outlandish promise to grow the Hebrews like sands on the seashore is starting to worry the magicians of surrounding empires who had heard of the perpetual fire of the menorah's lamp and feared its significance. No operation was too elaborate to attempt to extinguish the menorah's flame. The Assyrians attacked Jerusalem in the seventh century B.C. to extinguish it, and they failed. The Babylonians made the same attempt in 586 B.C., this time capturing the Ark of the Covenant, but not the menorah's flame. It was kept alive in a hidden location even as the Persians invaded fifty years after that."

"So before the Roman sack, the flame had never been extinguished?" Emili said.

"Right, and the closest call is justifiably still the most celebrated," Chandler answered. "Four hundred years after the Babylonians, the Greek empire attacked Jerusalem. The five sons of Mattathias, a Temple priest, repelled the Greek invasion with such force, they were called 'the hammers,' or, as the word is translated in Aramaic, *maccabas*, and we know them as the Maccabees."

"As in *the* Maccabees?" Emili said. "Their name comes from the word for 'hammer'?"

"Gives the phrase 'tough as nails' a whole new meaning, doesn't it?"

"*Chandler—*" Jonathan rolled his eyes.

"Fair enough, Marcus, but my point is that by the time the Maccabees regain control of the Mount, the desecrated Temple contains only enough oil to keep the hidden flame alive for one day. The problem is, preparing the sanctified oil for the menorah takes *seven* days. To keep the flame alive they need that little bit of oil to last seven days, or else."

"Or else what?"

"Or else the flame would extinguish for the first time since its kindling by Moses in the desert tabernacle a thousand years before. Miraculously, though, the day's worth of oil burned for not one, but eight nights, just in time for more oil to be pressed and the flame to be saved. It was the miracle of the Temple's rededication, or as the word is in ancient Aramaic, *hanukkah*, which is still celebrated by symbolically lighting the lamp that the Greeks tried to extinguish."

"So by the time the Romans surrounded Jerusalem in the first century A.D.," Jonathan added, "the story of the Maccabees was well known to Josephus, as was the preeminent significance of the menorah's fire inside the Temple."

"Not only that," Chandler said, "Josephus knew it was Titus's superstition that drove him to sack Jerusalem's Temple. After all, Titus knew its sanctuaries were not brimming with the golden statues of neighboring pagan provinces. He was not even after the menorah's eight feet of solid gold. What he was after"—Chandler paused dramatically—"was *its fire*. The menorah's flame threatened his divinity. That's why even after his legions stormed Jerusalem's inner walls and set fire to the Temple, Titus still ran through its burning walls into the Holy of Holies and thrust his sword through the sacred tapestries. Both Talmudic and Roman sources report that the tapestries miraculously began bleeding on the floor. Titus pointed to them, shouting, 'This is the blood of your god.'"

"And all the while," Emili said, shaking her head, "the authentic flame—"

"Was smuggled out," Chandler said, nodding solemnly. "Just think of the importance of a flame that has burned continuously since *Moses* tended it alongside the Ark of the Covenant during the Exodus. *I mean, can you imagine?"* Chandler leaned back in his chair, eyes up at the ceiling as though taking in the scale. "Even today, two thousand years later, the notion of a perpetual fire is more a part of our modern traditions than we realize. Nearly all synagogues keep an electric flame 'lit' above the sanctuary's ark at all times, often even connecting its trip wire to a separate generator in case the local electricity fails. Most Catholic and Lutheran churches display a continual fire kindled from the candles of older churches. The Daisho-in Buddhist temple's flame in Japan has burned continuously since the eighth century."

"Not to mention the secular significance of eternal flames all over the world," Jonathan added, "like the Eternal Flame on John Kennedy's gravesite in Arlington National Cemetery—"

"Or the one in Hiroshima's Peace Memorial Park to remain lit until all nuclear weapons are destroyed," Emili added.

"And think of how extinguishing any of them would be the ultimate statement," Chandler said. "Human rights protesters went so far as to climb the suspension cables of the Golden Gate Bridge to ambush the 2008 Olympic Torch en route to Beijing."

"So Titus needs to get inside the Holy of Holies to put it out *himself?"* Emili asked. "Like some kind of deicide?"

"Exactly," Chandler answered. "And it's why Josephus's priestly lineage made him the perfect operative to get inside the Holy of Holies before Titus did. Remember, only a member of the *kohanim,* the priestly caste, could run into the inner sanctuary to smuggle out the menorah and its flame through the hidden gate."

Emili thought for a moment. "So when Josephus added that line, *'But someone ran in before them,'* he was talking about—"

"Himself," Jonathan finished her thought. "Over the centuries, no one has realized he was talking about *himself* the entire time."

"Now if only we had some idea where this gate was," Emili said.

"Turns out, I think we do." Jonathan reached into his jacket pocket.

"The manuscript page said where the hidden gate was?" Chandler leaned in enthusiastically.

"No," Jonathan said, his voice distant, picturing the horrific photograph he had seen a half-hour earlier in Tatton's office. "The location wasn't written in the manuscript. It was written somewhere else."

From his jacket pocket, Jonathan removed his BlackBerry and accessed the photograph he managed to take in Tatton's office. The image spread to the four corners of the device's screen. Its small size did nothing to lessen the macabre nature of the preserved corpse lying in the liquid.

"What the—!" Chandler stepped back, recoiling as though the digital image were contagious. "What the hell is that?"

"The carabinieri found this corpse in the warehouse, beside the pages of Josephus," Jonathan said, and turned to Emili. "A preserved first-century Corinthian maiden."

"Sick bastards." Chandler leaned over to the image, pounced back, and then moved in closer. "What's she floating in? Olive oil?"

"It's probably amber," Emili said, "or another natural preservative."

"Did they cross-reference the photograph with Interpol's missing-persons database?" Chandler said.

"Not sure they'll have much luck there," Jonathan said.

"Why not? That database goes back many years. She can't be more than forty years old."

"I think she'd be flattered, Chandler," Jonathan said, "considering that you're probably off by a couple thousand years."

36

L ate for his meeting at the offices of the Waqf Authority, Salah
ad-Din moved with a clipped military gait through the narrow
corridors of Jerusalem's Old City. *I do not have time to talk politics over
tea and dried fruit,* he thought. But he agreed to meet with the *mutwali* on short notice. He knew the Waqf's support for his excavations had grown tenuous. Salah ad-Din must not let his pride
endanger his team's access beneath the Mount. *Not when he was so
close.*

In the arched doorway of the Waqf offices inside the Bab el
Nadme Gate, two guards in traditional Islamic dress averted their
eyes as they waved Salah ad-Din through. The imams appeared personally insulted that someone with his pedigree—a grandson of the
Grand Mufti Sheikh al-Husseini—wore Western clothes and disregarded the Quran's prohibitions daily.

I intend to honor the Mufti with more than empty words of prayer,
Salah ad-Din answered, but not aloud.

He stepped through the Waqf's weather-beaten doors and into
the two-story compound that had overlooked Haram al-Sharif since
the fourteenth century. Salah ad-Din felt like a stranger among these
imams, but he relished the Waqf's history, how its jurisdiction dated
to the expulsion of Richard the Lionheart and his Crusaders from
Jerusalem by medieval Islamic warriors in 1192. It was then that the
authority was created to administer the Islamic shrines of Haram
al-Sharif through a *waqf,* or charitable trust.

A young imam escorted Salah ad-Din past renovated offices with
granite floors, polished Herodian stone walls, and magnificent Ira-

nian rugs that announced the trust's recent prosperity. He knew of the large sums the al-Quds fund collected at the annual international Islamic conferences to support the Waqf's maintenance and construction inside the Mount. Saudi Arabia alone had donated more than $100 million to the Waqf's projects since 2000.

"It is an honor to have you in the Waqf's office," the imam said, walking toward him. He did not attempt to cover up the falsehood, eyeing Salah ad-Din's black wool slacks and white oxford with open disapproval.

"Chapter twenty-four of the Quran," Salah ad-Din said with a polite smile. *Lying incurs Allah's condemnation.*

The young imam led Salah ad-Din into a sitting room adorned with two prayer apses facing Mecca. Between the apses hung a framed photograph of the grand mufti of Jerusalem. In the 1930s-era photo, the grand mufti was a young man, and the resemblance to Salah ad-Din was unmistakable. A dish of olives and dried fruit had been set on a low table between two chairs in the room's center: a low red velvet armchair intended to accommodate the aging back of the *mutwali*, and a wooden chair for visitors. Salah ad-Din sat down and picked at the platter. It was a hospitality ritual and Salah ad-Din knew not to refuse. An engraved marble page of the Quran hung above an office desk.

A manservant opened the door and Tarik Husseini, the current *mutwali* of the Waqf, appeared in the doorway. For intricate reasons of Islamic law that Salah ad-Din did not care to learn, the Waqf remained technically a trust, and the chief trustee or *mutwali* administered its most delicate affairs.

The *mutwali* was a small, barrel-chested man who rarely removed his large tinted glasses. His ill-fitting dentures kept his lips permanently pursed, and his black mustache was so deeply dyed that it had long stained the skin above his mouth a cadaverous grayish blue. He walked across the room with a waddle, a constant reminder of the

war injury that crippled his leg in 1948 as he fought alongside Jordanian snipers to keep the Israelis out of Jerusalem. He grandly lowered himself into the velvet chair and made a quick gesture.

A servant wearing khaki pants and a military jacket came in with
a tray of black tea. As he leaned over, Salah ad-Din saw the man's
sidearm—a glinting black Beretta that announced his recent activity
in Iraq. The gun was the standard-issue weapon of American soldiers, and among insurgents, wearing the weapon of a killed adver-
sary hailed back to early Arab traditions of keeping the sword of the
vanquished. *At least that was one lesson they managed to learn from my
grandfather,* Salah ad-Din thought. *Keep the Mount protected, not with
treaties, but with warriors.*

The *mutwali* leaned forward, eyeing the door. The guard waiting
outside sensed the silence within and closed the door completely.

"Our work is nearly done," Salah ad-Din said.

The *mutwali* slowly poured the tea for them both.

"Not *our* work, young Salah ad-Din. *Your* work." The *mutwali* sat
back, sipping his tea. "Your efforts are not supported by the imams
of the Waqf Authority. They think you have gone too far."

"Too far? Two thousand years, *Mutwali*. And we are *hours* from
finding it. Where the Assyrians, the Babylonians, the Greeks, and
the Romans failed, *I will not.*"

The *mutwali* nodded, staring out the window; the golden Dome
of the Rock was brilliant even beneath the overcast sky. "You have
not found the path beneath the Mount where Josephus escaped
with the artifact," he said.

Salah ad-Din was taken aback by the *mutwali's* knowledge of his
efforts.

"You think I haven't been following your research?" The *mutwali*
labored to stand. "I admired your grandfather, traveled with him
throughout Berlin and the Balkans, seeking clues in the writings of
Flavius Josephus. But we cannot risk the Waqf's exposure because

you inherited his obsession of controlling the past." The *mutwali's* expression hardened. "Your excavations must end, Salah ad-Din. The World Heritage Committee may vote to grant UN inspection privileges for the Haram any day."

"Inspection privileges? But the Waqf has had complete sovereignty of the Mount for nearly a thousand years."

"The imams now view the Mount as being more a part of . . . *of the present.*" The *mutwali* waved his hand abstractly. "Their intentions are to fill a large cistern inside the Mount with water from the Sacred Well of Zamzam in Saudi Arabia, thereby raising Jerusalem to the holiness of Mecca. If they begin construction *before* the UN inspection, they can argue that as a religious project already in progress, it should continue. Your efforts, they say, are too preoccupied with ancient history."

"*Ancient history?* Remember the teaching of my grandfather, the grand mufti, peace be upon him." Salah ad-Din's eyes rose to meet the picture. "*Archaeology is politics.*" A moment of reverential silence passed. "Did my grandfather think it was ancient history when he excavated sixty years ago?"

"Your grandfather is the only reason the al-Quds fund has continued to finance your efforts outside Jerusalem." Another slow sip of tea, his eyes not leaving Salah ad-Din's. "Or have you forgotten how the United States Congress almost passed a law to withhold financing from the Palestinian Authority unless we halted our projects beneath the Mount?" There was a stack of paper in front of him, and he adjusted his glasses to read it more clearly. "U.S.C. Bill H.R. 2566. Do you remember how it took the careful strategy of our al-Quds fund's business interests to silently mobilize the oil lobbies to put out that fire?"

"I cannot stop my excavations yet," Salah ad-Din said. "I promised the grand mufti I would find it."

"Allah will forgive your promise."

"Allah is not my concern!" Salah ad-Din said, his voice strengthening. He stood up from his chair.

The door opened and the guard looked at the *mutwali*, who nodded paternally. *All is well.*

"You did not see my grandfather at his end in Beirut," Salah ad-Din said, stepping toward the window. "You did not hold his hand as he kneeled on the prayer carpet of the Al-Omari Mosque, watching the men assemble in the shadows. He knew who they were. The same Israelis who captured Eichmann in Argentina had come for him in Beirut. You did not see him remove a small cyanide pill from the binder of his Quran. He kept it close in case they ever found him." Salah ad-Din's tone softened. "You did not watch him slip it in his mouth and hold his hand as he fell onto his side, writhing on the floor. 'Do not make Titus's mistake,' he told me." Salah ad-Din's eyes rose to the picture above him.

"Do you know why your grandfather conducted his search with such passion? He believed the lamp was still *aflame*. He believed that the Romans failed to wipe out the Jews because Titus did not extinguish it, because he was betrayed and stole an ordinary fire while the authentic flame was squirreled to safety. He sought to finish the task Titus could not complete. Is that your aim, Salah ad-Din?" The *mutwali* removed his glasses, revealing eerie pale blue eyes. "Perhaps you have your grandfather's religious passion, after all?"

"The object is a historical symbol more powerful than any religious myth," Salah ad-Din said. "You know the historical claims that would follow if others find it. It would endanger the Waqf's control of the Mount overnight."

"Your expert from Rome, Professor Cianari, might have found it, but . . ." The *mutwali* held a strange, admiring gaze that finished the thought, *but you apparently have your grandfather's temper, too.*

Salah ad-Din looked down and noticed a small spattering of the professor's blood on the cuff of his shirt.

"I will have additional expertise," Salah ad-Din said. "Ramat Mansour."

"Your cousin?" the *mutwali* said.

"Ramat Mansour is more knowledgeable about the Mount than any professor."

"Except your cousin will not assist your efforts. He opposes your activities beneath the Mount."

"For this effort he will assist me," Salah ad-Din said. "I will see to it."

"You have until the *sabah*," the *mutwali* said, lowering his gaze to his tea.

Dawn.

"I am sorry, Salah ad-Din," he continued. "I cannot allow—" But the *mutwali* did not finish. When he looked up he saw that the young man was no longer standing by the window. As the consummate sign of disrespect, while the *mutwali* was mid-sentence, Salah ad-Din had walked out, leaving the door wide open.

37

"A n ancient dead woman," Chandler said. "Floating in a column. Congratulations, Aurelius, we're even. Now I think you've lost it. And have you any idea how much it takes for me to say that? A hell of a lot." He turned to Emili. "I mean, is it even possible? That level of preservation after two thousand years?"

"Actually, it is," Emili said. "In 2002, a highway construction team in eastern China uncovered a fluid-filled coffin, and a corpse just as well preserved was floating inside. Nearly perfect, except for the muscle tissue that got discolored from the alkaline fluid."

"This old?" Chandler said.

"Older. A queen of the Han Dynasty. Early first century. I bet she has this young woman's radio carbon numbers beat by fifty years."

"Fine"—Chandler tilted his head back—"let's say she's that old, Aurelius, what does she tell us?"

"The inscription tattooed around her navel indicates a location," Jonathan said.

"*'Phere Nike Umbilicus Orbis Terrarum,'*" Jonathan read.

"What does it mean?" Emili said.

"Well, *phere* or *pheros* refers to someone who carries or bears something, like phos*pheros*, 'a stone that bears light,'" Jonathan said, "or Christopher, as in 'bearer of Christ.' *Nike*, of course, means 'victory,' *umbilicus*, as you might expect, means 'navel,' and *orbis terrarum* means 'sphere of the world.'"

"Navel of the world." Chandler stood up suddenly.

"Wait," Emili challenged. "It says *'orbis terrarum,'* which means a round earth. That means this inscription couldn't have been written in the first century. The ancient scientific consensus was that the world was *flat*."

"But it wasn't the consensus among the ancient priests of Jerusalem," Chandler said slowly, thinking aloud. "The Kabbalists in Jerusalem knew a great deal of astronomy. They correctly modeled the solar system two thousand years before the European philosophers realized the earth was round. In fact, it's no coincidence that the six branches of the menorah make completely round orbits around a central fiery object. For the ancient mystics, the menorah represented the solar system, each branch embodying the revolution of visible planets around a central light, the sun." Chandler shrugged. "The Church may have tried to lop off Galileo's head for suggesting a heliocentric view, but Jerusalem's priests millennia before had been quietly using the menorah's symbolism to understand a more accurate depiction of the planetary alignment. The lamp's central light, a *shamash*, even uses the same Hebraic letters as *shemesh*, meaning 'sun.'"

"Chandler's right, Emili," Jonathan said. "Josephus himself says, 'The seven lamps upon the sacred candlestick refer to the course of the planets.' Anyone for whom this tattoo's message was intended knew—at the very least—that the earth was round."

"Center of the world?" Emili said. "Still doesn't exactly narrow it down, does it?"

"Oh, yes it does," Chandler said, grinning. "Ancient cosmology viewed Jerusalem as the geographical center of the world, and the Temple Mount as the center of Jerusalem."

"Of the entire world?" Emili said.

"'As the land of Israel is the navel of the world,'" Chandler recited from memory, his eyes obligatorily closed for effect, "'Jerusalem is in the center of the land of Israel, and the sanctuary is the center of Jerusalem.'" He turned to Jonathan. "Even through medieval times, cartographers portrayed the continents as cloverleafs and the Temple Mount in the center of the earth."

Emili looked suddenly skeptical. "But how do we know this woman is even connected to any of this? Maybe she was just—"

"Just what?" Chandler said, pointing at the tattoo. "Some ancient hipster, and 'navel of the world' was her favorite ancient punk band?"

Emili ignored him. "Jonathan, this woman may not even have been from the *same century*. Now you're the one making assumptions."

"No assumptions here at all," Jonathan said. He pointed at the corpse's abdomen in the photograph. "Look at the length of those five curved rows of gashes across the torso. They look like—"

"Claw marks," Emili whispered.

"Yes," Jonathan said, "and big ones, too. Perhaps a tiger. An urban woman this refined wasn't killed in the wild. She was most likely *damnata ad bestias*."

"Condemned to the beasts," Emili translated.

"Right, and most likely for treason. We know Titus reserved his tigers for traitors because he felt their calculated crime merited an executioner that stalked its prey."

"So you think she was a member of Josephus's network, one of the prisoners executed in the Colosseum?"

"Yes, and I think we can tell *who* she was." Jonathan looked up at Chandler. "Even without the Interpol database." He pointed at the inscription. "They've written her name on her."

"Her name?" Chandler leaned over the image. "I don't see a 'Hello, my name is . . .' sticker."

"Look at the inscription, it's a mere combination cipher."

"As in combining two words," Chandler said.

"Right, the words *phere* and *nike* mean 'bearer of victory,' referring to whoever managed to escape from the Temple with the menorah. But in combining those words we suddenly have a Greek name, *Pherenike*, which in the Macedonian dialect was written *Bherenike*."

"Berenice," Emili said softly, allowing the name to echo in her head.

"Titus's mistress and the last princess of Jerusalem. If her real name even was Berenice," Jonathan said. "Given its double meaning, Josephus may be revealing his plot subtly in his work, so as to avoid Roman censors, and he may—again—be using a pseudonym here to do it. Just as he gave the name Aliterius to that so-called stage actor so we could understand his true role as Jerusalem's spy in Nero's court, Josephus may have done the same with Titus's mistress, giving her a name that connotes her true role as a conspirator. *Bheronike*, a 'bearer of victory' who helped Josephus convey the menorah to safety after Jerusalem's sack."

THE LAST EMBER   187

"But the problem remains," Chandler said, "that even if her tattoo tells us *how* Josephus escaped through the Holy of Holies with the menorah, there's no record of where it went."

"That's true," Jonathan agreed. "The terms are too vague to be an archaeological guide. The slaves of Jerusalem would have needed to leave us a detailed map of first-century Jerusalem."

Across the table, Emili was unexpectedly smiling.

"And I think I know where it is," she said.

38

Comandante Profeta had just returned to his sixth-floor office at the Command. His trip to Dulling and Pierce had been more informative than he expected. A junior officer waited silently beside his desk as the *comandante* signed a series of Interpol requests, seeking information about the Geneva corporation that had loaned the Forma Urbis fragments to the Capitoline Museum. After receiving the final page, the junior officer bolted out of the room, nearly colliding with a paunchy, middle-aged man whom Profeta recognized at once.

Dr. Stanoje Odalović, Rome's deputy city coroner.

"Stanoje, come in," Profeta said.

Profeta had known Odalović since he joined the coroner's office as a slim Kosovar émigré with a black bushy mustache, a license in pathology from a bombed-out medical school in Prishtina, and no employment papers. In the twenty years since, Profeta had worked regularly with Dr. Odalović—more frequently now, as the antiquities trade had turned lethal. But Profeta had never seen the man this agitated.

"*Comandante*, it's a little early for a *pesce d'aprile*," Dr. Odalović said, referring to an Italian April Fool's Day joke.

Dr. Odalović opened the butterfly tabs of a large manila envelope and removed the photograph of the female corpse Profeta's men discovered in the warehouse raid.

"She is"—Dr. Odalović coughed nervously—"older than we thought."

"How much older?"

"Well, you can tell the people in Homicide to stop their investigation," he said. "Let's just say the statute of limitations has run out on this one."

"I'm not following, Stanoje." Profeta took off his glasses.

"We just received the preliminary dating results from liquid scintillation analysis. The follicle sample you gave me was . . ." Dr. Odalović shifted. "First century A.D. What you saw was no hoax, Jacopo. She was ancient."

Profeta stood up from his chair and Dr. Odalović's eyes followed him. He walked toward the window, looking more contemplative than surprised.

"And the liquid she was in?"

"A perfect ancient embalming recipe. Cedar oil, juniper, wood tar. Each organic component dated to the same period."

"Cause of death?" Profeta asked.

Dr. Odalović was surprised to hear the *comandante* ask a routine question as he would for a modern victim.

"Cause of death? I just told you she was from—"

"I heard your analysis, Stanoje. Do you have a cause of death?"

Dr. Odalović nodded and removed another slide from the manila folder.

"In the lock of hair you sent to my laboratory there was a strand that was . . . *different*. It wasn't human."

"What do you mean, different?"

"It was not human."

"Not human?"

Dr. Odalović handed Profeta an enlarged slide from the folder.

"This is a one-hundred-times–magnified picture of a single strand. Do you see those petal-like pattern rosettes? Those are from a large spotted animal. A jaguar or leopard."

Profeta inspected the picture.

"From the gashes across the torso, and the sand crystals present in the hair, I'd say the cause and place of her death is clear," Stanoje Odalović said, using the coroner's logic that had become second nature. "This woman was mauled to death in the sand."

Profeta looked out the window. "The Colosseum," he said.

"And one other thing, *Comandante*," Dr. Odalović said, standing to leave.

"Yes, Stanoje?"

"After we received the initial results, we thought our in-house machine was acting up. So we cross-checked the results with the carbon dating equipment at the Earth Sciences Department at Sapienza."

"And?"

"And they said an organic sample that yielded the same carbon results had been submitted only days before. The sample was from the left patella, her kneecap."

Left kneecap. Profeta's eyes drifted down to the photograph, where the corpse's left leg was still tented upward and the kneecap removed.

"Who submitted the sample?"

Dr. Odalović glanced down at his notes. "Cianari. Professor Gustavo Cianari, a professor of—"

"Biblical archaeology at La Sapienza," Profeta finished. He remained silent a moment, watching the afternoon sun rest on the curve of the Pantheon dome. Profeta leaned forward toward his desk phone.

"Damn it, Cianari," Profeta said. "What have you done?"

39

A *first-century* map of Jerusalem?" Jonathan challenged. "Emili, unless a map were stowed in an arid desert atmosphere like the Dead Sea scrolls, there's no way it could have survived."

"The map wasn't parchment. It was a painting on the wall."

"A wall painting?" Chandler was incredulous. "Doesn't that sound a little public?"

"Not where they painted it." Emili turned to Jonathan. "I think it's down in the Domus Aurea, Nero's Golden Palace. Beneath the inscription 'Sacred Tree of Light' those prisoners in the Colosseum inscribed a second line: 'Domus Aurea.'"

"And that's not public?" Chandler said. "A map painted on the wall of the emperor's palace?"

"Where a palace had been previously," Emili countered. "By the time the slaves from Jerusalem were marched into Rome, the Domus Aurea was no longer Nero's gem-encrusted paradise. Titus had buried the palace and built public baths over it."

"Interesting theory," Jonathan agreed, "but we'd need more historical information—"

"And we have it," Emili fired back. "In the 1500s, the first explorers of the Domus Aurea described an ancient mural of an unknown city with turreted walls and large public courtyards."

Jonathan knew that Emili's extensive preservation work in the 1999 restoration of the Domus Aurea offered her a front-row seat for the sprawling ruin's history of excavation.

"The map hasn't been found since, but from the explorers' descriptions, archaeologists once argued that the painting was of Rome before the great fire of A.D. 64, given how much the fire changed the face of ancient Rome. The fire leveled miles of warehouses and homes in the area that eventually became the space for the Colosseum and public baths."

"But you said the walls had turrets," Jonathan said. "The walls of Rome didn't have turrets until the Aurelian Wall of A.D. 270 to 280."

"Exactly," Emili said, "which is why recent commentators suggest the map they discovered in the Domus Aurea was of another ancient city. A city that was bracing itself for the full onslaught of Rome's force."

"Jerusalem," Chandler said.

"Yes," Emili said. She was leaning over the worktable with her arms straight, hands flat, and a mess of blond hair dangling just above the table's surface. It was the same intensity Jonathan remembered. "Jon," she said, lowering her voice, "the prisoners beneath the Colosseum wrote the second line of the inscription because they were *telling us where to go next.*"

"I've brought down some nineteenth-century expedition maps of the Domus Aurea!" Chandler said, quickly turning around, as though they might soon disappear. "Here." His eyes widened as he unrolled a large yellowed parchment on the table.

"Wait a second," Jonathan protested. "Even if there is a painting down there, you said it's lost. The Domus Aurea stretches for *two miles.*"

Emili remained silent, studying the map. Nero's ancient pavilions were drawn in red, marking where they lay deep beneath the Oppian Hill. Every time she took in the full view of Nero's sprawling palace, she understood the ancient satirist Martial's complaint: *Rome is now a single house!*

"Jon?" Emili's voice had raised an octave. The tone of an imminent discovery. "Down in the Colosseum. What was drawn on either side of the inscription?"

"Owls," Jonathan said. "They surrounded the second line of the inscription, *Domus Aurea.*"

"*Look here,*" Emili said, waving him over to her side of the map. "Look where this portico ends. The Vault of"—she leaned over farther to make sure she had the map's fine print right—"Owls. The Vault of Owls." She looked up at Jonathan. "They all but gave us directions."

Chandler disappeared into the back of the room and emerged from the darkness carrying a large navy bag. Jonathan recognized it at once.

"Why are you carrying that rope ladder?" Jonathan said suspiciously.

"Do you think fifty feet will be long enough?" he said. "It's the longest one back there, but parts of the Domus are pretty deep." He placed three heavy ten-inch black aluminum flashlights on the table. "And we'll need these Maglites," Chandler said. "It'll be pretty dark down there."

"Down there," Jonathan repeated, struggling to keep his composure. "Climb into the Domus Aurea?"

"Those brick well shafts in the municipal park of the Oppian Hill lead directly into the Domus's palace corridors."

"*Renaissance* explorers used those chutes to access the Domus Aurea!" Jonathan responded. "The only reason they even still exist is because the Domus Aurea museum used them for ventilation."

"Exactly," Chandler said, "and the museum has been closed for over a year."

Jonathan knew that the archaeological superintendent in Rome had completed a staggering twenty-year-long renovation to meticulously clean ten percent of the Domus Aurea's wall paintings for a subterranean museum. But within four years, the carbon dioxide exhaled by tourists discolored the ancient drawings, and the nighttime collapse of an interior wall revealed that the ancient bricks had begun to crumble. By 2006, the doors of the Domus Aurea had closed again, forcing most tourists once again to view its murals only in art history textbooks.

"Jon." Emili pointed at the map. "Chandler's plan actually works. If we take this path"—she ran her finger along a dotted line representing an ancient portico—"that would lead us directly into the Vault of Owls."

"*Us?*" Jonathan exclaimed. "Em, I'm not *roping* down anywhere." Emili saw the memory of Gianpaolo's death surface in his eyes.

"We don't need to rope down," Emili said soothingly. "The Domus museum is not entirely closed." She looked at her watch. "It still opens a few afternoons a week now for limited tours. Mainly just dignitaries and benefactors. I could see if there's something this afternoon. I have a friend at the Cultural Ministry who could—"

"Emili, even with museum access, you'd have to sneak hundreds of meters away from the restored corridors to access the Vault of Owls. Those tunnels haven't been seen by *anyone* in two hundred years."

"Then what do you suggest I do?" Emili asked, walking around the table toward him. "They're *erasing* history, Jon. They've been doing it beneath the Temple Mount for years, and now they've come to Rome to finish the job. If your thesis was right years ago, then Josephus and countless slaves gave their lives to protect the location of the menorah. I can't let the Waqf destroy that, too."

"*Brava.* I'm convinced," Chandler said, handing her his iPhone. "See if there's a tour."

I should contact the carabinieri alone, Jonathan thought. *But that might only put Emili and Chandler in greater danger in the Domus Aurea.* Both explosions, the dockside warehouse and the Colosseum, occurred just after the carabinieri were notified. *Someone was tipping them off.*

"Thirty minutes." Emili put down the phone, looking smug. "How's that for timing?"

"What's in thirty minutes?" Chandler said.

"A guided tour, some benefactors from London," Emili said. "So you're in luck. The tour's even in English."

"There's a guided tour in a half-hour?" Jonathan said. "Did you plan that?"

"*Audentes fortuna iuvat,*" Emili said, and shrugged, quoting Virgil. "Luck favors the brave."

A police siren blared outside the academy's gates.

"Or maybe not," Chandler said, looking out the window. "Today, luck favors the carabinieri."

"The carabinieri must have circulated a photo," Jonathan said, turning to Emili. "Did anyone see you come in here?"

"One of the carabinieri guards outside the American Vatican embassy across the street must have spotted Emili," Chandler said, swinging shut the Casa's wood-plank doors and locking them. "The officers in their jeep whistled and catcalled for a full minute as we walked by." Chandler turned to Jonathan. "I assumed it was for her, not me."

"But the American embassy is on Via Veneto," Jonathan said.

"That's the American embassy to Italy, ol' boy. Rome's the only city in the world with *two* sets of embassies, one diplomatic mission to Italy and another to the Vatican's one hundred eight sovereign acres. The American Vatican embassy is across the street."

The academy's iron side gate slammed shut, and a uniformed carabinieri officer walked onto the grounds. Jonathan joined Chandler at the window. The flashing light of a lone carabinieri car was parked outside the academy's back gate. The officer walked at a fast clip across the grass toward the Casa Rustica. Kossi followed, noticeably reluctant, gesturing argumentatively.

Jonathan could hear the carabinieri officer. "If there's no one here"—the officer spoke curtly to Kossi in Italian, pointing at the wet grass—"then what are these fresh footprints?"

The officer stopped walking and pointed angrily. As though following the order of a furious parent, Kossi skulked back to the academy's main villa. The officer continued alone. Jonathan could now see his face.

"That's him," Jonathan said.

"Who?"

"Lieutenant Rufio, the officer from the Colosseum," Jonathan said. "He knows we're here."

"There's no back way out," Emili said. She looked out the window. An ancient Roman stone wall towered over the gardens, casting long shadows over the academy's well-trimmed lawn.

"I can't believe this," Jonathan said. "Not even twelve hours ago I came here a lawyer, and now—*Chandler*, what on earth are you doing?"

Chandler had climbed beneath the table and was tapping on the Casa Rustica's slate floor tiles with the end of his pen.

"You're right, the walls are too high to go over them." Chandler crouched, using his pen to jimmy the tiles. One of them moved slightly, and he got his fingers under the crack and lifted a two-foot-square portion of the floor. The tiles were glued to the top of a hinged wooden trapdoor.

"But not under them. Here, help me lift this."

Emili helped raise the wood panel.

"It's an entrance to a Trajanic aqueduct."

They all knew that the emperors of ancient Rome had built aqueducts for miles inside Roman hillsides, using gravity to bring in water from streams miles outside Rome. But Jonathan had forgotten that the academy was built immediately over a Trajanic aqueduct, constructed in A.D. 129.

"Where does it lead?" Emili asked.

"It runs beneath the Aurelian Wall." Chandler grunted, lifting the wooden board. "Used over one hundred fifty years ago, when Garibaldi's men used these aqueducts as foxholes against the papal forces."

Jonathan quickly climbed the ladder to the stacks, and through the semicircular fanlight above the door watched Rufio approach. Rufio was walking slowly. He removed his gun from his holster.

"Why is he alone?" Emili whispered as she hurried to lift the tiles beside Chandler.

"Because he doesn't want witnesses," Jonathan said.

"Aren't you coming?" Emili called up to Jonathan.

"You've got to, Jon!" Chandler exclaimed in a loud whisper. "Josephus arranged the most important heist of the ancient world. It doesn't get much bigger than this."

Rufio stood outside the door and wiped his brow with his sleeve. He was sweating profusely.

"Hello!" he yelled, and banged on the door. "I know you're in there! This is the carabinieri! Open the door!"

Only the rusted shutter of the gardener's shed answered him, creaking in the wind.

Rufio moved from the front door and walked around the small structure, staring into its frosted windows. "You have no idea what you are in the middle of, do you?" He was now along the back of the house. It was unnerving to hear his voice from each side of the house, as though they were surrounded. A sudden yanking of the bolted back doors startled all three of them.

"Open the door and I will protect you," Rufio said, pointing his gun at the Casa's doors. Jonathan could see his forefinger on the trigger.

"Jon!" Emili said. "Let's go!"

Jonathan raced down the ladder, crossed the room, and lowered Emili through the black square in the floor. The doors exploded inward with a gunshot, just as Jonathan lowered the trapdoor over their heads, rejoining glued tiles to the floor's pattern.

Rufio stormed in to find the Casa Rustica empty. He yelled an Italian expletive and in his rage fired another deafening round into the half-light.

Jonathan, Emili, and Chandler stood completely still beneath the tile floor. A damp breeze carried the smell of stagnant water and mildew.

Beneath the Casa's floor, they heard a mobile phone ring, and all three of them gave one another panicked looks for a moment for fear it was one of theirs.

But it was Rufio's. They heard him answer the phone, speak one line into it, and then clip it shut.

"Tell Salah ad-Din they are gone," he said.

40

Beneath the Casa Rustica's tile floor, Jonathan, Emili, and Chandler could hear Lieutenant Rufio's stampede of boot steps as he searched among the bookcases and under the tables. Chandler clicked on his Maglite, illuminating Roman-era grooves in the walls that indicated water levels in antiquity.

A steel sewage pipe, caked in rust, ran across the ancient tunnel like a limbo bar.

The ancient Roman engineering graded the angle of the tunnel downward, allowing the water to flow toward the city. They walked, leaning backward to balance against the slope. After about a hundred feet, daylight seeped through a manhole above them. Chandler pushed it upward, revealing a street on the other side of the academy's gate. The oblivious driver of a royal-blue Smart car nearly clipped Chandler's arm, but the car passed harmlessly overhead. The afternoon light was startlingly bright.

Two carabinieri officers were stationed outside the embassy, deep in conversation. They stood less than twenty feet from Emili's motorcycle.

"You still have that thing?" Jonathan said, blanching at the sight of the motorcycle. "The Ducati?"

He remembered Emili's classic motorcycle, its handcrafted engine exquisite even by Italian standards. Their death-defying trips at sixty kilometers an hour down the winding streets of Janiculum Hill rushed back to him. "And you're still alive? Luck really does favor the brave."

"Listen, I'll go first," Chandler said. "I'll get their attention, and you two slip over to the bike. Got it?"

"Chandler, how will you get to the Domus?" Emili asked.

"There's always a cab at the Fontana dell'Acqua Paola." Chandler pointed down the road. "They circle like vultures to pick off exhausted tourists who underestimate the Janiculum's climb. I'll be lucky to get 'em to use the meter."

Chandler pushed himself out of the manhole, and within seconds he was walking toward the officers, yelling in a foreign language as he waved his hands to make a great fuss with the policemen. They gathered around him.

"Wait here," Emili said. "I'll pick you up."

Pick me up? Jonathan thought. Before he could say anything, Emili hopped out of the manhole and walked briskly toward the motorcycle. Soundlessly, she threw a leg over, but upon giving the engine some gas, one of the policemen called out. She revved the engine and darted down the side street toward Jonathan.

"Get on!" She briefly slowed down.

Scarcely had Jonathan thrown a leg over the saddle when the low growl blared into a roar. The bike fishtailed up on the sidewalk curb, just missing a shuttered flower stand along Via Masina. A group of locals miraculously parted as the bike's chassis scraped against the street curb. The bike's back tire clipped the charcoal grill of a vendor selling smoked chestnuts. Hunched over the handlebars like a jockey, Emili's small frame leaned forward, and the bike tore down the Viale Glorioso as though finding an open patch of sky.

Jonathan grabbed her waist and yelled in her ear, "Why can't you just have a Vespa like everyone else?"

41

From the Command, Profeta's drive to La Sapienza's gated six-teenth-century palazzo took less than two minutes, but he felt as though he had traveled back a lifetime. He had been here as a young graduate student in art-recovery and architecture before the carabinieri's first specialized team approached him in a dark library. It was a memory that now seemed part of this university's ancient past, just another historical fact, as distant as its founding by Pope Boniface VIII, who in 1303 raised taxes on wine to pay for the new college he christened simply Sapienza, or "wisdom." For Boniface VIII, wine may have paid for education, but for Profeta and his young colleagues who spent half their stipends at the local bars, education paid for the wine.

Profeta walked through the palazzo's main courtyard toward Sant'Ivo alla Sapienza, one of the school's original baroque build-ings from the mid-1600s. Its bizarre corkscrew tower, designed by Francesco Borromini, resembled a dark castle from the Middle Ages. During Mussolini's era, most of the university's faculty were moved to a spacious campus of stark concrete neoclassical design nearer Termini station, but not Cianari. His seniority allowed him to remain in these historic offices inside the palazzo, which now contained the State Archives.

"Cianari," Profeta said to himself, shaking his head. He had been a faculty member even during Profeta's graduate school days. Pro-feta knew that Cianari, as a biblical archaeologist, had always been marginalized by skeptics in his department. As academics, Cianari's colleagues disbelieved most of what was *in* the Bible, not to mention that it could ever be a useful archaeological text. Even graduate students chided him about his fieldwork in the hills of Turkey in search of where Noah's Ark ran aground on Mount Ararat. Cianari's ambition was epochal, and that was precisely what worried Profeta. If Cianari had finally found someone to believe in or, even more dangerous, *fund* one of his escapades, the parameters of the expedition could span countries.

An officer stood outside the partially open door to Professor Cianari's office. "None of the faculty have seen the professor in two weeks, *Comandante*. Traveling outside the country, they said."

"That will be all, Officer, thank you," Profeta said, now fearing the worst. He stepped into the office alone. It was wallpapered with books vaulting up to the ceiling. There was a tall wheeled ladder and a sweet, musty smell of oiled leather. Seven hundred continuous years of professors had inhabited this office.

The area near the desk was in total disarray. Not quite ransacked, but revealing the throes of a tormented man. Open copies of books in ancient Greek and Latin lay across the desk. Profeta circled the desk and, using a handkerchief from his pocket, lifted manuscripts to uncover a glossy photograph lying beneath.

"I don't believe this," he said, staring at the black-and-white image.

"What is it, *Comandante*?" asked Lieutenant Brandisi, who had just entered the office behind him. As Brandisi rounded the desk, no spoken answer was necessary.

The corpse from the abandoned pier of Civitavecchia again floated before them, this time in the center of a blown-up photograph on Gustavo Cianari's desk. The setting of the photograph was not the warehouse, but rather an underground grotto with a low-roofed ceiling of jagged stone. Only the top of the column's lid had been sawed off, revealing, like a partially open casket, the corpse above the shoulders. The rest of the column remained a unified single piece of fluted column, as first discovered in situ. A chain saw lay beside the column, the whitened, powdery teeth of its blades suggesting that it had chewed through the column's stone just moments before.

"This is where they found her," Profeta said, now looking at the tomb art paintings in the photograph's background. "Looks like a first-century catacomb."

"Who took these photographs?" Brandisi asked.

"I think it was Cianari, and it doesn't look like he was supposed to," Profeta said. "The red glow suggests he avoided using a flash."

Profeta picked up the picture.

He took off his reading glasses and held them an inch from the picture to magnify the image. His eyes focused on a fresco in the photograph's background, along the grotto's back wall. He could not make out the ancient drawing, but along its bottom he could see that someone had vandalized the painting with two words scrawled in red spray paint.

"To a grave robber that ancient painting would have been priceless," Brandisi said. "Why the graffiti?"

"I think Cianari did that," Profeta said.

"An archaeologist would vandalize an ancient painting?"

"It might have been Cianari's only method of identifying where these men had been digging. Whatever they were looking for, it was important enough that Cianari felt compelled to document its context."

Beneath Cianari's desk, Profeta noticed a large, map-sized piece of paper crumpled on the floor. He picked it up and spread it over the strewn papers. It was an aerial satellite image of downtown Rome. With a blue felt-tip marker, someone had circled two locations in Rome. One circle was drawn around the ruins across the Colosseum.

"Do you recognize this location, Lieutenant?" Profeta said. Brandisi detected an urgency rising in the *comandante*'s voice.

"The gladiator's barracks," Brandisi said.

"That's right, Lieutenant. Precisely the location of the explosion just three hours ago."

Profeta's index finger moved along the satellite image as though hovering above the city center. His finger stopped where the other circle was drawn around a church basilica on the Oppian Hill, a half-kilometer from the Colosseum. Beside the circle, someone had written a hurried note: *SPIV.*

"It looks signed," Brandisi said aloud. "Those initials, SPIV."

"That's not a signature, Lieutenant. From the location, I think it's referring to Rome's oldest reliquary church, San Pietro in Vincoli. Saint Peter in Chains. Lieutenant, these could be the same men who blew up the corridors beneath the Colosseum. Get the tourists out of that church."

42

The streets were barricaded at the bottom of the Janiculum Hill. Emili cut the engine, maneuvering her motorcycle down the jagged stone steps, its suspension absorbing each of the tiny ancient ledges carved into the hillside. They exited the staircase onto Via Goffredo Mameli, as though emerging out of the mountain's rock. Emili turned the ignition, gave the motorcycle some gas, and followed the tracks of the electric tram across the Ponte Garibaldi back over the Tiber.

A police car raced in the opposite direction toward the academy's gate. Emili sharply turned the motorcycle off Via Arenula, taking back streets behind Piazza Venezia. It was a bizarre reverse *Roman Holiday*, Audrey Hepburn gunning the engine and Gregory Peck clutching her waist for dear life.

Her motorcycle slalomed through Via Cavour's traffic, and reaching the dark side streets of the Oppian Hill, she eased off the gas, gliding into an overgrown municipal park with a panoramic view. Beneath them, Rome rose out of a sea of brake lights from the late-afternoon traffic. They could see police cars still flanking the Colosseum's outer arches like a wedge of geese. A tour bus traffic jam lined Via dei Fori Imperiali, caused by the sudden closure of the Colosseum piazza since the explosion hours earlier.

Jonathan looked at his watch. Nearly four-fifteen p.m. He watched Emili gracefully dismount the Ducati and stow her helmet beneath its seat. He could not believe it was only this morning in court that he had seen her for the first time in seven years. What did Tatton say? "For Rome, one lifetime is not enough." *Apparently.*

"I'll leave the motorcycle there," Emili said. She walked her bike over to some brick ruins where the ivy was three feet thick, and it disappeared beneath its tufts.

In the park, small brick chutes that looked like chimneys dotted the terrain in all directions. Jonathan knew they were ventilation grates for the ancient corridors of the Domus Aurea, which sprawled for a quarter-mile beneath this litter-strewn park. Jonathan remembered Pliny's fanciful descriptions of the palace: *"Even when the doors are closed, inside the gems glowed like daylight,"* but he knew that even when the museum was open to the public only one-tenth of the Domus Aurea's one hundred fifty rooms were excavated.

They crossed the park, entering another set of gates behind a glass gazebo that once sold tickets to the Domus Aurea Museum, but now a sign in its window read: "Guided Tours Only." A small private tour of seven British couples bundled in fur coats and cashmere scarves gathered near the ticket booth. In a cultivated accent, one woman expressed surprise that the entrance to this "palace" was an unimpressive steel gate leading underground.

"Where is Chandler?" Emili said.

"Maybe he's not com— Wait, there," Jonathan said.

A figure hurried up the hill toward the museum entrance. Chandler Manning was running awkwardly with a large folio under his arm.

"I . . . I brought it," Chandler panted, handing them the nineteenth-century cartographic renderings of the Domus Aurea. "Once you split from the tour you'll need it to find the map of Jerusalem."

Jonathan unrolled the parchment map while waiting for the rest of the tour group.

"The route of the guided tour goes right through Nero's octagonal dining room, which is connected to the corridor leading to the Vault of Owls."

"But how will we split from the tour?" Emili pointed at a security guard standing at the back of the crowd. She knew the museum corridors of the Domus Aurea were dim, and many passageways led abruptly to dried-up waterfalls, fake grotto cliffs, and other hazards. To ensure visitors stayed together at all times, each Domus Aurea tour had a security guard following at the rear.

"Not to worry," Chandler said, winking. "When the time comes, I'll get the docent's attention. You just get Aurelius here to tell me when you need to disappear."

"It'll be around here," Jonathan said, pointing at the map. "When the tour enters the octagonal room, the crowd will be gathered in a circle, and Chandler, that'll be your cue to get the guard's attention."

"Welcome to the Domus Aurea! Nero's Golden Fantasia!" said

the tour guide, a pretty Italian graduate student with the ebullient tone of a kindergarten teacher. She began stepping back. "'*Roma domus fiet!*' 'Rome is all one big house!' said one ancient historian in describing the grand corridors we are about to explore together!"

The tour moved deeper underground through barrel vaults. The guide pointed upward at circular holes high in the ancient ceilings.

"That's where Renaissance artists first roped down to discover this ancient ruin. Some of the sixteenth century's most famous Roman artists wrote their names in black candle ash in order to trace their way back through the corridors to avoid getting lost!"

The tour group cooed as the guide pointed out various names, Caravaggio and Raphael among them, scrawled across the ceiling.

Emili remembered seeing the Domus excavations as a graduate student, before it was opened to the public. She could picture where the scaffolding was, where the makeshift excavation tables were set up with maps of the sprawling ruin. Now, everything looked quite polished. Frosted-glass sheets depicted the construction of Nero's golden palace with three-dimensional blueprints. Emili's trained eye never ceased to be impressed by the more subtle aspects of the ancient corridor's state of eerie preservation: a piece of crystalline marble still shining inside a brick wall, a vivid wall stucco illustrating Achilles in mid-battle.

"And here," the tour guide said, projecting her voice louder to emphasize the location's importance. "Here we have come to the grand octagonal room. You can tell from the arched vault that this was probably an ivory ceiling that would shed flowers and perfumes on its dinner guests."

Jonathan nodded to Chandler.

"Or," Chandler exclaimed, "it may have been an *orgiastica* room created for royal bathing and marathon sexual practices."

"Excuse me?" the guide said.

"Oh, let's not be skittish here. Nero's dinner parties weren't exactly rated PG-thirteen, were they? C'mon, we're all grown-ups here!" Chandler stepped into the middle of the circle. "Rose petals would fall down from the ceiling onto rotating couches! Safe bet it wasn't just to encourage conversation." He pointed at an ancient mural of a nude man surrounded by three women. "And that's a picture of the mythical god Priapus. You know, as in call your doctor after four hours? It's called priapism for a reason, people!" The guide looked mortified as the entire tour turned toward him, and Chandler—as was his talent—became an instant spectacle, regaling the crowd with off-color legends of Nero's nightlife.

"This way," Jonathan whispered, leading Emili around the tour group along the perimeter of the octagonal room. He edged closer to one of the arches that led off into the darkness and, with Emili by his side, stepped backward. In a single moment they were cloaked in darkness. They waited a moment to make certain their disappearance was not noticed.

They were too close to the group to use their flashlights, and Jonathan felt Emili's warmth close to him. The back of their hands brushed against each other as they moved backward, and the unexpected softness of her skin reminded Jonathan it was the first time they touched since his return to Rome. In the half-light of a park grate overhead, Jonathan noticed Emili was not looking at the walls but at him, as though he, too, were a fresco of the Domus Aurea and buried under the sludge of many years, something vibrant and pristine had been revealed. She smiled, slipping her hand into his.

"We have a lot of ground to cover," she said, gently squeezing his fingers. "Let's go."

43

As a row of carabinieri sedans climbed the Esquiline Hill, Profeta could see the Colosseum at the foot of its western slope.

"Quite a view," Brandisi said to Profeta in the backseat.

"Something Nero took into account when building his palace on the hill," Profeta said.

At the end of the Via Eudossiana, the carabinieri cars slowed as they passed a fifteenth-century monastery, adjacent to San Pietro in Vincoli, the church of Saint Peter in Chains. Built originally to house monks, the building now contained the faculty of engineering of the University of La Sapienza. A banner hanging between two sixteenth-century columns welcomed engineering professors to an annual robotics conference. At the entrance to the old monastery court, students sat outside on the steps, smoking as they enjoyed a short break from the rain.

The carabinieri cars pulled in front of the two-story façade of Saint Peter in Chains. Even by Roman standards, the church exuded a deceptive obscurity, sitting at the northern end of an unadorned piazza that had been transformed to a neighborhood parking lot. But Profeta knew the façade was misleading. Behind its unassuming wrought-iron gate and Ionic columns were some of Christendom's most remarkable treasures. Under the main altar in a reliquary of gold and rock crystal lay the ancient chains that bound Saint Peter in Jerusalem, as recorded in the Acts of the Apostles.

"The church's evacuation is nearly complete," Rufio said, meeting Profeta and Brandisi as they stepped out of the car. "I was on

Janiculum Hill when I received Brandisi's message to have the church evacuated. We had a false sighting of Dr. Travia."

A stream of tourists funneled out of the church like refugees. A policeman argued with a gelato vendor to move his van from the piazza. The vendor's furor was audible from across the piazza as he stabbed at the permit he wore around his neck as if it were a war medal.

By the time Profeta stepped inside, all the tourists had exited the church. The long rectangular shape of the church had few windows, and even during the summer months, the interior was dark. Twenty-four columns converged on a single point, where the chains of Saint Peter lay in a brass *confessionale* beneath the altar. Profeta's trained eye recognized the ancient marble seat on top of the altar as being from a toilet-bath in ancient Rome, but he knew to say nothing, as the seat was now converted to an episcopal throne over the chains of Saint Peter.

Profeta stood in the middle of the aisle. *"Comandante,"* the church rector said from the far side of the aisle, "Father Zicino is ready to receive you."

Profeta walked through a small black door to a sconce-lit sacristy. He passed the stored vestments of the priests and attendants and descended a dim hallway lined with portraits of the Renaissance-era priests of San Pietro in Vincoli, among them Francesco della Rovere, who eventually rose to the papacy from this very office. Profeta stepped through a wooden door to find a middle-aged man, more athletic-looking than he had expected. Father Zicino was approaching fifty, still with many years before him to rise politically within the Curia. The priest sat at his desk with a large cross on the wall behind him. His face was clean-shaven beneath well-groomed black hair with gray forelocks. Saint Peter in Chains was an important parish, and Profeta could decipher from Father Zicino's immaculate office that he was an efficient man. He gestured for Profeta to sit down. He seemed at ease, as though evacuating his church were an everyday occurrence.

"Yes, *Comandante*, how may we help you?"

"My apologies for the disruption, Father," Profeta said. "We have reason to think your reliquaries could be in danger."

"*Comandante*, this church has been the custodian of some of Christendom's most valuable belongings for more than one thousand years. The chains of Saint Peter have been safe here since the early fifth century, when Empress Eudossiana placed them here, after her journeys in Jerusalem. They are behind half a foot of plate glass."

"Has there been any restoration or any construction here in the church's sanctuary?"

"Two years ago, the restoration of *Moses*."

Profeta knew of the restoration of the church's main attraction. Michelangelo's *Moses*, which sat in the church's southern transept as part of Julius II's unfinished tomb.

The Italian company Lottomatica had financed the cleaning of Michelangelo's statue. *Another corporate effort.* Profeta was unsure how the Renaissance master would feel about the restoration of his statue becoming a publicity stunt by one of the largest manufacturers of casino gaming equipment.

"And no construction beneath the church?"

"Not beneath the church, no." He paused for a moment. "Although the faculty of engineering has been conducting significant renovations along their eastern wing, the vibrations at times feel as though they are beneath this very church."

Profeta looked up from his notepad, and nodded to Brandisi, who slipped out the door. Profeta turned back toward the priest. "May I see the sanctuary again, Father?"

They walked down the aisle, just the two of them. In the church's dim interior, the beams of Profeta's officers' flashlights crisscrossed as they searched inside each transept for unmarked knapsacks or other potentially dangerous objects.

Father Zicino pointed at the transept where Michelangelo's *Moses* sat in relative darkness. During the day, tourists lined up in front of a small coin box and for one euro could activate a spotlight above the masterpiece for thirty seconds. But in the now empty church, in a dark transept outside the basilica's central nave, the statue appeared forgotten.

"He is a little large to steal, don't you think?" Father Zicino smiled.

Profeta turned from the statue and stared at the front of the sanctuary.

"What is below the altar?"

"Warriors, *Comandante*."

"Warriors?" Profeta repeated, looking around. "I thought the only graves here are the tombs of prior cardinals of this church."

"Oh, no, *Comandante*, beneath the altar is the exception. The Maccabees' graves," Father Zicino said.

Profeta stopped walking. "Maccabees?"

"Yes, in 1876, a restoration discovered Maccabee graves beneath the altar. The inscriptions revealed that in the sixth century, Pope Pelagius brought the seven Maccabee brothers to be reinterred here. The location of the Maccabees' graves beneath us is largely unknown, but we think their presence makes this church a fitting location for the tomb of Julius the Second, a man known as—"

"The warrior pope," Profeta said. He knew Julius II tried to gain support for a Fourth Crusade to search for reliquaries in Jerusalem.

"Yes, *Comandante*," the priest said through an apologetic smile, "Julius the Second was known for his *courage*, although some would say violence. He was a great admirer of the Maccabees as defenders of Jerusalem."

Profeta was silent a moment. "Josephus," he finally said.

"I'm sorry?"

"The first-century historian Josephus. He descended from Maccabean heritage—"

A junior officer interrupted, his rapid boot steps echoing down the aisle. He whispered in Profeta's ear.

Profeta turned to Father Zicino. "I'm afraid my men will need to go beneath the altar, Father."

"*Comandante,* I can't simply open th—"

"This church is in immediate danger," Profeta said. "Those vibrations you heard are not from next door."

"But we received notice from the engineering school," Father Zicino said, revealing his administrator's soul.

"Those vibrations are from beneath your church."

"How can you be certain?"

"My men just went over to inquire, Father. There are no renovations next door."

The priest escorted Profeta down a half-flight of steps to the well beneath the altar. He removed a decorative leather box from his frock and set it on the small table, where votive candles burned. From the leather box, he removed a key that resembled a fairy-tale prop. The key rattled inside the small grate's lock and the ratchet bolt groaned but stopped short. One of the church's maintenance staff appeared with metal lubricant and, throwing his weight into pulling the grate's metal lever down, got the lock to drop open.

Profeta studied the square-sized open hatch beneath the marble altar, ducking his head inside. His voice echoed from within. "It's massive in here," Profeta said. Rufio crouched beside him, shining his flashlight into the black air beneath the tomb. A narrow brick staircase seemed to descend into infinity.

Profeta went first, balancing himself against the wall of the stairs as he started down. His flashlight beam revealed an underground chamber hewed with ornate stone columns into the walls. Seven sarcophagi lay inside the room, each one carved with scenes of battle.

"The remains of the Maccabee brothers," Profeta said.

On the far side of the chamber, Profeta noticed some fresh rubble. A crude opening had been hacked through the bare rock. Profeta shined his light into the space. A massive tunnel stretched into the darkness.

"This tunnel is enormous," Rufio said. "It's large enough for—"

"An emperor's palace," Profeta said. "These tunnels were here long before the church was built on top of it. We're standing in Nero's palace, the Domus Aurea."

44

Jonathan cupped his palm over his flashlight to diminish its glare, just in case the tour group could see its glow in the corridor.

The ground steepened and Emili braced herself against the rock walls as they moved down the portico.

"Watch your feet; the rock is slippery," Jonathan said.

Emili's gray slacks couldn't have been more inappropriate for spelunking, but she was glad they were wool. The corridors of the Domus Aurea were ten degrees cooler than the surface temperature of Rome.

"This cistern must be sixty feet high," Emili said as they entered another chamber.

"Not a cistern," Jonathan said. "Look." Jonathan turned his flashlight's beam to the wall. A bright ancient fresco of reds and blues jumped out at them. The fresco was a country setting, with birds and trees, painted in remarkable detail, befitting the villa of an emperor.

Suddenly there was a slow rumble above them, gathering in intensity and volume.

"What is that?" Emili yelled above the noise.

Jonathan waited for it to pass. "I think we're below a metro station. That was a train."

Jonathan pointed above them and then to the map of Nero's palace that Chandler had given them. "This brick architrave here," he said, looking into the map, "it's the double barrel vault of the palace's portico. This is the right way."

They walked down a corridor, following the curve of a solid ivory wall until they reached a grand space meant to receive guests. Dust sifted down under the weight of another rattling train. The modern sounds comforted Jonathan as they descended deeper into the corridors. *I never thought I would be doing this again*, he thought.

While Emili wiped a thick layer of algae off the wall, to admire a remarkable stucco in the Pompeian style of landscapes, Jonathan felt the floor moving slightly. He pointed his flashlight downward and realized the floor was practically alive with worms, an endless bed of writhing pasta. Pinkish-white worms swarmed over his Ferragamos. One disappeared inside his shoe.

"This is part of grad school I haven't missed."

Jonathan and Emili penetrated deeper into the palace. The sounds of the passing metro trains faded to a soft, distant thunder. An acrid subterranean breeze singed their nostrils, and they both breathed in soft gasps. The air around them was fifteen hundred years old.

Jonathan walked in first, into a semicircular room. Seven radial passageways branched out of the curved far wall.

"How do we know which passageway leads to the map of Jerusalem?"

"These frescoes," Jonathan said. He trained his beam on a series of ancient paintings that lined one of the corridors. "They look recently excavated." In the first painting, the pigment had faded, but the figures were quite clear: a young man, in a neck chain hitched to other prisoners, pulled heavy stones.

"I don't recognize the myth," Emili said. "Sisyphys pushing a boulder?"

"No," Jonathan said. "Look at the next painting." The same young prisoner, Jonathan noticed, the chain still around his neck, but he was now standing before a king, who listened raptly. The prisoner was pointing above his head, where two rows of cows stood side by side among stars in a night sky.

"In this last frame, a slave has been brought from prison before a king," Emili said. "It looks like an Egyptian pharaoh."

"Yes," Jonathan said, "and he's interpreting the pharaoh's dream, pointing to skinny cows and fat cows."

"What Roman myth is it, then?" Emili said.

"Not Roman," Jonathan said. "It's a narrative from the Bible."

"The Romans were pagans, Jon."

"But the prisoners of Jerusalem weren't. The young man in the fresco is a prisoner in Egypt interpreting Pharaoh's dream. Ring any bells?"

"The biblical story of Joseph," Emili answered.

"Exactly. Look at the cows. Pharaoh dreamed of seven fat cows standing beside seven skinny cows, foreshadowing famine in the land."

"This must be the right tunnel," Emili said, picking up her pace.

As they moved deeper into the corridor, Emili shone her light along the tunnel floor.

"Jon, look at these tools." Old, rusted picks and saws with eroded wooden handles lay against the walls. "This equipment hasn't been used in a hundred years." Her flashlight caught the grooves of an Italian inscription.

"In honor of Pope Pius VII. Giuseppe Valadier. 1811," Jonathan translated, standing behind her.

"Pope Pius the Seventh is known as the first conservationist pope," Emili said. "He must have commissioned the papal architect, Giuseppe Valadier, to lead a restoration team here in this corridor."

The passage led to a small archway. Jonathan pointed his light above the arch, revealing a stone carving of a large owl perched above it. The owl's eyes were orblike, glowing gemstones that seemed to follow them through the door.

"The Vault of Owls," Emili said, exhilarated. "The map must be in here."

They entered a large circular room. In the high vaulted ceiling, the perforations of a steel manhole showered slim rays into the cavern like spotlights, illuminating—to their surprise—a large modern aluminum scaffold constructed against one of the room's bare rock walls. Among other rusted nineteenth-century excavation tools, the structure's gleaming metal was as out of place as a stage set from the wrong play.

"Looks a little modern for an excavation in the 1800s," Jonathan said.

"It was just built. There's scarcely any condensation on the piping," Emili said. She walked the circumference of the room. "Why build a scaffold when there are no ancient murals to restore?"

Jonathan pulled on the scaffolding's lower pipes, testing their sturdiness, and then scampered up several first rungs.

"Jon, what are you doing?"

"It's here, Em. It's huge!"

Emili looked around. "There's nothing on the walls."

"The scaffolding's not meant to look at the walls. It's to look at the floor."

Emili looked under her feet. She could make out the faint colors of an image beneath the green membranous veil of algae. She joined Jonathan on the scaffolding, and took in the size of the floor painting.

"It's a painting of Jerusalem," she said, "Drawn as large as the room."

The ancient floor painting portrayed Jerusalem beneath a brilliant blue sky, which was still visible as flaking blue stucco under the algae. Towering walls surrounded large public courtyards, and in the mural's center stood a large white structure surrounded by a rectangular columned portico.

"It's so . . . *peaceful*," Emili said, struck by such a soothing landscape of first-century Jerusalem. Repeated European paintings of Roman soldiers burning Jerusalem were her only visual references, most notably Poussin's seventeenth-century corpse-strewn *Destruction of the Temple in Jerusalem Under Titus*, but never had she seen a rendering of Herod's Temple *before* the destruction in such a pastoral setting.

"Those concentric colonnades are the priestly courtyards of the Temple Mount," Jonathan said. He pointed at the center of the painting. "The large, white building there must be the Holy of Holies." Josephus's description of the rectangular white marble structure was surprisingly accurate. *Like a snowy mountain glittering in the sun.*

Emili looked at the map. "Titus built his baths directly above this wing of the Domus Aurea. He used Jewish slave labor for its construction, just as he did for the Colosseum. The slaves must have spent months sneaking down here to work on this painting," Emili said.

"And I think I know why." Jonathan climbed down from the scaffolding and walked across the fresco. He knelt down and wiped the algae away from the depiction of the Temple's inner courtyard surrounding the Holy of Holies.

"This painting must show the path of Josephus's escape with the menorah . . ." he said softly, "through a hidden gate."

"But there's nothing drawn there."

Jonathan twisted the cap face of the flashlight, narrowing the beam until only a small bright circle concentrated on the painting. *Tropaeum Illumina*, Jonathan remembered the Forma Urbis's instruction. *Illuminate the monument.*

To his astonishment, a small row of red stones became luminescent beneath the thin layer of stucco, shimmering a fiery orange-red glow, lighting an electric path as his flashlight moved.

An inlaid trail of gemstones beneath the painting.

"Emili, get down here!" Jonathan said. "It looks like there's a row of—"

"Rubies?" Emili said, already standing beside him.

"Or pyrope," Jonathan said, "a red mineral, named from the Greek *pyropus*, meaning fiery-eyed." Jonathan tilted his head to see the line of stones only millimeters beneath the paint. "Completely hidden," he said, marveling, "but revealed through light, just like the carving inside the Forma Urbis instructed."

"The slaves must have collected these stones from Nero's gem-studded walls and buried them beneath this stucco to illuminate the path of Josephus's escape with the menorah," Emili said, trailing her flashlight's beam along the stones until the path came to an abrupt stop where water damage had lifted up the stucco. "The flaking surface of the paint exposed the other gemstones, and now they're gone." She looked up at Jonathan. "*Quae amissa salva.* Lost things are safe."

Jonathan held up his hand. "Do you hear that?"

The unmistakable sound of rushing feet emerged from the darkness around them.

Before they could react, a high-powered LED floodlight shined

through the archway and trained side to side like a prison search-
light casting for fugitives.

"Carabinieri!" Profeta yelled. "Do not move!"

Jonathan stood in the carabinieri's bluish light, as though frozen in ice. Emili grabbed his arm and pulled him into an adjacent
corridor.

"Jon, up there!" She pointed to a rock scarp ten feet off the
ground. There was a steep but climbable face of packed dirt. As
they clambered up, the sound of the policemen increased with every
second. Just as the flashlights turned the corner and flooded the
niche, Jonathan and Emili were lying on top of each other on a narrow rock shelf ten feet above the frantic rays of the flashlights.

The beams raced past them, and again they were in total darkness, fitting so compactly on the ledge that their lips nearly touched.
Jonathan caught an alluring scent from Emili's neck and would not
have minded being trapped on the ledge a little longer.

"There must be a way out," she whispered.

"Way out?" Jonathan whispered back. "They must have twenty
guards at the exit. We're a quarter-mile inside the Domus Aurea!
No, there's not a way—" The distant rumble of a metro train interrupted him. "Wait a minute," he said, the flicker of an idea taking
shape.

"What?" Emili said eagerly.

"The room with the map of Jerusalem," he said. "There was a
manhole above the vault."

"What about it?"

"I think it opens up to the train station."

"There are usually a dozen carabinieri outside the station."

"From the sound of those trains, I think that manhole opens *inside* the station."

"Let's go," Emili said, rolling her body off his.

The carabinieri had taken their search deeper into the ruin, and Jonathan and Emili quietly reentered the vault where they had discovered the giant fresco. Jonathan pointed at the manhole above them. Five feet beneath the manhole was a metal grate suspended by iron girders.

"Must be a maintenance platform to repair the tracks," Jonathan said. "We can get close to the ladder hanging from the bottom of the grate if we climb up the scaffolding, but it may be too high for us—"

Emili ran to the wall and began climbing up the scaffold.

"—to reach." Jonathan shook his head and followed her up the aluminum pipes. They were more than twenty feet above the ground when a carabinieri officer made his way back into the cavern beneath them. They both froze to stop the creaking sound of the swaying scaffold.

Beneath them, the officer walked slowly across the cavern. He took a few steps, his footfalls echoing as his flashlight swept the floor. He unsnapped his leather holster, and they could hear the sound of metal against leather. He unsheathed his gun.

Jonathan recognized him. *Lieutenant Rufio.*

Jonathan and Emili remained motionless on the wall. If he pointed his beam upward forty-five degrees, they would be exposed. As he walked around the scaffolding, the hard-packed stucco floor crackled under his feet.

Lieutenant Rufio beamed his flashlight inside the deep statuary niches that surrounded the room. He searched the perimeter of the cavern, clearly growing more frustrated. Jonathan realized he was not looking for them, but rather for *something else.* From inside his jacket, Rufio removed a pair of white carabinieri gloves, quickly slipped them on, and removed two plastic jugs from a dark niche in the wall. Gray dust covered the cartons; they appeared to have been there for some time. He unscrewed the tops of both cartons and began pouring the liquid contents onto the fresco, coating the floor. Within seconds, fumes carrying the strong odor of gasoline wafted up to where Emili and Jonathan remained still in the darkness.

No, Emili whispered.

Rufio pulled a lighter from his inside jacket pocket, lit a small piece of paper, and threw it onto the center of the floor. Like a flood of fire, the flames spread across the floor. Plumes of smoke billowed upward.

"Go!" Jonathan yelled, shoving Emili up the scaffolding to reach the service ladder that hung from the maintenance grate. She jumped and grabbed the bottom rung and lifted herself up.

"Keep going!" he shouted. The fire spread across the floor and Jonathan looked down, his panic dredging up the imagery of Homer, *a pouring fire sweeping the earth beneath it.*

Rufio heard the shouting and cast his beam upward. Through the smoke, he could faintly see Jonathan on the maintenance grate desperately trying to push up the manhole in the ceiling. Rufio sprinted around the burning fresco and began climbing up the scaffold. The aluminum had become hot, even beneath his white officer's gloves.

Now crouching on the grate beside Emili, Jonathan pushed the manhole up with all his strength from below. Smoke sieved upward through the grate, and he could feel the heat of the steel through his shoes. He managed to scrape the manhole aside far enough for their bodies to slide through. The sudden sound of an oncoming train was deafening. The grate shook uncontrollably.

"Jon! There's a train coming!"

Jonathan saw Rufio, now only ten feet beneath them. He lifted himself through the hole and found himself in the middle of the subway tracks. The train was closing in with such speed he could feel its push of tunnel air.

"*Shit,*" Jonathan said.

45

A t the end of the hall, Profeta saw smoke billowing. He ran toward the smoke-filled vault, covering his mouth with his sleeve. Brandisi emerged from the room, coughing.

"Someone set the room on fire, *Comandante!*" Brandisi yelled.

"Get extinguishers from the museum!" Profeta yelled at the surrounding officers. "Where's Rufio?"

Brandisi pointed upward. "There's a service grate beneath a manhole in the ceiling. I saw Rufio climbing up the scaffold, chasing a man in the smoke."

"What's above the manhole?" Profeta asked.

In his shaking flashlight's beam, Brandisi unfolded a large urban map big as a tent. *"Aspetti, Comandante,"* he stammered. "It must be the metro station! The Colosseo station!"

Profeta whipped the radio from his belt. Static. There was no reception. "Brandisi, get out of here and radio for backup in the Colosseo station. Stop all trains."

46

J onathan knew they could not wait for the train to pass. The metal service ladder rattled as Rufio rapidly climbed up after them. There was no time.

"Give me your hand!" he shouted to Emili.

Inside the oncoming Linea A train, the aging *capotreno* blinked. He could see a young man on the tracks in a billowing circle of steam—or smoke? He seemed to have appeared from nowhere. The *capotreno* laid on the blaring horn, knowing in moments the train would plow through the young man.

In that final second, the *capotreno*, blasting his horn and flashing the train's headlight, feared it was too late. He had seen similar tragedies before in his long tenure on the metro; the violent shudder from the body smacking the front of the train, the blood smearing the tracks for a hundred meters. But those cases had been suicides. This was different. There was no peace about this. The young man was desperately trying to pull someone out of a manhole. The conductor could see the ferocity of his will to live.

The train's horn was now a continuous bray, and just as the grille skirt of the train was about to plow over the manhole, Jonathan lifted Emili with an adrenaline born only from the fear of death. He clasped her forearms, managing in a single throw to heave her frame upward to a metal platform along the metro tunnel wall and propel himself, landing squarely on top of her.

The train roared past without even slowing, a chain of subway cars, deafeningly loud, and so close that their metal siding touched the fabric of Jonathan's suit.

Lying beneath him, Emili could feel Jonathan's heart pounding so hard it seemed to pulse through her. She looked into Jonathan's eyes, wide with terror, and rubbed his back.

"No wonder Nero built his palace here," she said with a relieved smile. "Good access to public transportation."

Pulling herself to her feet, Emili spotted an electrical pipe soldered to the wall. She found the switch and a string of caged lightbulbs flickered on, one after the other, running along the tunnel wall. They could see the white lights of the metro Colosseo station at the tunnel's end. They walked toward it and climbed over the orange *"Passaggio Vietato!"* sign, entering the bright white fluorescence of the station. Amid the bustle and the occasional odd glance at their faces, which were blackened from the smoke, they both relaxed in the anonymity of moving through the torrent of commuters on the platform.

They were walking briskly toward the exit stairwell, when Jonathan felt a sudden force in the crowd grab his arm. He whirled around and saw Rufio's blackened face only inches in front of him, his gun pressed hard against Jonathan's stomach.

"So that's who you are," Rufio said. *"Quell'avvocato."* That lawyer. The rush of commuters swarmed around them, hurrying to catch the train.

Jonathan could hear Emili up ahead, calling his name in the crowd.

A ring tone over the loudspeaker announced the closing of the subway doors.

"I'd like to speak with someone from the American embassy," Jonathan responded in a formal tone.

"Embassy?" Rufio laughed. "I don't plan to arrest you." Rufio jammed his pistol even harder into Jonathan's side. He pointed at the stairs leading up from the platform. "Walk toward that exit."

A commuter stepped between them to ask Rufio for directions, giving Jonathan a half-second to free himself. He bolted into the crowd, following the sound of Emili's voice.

"Jon! Where have you—"

"Keep moving," Jonathan said, walking tightly near her alongside the train. "He's here, on the platform."

The subway doors were about to close when Emili unexpectedly threw out her leg, catching the doors with her foot, keeping them open momentarily as she slid through.

"Get in!" Emili yelled. Jonathan stared at the gap between the platform and the subway. This six-inch space of air was the point of no return. *This was his Rubicon.* Two surveillance cameras were directly overhead. He would be identified, that was without question. With an ease that suggested it took no great deliberation at all, he joined Emili on the train. Rufio lurched toward the door, managing to get a hand between the black rubberized padding to muscle the doors open. The strained look on Rufio's face faded as he pushed them apart with a malevolent smile.

"Did *you* really expect to—"

Emili wheeled a right fist through the door's sliver and hit him square in the face. Rufio hurled back onto the platform as the door exhaled shut.

47

Ramat Mansour stood in the doorway of his house at the top of Silwan, an Arab village on a dry white hillside in the shadow of the walls of the Temple Mount. Mansour was a neat, thin man with a well-trimmed black mustache. After an afternoon nap, his kaffiyeh and black coil were still unfurled and draped around his neck as he passed his youngest child, a baby boy, back into his wife's arms. Reluctantly, he buttoned his cotton *dishdasha* and fastened his sandals. Walking across a loose-gravel path, he passed his small shop of ancient coins and pottery, and checked the corrugated steel door padlocked to a bolt in the stone.

He lit a Parliament cigarette and scratched his mustache where his first hairs of gray were beginning to show.

He continued up the gravel slope of the Bab Huttah road to the Dome of the Rock. The ascent used to be a journey of immense joy for Mansour. He remembered making the pilgrimage with his father at the start of every day from their home in Silwan. But now Mansour was scarcely able to look at the al-Aqsa's minaret without regretting the so-called excavations of the Waqf.

It had been more than a year since a man from the Waqf came into the shop and said Mansour's graduate work in archaeology at Birzeit University could be useful. Mansour had naively hoped the Waqf was interviewing for an archaeologist's position. He quickly closed up his shop and ran home to get his academic recommendations, kissing his new wife and newborn son for *bet-tawfee inshallah*, good luck.

But when he returned home to them that next morning, he was dazed, his face caked in gray mud. It was as though he had been forced unwittingly to commit a crime greater than he could have imagined.

"They said it was for excavation," Mansour told his wife in a frightened whisper. "But they had bulldozers and dozens of men with pickaxes." Fists clenched, he described how they instructed the men to rip up delicate Herodian mosaic floors and Byzantine glass, how they bulldozed through an ornately designed dome in the anteroom of Solomon's stables. They were told to mix up the strata to make certain no one could sift through the piles and determine a useful archaeological record. Mansour had been raised by his father with the Islamic virtue of respecting the remains of the two Temples that once stood on the Mount.

When he was finished speaking he opened his hand and his wife gasped, for Mansour held the one piece of antiquity he had been able to save. Shimmering in the morning light, it was a beautiful piece of Roman glass, green as jade with an inset carving of the Temple columns on its bottom. The next day, Mansour anonymously left it at the door of the Bible Lands Museum in West Jerusalem. Months later, he brought his wife and children to the museum. He was proud to see the glass safely resting in a shaft of light in the center of a display case.

It did not surprise Mansour that most of the destruction beneath the Temple Mount was done without the knowledge of many religious clerics who pray on the Mount. Respecting other cultures and their heritage was the highest calling of the noble religion he knew. Did Muhammad himself not seek to pray there because of the holiness created by the Jews? Did Suleiman the Magnificent not take on the very name Solomon because of the deep impression left upon him by the ancient leader? Did Suleiman not order the Temple Mount to be cleaned of all the Roman rubble to honor the Temples that stood there before his time?

One year had passed since Mansour had been approached, and Mansour now found himself returning to the Waqf's offices in East Jerusalem.

The Waqf assistant who called an hour earlier knew better than to ask him to "excavate." Instead he asked Mansour to inspect an excavation that was already completed. The man offered more shekels than Mansour had seen in half a year. His antiquities shop had been empty since last week. Christian tours were down since the violence in Gaza had increased a year earlier, and that meant fewer customers.

The man from the Waqf could sense Ramat's hesitation over the phone and asked him to come to the office as a personal favor, as well.

"Your cousin, Salah ad-Din, would like to speak with you immediately."

Don't go," Mansour's wife had said as he left the house. She spoke to him from the doorway of their bedroom, wearing a dark robe and a *hijab* over her hair. "I don't care that your mothers were sisters, I don't care you were like brothers once. You don't have to go. What if something should—" She broke off, covering her mouth with the back of her hand. "Who would protect us?"

"I must go," Mansour said. "He is still family." Mansour remembered the day his parents took in the little boy as one of their own after the death of his grandfather, who had been the boy's only remaining guardian. An unbathed, twice-orphaned six-year-old, smuggled in from Beirut. Mansour's father quickly made a rule that no one ask a single question about the boy's past.

From their prayers at the al-Aqsa Mosque, his father would take both boys to his small antiquities shop at the base of the Pool of Siloam. Ramat played with his younger cousin in the shop, both of them darting among the shabby glass cases. They spent hours studying the ancient coins in the shop, repositioning them like a game to be more attractive to the tourists who emerged from their tours of the Pool of Siloam. A devoutly religious man, Ramat's father had a deep respect for the archaeology of the Judeo-Christian tradition still beneath Jerusalem's stones. The pool located immediately beneath the shop was the wellspring in which, according to the Christian Gospel, Jesus once cured the blind. The site was heavily trafficked by Christian tours, and Mansour's father would encourage both boys to follow the tours to practice their English.

Looking back, Mansour realized he should have known. The boyhood innocence that can ignore a horrific past cannot erase it. As early teenagers, Ramat and his cousin shared a room, and he would find his cousin gone from his bed in the middle of the night, sneaking to the basement to study their grandfather's drawings, which Mansour's father forbade them to see. Ramat pretended to sleep as his cousin returned and mumbled, as though speaking to someone else. The only word Ramat could make out was *jeddih*. Grandfather. Years later, they both entered graduate school for archaeology, Ramat at Birzeit University and his cousin at various schools in Europe. They had lost touch, but he knew his cousin had become dangerously involved in the political aspects of archaeology. Even in those days, close friends had begun calling him Salah ad-Din because of his extreme views.

Two guards now escorted Mansour upstairs, into the open-air plaza of Haram al-Sharif and into the dusky light of the Islamic Museum. The guards waited at the museum door and Mansour walked in alone. A wide Templar-era corridor housed the museum's main gallery inside the Mount. Mansour walked past a collection of seventeenth-century decorated swords and daggers, as well as a rare eighth-century version of the Quran, ascribed to the Prophet's great-grandson.

In the center of the gallery, an enormous Crusader-era wrought-iron screen that had surrounded the Foundation Stone from the twelfth to the twentieth century obscured the man who stood behind it.

"Too long, Ramat," a voice gently reprimanded him from behind the screen. "It has been too long." Salah ad-Din stepped out of the shadows. "I know we differ about how to preserve the archaeology here on the Haram al-Sharif, but we are family. Our mothers were *sisters*. We share the same *jeddih*, peace be upon him."

"I will not assist your destruction, cousin. The construction of another subterranean mosque that seats ten thousand pilgrims beneath the Mount does not preserve archaeology." He knew that, despite the UN agencies' protest, the mosque was nearly completed, and now caused the southern wall to bow out nearly fifteen centimeters, a potentially fatal degree.

"The Waqf's religious projects are outside my interest," Salah ad-Din said, pacing between the display cases. "I have merely an archaeological question for you."

"Archaeological," Ramat repeated suspiciously.

"Yes, one that would allow you the rare opportunity to preserve the Temple Mount platform, rather than destroy it," Salah ad-Din said. He walked over to one of the display cases and unrolled a structural map of the Temple Mount over its glass.

"You are the best archaeological dig foreman in Jerusalem. I will require your assistance."

"I am sorry, cousin," Mansour said, turning to walk out of the gallery. "Digging some giant cistern to contain well water from the Zamzam in Mecca is not archaeology."

"That little project is the Waqf's, not mine."

Little project? Mansour thought. *The day laborers have probably removed thousands of tons of archaeologically rich soil.*

"The work I am suggesting for you is strictly archaeological. I have discovered the ancient tunnel in Josephus," Salah ad-Din said. "The one sought for a lifetime by your grandfather."

Mansour stopped, but did not turn around.

"It runs from beneath the Foundation Stone to the Royal Cavern, but we must find where it continues. We thought it would extend directly across the cavern, following the path of an aqueduct, but our most recent excavation revealed just solid rock. Our archaeological expert is unavailable. *Buried* with work, I'm afraid. We need your expertise, cousin. Our grandfather, Haj Amin al-Husseini, dedicated his life to this."

"My father forbade you from seeing the mufti's research."

"As boys, he forbade us. Times have changed, Ramat. The Waqf waited until your father died to remove the mufti's research from the basement. Our grandfather researched for decades to locate this tunnel. His archaeology—"

"It was not archaeology," Mansour said, his back still turned. "It was revisionism."

Salah ad-Din winced. "As children, I followed you up streams from the Pool of Siloam to the legendary subterranean reservoirs beneath the Mount. You hiked in the blackness for hours before lighting a candle to show me the Fountain Gate mentioned in Isaiah or the Serpent's Pool in Josephus. By the time you were eleven, cousin, you could reconstruct ancient Jerusalem better than almost any archaeologist."

Mansour remained silent.

"Tell me, cousin," Salah ad-Din said, noticing that Mansour had become suddenly contemplative. "How much rent do you owe on your shop?" He again began pacing, this time circling around Mansour. "My sources say you have not been able to pay for twelve months. I can wipe clean *half* of that debt."

Mansour's eyes closed, searching his own morality. The back rent of the shop overwhelmed him every day, and his wife was expecting, yet again. . . .

"You grew up running through the tunnels beneath the Mount. You know them better than anyone."

Mansour could see their grandfather's drawings in the dusty cardboard boxes beneath their childhood home. He knew of their grandfather's obsession with Flavius Josephus, searching his works to locate a secret tunnel that led to some kind of *hidden gate.*

"I will ask for your assistance one more time. In exchange for which I will wipe clean the *entire* debt of your shop's rent. The entire year." Like a bargainer of the souk, Salah ad-Din watched Mansour's eyes. "I have consulted nearly every historical source to find where the aqueduct exits the Royal Cavern, and cannot find it."

"That is because the aqueduct's direction is described in the one historical source you would never read," Mansour said, his softened tone reflecting his moral defeat. "The Old Testament."

48

E mili and Jonathan slipped out of a service exit at the next metro
stop, the Circus Maximus station. They crossed the street to
the shadows of a tree-lined field, and looking back, were surprised
to see only a few uniformed officers outside the station. Emili expected to find officers combing the station, hurdling the turnstiles
in pursuit, searching every subway car. As they walked farther down
the street, they watched the headlights of cars flash past, each one
presenting the fear that it was a carabinieri car.

"Why didn't that officer stop the train?" Emili said. "Or alert the
next station?"

"Because Lieutenant Rufio doesn't want us arrested," Jonathan
said. "If I end up in an interrogation room, he's afraid I'll expose
what he said beneath the Colosseum."

"Then maybe he won't circulate your picture," Emili said.

"And that's supposed to make me feel better?" Jonathan stopped
walking. "That I have a ruthless carabinieri officer probably by now
in my hotel room waiting to kill me?"

"At least we both agree that there's no going to the carabinieri
now," Emili said, her face determined. "And we're now a step closer to
proving a connection between the illegal excavations in Jerusalem and
Rome. That map in the Domus must be the reason Salah ad-Din was
digging here. He was trying to piece together Josephus's escape."

For a moment, Jonathan said nothing. Like the merits of a strong
legal case, the vast ancient effort to protect the menorah had further
unfolded in the Domus Aurea. *Inscriptions beneath the Colosseum. An
illuminated path beneath a mural of Jerusalem.* He felt a sudden weight

of responsibility, as though history itself had become critical evidence that someone was trying to destroy.

"Remember that old drawing I showed you of the unnumbered gate in the Colosseum? Valadier sketched it while excavating for Napoleon in 1809. He must have found the prisoners' inscriptions just as we did, and followed them to Domus."

"But whatever that floor painting revealed," Jonathan said, "there's no way to reconstruct it. It's ashes by now."

They walked past teenagers playing guitar around bonfires in the grassy ruins of the Circus Maximus.

"We might be able to get a better view of that mural," Emili said, quickening her pace.

"You're going *back* to the Domus Aurea?" Jonathan stopped walking. *Then you're going alone.*

"We don't have to. Valadier may have drawn a sketch of that mural just as he drew a sketch of the Colosseum."

"And let me guess," Jonathan said. "You know where he left it."

She pointed in front of them at the Great Synagogue's square aluminum cupola rising against the purple dusk.

"The Great Synagogue?" Jonathan looked incredulous. "You're saying a restorer leading a *papal* excavation of the Domus Aurea bequeathed his sketches to the Jews?"

"Valadier probably realized that the gladiators' gate in the Colosseum contained messages revealing the menorah's location. He left all related sketches to the Ghetto in an attempt to restore the sacred relic to its rightful heirs."

"Without telling *the pope?*"

"He wouldn't have been the first well-known artisan in the employ of the pope to secretly leave his sketches to the Jews," Emili said. "In 1480, after falling out with Julius the Second, Michelangelo stopped all his work here and went back to Florence, telling his assistant, 'Sell all my belongings to the Jews.'"

Across the street from the synagogue, they walked in the shadow of a small Renaissance-era church with Hebrew and Latin passages inscribed boldly above its large double doors, the Latin translation above the other. Jonathan glanced up at the Latin as they passed beneath it.

"Not a very welcoming passage from Isaiah," Jonathan said. "'You are a people that provoketh Me to anger continually to My face.'"

"For four hundred years, this church's walls served as one of the Ghetto's entrance gates," Emili said. "In the 1990s, the pastor of San Gregorio petitioned the municipality of Rome to alter the façade, embarrassed by the Church's history of intolerance. Our office opposed the change, and we had an unlikely ally: the archivist of the Great Synagogue, Mosè Orvieti. Orvieti took issue with the Church's desire to remove a lasting remnant of Jewish persecution." She pointed upward. "And there it remains."

From across the street, Jonathan could see the high window beneath the cupola of the synagogue. Its crosshatched yellow light resembled the top window of a lighthouse, or a prisoners' tower.

"Orvieti still works up there?"

"Signore Orvieti has worked in the belfry for more than sixty years."

"During the war?"

"Yes." Emili turned her jacket collar down as they walked through the courtyard toward the synagogue's back steps. "He has been an invaluable source for the Holocaust restitution suits brought by the International Centre for Conservation. He possesses a near-encyclopedic memory of the archive's collection before the war."

"Sounds like his life's work."

"That archive is all he has left." She pointed to a public square outside the synagogue and bordered by the moldering brick arches of an ancient amphitheater. "The Nazis rounded up two thousand ninety-one Jews in that square and took them away. He lost his wife and his five children."

Jonathan said nothing.

"Years later, in 1948," Emili said, "many of the Holocaust survivors held a rally in the Roman Forum to show support for the establishment of the state of Israel. The local Jewish community lined up in front of the Arch of Titus, beneath the relief depicting the procession of the prisoners of Jerusalem being marched as slaves through the Roman Forum. "Do you know what they did then?" Emili paused.

"They marched the other way. Not into the Forum, as their ancestors did, but out of the Forum, like free men, women, and children. Eighteen hundred years later, they made a single file and marched right back through the arch. For many of the Roman Jewish families it was not merely symbolic. Many left Rome and emigrated to Israel."

"Orvieti was there?"

"Yes, he was in the procession. As the story goes, he approached the arch, but the thought of his wife and his five children all incinerated at Auschwitz overwhelmed him. He just stood there, watching the children and their parents walk through the arch, until he was the only one left. The crowd hushed and people gathered on the other side of the arch, waiting for him."

"And what did he do?" Jonathan asked.

"They say he stared at the arch for a long time and turned around and walked back to the Ghetto. To the synagogue."

Somberly, Emili led the way through the heavy iron gate of the synagogue to the Dutch oak doors, where Orvieti stood waiting for them in response to Emili's hurried phone call.

He closed the door behind Emili and Jonathan, lowering the thick metal bar across the inside of the synagogue's huge doors. Emili introduced Jonathan and they followed Orvieti up the stairs into the archives. They entered the octagonal belfry, where the sky-light in the square dome ceiling illuminated the walls' oak cases. Jonathan stared at hundreds of clothbound volumes that lined one wall.

"That's correspondence," Orvieti said, sitting down to rest.

"Long correspondence," Jonathan said, turning around. "Between?"

"Roman Jews and the Catholic Church from 1555 to 1843. Thousands of letters from parents pleading with the Church to return children who had been kidnapped and forcibly baptized."

Emili walked over to the table and sat beside Orvieti.

"I think I've discovered why the grand mufti was searching for this sketch, along with the manuscripts of Josephus," she said.

"Then I've waited sixty years for this moment," Orvieti said.

"The drawing of the Colosseum you gave me this morning depicts the arch in the Colosseum where prisoners awaited their execution. Beneath the Colosseum this morning, Jonathan and I saw many of their names still carved on the wall. One of the names was Joseph ben Matthias."

"Josephus," Orvieti whispered.

"Right," Emili said. "He was apparently one of the accused spies executed as part of a blown network inside Titus's imperial court. Berenice, Epaphroditus, and Aliterius were among the other names."

"You saw their *names*?"

"Not only their names, but a nearby inscription that suggests the reason for their conspiracy in Titus's court: 'A sacred tree of light.'"

"Are you certain those were the words?" Orvieti said, his eyes widening.

"You know its meaning?"

"Yes, but it's just a *myth*. The ramblings of the previous archivist, who said those words described . . ." Orvieti's voice trailed off.

"The menorah?" Emili said.

"Yes, the menorah of Herod's Temple," Orvieti said, smiling wistfully. "But legends have been a part of this Ghetto for centuries."

"*Signore,* there may be more history here than legend," Emili said. "Which may explain why the grand mufti was looking for Josephus's manuscript."

"But he only took certain pages," Orvieti said.

"They were the only ones he needed. Those pages in Josephus's medieval manuscripts included an additional line of text describing a hidden gate inside the Temple Mount. We think Josephus smuggled out the original menorah moments before Titus and his men infiltrated the Holy of Holies. The inscriptions beneath the gladiators' gate led us to a vault inside the Domus Aurea, where we saw an enormous mural of Jerusalem that may indicate where the menorah was laid to rest."

"The slaves of Jerusalem left messages," Orvieti whispered.

"Concealed ones," Jonathan said, "so that the Roman censors would not detect them."

"And when, eighteen hundred years later, a member of Napoleon's excavation team found the names of the spies in Josephus's network beneath the Colosseum in 1809, he realized their importance, and left a sketch of their location—"

"Here, to this archive," Orvieti finished, the wrinkles in his forehead lifting like a great curtain. Emili knew such archaeological discoveries would have sent anyone's head spinning, let alone someone who had spent his life turning over the pieces of this puzzle.

She began to describe in more detail the biblical frescoes that led them to the map of Jerusalem in the Domus Aurea.

"I thought it was impossible," he said softly, nodding as though working through a logic problem that had become solvable at last.

"You are certain the frescoes in the Domus Aurea depicted seven lean cows beside seven well-fed cows?" Orvieti asked.

Emili nodded.

"Then it all makes sense now. He was the Joseph of the Roman world," Orvieti said.

"Who?"

"Flavius Josephus." Orvieti paused, lost in his own thoughts. "The Roman version of the biblical Joseph."

"You know what those frescoes mean?" Emili asked.

"Think of Joseph's story for a moment. He was imprisoned and recruited out of jail. How? Pharaoh required an interpretation of a dream of seven well-fed cows standing beside seven lean cows. Joseph used his vision to foretell the future, working his way up from prison until he became Pharaoh's second in charge, right?"

"Right."

"This is also the story of Josephus. He, too, was in jail and worked his way into the royal court. How? He foretold that Vespasian would be the next caesar, which fortunately for him proved out. Like Joseph, Josephus moved from jail to the emperor's side as prophet and interpreter. Even his *name*, Josephus, is a clue to his underlying ambition, retaining the root of his biblical namesake, Joseph."

"But what does this have to do with Josephus's strategy to hide the menorah?"

"Think of Pharaoh's dream represented in those frescoes. Seven lean cows standing beside seven well-fed ones. Even Pharaoh's magicians knew the cows represented seven years of famine and seven more of plenty."

"If the magicians already knew that, then why was Joseph's interpretation so important?"

"Because the magicians still had a problem of logic. If the cows represented years, Pharaoh's magicians were stumped why the two rows of cows were standing *beside* one another." Orvieti stood up with a spring that surprised Emili and Jonathan. From the stacks he brought a tattered copy of the Old Testament. He rifled through the pages until he finally rested on one, reading it for a moment before speaking.

He pointed at the Hebraic text. "The biblical Hebrew, here, *eytzel* means 'beside,' not one in front of the other. How do years of plenty stand *beside* years of famine? How do they happen simultaneously?"

"How do they?" Emili asked.

"That's what Joseph explained. He realized that the answer was already inside the dream," Orvieti said. "They had to begin storing the grain *now*; they had to prepare for the famine *during* the time of plenty."

"So you're saying that Joseph's foresight was to store something before it was endangered," Jonathan said.

"Yes. And like his biblical role model, Josephus foresaw a desolate time. He put a plan in motion to store the menorah before it was too late."

49

The head station manager of the Colosseo metro station, Carlo Pavan, had been hunkered over the pink pages of *Gazzetta dello Sport* when a furious carabinieri officer, his nose caked in dried blood, screamed something about two fugitives' having entered the station. That was twenty minutes earlier. The longest twenty minutes at work he could remember since the London rail bombings in 2005 sent every Roman commuter fleeing from the station.

Pavan's small glass office, no larger than two conjoined phone booths, had since become its own small Termini station for the carabinieri, who rushed in and out, frantically passing around an emergency contact list of neighboring stations to set up security perimeters.

As instructed by the carabinieri, Pavan had ordered buses to line up outside the station for transportation to the nearest metro stop, Piazza Cavour, but the crowds were defiant and few people were taking the buses. Platform security officers heard murmurs of a riot if another train was ordered to bypass the station. *A riot on my watch,* Pavan thought. *Why couldn't these fugitives have chosen another station?*

Comandante Profeta found Lieutenant Rufio in the station manager's office.

"Lieutenant, you're certain it was Dr. Travia? You got a good look?"

Rufio pointed at the dried blood beneath his nose. "A very good look, Comandante."

"And you saw her accomplice?"

Rufio nodded solemnly. "The same one who attacked me beneath the Colosseum."

"We've submitted the images from the surveillance cameras to the Interpol. We should have him arrested within hours."

Not if I get to him first, Rufio thought, though he nodded obediently.

"Go get cleaned up, Rufio," Profeta said warmly. "Nice work out there."

Rufio exited the station manager's office and stood beside the ticket-vending machines, holding a bloody tissue in one hand and his mobile phone in the other.

Rufio turned on his phone, and his racing adrenaline made the mobile data connection seem even slower as he navigated the Internet on its small screen.

Rufio knew the young man looked familiar when he visited Dulling's office with Profeta. Now it all made sense. The suit he wore beneath the Colosseum, the cut on his hand in the office.

The law firm's website steadily uploaded, revealing a gray marbled backscreen and stately block letters that slowly materialized in the margin: DULLING AND PIERCE LLP. The background of the website sharpened: an elegant sepia photograph of a glass skyscraper. Rufio clicked on various hyperlinks, "Offices," then "New York," and finally "Our Attorneys."

As Rufio navigated the page he felt the heightened awareness of a stakeout, effortlessly drawing closer to his quarry with each click.

Photographs. He smiled. Passport-sized photographs accompanied each name.

His thumb wheeled along the side of the mobile device and he marveled at the sheer numbers of pictures. *Una fabbrica,* he thought. *A factory.* He scrolled further down until . . .

There. The dignified black-and-white photograph was a cleaned-up version of the panicked young man he had just seen in the fluorescent light of a metro car. In the photograph, he was in a dark suit, head turned slightly to the side. "Jonathan Marcus," the caption read.

"That's him." But Rufio's silent moment of triumph was interrupted by a group of approaching officers.

"Quite a day for you, Alessandro!" one of the other lieutenants called out admiringly, as the others applauded.

Rufio nodded. "You have no idea."

Comandante." Brandisi entered the station manager's office. "Your office just received a call from the Curia. Cardinal Inocenti has been trying to find you."

"About trespassing beneath the altar of San Pietro in Vincoli?" Profeta asked, looking surprised. Inocenti was not one to press him on formalities.

"No," Brandisi said. "He reviewed the images from the raid that we sent the Vatican Library."

"The Josephus manuscript pages," Profeta said.

"He's requested you meet him at the Vatican Library as soon as possible."

50

Emili remained seated beside Orvieti at the table.

"And that's why the prisoners of Jerusalem created the floor painting inside the Domus Aurea," she continued. "They wanted a map of first-century Jerusalem to stay in the hands of Josephus's descendants."

"And I believe it has," Orvieti said.

"But the map in the Domus Aurea was too damaged to read," Emili said. "And you said all of the other Napoleonic-era sketches were stolen by the grand mufti."

"It was not passed down to us as a sketch. It was too important."

Jonathan and Emili exchanged looks. "Then how do you still have the map?"

"I believe it was painted as a mural in the synagogue on the other side of the Portico di Ottavia," Orvieti said.

"*Signore,*" Emili said gently, "there are no synagogues left in the Ghetto other than this one."

"It is still there across the street," Orvieti said. "Beneath the Ghetto."

"Beneath?" Emili and Jonathan chorused.

"This area of Rome along the Tiber was twenty feet lower than it is today. In 1872, the pope raised the level of the Jewish Ghetto. The roofs of stores and houses became the support for a new foundation of streets and buildings. The Renaissance Ghetto, including its alleys and first story of storefronts, was never demolished. They were just built over."

Orvieti disappeared into the stacks and returned with a worn oversized book. Seeing the frontispiece or a red wax seal of the Vatican, both Jonathan and Emili knew it was a map of the Ghetto, as established in 1516. Orvieti's small frame tented over the folios as he turned the pages, his arms straight against the desk on either side. The gray-blue sketches detailed the Ghetto's narrow streets.

"You can still access the Ghetto's original streets."

"From where?" Emili asked.

"Beneath the furnace room of this building," Orvieti said.

Orvieti led them down the spiral stairs from the belfry to the synagogue's subbasement, which until the turn of the century had been a furnace room. Orvieti pulled a string, illuminating the room with a dim, swinging bulb. They stepped past some rusted flue piping and a rotted-out oil tank.

At Orvieti's direction, Jonathan slid his fingers through the iron mesh of a heating grate at the base of the wall and pulled it delicately, as though removing a fragile painting. The grate snapped out, and granulated concrete crumbled on his shoes. A damp breeze exited the dark square hole.

"This is as far as I can go," Orvieti said, smiling weakly. "My doctor tells me the air is too thin."

Jonathan crawled through the opening first, and Emili followed. The crossing beams of their flashlights illuminated the nineteenth-century iron pylons that raised the streets to their modern height.

They descended a staircase leading farther underground. The odor of coal dust and rat droppings condensed around them like a mist. The underground landscape stretched out before them like a lost city, street after street winding deeper into the earth. Occasional gusts of fetid air made it difficult to breathe. It resembled an underwater street scene: rotted casks lay half buried in the silt; dust motes floated across the flashlight beams like plankton; algae-covered signs still hung outside small storefronts. The ghostly, intact streetscapes sprawled for dozens of meters. These Roman streets had been buried alive.

"The portico," Emili said with awe.

Before them, giant granite columns stretched upward twenty vertical feet, a double row of columns built by Augustus for his sister, Octavia. "At the street level," Emili said, "only the top portion of these columns are visible."

To the right, they saw the slouching marble lintel of a brownstone, its wooden doors collapsed and bowed, softened by the centuries.

"Here," Emili said, pointing above the doorway at two conjoined, rounded tablets with lions on rear legs, flanking either side. It was an unmistakable image of the Ten Commandments. "This is it," she said. "A house of prayer."

They moved through the doorway, and the darkness seemed to thicken around them. Their beams caught glimpses of the sanctuary's grandeur, as though entering the once luxurious confines of a sunken ship.

Above the overturned pews there appeared to be a large hole in the ceiling filled by the cement foundation of a building above it.

"Look." Jonathan pointed his beam at a mural along the wall. In front of them was a breathtaking replica of the painted image of Jerusalem from the Domus Aurea. They both stood silent, stunned not only by the artistic mastery of the landscape but by the foresight of its artist, who despite his role as papal architect secretly salvaged Josephus's legacy by reproducing this ancient painting on the wall of a Ghetto synagogue in 1825.

"Imagine the irony," Emili mused. "Valadier's employer, Pius the Seventh, was the very pope to reinstitute the Ghetto Napoleon had just abolished. He must have had no idea what his papal architect had done."

"I'm not sure anyone did," Jonathan said. "No one inside the Ghetto would have dreamed that the mural before them illustrated the path of the menorah's escape from the Temple Mount two thousand years before."

"Look at the detail of the Cardo Maximus," Emili said, pointing at the central thoroughfare of ancient Jerusalem. "He even drew the porticos on each side leading into the Temple Mount." The map's detail was a precise, vibrant version of the faded mosaic they had discovered only an hour before inside the buried walls of the Domus Aurea.

Jonathan walked to the center of the mural, dwarfed by the portrayal of the Temple Mount's four massive retaining walls, with turrets drawn at each corner. "There's a faint red line here," he said, pointing at the center of the Temple Mount. "It continues where the row of gemstones stopped in the Domus Aurea's mural." He moved his hand along the mural, scraping off gray fungus with the face cap of his flashlight.

"That path goes through the modern-day Muslim Quarter of Jerusalem," Emili said. "It looks like the tunnel runs from the center of the Mount to Antonia's Fortress." She pointed at an ancient tur-reted fortress drawn along the painting's northern edge.

Beneath the red line leading into the fortress, a small Latin cita-tion was written.

CVNICVLVS EZEKIAE

Sotto Cannone Chiesa

"*Cuniculus* means 'tunnel' or 'subterranean passage,'" Jonathan translated. "The second word is the Latin genitive of the name Hezekiah."

"Hezekiah's tunnel," Emili said. "And below that, Valadier wrote an additional line in a modern Italian: "*Sotto cannone chiesa,*'" she read aloud.

"'Beneath a canonical church'?" Jonathan translated.

"Yes, and notice how Valadier used a different font and color. He was one of the first preservationists to distinguish his modern additions from the original. When he restored the Arch of Titus in the Forum, he intentionally used a travertine distinguishable from the ancient marble."

"Hezekiah's Tunnel," Jonathan said. "What does it mean?"

"I think it's telling us how Josephus moved a lamp made of eight feet of solid gold out of the Temple Mount." Emili marveled. "Through the tunnel dug by King Hezekiah in the eighth century B.C."

51

With a sense of urgency, Emili and Jonathan hurried back through the underground streetscape and climbed into the synagogue's furnace room. By the time Jonathan put the grate back into place and followed Emili up the stairs, she was already sharing the discovery with Orvieti, showing him the flashlit photographs of the mural on the digital screen of her camera.

"Hezekiah's Tunnel," Orvieti said. "Of course, it would have to be."

He walked to the bookshelves and reached up to pull a volume from a high shelf. Jonathan walked over to help, but Orvieti waved him off. "This is my exercise," he said kindly.

He opened the volume and returned to the table.

"The Book of Chronicles," Jonathan said.

"Are you familiar with the story of King Hezekiah?" Orvieti asked.

Jonathan shook his head, always somewhat guilty that his historical knowledge of the biblical era lagged behind his knowledge of pagan civilizations such as Rome and Greece.

"The year was about 700 B.C.," Orvieti said as he flipped through the tissue-thin pages of the text. "King Hezekiah of ancient Israel decided to stop paying the king of Assyria *tangenti*." He looked up to Emili for a translation.

"Protection money," she said, smiling.

"Hezekiah knew the Assyrian forces wouldn't waste any time laying siege to Jerusalem," Orvieti continued. "Knowing the city would be surrounded, Hezekiah designed a water supply that ran beneath the Mount to the Gihon spring, located outside the city walls."

"And the tunnel has been discovered?" Jonathan asked.

"Only the southernmost tip," Emili replied. "In the nineteenth century, a boy bathing in an Arab village near the Gihon spring discovered the tunnel along with an eighth-century-B.C. plaque describing the tunnel's construction, just as in the biblical text. But where the rest of the tunnel runs beneath the Mount is still a mystery."

"But it probably wasn't a mystery to Josephus," Jonathan said. "That's why he could escape from the Mount without the Romans' hearing any digging. They used a tunnel that was already there."

"Unfortunately, even if this theory is correct," Orvieti said, "there's no way to figure out where Hezekiah's tunnel is."

"Not unless Valadier told us," Emili said. "There was another line written in modern Italian? *Sotto cannone chiesa.*"

"'Beneath a canonical church'?" Orvieti asked.

"That must be referring to the modern location of the tunnel," Jonathan said. "'Beneath a canonical church'."

Emili zoomed in the image on her camera's digital screen. "The only problem is, at least twenty churches now span the Muslim Quarter of Jerusalem. Greek Orthodox, Catholic, Franciscan, Armenian. All of them are considered part of one Christian canon or another."

"Keep zooming," Jonathan said, staring at the digital image from over her shoulder. "The word *cannone* has two *n*'s here. I don't think that's just an antiquated spelling. Like English, *canone* with one *n* means 'tradition,' but with two it's a—"

"Gun," Emili said.

Jonathan nodded, but then looked askance. "Wait, this inscription is telling us to look for a church with a big gun sitting on the top of it? That doesn't make sense."

"But it might have when this mural was drawn in 1825. The

Ottoman hold on Jerusalem was precarious," Emili said. "A cannon could have sat on a church and pointed over the city walls of Jerusalem as a defense."

"We may have some maps of Jerusalem here," Orvieti said, searching the far side of the archive.

But Emili was too deep in her own calculations to respond. She stared at the digital image of the fresco, a mischievous glint lighting her eyes from within.

"Whoa, whoa," Jonathan said protractedly. "You're not thinking of—"

"Of course I am."

"Emili, we're talking about a church in Jerusalem from nearly two hundred years ago? *Even* if you made it to Jerusalem, the church may not even exist anymore. You're acting like you can just return to nineteenth-century Jerusalem by hopping on a plane."

"As a matter of fact, I can," Emili said. "In the Old City, there's an elaborate model of Jerusalem built for the 1873 World's Fair. It depicts every small structural detail of nineteenth-century Jerusalem in beaten zinc, down to the colored flags of the consulates. It's exactly how a nineteenth-century pilgrim would have seen Jerusalem."

She saw interest flash across Jonathan's face.

"You don't even have a way of getting there," Jonathan protested. "The carabinieri have probably identified us from the metro surveillance cameras. You'd be stopped on the first commercial flight to Jerusalem tomorrow."

"I'm not thinking of a commercial flight, Jon." She stepped toward him. "There's the World Food Programme based here in Piazza del Popolo. Cargo planes leave every week from Ciampino to Ben-Gurion, shipping food packages en route to Gaza."

"And that's tonight?"

"I'm scheduled to be on it anyway," she said.

"Emili, at the very least, just wait a day to see if we can speak to someone at the—"

"Carabinieri?" she interrupted. "And tell them what? That we've discovered a series of embedded messages from a first-century historian whom every scholar in the world is dead wrong about? That he wasn't a traitor at all, but really running Rome as a double agent so he could smuggle the tabernacle menorah to safety? And, by the way, just when his messages were about to be discovered by Napoleon's megalomaniacal expeditions two hundred years ago, an eighteenth-century architect working for the pope quietly saved them by painting a copy of an ancient mural in the Jewish Ghetto?"

Jonathan exhaled, shaking his head in disbelief.

"Then I'm going with you," he said, feeling his chest tighten. "I won't let you go alone."

"Just this morning, in the courtroom, you said you were here for a 'legal case'—that's it. And now because of a *theory*, you'll go with me? To Jerusalem?"

"I'm no longer worried your theory is wrong. I'm worried it's *right*. There's no telling what these men are capable of. They *detonated* beneath the Colosseum."

"And the firm?" she said tauntingly. "You said the firm *needs* you."

"Right now, *you* need me," Jonathan said. "And I don't just mean because my Latin is better than yours. I mean because I can help you make sense of all this. I can keep you grounded, keep you . . . *safe*."

Emili walked toward him, her solemnity and quickness suggesting that he had angered her or taken her for weak. She pushed his right shoulder, shoving him into the stacks and out of view.

"Okay," Jonathan said. "So my Latin's not *much* better than—"

But Emili did not let him finish. She opened her mouth and kissed him deeply, her hands clutching at the back of Jonathan's hair.

"Wait," she said, stepping back. "There's a problem."

"What problem?" Jonathan said. "That was the *opposite* of a problem."

"You don't have travel documents to fly aboard a UN aircraft. To even step on the tarmac you need a *laissez-passer*."

Jonathan knew it was comparatively easy for those with the coveted light-blue UN passes to move across the most complicated borders in the world.

"They're only issued to international civil servants, aren't they?"

Emili thought a moment, a conspiratorial smile not far behind. "Well," she said, "we're about to change that."

52

Inside Vatican City, Profeta walked through the papal apartments' back corridors, far from where tourists are permitted. A ceremonial papal guard in Elizabethan dress snapped to attention, unlocking a series of oak doors leading to the Sala Consultazione Manoscritti, the reading room for Vatican drafts and manuscripts. Profeta knew only an exclusive club of independent Christian scholars and Vatican researchers had ever seen the breathtaking size of the reading room for drafts and manuscripts. The walls of ancient books were impossibly long, as though two mirrors reflected panels of rococo vaults stretching into infinity. Across the ceiling, angels danced with books and keys as parchments rained down from heaven in remarkable trompe l'oeil stuccowork.

Nestled between two card catalogs, Cardinal Francesco Inocenti's girth nearly filled the width of a small niche in which his desk sat. Profeta wondered how someone with such an affection for old-style Roman cooking had reached Inocenti's old age. More than a half-century ago, the cardinal started his career in the Church as a librarian, and now, having retired from the College of Cardinals, where he had spent twenty years, he returned to his true passion, cataloging the world's rarest cracked and faded books behind the Vatican's walls, where his career had begun.

On his desk was a manuscript hundreds of years old, its metal locks blackened from fire.

"Jacopo, thank you for coming so quickly. You brought the manuscript page I requested?"

Profeta handed him the page inside a laminated sheath. With extra care, Cardinal Inocenti removed the page from its protective covering and laid it down inside the open medieval manuscript in front of him. The inside jagged edge of the manuscript page matched perfectly with the long ripped stub that protruded inches out of the binding.

"How did you know this page belonged to this book?" Profeta asked.

"For two hundred years, pages from many of our Josephus manuscripts have been missing," Cardinal Inocenti said. "In 1809, Napoleon stormed Rome's walls and brought the Vatican to its knees. He had all the Vatican treasures at his mercy, but what did he take? Not the Vatican's most prized possessions, the statue of Augustus or the Laocoön. Instead, his archaeologists came to the library and examined the manuscripts of Flavius Josephus."

"Flavius Josephus as an archaeological guide? But Emperor Titus commissioned Josephus to write his history as propaganda. They are as biased as one of Berlusconi's newspapers writing on politics."

The cardinal laughed, but his solemnity returned as he lifted the manuscript page. "It was certainly Titus's intention for Josephus to write a flattering Roman history, but what if Josephus had something else in mind?

"The parchment was treated with potassium nitrate. They were looking for writing rubbed out under the vellum beneath the current script. Apparently, there may be more to Josephus than meets the eye."

"Your Eminence, these efforts sound more appropriate for a scholar, not an antiquities thief. These men do not share your love of history."

"I am not speaking about history," Cardinal Inocenti said, his gaze anchored on Profeta. "I am speaking about greed, *Comandante*. Treating Josephus's manuscripts with chemicals?" He pointed at the circled letters of text. "Searching for equidistant letter sequences in the Greek? What is the adage you once shared with me about stolen antiquities?"

"The greater the relic, the greater the thief," Profeta said.

"Veramente," Cardinal Inocenti said.

He swiveled in his chair, reaching for a manila envelope behind him. "For years, our monasteries in Jerusalem have been tracking illicit archaeological activity beneath the Temple Mount. Unfortunately, the Waqf's jurisdiction makes the inner workings of the Vatican look like an open book."

He removed pictures from the manila envelope and handed them to Profeta. Each depicted large piles of rubble amid olive groves. Inside the huge piles of dirt, Profeta could make out crushed marble and terra-cotta.

"What is this?"

"Priceless ruins from beneath the Temple Mount," Cardinal Inocenti said. "We found them dumped in the valley of Kidron. The piles were systematically mixed together to prevent future excavation."

"And the Waqf is conducting these excavations?"

"Not directly, no. There are many honorable and religious imams within the Waqf Authority who know nothing of these excavations. But a small few within the Waqf have used the trust's jurisdiction over the Mount to permit an ongoing excavation of catastrophic proportions, led by a man named only as Salah ad-Din."

"Salah ad-Din as in the twelfth-century warrior?"

The cardinal nodded. "Our Christian informants in Jerusalem report that this man Salah ad-Din has been researching priceless Josephus manuscripts as well as detailed topographical maps of Rome."

"And you think this relates to the excavations we've discovered in Rome?"

"Yes, our sources report that he was digging here to find a location beneath Jerusalem. Jacopo, he will use methods of excavation cruder than you can imagine."

"Cruder than what I saw beneath the Colosseum? I'm not sure that's possible."

"Our contacts in Bethlehem report nitrocellulose explosives, as well as rubber suppression mats, smuggled in through Syria. Whatever he is looking for, he will detonate to find it."

Comandante Profeta reached for his two-way radio. "Brandisi, get me Eilat Segev at the Israel Antiquities Authority, immediately."

53

On the outskirts of Rome, Emili's motorcycle approached a ramshackle postwar apartment building. The building's rust-stained concrete walls rose six stories, and the chipping around the first-floor windows indicated where security bars had been ripped off.

"I'm guessing this isn't on most tourist maps," Jonathan said.

A sign in the shape of a heraldic symbol was glued to the door. RAOUL FRADELI, MASTERPIECES, PORTRAITURE.

"Here we are," Emili said.

"Fradeli?" Jonathan said. "That name seems familiar."

"You'll be UN personnel in no time."

Jonathan looked at the hand-painted sign.

"Masterpieces?" Jonathan shook his head. "Please don't tell me he's a forger."

"Look at the bright side, you're about to have one of the best imitation UN passports in the world."

Jonathan knew that for most forgers, with their steady hand and eye for signatures, it was more lucrative to imitate green cards and EU passports than to spend months repainting a Monet only to compete with the poster shop down the street.

"The name, it just sounds so familiar," Jonathan said.

She pressed the apartment number.

"*Quem é?*" said a gruff voice in Portuguese.

"Raoul, it's Emili."

The metallic sound of a buzzer answered. They walked up creaking steps, each one worn into a trough-shaped plank. The grainy sound of an opera playing on an old phonograph echoed in the stairwell. There was a sharp odor of mildew.

"Wait a minute . . . Raoul Fradeli," Jonathan whispered. He remembered a case three years before, in which Dulling and Pierce represented a museum in Detroit against a small Italian dealer. The museum's insurance company investigated a piece and traced it back to the studio of a Raoul Fradeli. Fradeli claimed to have just restored the painting for the dealer, but it was clear he painted the thing from scratch.

Jonathan stopped on the staircase landing. "Emili, I know this guy from a *case*."

"I wouldn't mention that if I were you," Emili said.

"What if he recognizes me?" Jonathan whispered.

Jonathan pictured himself in a New York office conference room at Dulling and Pierce. He sat directly across from Raoul Fradeli, watching the firm's senior lawyers grill him with questions about his restoration. The expert witnesses could not agree which quadrants of the canvas were original.

"The case against him was dismissed," Jonathan said.

As Emili was about to knock, she turned around and smiled. "I told you he was good."

Raoul opened the door, the collar of his white coat upturned, a beret tilted to one side, three days' scruff of beard on his face. He looked the consummate bohemian artist. His demeanor immediately changed when he saw Jonathan.

"Who the fuck is this?" Raoul said in Portuguese-flavored English.

Emili stepped past him. "A friend who needs a favor."

Raoul stared at Jonathan uneasily, narrowing his eyes, as though faintly recognizing him.

"And who is willing to pay handsomely for it," she added.

Raoul grinned suddenly. "In which case, any friend of yours is a friend of mine. *Benvenuto.*"

Behind him, replica paintings of Goya, Picasso, and a half-finished Jackson Pollock lined the walls. In a sink, a small penciled sketch soaked in soapsuds, a technique used to age parchment a few hundred years in a matter of hours.

Emili pulled Raoul aside, showing him her *laissez-passer*, issued to international civil servants of the United Nations. He nodded reluctantly and took the papers from Emili's hand. He whispered to her in Italian, "Do I know this guy?"

"No, Raoul, you don't."

"Are you sure?"

"I'll pay you what you want, and get out of your life," Jonathan said with an abrupt confidence as false as the art around him.

"I like him," Raoul said to Emili. He turned to Jonathan. "I like you, so I give you discount." He took the papers from Emili and walked over to his stove, and stirred the boiling water where he was making pasta. He walked back over to the table where Jonathan was sitting.

"For *le bleu?*" Raoul said, looking at Jonathan.

"What's *le bleu?*"

"The most coveted," Raoul said. He held up Emili's small blue UN passport. "The UN *laissez-passer.*" He lowered his voice reverently. "It unlocks every border in the world."

"How much?" Emili asked.

"*Mille.*"

A thousand euros! Jonathan yelled, but only to himself. Emili nodded that the price was fair.

"Reasonable enough," Jonathan heard himself say, counting out the bills. It was nearly all the cash he had withdrawn before leaving for Rome.

Raoul went to snatch the money, but Jonathan pulled back his hand as he glanced at the stove. "That pasta?"

Raoul nodded.

Jonathan handed him the money, remembering they had not eaten all day.

"Then this better include dinner."

Raoul grinned, leading them into a back room, where lamination and scanner equipment lined the walls. The rest of the flat was a dusty artisan's studio, and Jonathan was stunned by the contrast of this room's technology. Emili took in the equipment, shrugging, "At least he's a professional," she whispered.

"It'll be a real person," Raoul said, putting on glasses with jeweler's loupes flipped up. "Even if they run the passport through a scanner, it'll correspond to one of the UN's fifteen thousand passports currently issued." He pulled out a blank shell of the UN's light blue passport backing, and a straight-edge razor and fine-point marker; he flipped down the magnifying lenses of his glasses and got to work.

Emili and Jonathan waited at a small table beside the stacked dirty dishes in the sink. They heard the cutting of a board and the sound of a scanner. Half-drawn Chagall sketches lined the kitchen wall, emitting an inky smell of ash and chalk. When the pasta was cooked, Emili returned with two steaming bowls.

"I have a question for you," Emili said.

"If it's whether I remember how to twirl the pasta like you once taught me," Jonathan winced, "prepare to be disappointed."

"About your work at the firm." Emili sat back down at the table. "I'm still surprised you represented that antiquities dealer a couple of months ago."

"Which?"

"Andre Cavetti. You knew the guy wasn't clean," Emili said. "He's running illegal excavations just outside Naples bigger than a soccer stadium."

"But that bronze nude statue wasn't illegally excavated. And it certainly didn't belong in some museum in Italy."

"How can you be so sure?"

"Because it was a fake."

"What?" Emili's eyes widened.

"The Latin inscription used grammar that wasn't invented until the tenth century, and her hairstyle looked like a Renaissance pinup girl's."

"None of the other experts saw it?"

Jonathan shrugged. "Someone will. Eventually."

"So you managed to prevent the Italians from embarrassing themselves by having a fake on display in their museum, Cavetti saves face in the art world, and Dulling wins again."

"Not exactly the heroic solution, but justice isn't done by heroes with swords anymore," Jonathan said. "It's done by lawyers."

"Coming with me to Jerusalem is the heroic solution." Emili's tone softened. "So how do you explain that choice, Counselor?"

"We're talking about one of the greatest treasures of the ancient world here, Emili."

But both of them knew that the answer was a placeholder for one that couldn't be spoken, although it hung thick in the air of the kitchen. *Because I nearly lost you down there. Because I've pictured you a hundred times, lying in the catacomb's rubble, blood seeping out the side of your lips. Because I remember grabbing your wrist, frantically searching for a pulse, whispering in your ear, "Just stay with me. . . . Just stay with me."*

"Did you say something, Jon?" Emili asked, sitting in the kitchen. "You just said, 'Stay with me.'"

"I meant, *stay with you*," Jonathan said, fumbling. "I'd like to stay with you."

"I need your real passport." Raoul's voice from the other room was a welcome interruption.

"Why?" Jonathan said.

"Just going to borrow the picture, image it, then put it back." Raoul flipped down his loupes again. "The picture's lamination must look creased and matted. New picture is a dead giveaway."

Jonathan watched Raoul cannibalize his real passport, peeling back his current identity. He remembered how ancient Romans scraped and washed leather parchments to reuse them, but often the underwriting, the *scriptio inferior*, resurfaced years later as the animal hide aged. As Emili took Jonathan's hand, rebuking him to properly wrap the pasta around the fork, he realized just how much the *scriptio inferior* of his own past had resurfaced with a startling legibility.

"And *please* don't get any tomato sauce on the Chagall lying on the countertop," Raoul said, looking up at them. Through the magnifying lenses of the loupes, his eyes looked comically large. "The British Museum just bought it."

54

In East Jerusalem, General Eilat Segev sat in her office at the Israel Antiquities Authority in the Rockefeller Museum, a nineteenth-century Byzantine-style building that looked etched from a solid piece of sandstone. In the hallways outside her office, priceless Greek sculpture and Roman-era capitals were propped against wooden crates as though in a storage depot. Whether or not the Israel Antiquities Authority intentionally decided to preserve the ascetic habits of tent-housed British archaeology of the 1920s, or whether the Israeli government was simply reluctant to invest in a public building so deep inside Arab Jerusalem, the no-frills classical ambience of the Rockefeller Museum could not have better matched the strength and simplicity of General Eilat Segev: the woman in charge of Israel's only organization to prevent illicit excavations and the illegal trafficking of ancient artifacts.

General Segev leaned over her desk, her long gray hair pulled back from her face, which was tanned and creased from thirty years of fieldwork. She still wore the same dust-covered white blouse and trim olive pants from her site work earlier in the day. Her outfit had a vaguely military appearance, and the image of her leaning over her maps with such intensity resembled her days in the military, when, as the commander of an elite team, she studied Syrian troop movements along the border late into the night.

Archaeology for her was a first love, but a second career, not realized until her military role as a high-ranking officer of foreign dignitary security details came to an abrupt end in Sharm el-Sheikh, when a bullet meant for the Israeli foreign minister found her abdomen instead. Her passion for archaeology, coupled with obvious praise from the foreign minister's office, allowed Segev to transfer with commendation to the ranks of the Israel Antiquities Authority.

She thought pursuing her passion for archaeology would mean a milder career. But Segev found herself running an organization that had begun to more closely resemble the Mossad than an archaeological parks department. Almost daily her undercover agents in the Israel Antiquities Authority were discovering new tunnels that were used to smuggle antiquities and arms from Egypt to Gaza. And her department now fielded Hasidic informants to keep tabs on fringe religious groups looking to harm historical Islamic sites. Segev may have fought in every war for Israel since 1967, but as far as her professional dedication was concerned, she protected Islamic minarets with the same vigor that she did the Western Wall.

Her desk phone rang.

"Segev," she answered

"*Generale Segev?*" Profeta's thick Italian accent and raspy voice were immediately identifiable. Not to mention his insistence on still using her military title.

"Jacopo," Segev said. She spoke in English, their best shared language.

Under different circumstances they would have traded memories of their younger days, when the Tutela del Patrimonio Culturale cooperated with the Israel Antiquities Authority to bust a geniza scroll ring in Amman. But Profeta knew the increasing demands, and dangers, of Segev's schedule. She had recently stunned an audience during a panel discussion with Profeta in Rome's Palazzo dei Conservatori. She was asked to describe the difference between the ruins of Rome and those of Israel.

"Simple," she told the crowd. "In Rome, the ruins are dead."

"*Generale,*" Profeta began, "our team here in Rome has uncovered a series of illegal excavations that we believe may be related to excavations beneath the Temple Mount. Have you detected any unusual activity?"

"Jacopo, I can't send a single officer up there, but we've been receiving reports of massive demolition inside it."

"Demolition?"

"In the Islamic political world, the idea has gained traction to remove any Judeo-Christian archaeology from the Mount. On a daily basis, Yasser Arafat would deny that there were any Temples ever there."

"And you can't send archaeologists up there even for a brief UNESCO review of their activity?"

"Ariel Sharon went up to the Mount for ten minutes and we were putting out riots for six months. Of course, many think that his stepping foot on the Mount gave him mystical power to revive his political aspirations. He became prime minister less than two months after setting foot on the Mount. We were worried we'd have politicians lined up, waiting their turn to touch the soil of the Temple Mount."

Their laughter died and Profeta's tone turned serious. "General Segev, these are not mere *tombaroli*. Our investigation has turned up the name Salah ad-Din."

"Jacopo, are you near your fax machine?"

Profeta immediately understood the reason for the low-technology request. *Too sensitive for electronic transmittal. Read and shred,* her tone implied.

Beside Profeta's desk in Rome, his secure office fax came to life, unspooling a black-and-white photograph.

In the image, four men stood on a restoration scaffolding outside the Dome of the Rock.

"Have you received it?"

"A photograph of a restoration?" Profeta asked.

"A front," Segev said. "A restoration effort that is merely a means to gain entry beneath the Mount."

Profeta noticed that one of the men on the scaffolding had his back turned to the camera. Only the back of his head, its stubble-length black hair, was visible.

"The one with his back turned," Profeta said. "He knows the camera is there."

"We believe that's him. That's Salah ad-Din."

"Does Interpol have a better photograph we could circulate?"

"In five years of surveillance, this is the only picture. But our intelligence inside the Waqf reports that many imans believe Salah ad-Din has gone too far. Whatever he is looking for, he is running out of time to find it."

"Which has apparently made him only more dangerous, *Generale.* There are reports of him smuggling nitrocellulouse explosives from Syria. He may detonate."

"What other data have you learned, Jacopo?"

"Only that."

"He's had one hell of a classical education," Profeta said. "His team was able to excavate a female corpse in ancient garb and preserved in oils that perfectly matched Pliny's embalming techniques."

Segev was silent. "Jacopo, was there an inscription tattooed on her torso?" All trace of exhaustion disappeared from her voice.

"Yes, combining Greek and Latin. 'Through the navel of the world.'"

"Those were the words?" Segev asked, the awe in her voice detectable even over the phone. "You are certain?"

Profeta felt he had stumbled into particularly sensitive territory. A sudden barrier of information rose between them.

"Something tells me I have wandered into waters deeper than I imagined."

Eilat Segev was silent another moment. "Jacopo, they call you the Prophet for a reason."

55

Although it was midnight, Rome's Ciampino Airport was crowded with passengers delayed because of the daylong rain. Jonathan pulled a Roma soccer-team cap farther down over his face and they walked toward the *imbarchi*, or gates, blending in with a church group from Devonshire. "For a thousand euros, he could have let me pick my native country." Jonathan turned to Emili, holding the faux-leather UN passport in his hands. "I don't know a thing about *Canada*."

Unlike Rome's larger international airport in Fiumicino, which offered strictly commercial flights, Ciampino was a joint civilian and military airport, and the dozens of soldiers in full regalia milling through the duty-free shops did nothing to calm Jonathan's bristling nerves.

He followed Emili through the crowd to a small flight of stairs that led to a mezzanine floor housing the Plexiglas cubicles of airline corporate offices, customer service, and UN agencies.

The UN agency was immediately next to airport security. The security officers sat around eating panini, watching an episode of *Law & Order* dubbed in Italian. None of them looked up as Jonathan and Emili walked past.

"Ciao, Andre," Emili said to the UN administrator sitting behind his desk. He was clad in the UN's powder-blue uniform, his tie was undone and pulled to one side, and one of his epaulets was hanging off his shoulder. Apparently, no one from the main office was coming by for an inspection anytime soon.

"Could you walk us through customs? We're trying to make the 12:00 a.m. charter to Ben-Gurion."

Andre shook his head, laughing, "That's in forty minutes! When will you ever learn?" He put down his sandwich. "As usual, it'll be tight. No promises."

Emili introduced Jonathan, who couldn't help thinking that on the other side of this piece of drywall, eight carabinieri watched American television dubbed into Italian. Jonathan heard gunshots and jumped. The bass guitar theme music of *Law & Order* reminded him it was the show.

"Too much coffee?" Andre smiled.

Andre walked Emili and Jonathan through the airport's brick-walled employee corridors. Excited to practice his broken English, Andre shared with Jonathan meaningless trivia about the airport. "Airport of the most age!" he said proudly.

"He's trying to say Ciampino's the oldest commercial airport in the world," Emili said in Jonathan's ear. "From 1916."

Jonathan nodded politely. *Hope the planes are more recent.*

They stepped through automatic doors onto a stadium-lit tarmac and walked to a roped-off area behind a row of generators. Faint green lights stretched into the darkness, and Lufthansa Sky Chef trucks with orange blinking lights whizzed past them. They approached the UN plane, a Russian-made Antonov AN-30 turboprop cargo aircraft with a fat, pill-shaped front and archaic circular windows that looked vaguely nautical. Emili was talking to Jonathan, but her voice was completely inaudible under the roaring noise of the revving engines. The faded emblem of a Croatian flag on the tail suggested the plane had been retired from military service and refitted years before to make small UN cargo runs across the Mediterranean.

Jonathan pointed at the bright red insignia. "UNFAO?"

"The plane belongs to the United Nations Food and Agricultural Organization. The one with their headquarters here in Piazza del Popolo."

Two pilots stood underneath the belly of the plane, chatting with the mechanics like two cabdrivers catching up at dispatch before moving along for the day.

Emili and Jonathan climbed an orange ladder to the hatch door. The inside of the plane was thinly carpeted aluminum siding. In the electric glow of the cockpit's buttons, the contents of the airplane's hull revealed itself: long rows of stacked freeze-dried meals. In front of the cargo, two single jump seats faced each other.

After the pilots boarded and Emili and Jonathan took their places, the plane moved unexpectedly, accelerating without a word from the pilots.

"I guess there's no safety demonstration, then," Jonathan said.

Shaking under its own weight, the plane's contracting metal groaned like a rusty fairground ride. The engines shrieked, loud as teakettles, and every joint in the metal hull made a snapping sound, as if the whole plane would split apart at any second. Emili flipped through the maps of Jerusalem in her lap, immune to it all. The wheels went up, there was a sudden tranquillity. Rome's nighttime shoreline was dotted with lights beneath them.

"That's right," Emili said, as though soothing a large animal, her eyes resting on the metal ceiling of the plane, "you're just a little rusty, that's all." As her gaze fell, it rested squarely on Jonathan, and he realized her last comment wasn't about the plane at all, but about him.

The plane banked over the blackness of the Mediterranean. In the slender shaft of light from above her seat, Emili circled various convents on a map of Jerusalem.

She looked up. "What did you see down there, Jon?"

"Down where?"

"That night seven years ago in the catacomb before it collapsed," she said. "You saw something, didn't you? A fresco, an inscription."

Jonathan averted his eyes. They had never spoken so directly of the tragedy. She knew how carefully he guarded the memory, trying to keep it in some distant chamber of his mind.

"After you roped down into the catacomb, Gianpaolo and I were a few feet ahead of you," Jonathan said. He remembered walking through the tomb's low-ceilinged corridors with Gianpaolo. As usual, the memory was intermittently hazy, like poor analog reception on a television and, by turns, was startlingly vivid.

"Gianpaolo and I entered a large cavern, and all three walls of the tomb were covered with a large ancient mural. The first wall's painting depicted a large arena and an elderly bearded man standing in its center, *damnatio ad bestias*."

"Condemned to be executed by beasts."

"Exactly," Jonathan said, his eyes distant, as though still seeing the paintings before him on the tomb's wall. "On the next frame, the man escaped, dropping through the floor of the arena."

"Like a trapdoor?"

"Yes," Jonathan said. "And on the third wall, he carried a torch through an underground tunnel exiting the Colosseum. The man wore an aristocratic toga, which suggested a role in the emperor's court."

"And now you think the man in the painting was Flavius Josephus, don't you?"

Jonathan nodded. "Beneath the painting was Suetonius's famous quote. 'After a certain prisoner escaped the Colosseum, Titus wept bitterly.' From what we've seen today, Titus's despair seems not only because of Josephus's betrayal, but because Titus realized that the authentic menorah had eluded him."

Jonathan's face was set with concentration, as though he were trying to prevent the memory from overrunning its banks.

"Gianpaolo then radioed up to Sharif that we had found wall paintings, and that's when the tomb began to collapse."

Jonathan stared out the window at the wing's fog light, and in the blackness outside the plane, the fateful night felt as real to him as seven years earlier.

In the cloud of debris, Jonathan slung Emili's unconscious body over his shoulder and ran one step ahead of the catacomb's collapsing roof. They reached the cavern where they had climbed down. The rope ladder dangled a foot from the floor, reaching up to a manhole where Sharif's head was visible.

"What the hell happened down there!" Sharif screamed down to them. "Sounded like a bomb!"

"The catacomb collapsed!" Jonathan shouted. "Gianpaolo's coming up first!" He turned to Gianpaolo. "You go first, then I'll bring her up!"

"She needs help!" Gianpaolo said. "Take her up first!"

Jonathan grabbed the first rung of the rope ladder, shifting Emili over his shoulders to use both hands.

"Oh, Jesus," Gianpaolo said.

"We'll be all right, Gianpaolo," Jonathan grunted, stepping up another rung of the rope ladder. "We'll all be fine, I promise." Just

at that moment, a large piece of ceiling fell, sending chunks of stucco splashing against the walls of the cavern.

Jonathan continued to climb, feeling the strain of their combined weight in his thighs as he moved one foot above the other. Jonathan could feel his veins nearly explode through his forearms with each haul upward. He neared the manhole and Sharif reached down, pulling Emili up and laying her limp frame on the grass.

Sharif stood up, hands on his head. "What the hell happened, Jon!"

"Get help, Sharif. There are policemen near the villa's front gate."

"But we're not supposed to be—"

"Go, now! She needs to get to a hospital!"

Sharif disappeared down the rain-slicked path.

"Gianpaolo, can you hear me?"

"Yes, I tried to climb, Jon. I can't do it." Jonathan could hear the tremble in his voice. He was crying.

"Listen to me, Gianpaolo, I just need you to hang on to the rope ladder. Just hang on and I will pull you up!"

A huge piece of ceiling fell, and there was a raw shriek from inside the catacomb.

"GP, are you okay!"

"It's all coming down in here, Jon!"

Jonathan stared into the manhole. He could see only gray dust.

"Just hold on to the ladder, okay?"

There was silence, but Jonathan felt the resistance of Gianpaolo's weight. Slowly, with agonizing deliberateness, Jonathan pulled up the ladder carrying Gianpaolo. After four or five hauls, Gianpaolo's face emerged from the gray dust, covered in powdered stucco. He squinted at the streetlamp behind Jonathan as though he had never seen a light.

"Stay right there!" Jonathan screamed.

Jonathan moved toward the hole, managing not to lose any slack on the rope ladder, and swung his arm down, gripping Gianpaolo's hand.

"Your other hand, Gianpaolo," Jonathan said, grunting. "I can't hold you!"

In Gianpaolo's other hand, he held a piece of notebook paper clenched in a tight fist. Before the tomb's collapse, they found a paragraph of Latin text painted on the wall, and Gianpaolo had written it down.

"Drop the paper and give me your hand!"

"I . . . I can't." Gianpaolo's eyes widened, confused that his own muscles were working against him. "My hand won't open, Jon."

"You're slipping, GP! Please," Jonathan said, feeling the popping of his arm socket. "Just let go and take—"

But the emotion in Gianpaolo's face had already changed into something strangely tranquil, an expression that would recur often enough in Jonathan's nightmares that he at least thought one day he would make sense of it—the sudden transformation of a tight grimace to a portrait of someone sleepy, unconcerned, at peace.

"Jon?" was all Gianpaolo said.

It was the last word he ever spoke. He said it softly and phrased it like a question, as though recognizing someone he did not expect to see. Or more haunting, as though expressing surprise that someone he had so completely trusted could let this happen.

Jonathan felt Gianpaolo's fingers slip through his one by one. He remembered the feeling of the last fingertip as Gianpaolo began to free-fall, his head tilted like a confused child just before he was eclipsed by the cloud of dust.

Jonathan knelt there, quivering over the manhole, still reaching through the manhole as though hanging on.

"Get back from her!" The carabinieri now surrounded him,

screaming instructions at Jonathan, who remained kneeling by the manhole with Emili's unconscious body in front of him like an offering.

Jonathan Marcus, Rome Prize winner in classical studies, used his last bit of strength to place his hands behind his head.

"She needs a hospital," he rasped, looking down at Emili. "Please."

Jonathan woke with a start. It was night outside the plane. The plane's engines rumbled like distant thunder, and the wings' fog lights flickered in the darkness. The red emergency lever of a steel door had burrowed into the small of his back. In his exhaustion, Jonathan wiped his eyes, but not with the fogginess that usually attends waking in a foreign place. His ears felt a sudden drop in cabin pressure. The plane was descending.

Jonathan jolted back in his seat, realizing Emili's seat was empty.

Suddenly, the cockpit's door opened, and there she was, apparently having just conferred with the pilots. Cheeks flushed and her blond hair falling lightly over both shoulders, she somehow looked refreshed. In the cabin lighting, her full lips had a shine and Jonathan remembered once calling them—amid admiring laughter—the pink hulls of an ancient Roman ship, a trireme, their voluptuous folds like the hundred oars that slanted from each side.

"Landing in less than ten minutes," she said, plopping back in her seat, completely unconscious of her beauty. "Just before dawn."

"No meal on this flight, then?" Jonathan pointed at the cartons of food relief packages. "I can make a mean omelet with a metric ton of powdered eggs."

The pilot was speaking loudly into a walkie-talkie. Landing procedures were now transferring control of the aircraft from Cairo air-traffic control to the Israeli Southern Command control tower.

"We're approaching Tel Aviv," she said. Jonathan could see the row of lit beachfront hotels as the plane banked sharply east, and within minutes the illuminated glass walls of the airport came into view, a strange modern architectural oasis in the dark desert landscape. A recent $100 million renovation had transformed Ben-Gurion into a sprawling, multilayered glass-and-chrome structure supported on a base of Jerusalem stone.

As the UN plane approached the runway, the cabin was half as pressurized and the descent twice as steep as a commercial airline. Jonathan was still catching his breath when the plane slowed to a stop and the pilots were busy filling out paperwork.

There was a light blue tinge on the horizon. The pilot opened the door, and they were greeted by a strong whiff of jet fuel and three Israeli soldiers who clanked up aluminum stairs to secure the inside of the UN aircraft, which was standard procedure for all World Food Programme cargo arrivals at Ben-Gurion.

Emili and Jonathan climbed into the backseat of a small tram on the tarmac as carts whizzed past to unload the UN foodstuffs.

The tram drove Jonathan and Emili beneath the belly of a plane with African insignias that was parked on the runway. A dozen people in tattered clothing were exiting down a staircase to the tarmac.

"What other plane arrives at"—Jonathan looked at his watch—"five a.m.?"

"New Ethiopian émigrés," said the driver of the tram, pointing at an old African man in a knit white skullcap, barely able to descend the stairs of the plane. Jonathan remembered, from his international law textbook, Israel's complex history of requesting that the Ethiopian government permit the return of the millennia-old Jewish community in Africa, widely viewed as the lost tribe of Dan. Jonathan watched as the man reached the base of the aluminum stairs, two young Israeli soldiers holding on to his frail arms. The old man knelt down and kissed the tarmac. Emili saw it, too.

Terra Sancta, Jonathan thought.

"Welcome to the Promised Land," she said.

The marble expanse of Ben-Gurion's central terminal stretched before them, multiple stories of a crescent-shaped atrium ringed by the Hebrew script of American brand names in neon. A large English sign, KOSHER, hung above a McDonald's in the food court.

A bank of fifteen passport-control booths came into view.

"Passport, please?"

Jonathan slid Raoul's handiwork beneath the plated window of the UN customs booth and his heart might as well have pounded against the glass. A pretty Israeli official offered a warm smile and removed a pen from her ringlets of brown hair to write a brief note. Jonathan offered a tight smile, but his lips were becoming pale from being pressed too hard together. *A day ago, I was practicing law, and now I am traveling on a forged passport.* Jonathan envisioned plainclothes Israeli security guards appearing out of nowhere hauling him into a backroom at Ben-Gurion, and giving him a military escort back to Rome. But uneventfully, the young woman just handed the altered passport back to him. *"Todah,"* she said with a polite nod. Her eyes turned to the next person in line. Despite his best efforts, Jonathan appeared visibly surprised as she waved him through.

They stepped through the airport's glass doors, and Jonathan's tie blew over his shoulder in the dry Levantine wind. The sun was rising over the coastal plains, illuminating a line of Kia taxis outside the baggage terminal.

"Emili!" yelled a voice from behind them, and both of them spun. A slender young Arab man with dark good looks and aviator sunglasses stuck his head out the window. He waved frantically from an old dusty Mercedes limousine, its flaking beige paint blackened from its own diesel fumes. Ratty curtains hung inside the windows. It was the kind of car the dictator of a third-world country might have had twenty years before.

He hopped out and gave Emili a hug. They exchanged a few words in Arabic.

"Jonathan, this is Yusef Rashid. He's been with us at UNESCO for five years. Yusef, Jon Marcus is an old friend."

Old friend, Jonathan thought. *A promotion.*

Yusef took off his glasses and his youth—his fresh face, his wide, light brown eyes—became much more apparent. Jonathan noticed the car's hood had the letters "TV" in black masking tape on its hood. The paint was sharper where the tape had previously spelled "UN."

"You've switched to the press?" Jonathan said.

"No." Yusef smiled. "I had 'UN' there to prevent being shot at. But that stopped working." He held up a slender finger as though discerning a secret far beyond his years, "Then I realized no one around here likes bad publicity."

56

Blindfolded, Ramat Mansour felt the tight grip of two of Salah ad-Din's men, one lifting each elbow as they rushed him.

He stumbled along the corridor's uneven ground until the floor beneath his shoes felt smooth, metallic. One of the guards pushed a button, and the sound of an electric ping accompanied the sensation of a descent. *An elevator.*

When the elevator doors opened, the men removed his blindfold. Ramat found himself standing in a large subterranean hallway. He marveled at the massive stones lining the underground corridor, trying to match up his surroundings to the hypothetical sketches of what archaeologists suggested lay beneath the Temple Mount. The hallway was empty, except for a few clerics sitting on small wooden chairs with rifles across their chests, a testament to the secret nature of this world. Salah ad-Din demanded loyalty from all those inside the Mount. Ramat knew all too well of local fatwas issued against families of even suspected traitors.

One of the clerics watched Ramat as he passed.

"Hope he keeps you longer than the last one," the cleric cracked.

At the end of the corridor, a large guard with a semiautomatic slung across his ample stomach patted down Ramat's chest and legs.

"I don't own a gun," Ramat said to the guard as he frisked him.

"Not for guns," the guard said. "For cameras."

Ramat was reminded that any documentation of their excavation proved a threat far greater than any weapon.

The guard's search for recording equipment renewed Ramat's sense of guilt, reminding him of the work he had done a year before, when he assisted the beginning stages of "this excavation." Back then, only ten feet of the cavern had been cleared, and in many places the men had to duck to swing their picks, so as not to hit the ceiling.

The guard bent his knees, using his strength to lift up the bolt lock of the iron door behind him. At first Ramat became disoriented, certain that he had been marched back outside. Only when he saw the cavern's ceiling distantly above him did he realize the scale of work that Salah ad-Din had managed to complete. The guards pushed him forward.

Give him the information and get back to your family, Ramat thought, panicked that he had even witnessed the scale of the operation. He navigated through the heavy construction equipment, stepping over drills and walking around a bulldozer to reach a wooden saw-horse table, where Salah ad-Din stood hunched over an architectural map.

"Up there." Salah ad-Din pointed toward a tunnel opening forty feet up the cavern wall. "That is where the tunnel came from beneath the Foundation Stone, but where does the aqueduct continue?" He drew an imaginary line across the air of the cavern. "Our technological equipment projected that the aqueduct would continue there." Salah ad-Din pointed at an enormous gash in the far wall, indicating very recent destruction by bulldozer. "But those calculations were apparently *imprecise*," Salah ad-Din said. The solid rock wall was evidence enough of his predicament.

Ramat walked a few feet, his head tilted down at the cavern floor. He knelt and felt a slight curvature separated by two lips of carved stone a foot apart. *A sluice.* "The ground is uneven here, and there are remains of a water drain, although"—*although the tire tracks of your machinery nearly obliterated it*—"they've suffered some damage," Ramat said, containing himself. He crossed the cavern, following the remains of the drain. "And notice the discoloration of these few feet of rock." He pointed at a vein of darker rock running across the floor of the cavern.

Salah ad-Din looked back up at the high opening to the tunnel. "The water cascaded from the tunnel and flowed along the bottom of this cavern."

"Yes, and that explains the slope of the floor toward the opposite wall," Ramat said.

"But there are no records of a Roman tunnel there," Salah ad-Din said, pointing to the foot of the far stone wall.

"The Roman-era priests must have used a drainage system from the First Temple, from the Assyrian age of the eighth century B.C.," Ramat said. "If there is a tunnel behind there, it was dug by the biblical king Hezekiah."

Salah ad-Din gestured for the men to drill through the cavern wall, giving out instructions with the efficiency of a military commander. But in his cousin's eyes Ramat could see an anxiety. *He is running out of time.* Sixty years of the grand mufti's research had brought Salah ad-Din to this moment, but Ramat knew his cousin had made the obsession his own.

Two men lifted a jackhammer to position it diagonally a few inches above the floor. After a few deafening staccato blasts, the drill bit quieted, finding the air of the tunnel behind the wall.

"Enough!" Salah ad-Din shouted, and the gurgling noise of the drill's motor silenced. Salah ad-Din walked over to the wall and knelt at its base. A thin stream of water trickled out of the wall.

"This is the aqueduct leading to the hidden gate," Salah ad-Din said. He turned to Ramat. "Cousin, you have found it."

57

Leaving Ben-Gurion Airport at dawn, Jonathan watched the winter rains assemble over the Judean Hills, their gray cumulus clouds underlit by the rising sun like great bales of wool set aflame. Through the car's open windows, Jonathan could taste the aridity of the desert air and smell the cypresses. But within minutes, they began a steep ascent and the climate changed from the low coastal lands of Tel Aviv to the higher elevation of Jerusalem. Yusef did not bother to slow the Mercedes around the mountain road's turns, sending Jonathan and Emili gently into each other, left and then right, as they exchanged nervous glances. Jonathan caught sight of a restored Roman marker carved in stone on the roadside. *Colonia Aelia Capitolina XXIV.* Aelia Capitolina, the Romans' pagan name for Jerusalem after its conquest. The ancient marker indicated they were roughly twenty-four miles from the Old City walls.

The sunrise lit Emili's pale brow, and, watching her, Jonathan knew there was something not only life-threatening about his having been hurled backward as through a portal—to Rome, to the academy, to her—there was something life-sustaining, too. A sense of self restored to him, unburied. He remembered what Emili had said in the courtroom not even one day before: *"I can see you buried under that suit, Jon. Like ruins."*

The Mercedes glided through a narrow canyon corridor, missing each rock face by inches. It looked as though these rock walls had been blasted through, but the slit in this mountain was natural, having been described in Josephus as "the mountain gate." As the only direct route to Jerusalem from the coastal lands, these walls were one of the most famous military bottlenecks in history, assisting to defend Jerusalem by slowing down the Assyrians in the eighth century B.C., the Babylonians in the sixth century B.C., the Greeks in the second century B.C., the Romans in the first century A.D., the Crusaders in the eleventh century A.D., the Ottomans in the sixteenth, and the Jordanians in the twentieth. Each force had looked to attack Jerusalem, and burned-out skeletons of Israeli tanks and vans still remained as memorials to the Israeli soldiers killed by Jordanian snipers who lined these mountain walls in 1948, during Israel's War of Independence.

"Can the Israel Antiquities Authority secure us safe passage beneath the Temple Mount?" Jonathan said.

Emili shook her head. "The best they can do is give us copies of the maps that Charles Warren and other British explorers used."

"Emili, those men came to Jerusalem in 1872," Jonathan said.

"They were the last to survey beneath the Temple Mount." Emili shrugged.

They made a turn around a mountainside, and there it was, the panoramic view of the Old City of Jerusalem suspended over the Valley of Kidron like a storybook image, the parapets of its stone walls laced with turrets like giant rooks from a chessboard. The enormous city walls, especially in the dawn light, looked transported from medieval legend, as they were still thick enough for ten archers to stand one behind another. Beneath the defensive walls, the lower ridges were terraced with vibrant rivers of wildflowers. When the grade of the road steepened, Yusef threw the diesel limo into second gear.

The car passed the whitewashed Monastery of the Dormition, where, according to most Christian traditions, the Last Supper was held, and now traced the circumference of the Old City's walls. Jonathan pointed at a curious site, where one of the monumental ancient gates to the Temple Mount had been blocked up with sixteenth-century stones.

"The Golden Gate," Emili explained. "It was walled up in the sixteenth century by Suleiman the Magnificent, who publicly dismissed all religions other than Islam but, after learning that it was prophesied in the Bible that the Messiah would one day enter through that gate, became secretly terrified and ordered his masons to brick it up. He even surrounded the arch with cemeteries, on the off chance that the Messiah would be from the priestly caste, whose members are forbidden by Jewish law to tread over human graves."

"A good way to cover your bets," Jonathan said.

As the car made its final ascent, along the narrow road above the Valley of Kidron, the road's shoulder gave way to a two-hundred-foot drop, and the dawn's morning mist created the momentary illusion that the Old City's walls presided over the edge of the earth.

"Here we are," Yusef said, slowing the car to a stop. "The Jaffa Gate."

Yusef had parked directly in front of a wonder of pure Turkish architecture, one of the city wall's oldest gates, its delicate stone turrets resting atop a pointed arch.

Jonathan stepped out of the car, and the mountain air of Jerusalem was unexpectedly cool. Jonathan followed Emili through the gate. An old taxi driver wearing a kaffiyeh watched them with curiosity, his idling taxi taking up the entire width of an ancient stone street. Emili thought of how even learning to drive in the center of Rome wouldn't prepare her for managing the Old City's labyrinth of streets.

A group of shops lined the interior of the gate, each inside its own shuttered stone archway. The Emmanuel Messianic Bookshop, the Franciscan Corner, Hali's Kabob. Above the shops was the Petra Hotel, its cracked beige stone and crooked wooden shutters looking as dilapidated as when Mark Twain described it during his stay in 1871.

They approached a dark stone fortress, built like a castle and surrounded by a grass moat. Its sloping stone façade and the turrets of its battlements dated back centuries, but the building looked as though it could survive another medieval siege, its walls still outfitted with slits for archers.

"We're going in *there*?"

"It's a museum," Emili said.

"The building looks older than the artifacts."

"It is," Emili said, smiling. "This citadel was built as the Tower of Phasael in Herodian times, then became a Roman temple to Jupiter in the third century, an Umayyad fortress in the seventh century, a Crusader camp in the eleventh century, Salah ad-Din's stronghold in the twelfth century, a Turkish mosque in the sixteenth century, and even a British social club in the 1920s."

"In other words," Jonathan replied dryly, "this museum belongs in a museum."

Emili led the way up the high stone steps of the citadel, reaching a thin wooden bridge that crossed a fifty-foot-deep moat, which at this hour was a well of darkness. The museum's front doors were two sleek frosted panels of glass inside a stone Gothic arch, an interesting fusion of modern and ancient architecture. Emili reached for the door's handle.

"Emili, it's not even six a.m. The museum *can't* be—"

The handle turned easily and the door pushed open.

"—um, open," Jonathan said.

"We're meeting my contact inside."

Inside the museum's entryway, Jonathan could make out the figure of a woman beneath the dim halogen lights of the stone foyer. As they drew near, he realized she was older than her athletic silhouette suggested. From her gray hair and creased face, he put her somewhere in her early sixties. In a relaxed pose, she leaned against the wall.

"Emili, what have you gotten yourself into?" Eilat Segev said.

58

Y ou wanted to see me, Comandante Profeta?" Lieutenant Rufio
said, standing in the threshold of Profeta's office.

"Yes," Profeta said. "We have an image of the male suspect from
the train station."

Profeta pushed a grainy surveillance image across his desk. It was
a photograph from inside the Colosseo metro station, a still of a
young man in a gray suit. The image caught the young man in profile, but his face was visible beneath his dark windblown hair. The
image to Lieutenant Rufio was clear: Jonathan Marcus.

"Does this man look familiar to you?"

"Yes," Lieutenant Rufio said reluctantly. "That's him, the one
from the Colosseum."

"The image is from a security camera above the platform," Profeta said. He stared at the subject of the photograph. Then Profeta
turned his gaze out the window, toward the dome of the Pantheon,
a block away. "He has escaped us three times now."

"Three times?" Rufio asked, hoping Profeta had not made the
identification yet. "Even if he was the suspect in the Colosseum,
that's twice, *Comandante*. Once in the Colosseum and once there in
the metro station. When was the third time?"

"When I sat across from him at the law firm of Dulling and
Pierce," Profeta said. "Jonathan Marcus. An American lawyer who
arrived in Rome last night at eleven-fifty p.m. and checked into the
Hotel Exedra at four-fourteen a.m."

He placed the black-and-white photograph of Jonathan Marcus
from the Dulling and Pierce website beside the surveillance shot.

"An American lawyer was involved in the Colosseum explosion?" Rufio asked, acting surprised.

"Not just any American lawyer," Profeta said. "Seven years ago, he was a Rome Prize winner here at the American Academy, conducting research on Flavius Josephus. It's all right here," Profeta said, handing Lieutenant Rufio a red file. Rufio knew the color codings of the files. Red indicated a prior arrest.

"He has a police record?" Rufio raised his eyebrows, his surprise now genuine. He opened the file and lifted a clipped Italian newspaper article. He read the headline aloud: "'Late-Night Excavation Takes Tragic Turn.'" Rufio flipped through the file's pages and looked up at the *comandante*.

"For trespassing?" Rufio asked, his eyes still in the file.

"He was lucky to escape without a charge of *omicidio*," Profeta said.

"Homicide?"

"It seems we've underestimated Mr. Marcus's knowledge of the ancient world," Profeta responded. "He brought three other graduate students to the outskirts of Rome, seeking a tomb of some kind. They climbed a fence onto the grounds of an abandoned eighteenth-century villa called the Villa Torlonia and roped into an ancient catacomb."

"According to the carabinieri investigators, they rappelled into the ruin at twelve-thirty a.m.," Rufio read from the file. "The ruins collapsed shortly after one a.m."

"Killing one of the graduate students," Profeta added factually. "A Roman native, Gianpaolo Narcusi, was pronounced dead on arrival at Rome's San Pietro Fatebenfratelli at one forty-one a.m.," Profeta continued from memory. "But more important for our purposes were the other two graduate students present that evening."

Lieutenant Rufio read aloud the first name, typed on the police report in courier print.

"Emili Travia, sir," Rufio said. "That's the UN official from the Colosseum."

Profeta nodded. "And the fourth graduate student?"

"I don't believe this," muttered Rufio. "'Member of the International Center and former fellow of the Palazzo Conservatori' . . ." Rufio looked up. "It was Sharif Lebag."

"But even more relevant to our investigation is not *who* joined him last night, but *where* they excavated."

Profeta handed Rufio another photograph of a crude excavation. A chain saw lay beside a sawed-open column.

"It's a photograph recovered from Professor Cianari's office earlier today. We suspect Cianari realized the importance of his discovery, and documented its location across the catacomb wall in spray paint."

"It's too dark to read."

"The quality is poor," Profeta agreed, handing another version to Rufio. "Copia's team managed to digitally lighten it."

In the zoomed image, the scrawled words became instantly legible.

"Villa Torlonia," Rufio said.

"That's right, Lieutenant, the column we discovered in the warehouse was found—"

"Precisely where Jonathan Marcus was illegally excavating seven years ago," Rufio completed.

"I don't know what research Mr. Marcus began seven years ago, but it looks like someone is trying to finish it."

Rufio stood up to leave.

"One more thing, Lieutenant."

"Yes, *Comandante*?"

"I'd like you to head up the manhunt for the suspect. Use whatever force is necessary to bring him here for questioning."

"Yes, sir," Rufio said honorifically. "Whatever force is necessary."

59

Eilat Segev led Emili and Jonathan into the ancient citadel's museum courtyard, still floodlit from the night before. They climbed a flight of outdoor metal stairs to the parapets of the Old City's wall. A gauzy morning mist settled along the bottom of an adjoining valley and the sun was still low over the Judean Hills' haze in the distance.

For Segev, the view was different. She remembered battling the Jordanians for control of this ancient citadel in 1967, before it was repurposed as a museum. On these high ancient walls, Jordanian snipers lay in wait between the parapets like medieval archers, hurling back Israeli battalions as they scaled the citadel at night. To this day, Segev watched families and their children on these ramparts. She watched them linger at picture points on the afternoon museum tours, secretly remembering all the men who gave their lives for that view.

Segev punched a code into a keypad in the stone and the lattice gate slid open silently. They entered a large hall, where models of ancient Jerusalem lined the corridors. The Solomonic period, tenth to the sixth century B.C.; the Second Temple period, sixth century B.C. to the first century A.D. Display cases contained silver coins from Hadrian's reign of Jerusalem; an ancient sword excavated from ruins near the Temple Mount. Along another wall of the foyer, stood a brass replica of Verrocchio's David, a gift by the city of Florence on the occasion of the Israeli recapture of the Old City from the Jordanians.

"Did you tell Comandante Profeta of our conversation?" Emili said.

"Of course not. I couldn't expect him to understand. I am not sure anyone in Europe, or the UN for that matter, understands the situation beneath the Temple Mount," Segev said. "Our infrared film taken from a helicopter above the Mount indicates there are bulldozers and dump trucks inside the Mount, raking the walls as we speak."

"But Israel is a UNESCO-compliant nation," Jonathan said. "Isn't there something that—"

"No." Segev slowly shook her head. "The Waqf Authority has claimed continuous jurisdiction over the Temple Mount for nearly eight hundred years. Well, the last eight hundred years, except for a couple of hours."

"A couple of *hours?*" Jonathan said.

"In 1967, we repelled an invasion by Jordan and captured East Jerusalem, including the Temple Mount, unifying Jerusalem for the first time in two thousand years. You can still see the bullet holes in the Zion Gate where we shot our way into the Old City. I remember the ranking colonel's voice crackling through the army wireless. 'The Temple Mount is in our hands! The Temple Mount is in our hands!' But within days, the military ceded sovereignty of the Mount back to the Waqf."

"Why return control of the Temple Mount to the Waqf?"

"Some historians say the Israeli politicians at the time were wary of the Mount's religious poignancy. They wanted to prevent ideas of messianic redemption from disrupting the building of a practical, modern society in East Jerusalem and the West Bank."

"So they let the Mount stay in the hands of the Waqf?" Jonathan said.

"Well, technically, the administration of the Mount was to return to the Jordanian king, who controlled the Mount nominally under Jordanian occupation before 1967. At that time the king delegated to the Waqf only the most ministerial tasks of its daily administration. But after the Oslo Peace Accords, the Palestinian Liberation Organization, under Yasser Arafat, tried to reinvent itself as more than a terrorist organization. In order to imitate an actual government and demonstrate some organizational capacity, Arafat encouraged some members within the Waqf to wrest control from the Jordanians. Even the Jordanians do not know the level of archaeological activity beneath the Mount for the last fifteen years. The Waqf has descended into a secrecy not known since Ottoman times. To this day, the Temple Mount remains an island of the Waqf's sovereignty, its funding routed through clandestine Saudi cultural groups and obscure corporate funds."

"The grand mufti's legacy continues." Emili shook her head. "And to think they are close to finding—"

"Emili," Segev said, "the Israel Antiquities Authority has spent years researching possible locations for artifacts from the Roman sack of Jerusalem. I just listened to your entire theory on the phone. There is no hard evidence that Flavius Josephus or any other historical figure managed to escape with the menorah of the Temple. After exhaustive research in France, the Israel Antiquities Authority decided to stop excavating for the relic."

"Why France?" Jonathan said.

"Carcassonne, to be exact. I was still in intelligence on foreign security at the time," Segev said. "In 1979, an Israeli secret service security detail was dispatched to Carcassonne, where myths had circulated for centuries that the menorah was buried. I suppose the premise is laughable, but from my own graduate work at Hebrew University I thought the location made sense. The Goths sacked Rome in A.D. 410, forty-five years *before* the more famous sack by Carthage. So it would have been the Goths who took the menorah, in which case the menorah would have followed the Goths to southern France—Carcassonne, to be exact. Golda Meir approved the project, but only if the operation could be done quietly enough, without Israeli taxpayers knowing the Mossad was chasing after legends." She shrugged. "Of course, their two weeks of investigations turned up nothing but local madmen and cheap relic shops playing up the mystery of buried treasure. The only remaining possible location, of course, is beneath the Temple Mount itself." Segev shook her head, crestfallen. "Which in this political climate makes it—"

"All the more important for us," Emili interrupted, "to find which convent in Jerusalem was described as the 'canonical convent' on the mural of the Roman synagogue. We need to see the model."

Emili and Jonathan followed Segev down a spiral stairwell into a storage area. Lights flicked on one after another, illuminating a damp vaulted cellar. In the middle of the room, a sprawling metallic model of a city spread thirty feet in each direction.

"The detail is remarkable," Jonathan said.

"It weighs more than a ton." Segev pointed at the model. "You should be able to find the convent here."

Find the convent? Jonathan leaned over. *You could find a nineteenth-century piece of litter on this thing.* Along the perimeter of the model, the outer Ottoman walls made a rectangle on the ridge along the Valley of Kidron. Inside the city walls, the model portrayed every street and alleyway, even the flags on the various monasteries as well as small crescents that stood on top of one of the Ottoman fortresses. Perched atop a high plateau overlooking the alleyways, the ruins of the Temple Mount were in a relative state of abandonment. The model portrayed the crumbling wooden dome of the Dome of the Rock as it was in 1873.

"These retaining walls built during the Roman era still support the Temple Mount platform," Segev said. With a red laser pointer, she indicated the Temple Mount area. "Each is roughly seventy feet of Herodian stone in height. Although it is a secret where this man Salah ad-Din bases his operations, we know the Waqf has renovated subterranean vaults in the cisterns along the northwest corner of the Mount here." Her laser pointer now moved along the northern wall of the Mount. "We believe the dump trucks come in through here, Bab el-Asbat, known as the Lion's Gate, which is not in view of any of the churches or synagogues of the Old City. When the trucks exit, they dump the archaeological finds in the Valley of Kidron, here"—her laser pointer circled an area in a valley hundreds of feet beneath the Old City's outer walls—"among this grove of olive trees." A copse of olive trees with their gnarled trunks was represented in the model with exquisite detail.

"They have hollowed out so much of the Temple Mount that this wall, here"—Emili pointed at a section of the southern wall of the model—"is in danger of collapse. For years, UNESCO teams have been working on stabilizing the wall from the outside. That is what first brought Sharif here as a visiting staff member."

Jonathan wandered around to the other side of the model.

"Emili!"

"What?"

"There is a cannon on top of this steeple." He pointed at a miniature stone convent half a foot along the model's scale from the Temple Mount. There was a shiny silver cannon above the domed convent roof.

"The Sisters of Zion Convent," Segev said. She could see Emili's plan beginning to materialize.

"Don't even think about it, please," Segev said maternally. "We cannot protect you inside the Mount. You are crossing into a place beyond our law. I will not even be able to say I have assisted you in getting inside."

60

Salah ad-Din moved through the tunnel as though blasting through the rock with each step.

"From this point," Salah ad-Din said, exhilarated, "the tunnel should have been sealed since the first century."

Unfortunately, Ramat thought, *it almost certainly has been.* He knew the earthquake of A.D. 363 closed off most of the passageways beneath the Mount, protecting many of its vaults from mystics, medieval souvenir hunters, and even the famed Templars. Ramat's guilt swelled. *Because of me, the first man walking through this aqueduct since the Roman era is no better than Titus.*

The tunnel was chipped from bedrock, not limestone, so there was little detritus. Salah ad-Din's men were running ribbed yellow hoses along the center of the tunnel to remove the dust.

The tunnel's ceiling grew higher, and with his flashlight Salah ad-Din illuminated Roman-era carvings of intricate biblical imagery and fantastical animals: a lion with wings and the talons of an eagle, a snake that walked like a man. As they passed, one of the men behind Salah ad-Din sprayed large red X's on each carving, identifying them to be destroyed.

Salah ad-Din led the team farther into the corridor. He rounded a corner and stopped. Dark and shaggy moss, thick as an ancient beard, coated a wall in front of him. He traced his flashlight's beam along the top of the ceiling, exposing a brightly patinaed metallic trim.

Salah ad-Din stepped carefully toward the moss, studying the ground's stones as he walked. Moving his arm slowly, he pulled a long knife from his waist and reached into the moss, his arm disappearing nearly to his shoulder. He reached something solid and tapped it with the point of the blade. It tinged with the sound of metal against metal.

"The hidden gate was a bronze gate, according to Josephus," Salah ad-Din rasped, out of breath. "This must be it."

"That door is three meters high," Ramat whispered, standing behind Salah ad-Din in awe. "It will take days to unhinge."

Salah ad-Din ignored him, taking in the size of the ancient structure with a clinical gaze.

"Evacuate all men from inside the Mount," he said. "Removing this door will require our largest blast." He turned to Ahmed. "Place the spices under the ticket counter in the Western Wall plaza by eight a.m." His eyes returned to the ancient bronze door. "The distraction must be simultaneous."

61

In East Jerusalem, Jonathan and Emili followed Segev through the Arab souk toward the Sisters of Zion Convent. Even at seven in the morning, the Old City market had an animal breath all its own. In its labyrinth of stone alleyways, an open-air butcher assaulted the carcasses of sheep and goats for the morning market. The butcher cautioned them to watch their step, pointing to stones slick with animal viscera. The only sound was his transistor radio, softly playing Iranian pop music.

Deeper into the souk, among the shuttered stalls nestled beneath intricately carved stone balconies, some booths already had a carnival atmosphere, where old men argued furiously over the day's first fruit deliveries stacked between the stone ramparts. Kaffiyehs and *tabus*, long dresses for men, dangled from the ceiling, and Jonathan and Emili pushed through them as through vines of a thick, disorienting jungle. Under a bare lightbulb, one shopkeeper took inventory of his goods before the morning market. Jonathan noticed him stacking framed pictures of Yasser Arafat, alongside T-shirts emblazoned with "My Bubby Loves the Kotel."

"Now, that vendor is diversified," Jonathan commented.

"Commerce doesn't have the luxury of intolerance," Emili said. She knew that some of the most successful illegal relic trading in the world was between Sunnis and Shiites who overlooked their religious differences to smuggle antiquities out of Iraq.

"Here it is," Jonathan said when they reached the façade of the Sisters of Zion Convent.

They knocked on the heavy oak door.

Silence, then the unlocking of a bolt. The door was opened cautiously.

Through the opening, a tall, thin woman appeared. From her mid-length blue dress, gray sweater, and flat white shoes, Emili knew she was a member of the Sisterhood of Zion, a Roman Catholic sect dating to the mid-nineteenth century. She appeared to be in her late forties, despite the youthful auburn hair that ran down her back.

"May we speak with the abbess?" Emili said in English. "I am afraid the matter is urgent."

"The abbess is unavailable at the moment," the woman replied in an Australian accent.

"But the matter is quite—"

"I am sorry. The convent is only open to visitors from the hours of—"

"We have information about an illegal excavation near your convent's basement," Emili said.

The door stopped just short of closing shut. "Excuse me?" said the woman.

Emili sensed her sudden interest. "An illegal excavation. It may pose a danger to the convent."

The woman opened the door wider, so that both her eyes appeared. Jonathan knew the two of them were not exactly an impressive sight. His sweat had made his shirt cling to his chest. Emili was still in a pair of blackened gray slacks, her silk blouse stained from the fire beneath the metro station in Rome.

"Come in," the woman said.

She led them down a long hallway with unpainted walls and chipped mahogany wainscoting. A corkboard displayed service schedules alongside a tacked-up postcard of a Raphael from the Vatican Museums.

They followed her into the convent's large lecture room, where she explained that the convent welcomed church groups from all over the world to view the *lithostrotos* in the basement.

"Pavement?" Jonathan said, translating the Greek. "They come from all over the world to see *pavement*?"

The sister smiled. "The *lithostrotos* beneath the convent are said to be the original first-century stones where Pontius Pilate held his infamous trial of Jesus. It has always been a place of quiet reflection." She looked away. "Until now."

"You have heard noises while down there?" Emili asked.

"For months," the sister said wearily. She managed to find their eyes briefly as she spoke.

"What sorts of noises?" she said.

"They sound like high-powered drills, and engines of large construction equipment."

"Construction equipment?"

"I raised the issue with Rome immediately," the sister said. "I received a letter in return, saying the land that surrounds this church belongs to the Muslim religious authority. I wrote back, suggesting the underground caverns adjacent to this monastery are beneath the Temple Mount, that it is the duty of all religions to protect it. I was told never to speak of the matter again." A mournful silence fell over her. "But I have never heard the drilling louder than . . ." She fell silent again, unsure how much to disclose.

"Louder than when, Sister?" Emili said.

The sister leaned in—"than last night."

62

Ahmed Hassan walked through the spice market's riot of noise and color, watching the vendors unload heavy sacks of black cumin, coriander, fennel, and curry from wheelbarrows. In the market's last booth, the vendor nodded as Ahmed approached, permitting him to inspect a sack of turmeric. Ahmed bent over and reached into the mounds of its bright ocher powder. He appeared to be testing the consistency of the spice, but inside the powder he felt three tubes containing red phosphorus mixed with nitrocellulose, a weapons-grade explosive. Ahmed tied and lifted the bag, his scrawny frame straining under the burlap sack's weight on his shoulder. The nitrocellulose did not increase the weight of the burlap sack substantially, although its explosive power was equal to that of two hundred pounds of TNT. Ahmed moved through the maze of Jerusalem's streets, past the Via Dolorosa, with its rows of shuttered Christian souvenir shops, and down Bab el-Hadid until he reached a small shawarma stand in the heart of the Muslim Quarter.

"We have been waiting for those spices!" said an old man, who sliced up a lamb outside his half-shuttered shop. He spoke loudly for the benefit of the Israeli surveillance that dotted the Muslim Quarter. Ahmed slipped into the shop and placed the sack of spices behind the counter, carefully removing the three vials of nitrocellulose. He opened a steel hatch in the shop's floor and the smell of animal carcasses wafted out with a dizzying force.

Ahmed climbed down through the hole into a stone-cooled grotto with skinned goat carcasses hanging from hooks on the wall. He immediately spotted the plastic bag, which contained the clothing Salah ad-Din had prepared for him.

Ahmed took off his madras and over his scrawny naked frame he carefully buttoned the white, Western-style shirt he removed from the bag. Next he put on tzitzit, the woolen fringes worn by Orthodox Jews, wrinkled black pants, and a black suit jacket, then clapped on a black velvet skullcap and above it an oversized, wide-brimmed black hat. Finally, he removed a stolen Hebrew prayer book, a *siddur*, from the bag, opened it, and neatly placed the vials of nitrocellulose where the pages had been cut out. Knowing the fragility of its explosive contents, Ahmed gently tucked the *siddur* in the inside jacket pocket of his suit and headed back up the stairs.

As he left the shawarma shop and walked down Bab el-Quattan, two Israeli soldiers waved him through an initial security checkpoint toward the Western Wall plaza. Ahmed's disguise as a thin-bearded Sephardic yeshiva student was so convincing that neither guard asked him a single question.

63

In the convent, Jonathan and Emili followed the sister into the chapel. They walked up to the altar and then behind it, where a thin steel chain hung between two short metal posts at the top of a spiral staircase. The sister unclipped the chain and led them down into the darkness.

"I heard the drilling while cleaning the *lithostrotos,* which I do every night in the basement."

The stone floor at the foot of the staircase was heavily marked by ancient graffiti. Drawings of concentric boxes were etched into the stones.

"What are these drawings?" Emili said.

"The Saturnalia games," she answered. "These stones were the floor of a Roman prison inside Antonia's fortress. The Romans were cruel captors and forced prisoners to play the 'Game of the King.'"

"The Game of the King?"

"Jewish prisoners were often mocked by Roman soldiers and guards. It was a game in which the Roman guards would make you king for a day or a week, and then crucify you. Why do you think the last images of Jesus show him with a crown of thorns? The Roman captors would transform the Jewish prisoners into mock royalty. Here"—she pointed to the floor—"some of our finest preserved inscriptions on Roman *lithostros* are etchings by the prisoners, forced to play the Game of the King on the day of their death." The boxes were filled with various astrological and pagan symbols.

"That's why our convent is so important for Christian pilgrims.

It is entirely possible that one of these stone etchings was done by Jesus himself. He was kept here, condemned by the Romans, along with other Jewish prisoners who were causing political trouble. That is why we lavish great care on the *lithostrotos*."

The stone floor led into a large, Roman-era chamber. Broken columns lined either side of the walls. The floor of the cavern was the original—Roman tiles with shiny gray enamel. The only light came from a tall solitary candle atop an altar in the center of the room.

"This is remarkable," Jonathan said, pointing into the darkness. "The bases of these columns are in the late Attic style, just as Josephus described." The scholar in him couldn't resist admiring their construction. "They are monolithic, and their capitals are carved with a Byzantine variation on the Corinthian style." He raised his flashlight's beam toward the cavernous ceiling.

"These arches are the support for the entire city. Jerusalem is literally a city built on stilts above vast valleys." The sister pointed to an enormous boulder. "There was so much debris from the Roman destruction in A.D. 70, the Romans simply built a new city over the rubble."

At the far end of the cavern, the basement's stone pavement ended with a large body of water. The white beam from Jonathan's flashlight stretched into blackness, not strong enough to illuminate the other side of the water.

"This water must flow beneath the Temple Mount," Emili said. "Was it an ancient cistern that serviced the fortress?"

"Not a cistern," the sister answered. "It was a moat that separated the ancient fortress from the Temple Mount."

"These waters lead directly to passages beneath the Mount?" Emili asked.

"In the early 1860s they did, and it was possible to raft across this water to the other side of the subterranean vaults. But in 1862 the

British expeditions of Charles Warren accidentally floated into this basement with a stick swaddled in kerosene. The nuns mistook him for a ghost, and they ordered a wall built to close off the water tunnels." She pointed at one of the archways above the black water. "But through that arch, there is rumored to be one tunnel that still leads into the vaults beneath the Mount."

"That tunnel?" Emili pointed to where the water stretched into the darkness beneath a large stone arch.

The sister nodded.

Emili walked toward a decrepit wooden rowboat, floating in the algae, its bottom caked with the sediment of the water's edge.

"May we borrow this?"

"Wait a minute," Jonathan said. His eyes edged over to the old small boat and then back at her. "You're not suggesting we go in that thing?"

"It's the only way, Jon." Emili flashed a pained smile. "We'll have to go beneath the Mount on this boat."

"Boat? Even if that thing was *ever* a boat," Jonathan protested, "it's now more like a *raft*. We don't even know if it floats!"

Emili turned to the sister. "Does it float?"

"I think so, but I wouldn't—"

"See?" Emili smiled at Jonathan. "It floats."

Without another word, she stepped inside the small wooden dinghy, crouching for balance.

Jonathan held up his index finger, trying desperately to come up with an argument to talk her out of this, but reluctantly stepped in behind her. The boat was wobbly on the water, and they gently guided it by pushing off the stone columns that emerged from the water's surface. Their weight in the small boat made it lie low in the water, scraping against some ancient rubble. After a minute, the water deepened and a slow current formed as they moved from the shore in the convent's basement into the darkness.

The ceiling, now higher than either of them would have imagined, was the underside of the street level. The daylight through the grates of the alleyway flickered on the water like moonlight.

The pace of the boat picked up in the dark current, knocking the dinghy against the walls of the tunnel.

The boat plummeted forward as though over a waterfall, reminding Jonathan of the stomach-drop feeling of a log ride. He instantly leaned back to shift the boat's weight. Just when Emili was nearly thrown over the boat's front end shot upward, hitting the water, and flinging her backward into Jonathan's lap. The boat righted itself, heaving back and forth, bobbing along a water channel between low stone embankments.

Jonathan steadied himself and leaned over the boat's edge. The beam of his flashlight descended into the blackness. As though floating through midair, the boat glided across an ancient aqueduct bridging an abyss.

The boat reached the other side of the aqueduct, running aground on the sandy floor of a narrow passageway. The eastern wall resembled a canyon's rock face, its jagged rust-colored stone vaulting upward. Facing the rock wall, on the corridor's other side, a manmade wall of enormous rectangular stone blocks rose to a dizzying height. Sunlight seeped through the blocks, casting pinpoints of light on the Temple Mount's original rock face.

"This giant retaining wall was built by Herod to extend the Temple beyond the edge of the mountain's rock face," Emili said, moving down the corridor. The sound of dried leaves rustled at their feet. Jonathan flashed his light down, and saw they were standing in an ankle-deep pile of dried-out paper scrolls.

"It must be the western fortifying wall," Emili said.

"How do you know?" Jonathan asked.

"For centuries, Jews have put written prayers between the stones of the Western Wall." She patted the stone blocks. "Before some crevices were reinforced, the scrolls must have pushed others further in until they wound up here, inside the Mount."

The corridor led away from the light, and the floor was covered in litter, soda cans, and plastic bags. Evidence of a dig site became clearer. Picks, crowbars, shovels, hand augers, and metal scrapers all lined the walls.

"Not exactly scientific instruments of excavation," Emili said, anger rising in her voice.

On the wall, a small inscription describing priestly duties glistened with a clear gel that had been recently applied. Jonathan leaned closer to the wall and lifted his hand to touch it.

"Don't!" she said. "It's a highly concentrated compound of hydrochloric acid."

"How do you—"

"The smell. It's a sulfur-based acid with vitriol. It's been used to dissolve stone since the Middle Ages." One more application of the chemical and the ancient inscription would be no more legible than any other crack in the jagged rock surface.

The strategic destruction became more apparent as they walked farther, past random piles of dirt, clay, silt, and topsoil, as though entering the mind of the Waqf Authority itself. Along one corridor, ancient painted pottery lay in pieces amid pickaxes and empty gallon jugs of solvents. A handsaw lay on top of a half-mutilated mosaic. The teeth of the saw were halfway through the sky-blue tiles that once illustrated what appeared to be a priestly service of some kind. Jonathan looked closely and saw blue enamel along the side of the pickax. Emili ran her fingers across what was left of medieval Templar emblems. Many of the tiles were already removed and thrown in a bucket.

Emili removed her digital camera and documented the destruction, photographing the crude equipment, the destroyed artifacts, the plastic gloves for handling destructive solvents.

"Do you hear that?" she said. The sound of drilling hummed faintly in the distance. "That way." She pointed down the corridor.

"Em, you have evidence now." Jonathan glanced at her camera. "I'm not sure we should go any furth—" But she was already charging down the corridor.

"You know, it's quite rude when you do that," he called out, following her.

The humming sound gained in volume and energy. The corridor led to an ornate flight of ancient stairs carved out of the rock wall.

At the top of the stairs, bright light seeped in around the edges of a modern steel door.

"What do you think is behind it?" Jonathan said.

"The Royal Cavern," Emili said. "It must be where they are excavating."

"The Royal Cavern mentioned in Josephus?" Jonathan said, an eyebrow up. "That supposedly stretched one thousand feet in diameter. That's nearly the width of the entire Mount. No one has seen it since antiquity."

"*Almost* no one. In the 1880s, some British explorers snuck in without the Ottoman overlords' knowing, and claimed to hold Masonic meetings inside there."

"And they are your scientific sources?"

"You have a point," Emili said.

They approached the door's hem of light. The stairs were narrow and steep, almost a stone ladder. Jonathan climbed first, leaning into the rock face to keep his balance.

Once at the top, he put his hand on the door's cold metal handle. The dark corridor they had just walked through, the steep stone staircase, the bright light from behind the metal door; it all seemed eerily like a posthumous vision.

One thousand feet in diameter, Jonathan thought, turning the knob. It must be a myth.

64

Ahmed Hassan straightened his black hat as he waited in line for the last security check before entering the Western Wall plaza. A large American synagogue tour stood in front of him, dozens of teenagers taking pictures with the Israeli soldiers as their colorful knapsacks moved through the X-ray machines. Amid the chaos, Ahmed stepped through the metal detector unnoticed. Now, standing on the other side, he watched the prayer book follow behind him on the X-ray belt, knowing that if it was mishandled, its contents would detonate.

"Where are you from, *habibi?*" asked a tall, thin Israeli policewoman about ten years older than Ahmed. His large brown eyes turned glassy, frozen with fear. *Why is she speaking Arabic to me? Habibi* was an Arabic word, meaning "my darling." But the policewoman's smile thawed Ahmed's nerves, reminding him that he had heard countless young Israelis adopt Arab words as endearing slang. The usage infuriated many of Ahmed's friends. *First they take our land and now our language.* But Ahmed enjoyed hearing these strangers speak his language. If only for a moment, Ahmed could understand them.

"From Yemen," Ahmed said, as instructed by Salah ad-Din. The immigration wave of religious Yemenite Jews to Jerusalem made Ahmed's answer to the policewoman not only believable, but common.

She swiped up the prayer book from the X-ray belt and held it loosely from its binding.

Ahmed began to sweat.

"One more question," the Israeli policewoman said.

The boy's wide, attentive eyes watched her.

"What is this week's *parasha*?" she asked, using the fast-track security check reserved for religious Jews who should know the weekly Torah reading.

Ahmed exhaled in relief, grateful that Salah ad-Din had prepared him for this singular question. Effortlessly, he pronounced two words of Hebrew, and the Israeli woman grinned. She handed him the prayer book and gestured toward the Western Wall.

"Pray for me," she said somewhat cynically before turning to the next tourist.

Ahmed nodded uncomprehendingly.

A department-wide investigation would eventually reprimand the policewoman for using a fast-track security question known to have been circulated by Hamas after a list of training questions from El Al security personnel had been stolen two months before. The investigation also reprimanded her for not picking up a number of clues that surfaced on the surveillance video. The clip to Ahmed's skullcap was too long, befitting a kaffiyeh clip. The woolen tzitzit had the washed-out pink stain of blood in the chest where a messy sewing job stitched together a tear in the fabric, roughly the width of a *shafra*, the serrated knife that had been used frequently in recent attacks on West Bank settlers.

Ahmed crossed the plaza and walked toward the ticket booth for the Western Wall Tunnel tour along the northern wall of the Western Wall plaza. Unexpectedly, the lights inside the booth were on and a teenage Russian girl wearing a cleaning uniform was wiping the windows from the inside. Without glancing up, Ahmed walked past her and around to the back of the booth. He took the vials of nitrocellulose from inside the prayer book, and noticed the adhesive side of the duct tape was so covered in jacket lint he was not certain they would stick. He bent down and pressed the tubes to the wall of the booth, careful not to shatter them. He unbuckled the cheap Casio watch from his wrist and opened the reverse side of the watch face, removing a coiled copper wire, which he wove between two of the vials.

He gingerly removed his hand and offered a brief prayer in gratitude that the duct tape adhered to the wall. He walked away from the booth in the direction of the Western Wall, as instructed, in case anyone was watching. After spending a minute at the wall feigning silent devotion amid a crowd of young men dressed identically to him, Ahmed walked out of the plaza.

65

The size of the cavern was no myth. The scale of the destruction raised the hair under Jonathan's collar. Emili stood next to him, frozen. The sprawling cavern was empty, but even in its silence, the dormant bulldozers, the dozens of wheelbarrows lying on their sides, and the large blue steel hull of a crane indicated its volume of daily activity. Multiple wooden platforms swung like primitive scaffolding from the giant cavern walls. On their planks, Jonathan could see chain saws beside buckets of potsherds and broken ancient glass.

"It's archaeological terrorism." Emili finally spoke.

Jonathan and Emili had stepped through the door onto a narrow aluminum walkway that circled high above the cavern's floor.

Jonathan said, pointing down at huge gashes that lined the circumference of the cavern's wall. "They have been trying to find the tunnel that Josephus used to escape Titus's troops."

"And I think they found it," Emili said, pointing at a newly excavated tunnel near the cavern floor. Beside the opening, blueprints lay strewn on a wooden table. Rubber blasting mats covered the mouth of the tunnel. Beneath the rubber, thick rows of yellow tubing extended outward, connecting to an industrial-sized floor fan.

"What's all that equipment?" Jonathan said.

"Those rubber mats over the arch are meant to suppress the spread of debris during an explosive blast. And those tubes are hydro-excavator vacuums. Those steel debris tanks at the end will vacuum up dust and pump fresh air into the tunnel within a half-minute of a detonation."

Two Arab men wearing UNESCO restoration jumpsuits rushed out of the arch and fastened the rubber mats to the side walls of the arch. Emili and Jonathan moved away from the ledge and back into the darkness. They watched the men rush to finish sealing the rubber mats around the sides of the mouth of the tunnel. They jogged up a wooden staircase of six flights to exit the cavern. One of the men began going back down, but the other yelled at him, pointing at his watch.

"Looks like they're in a hurry," Jonathan said.

"They just planted charges inside that tunnel. They are going to detonate."

66

Ramat Mansour removed his blindfold. He was alone, standing outside the Temple Mount's walls among the gnarled trunks of the Valley of Kidron's olive groves. His memories of the last two hours—the sensation of being rushed through corridors, squinting under the bright klieg lights of a massive excavation, uncovering a Temple-era door of solid bronze—seemed like a strange string of unconnected dreams. He had been known to sleepwalk, and he hoped the entire last two hours had been one unpleasant *hulum*.

But the small wooden carton at his feet was an unwelcome reminder it was not. The box label was for Lebanese strawberries, but Mansour could guess the carton's current contents. He lifted the top and in three neat stacks of crisp riyal notes was more Saudi Arabian currency than Ramat had ever seen. Each stack must have been a hundred bills thick, which at the local exchange rate would cover Ramat's rent for two years, not one. But instead of consoling him, the payment confirmed the frightening importance of what Ramat had done. He had led Salah ad-Din to the hidden gate described in Flavius Josephus. He pieced together in his mind what Salah ad-Din had told the teenager at that moment of its discovery.

Prepare the spices for eight a.m. . . . In the Western Wall plaza at the ticket counter. The distraction must be simultaneous.

Mansour stood up, now carrying the carton under his arm. He walked away from the Temple Mount, across a paved road, and down a gravel path into his hometown of Silwan. *Simultaneous,* Mansour thought. He stopped walking. That is how they plan to blast through the hidden gate. *A simultaneous explosion.* In his mind, he could see the boy Ahmed and remembered the missing portion of his lower ear. *A young bomb maker.* Slowly, Mansour realized how Salah ad-Din intended to excavate through the Bronze Gate: another detonation inside the Mount would require a second explosion as a diversion.

The Western Wall Tunnel's ticket counter, at eight a.m. Ramat remembered. He looked at his watch: 7:56 a.m. *Four minutes.*

Ramat Mansour ran back up the gravel path, jogging beneath the

Moghrabi Gate. Beyond the entrance to the Western Wall plaza and its bank of X-ray machines, he could see the ticket counter to the Western Wall Tunnel tour. Teenagers from a dozen nationalities leaned against it, sitting or lying on their knapsacks.

What have I done?

Mansour pulled out his pocket watch: 7:57 a.m.

With his adrenaline pumping, he ran through an unattended metal detector and sprinted across the plaza, yelling, *"Ashwik qun-bula!"* There is a bomb!

"Hafsik!" echoed the hollow electrical voice of a policeman's bullhorn behind him. And again in Arabic. *Halt or we will fire.*

Mansour stopped running.

The young Israeli policeman who chased Mansour into the plaza raised his gun. He heard the word *qunbula*. As part of his training, he knew a dozen Arabic words for "explosive," any of which were a license to fire in this political climate.

But when Mansour turned around he did not have the glazed look of a brainwashed Hamas teenager. In his right hand, he waved his Israeli passport, a coveted possession among the inhabitants of local Arab villages that entitled him and his family to full citizenship. *Why is he showing this?*

"A bomb will go off there in two minutes!" he screamed in Arabic, pointing twenty feet behind at the tourist gazebo.

Not understanding a word, the officer screamed back. "Open your coat!"

"There is a bomb there!" Mansour shouted again in Arabic, pointing across the plaza.

The policeman was squinting to identify a bomb belt stuffed with nails under Ramat's clothing. *If the bomber is confirmed, shoot to kill.* The no-warning tactic had saved dozens of lives outside street cafés of Ben Yehuda Street and shopping malls of Tel Aviv.

But something told the policeman not to fire.

"Translator!" the policeman yelled across the plaza, his gun still pointed at Mansour's head. "I need a translator now!"

Fifty feet above them, Salah ad-Din watched the commotion in the center of the plaza. He stood behind a tinted window built into a medieval arrow slit along the southern end of the Mount's western wall. The room was an administrative office of the Islamic museum, but its view over the plaza would allow Salah ad-Din to see the detonation of the tourist gazebo. He watched Ramat flail his arms to communicate with the Israeli policeman.

Salah ad-Din looked at his watch. One minute left. *Too much time.* If the police stopped the explosives beneath the ticket counter, the detonation beneath the Temple Mount would resonate for half a mile. An international incident. Salah ad-Din could not let that happen. *Cousin, you have done this to yourself.*

He stepped away from the window and nodded to a short, fat man wearing a green argyle sweater. From a Styrofoam-lined suitcase, the man removed a long black 7.62-mm Dragunov sniper rifle with a black steel butt assembly and digital optics. As relaxed as if he were cracking the window for fresh air, the short man rested the rifle's black suppressor and front sight base on the deep stone sill. He sharpened the telescope's viewfinder and wrote a mathematical equation on a small notepad to calculate windage and elevation variables. He adjusted the magnification from 3X to 9X, and in the crosshairs of the optic sight he was able to see the birthmark on Ramat's neck.

The police officer watched Ramat. "What are you trying to tell me!" he yelled. "Is there is a bomb in the plaza?"

Ramat nodded, yelling in Arabic, stabbing the air with his index finger in the direction of the tourist ticket counter.

"There, near the tourist gazebo?"

With so little warning that the officer thought for a moment it was an accident from his own gun, a bullet exploded through Mansour's neck. Mansour gripped the bloody aperture with both hands, his eyes wide with terror, gasping through the new hole in his neck. Blood spurted out with a horrific gargling sound as his reflexes tried to gulp in air.

The officer knew immediately what had happened. "*Tzalaf!*" he yelled. Sniper!

Collapsing to his knees, Mansour found the officer kneeling next to him, putting additional pressure around his throat. But Ramat still managed to point violently at the tourist gazebo. The officer sprinted toward the gazebo, screaming at the tourists to evacuate the entire northern end of the plaza. Dozens of teenagers fled, leaving their belongings.

The officer ran back to Ramat, again pressing hands over his neck. *We are too close to the ticket counter*, Ramat's eyes said.

"Go," he gurgled softly. "Please." His pocket watch lay open in his hand: 8:00 a.m.

Ramat lay alone now in the evacuated plaza. Inside the gazebo, a white light burst like a filament, its windows lit like a giant lantern, as the metal bent outward and the structure distorted and expanded, as did the last moment of Ramat's life. A sea of shattered glass oozed forward, washing over him like a glistening wave, and he closed his eyes to a final vision of holding his son in the Gaza surf.

67

Emili and Jonathan moved along the narrow walkway in the brightly lit cavern, hugging their backs to the rock wall. Jonathan looked down. It must have been a drop of five stories to the cavern floor.

Emili was photographing the site.

"Kodak moment's over, Em. You've got pictures for the World Heritage Committee meeting," Jonathan said. "Now let's get out of—" But the sudden sound of shouted Arabic interrupted him.

At the other end of the walkway, a middle-aged Waqf guard shouted at them, pointing his Kalashnikov rifle directly at Jonathan.

"What's he saying?" Jonathan said.

"You are a trespassing dog," Emili said.

"The gist would have been enough," Jonathan said, slowly raising his hands.

A low, thunderous rumble began shaking the cavern walls. Dirt sifted down from the high ceiling.

"They've detonated," Emili said.

The tremor intensified, and the guard lowered his gun to grab the railing. Emili and Jonathan exchanged glances, wondering if the scaffolding was sturdy enough to handle the vibrations. *Is the Mount even sturdy enough?* Emili wondered. She knew that in the past earthquakes had swallowed tunnels and large caverns beneath the Temple Mount, and that the Israel Antiquities Authority had publicly warned that the ongoing illicit excavation could weaken the Mount structurally to the point where a minor tremor could cave in the entire Mount, swallowing the Dome of the Rock whole.

Beneath them, a cloud of debris and powdered limestone burst forth from the tunnel's mouth. The rubber mat failed to hold, and flew into the cavern. A rolling fog of dust followed, carpeting the floor, and reaching as high as the oversized wheels of the bulldozers. The industrial fans pushed the cloud upward in a plume.

The guard raised his gun and fidgeted with his two-way radio, screaming in rapid Arabic.

"Can you still see the stairs?" Jonathan asked quietly. He glanced at the six flights of wooden stairs that led down to the cavern floor from the scaffolding.

"Jon," Emili whispered, unable to move her eyes from the Waqf guard's Kalashnikov, "that man has a gun pointed directly at you."

"In a moment he won't be able to see us," Jonathan said. The dust cloud from the blast quickly rose toward them. Already, Emili could barely see her own shoes. "Those fans are pushing the dust up here. The bottom of the cavern is already clear. We can get to the tunnel."

"And if the painting in Rome was right," Emili said, coughing, "that tunnel—"

"Will lead us straight to the pool of Silwan outside the city walls," Jonathan said. "The same route Josephus took two thousand years ago."

The man holding the Kalashnikov was now no more than a shape in the dust cloud.

"Let's go," Jonathan said above the guard's yelling. "Take a deep breath, Emili."

If I can, she thought, already wheezing.

They quickly moved around the aluminum walkway, and Jonathan placed Emili's hand on the pipe railing. They switched back and forth on the stair landings until reaching the cavern floor.

Jonathan's lungs were nearly depleted of air, and he swallowed to keep holding his breath. He knew Emili was running out of air, too. He could feel her grip weaken as he led her around the yellow hull of heavy machinery. Jonathan followed the sound of the vacuum generators, and just as he considered turning around, the dust began to clear, until it dissipated completely.

They breathed deeply inside the tunnel, hurrying past intricate Assyrian-era inscriptions that covered the walls. It pained Emili to rush past them; she knew this was a once-in-a-lifetime opportunity to see original First Temple–era inscriptions inside the Mount. Farther into the tunnel, the walls were jagged from the recent detonation, and the corridor smelled like burned rock.

"And that's why they detonated here," Jonathan said. He pointed at the massive bronze gate that had been blown off its hinges and was now lodged diagonally between the walls. Ducking beneath it, Emili's fury at the destruction alternated with wonder as she took in the gate's size and workmanship.

Emerging from beneath the gate, they saw elaborate reliefs covering the walls. The wall carvings portrayed open palms with fingers partially spread.

"It's the insignia of the priestly blessing," Emili said. "The *kohanim* used this corridor."

They walked in silence, reminded not only of the sacredness of where they stood, but of the possibility of their imminent discovery. With each step, the reality grew closer. Jonathan's adrenaline caused a momentary loss of skepticism. *Could this have been where the priests hid the tabernacle menorah?*

The next room was round and not large, twenty feet in diameter with a vaulted ceiling. The explosion shattered the room's pilasters, but even the rubble indicated how ornate the walls had been.

"This was an underground sanctuary," Emili said. "Judging from the designs, it was dug during the First Temple period in the eighth century B.C."

"And seven hundred years later, during the Second Temple, the priests probably used it as a hidden vault."

In the center of the room, three high steps were carved into a solid block of Jerusalem stone, leading to a flat, empty platform that gave Jonathan the impression that a large object once stood on it.

Three steps, Jonathan thought, remembering what Chandler said. *The high priest ascended three steps to reach the menorah's lamps.*

"They hid the menorah here during the siege," Jonathan said awestruck. He pointed at the ceiling darkened from smoke. "And tended its flame here."

Jonathan trained his flashlight on the top step as he walked toward it. "There's an inscription."

A CAPTIVO AD OSTIA ROMAE

יוסף

"From captive to mouth of Rome," he translated, "and it's followed by a name in Hebrew *Yoseph*, which, since the recent addition of the letter *j* to the Latin alphabet in the sixteenth century, is—"

"Joseph," Emili said, "as in Josephus."

Jonathan nodded. "His name was still Joseph at the time of the Temple's destruction. He changed it to Josephus only after he received Roman citizenship, after the war."

"But Joseph wasn't a rare name in Jerusalem in the first century," Emili said.

"How do we know this was the person who became Josephus?"

"Because Josephus has all but written his autobiography in these five words. 'From captive to the mouth of Rome.' One moment Josephus is captured and imprisoned, and the next he's the top negotiator for the Roman Empire."

"He *negotiated* for Rome?"

"His autobiography described his attempts to represent Titus in making a treaty with Jerusalem. The military leaders in Jerusalem agreed to send a diplomat equal in stature to Josephus. When Josephus waited outside the gates of Jerusalem to receive him," Jonathan paused, "they released a pig."

Emili smiled. "I'm guessing those negotiations didn't go very well."

"Nor did Josephus expect them to—at least secretly. But his public face to the world was as Rome's negotiator. Literally, 'the mouthpiece of Rome.'"

"But let me guess, knowing you, there's another meaning here."

"That predictable, huh?" Jonathan grinned. "It's true, I don't think Josephus is giving us his résumé just to identify himself. He could have done that in other ways. I think he's identifying a location, telling us where he smuggled the menorah next."

Emili stared at the phrase and suddenly lit up. "Ostia," she said. "It's a geographical marker. Not *ostium* as in the word 'mouth.' This is a reference to Ostia, the ancient harbor of Rome! The port was called Ostia, named for its location where the mouth of Rome's Tiber River flowed into the Mediterranean Sea."

"And '*captivoe*' doesn't refer to Josephus only as captive but to the relic. To the menorah," Jonathan said. "The menorah was surrounded, a captive, until someone smuggled it not just out of the Mount, but out of Jerusalem entirely."

"To the port of Rome," Emili said, her eyes widening at the sheer scope of the ancient operation.

"Josephus knew that only a priest could tend the flame in exile," Jonathan said, just as stunned by their discovery. "He had to bring it with him."

68

Along the Via Nomentana, Profeta stood in view of the skeleton of the Villa Torlonia. The carabinieri cars behind him idled in front of the high gates of what seemed an abandoned, overgrown park. The dark mansion was faintly visible in the morning fog. Rufio stood beside him, staring into the grounds. Weeds had overtaken the formal gardens that surrounded the abandoned, ramshackle villa.

"According to the police report," Lieutenant Brandisi said, "Jonathan Marcus was excavating over there seven years ago." He pointed near the villa.

"Looks haunted," Rufio said.

"It is," Profeta said. "By political ghosts, at the very least. Mussolini commandeered the villa as his private residence, and during the German occupation, the SS officers took up residence there in 1943."

"Not exactly owners to brag about," Brandisi said.

"It explains why the city let the villa fall into disrepair. Rome is still selective about what parts of its past it chooses to preserve."

"Where are the tombs, *Comandante?*"

"All around us. Eight miles of catacombs are buried under here."

"*Eight miles?*" Brandisi said.

"The areas outside ancient Rome were giant cities of the dead," Profeta said. "Eventually, palazzos and embassies were built over them."

A security guard opened the villa's gate.

"*Comandante,* maybe we're wasting time," Rufio said. "Why are we here?"

Brandisi's walkie-talkie came to life. "An officer just located some excavation at the foot of the villa," he told Profeta.

They approached the excavation, walking through abandoned gardens that resembled the dark wood of a fairy tale. Black moss covered the villa's pathway. A white tomb no higher than an altar protruded from the ground. One of the tomb's marble walls was missing.

"Look at this," Brandisi said, shining his flashlight to the right. A two-foot trench had been dug alongside the tomb, where a heavily rusted pipe had been extracted from the earth, revealing a broken pipe joint.

"It could have been a utility crew fixing a gas leak," Rufio suggested.

"Not a utility crew, Lieutenant." Profeta knelt in the grass. "Someone applied an acidic compound to the tombstone to make it illegible."

Profeta shone his flashlight into the tomb. He immediately recognized the inside chamber from the photographs taken by Professor Cianari. Missing from the center of the chamber was the column containing the woman they had found in the warehouse the night before. The top half of the column lay in the cavern, cut into small pieces.

"So this is where they found her," Profeta said, his voice echoing in the chamber.

"Her?"

"The woman we discovered in the warehouse," Profeta said. He pointed to a faint marble inscription that had been partially rubbed out: "*Sepulcrus Berenice Regina*." Princess Berenice's Tomb.

"Her name explains the extravagant burial. She was Berenice, the last princess of Jerusalem."

As Profeta stepped back from the tomb, he saw a piece of evidence

he did not expect to find. Lying in the wet grass was a small un-
bleached piece of paper, doused from days of rain.

Cigarette rolling paper.

Without Lieutenant Rufio's noticing, Profeta put it in his
pocket.

69

Emili heard the sound of feet scraping down the corridor. "That
guard isn't far behind."

Above the shouting, the sound of bullets now clamored against
the rock walls.

"Let's go," Jonathan said.

But even as they ran, Emili could not help marveling how this
tunnel confirmed the biblical story of Hezekiah's mysterious water
source during the Assyrian siege. *It will only be a matter of time before
Salah ad-Din destroys this, too,* she thought.

"Can you hear that?" Jonathan asked, close behind her.

"I know, the guards are getting closer," Emili said.

"I mean the water," Jonathan said. They both stopped. The sound
of an underground stream was unmistakable. "We must be close to
a water source." He shone his flashlight in front of them.

The corridor extended for another few inches. Emili had been so
close to the edge that one of her shoes stuck out into the blackness.

Beyond the edge of the tunnel, Jonathan's flashlight revealed a
strange forest of white vines descending from above.

"They're the roots of the olive trees in the valley above," Emili said. "Some of those trees are over a thousand years old."

The bouncing beams of the guards' flashlights were now visible behind them.

"These roots must have followed the water level of the stream as it lowered over the centuries," he said. "We can use them to rappel down to the stream, using the rock wall."

"*Rappel down?*" Emili said. "Those roots will never hold us."

A gun shot whizzed past them.

"Okay, you first," Emili said.

Jonathan reached for the olive tree's roots, but they were too far from the tunnel's edge. He jumped and clutched a lacy tangle of roots as he swung between the walls of the shaft. The roots were surprisingly dry and brittle, and he could feel the strain of his weight on them. But they were strong enough to hold. He slid down the roots a half-foot and found a crook in the rock wall to rest the weight of his legs.

"Now you!" he called to Emili. "Jump above me!"

Emili threw herself toward the roots. With both hands she grabbed the same shoot Jonathan had, and rested her feet on Jonathan's shoulders.

"Don't move," Jonathan whispered. "They're right above us."

They could hear the rushing water below; above them the guards' flashlights were only a few feet away. The guards were now yelling, blaming each other for choosing the wrong tunnel.

Jonathan and Emili remained still, hanging in the darkness. The only sound was the crackling of the olive tree's roots, withstanding the strain of both their weights—for the moment.

"It's not holding." Emili's frightened whisper was barely audible. Some of the roots snapped, lowering them a few unnerving inches before they stopped. The Waqf guards stood at the edge of the precipice, their beams searching the darkness, but not below the tunnel's edge where Jonathan and Emili swung from the roots.

Jonathan could hear the roots beginning to crack. He looked up. They were now hanging from a single, unraveling shoot.

One of the guards must have heard the sound because he shone his flashlight over the edge and exposed them hanging there. But there was no time for the guard to react.

The root snapped, the sound as sharp as a breaking stick. And like deadweight, their bodies fell, twisting, into the chasm.

70

Within seconds of the blast in the Western Wall plaza, a black armored Volkswagen with tinted windows and Palestinian plates slowed to a stop in front of the Damascus Gate. A young bearded mullah jumped out and opened the Mercedes' polyethylene-reinforced steel door. Salah ad-Din ducked into the backseat, which was outfitted with a customized ViaSat satellite terminal for streaming data and a satellite phone the size of an early-model, large cellular. Salah ad-Din turned his attention to the screen, where he received a live streaming feed from a video camera inside the tunnel's blast site.

The Israeli police was already setting up parameters around the Old City—standard procedure after a terrorist bombing—and Salah ad-Din's immediate departure was a necessary precaution.

Ostia, Salah ad-Din thought.

The car traveled toward the Gaza border, and Salah ad-Din held a mobile phone in one hand and his grandfather's lifetime of notes in a tattered leather book in the other. If the grand mufti only knew the critical information his grandson had just discovered, his wonderment would be rivaled only by the technology that streamed information to the computer screen in front of him.

"Keep searching for other inscriptions," Salah ad-Din said. "We must be sure it is in Ostia."

On the screen Salah ad-Din could make out the craggy limestone walls of the vault lit by the purple floodlight. The hidden gate came into view, blown diagonally across the corridor's walls.

"We are still in the circular room, Sheikh," said a voice behind the camera. He tilted the camera up to show the vault. A large block of stone sat below the center of the vault. Stairs had been carved into the stone. "It is the only inscription in the room."

"Show it again."

The camera bore down on the stone, and the inscription came into view, but the light directly on the smooth limestone created a glare that made it illegible on the screen.

"Dim the floodlight," Salah ad-Din said evenly, but there was anticipation in his voice.

As the light softened, the inscription came into sharp view, just as he had seen it himself a minute before.

A Captivo ad Ostia Romae.

So the menorah is not beneath Jerusalem. Salah ad-Din had suspected the ingenious nature of Josephus's plan for years, and calculated accordingly.

Salah ad-Din dialed the number of his exchange server in Paris, which connected him through to a cell phone in Rome.

The other line answered and Salah ad-Din uttered one word.

"Ostia," he spoke into his satellite phone.

"You saw the inscription? You are certain?" a nervous female voice said.

"Yes, it is in Ostia. When will the plane arrive?"

"Forty minutes. The Gaza border, just as you arranged."

"I must excavate today. I require maps immediately."

"Ostia spans three miles," the voice said. "How will you know where to dig?"

"Josephus disclosed the menorah's location in a line of text."

"But to see the Renaissance manuscripts of Josephus, you will require access to the Sala Consultazione Manoscritti in the Vatican Library."

"The information I need is not in the Vatican Library," Salah ad-Din said. "It is in the archives of the Great Synagogue in Rome."

71

Jonathan tumbled through twenty feet of black air before splashing feet-first into a thick bed of pond scum. The algae nearly immobilized his arms, but his legs moved more freely, treading in the water. A slim curtain of daylight illuminated the cavern through a crevasse.

"Emili!" Jonathan yelled.

A hand tightly gripped his arm and he whirled around. Emili surfaced beside him, her face covered in thick ropes of pond scum.

"So the roots will hold us, huh?" Emili slowly shook her head.

He wiped a piece of algae off her cheek. "You okay?"

"*Okay?* A crazed man with a Kalashnikov is thirty feet above us, and I don't see a way out of here. 'Okay' would be an exaggeration."

They waded through the sludge and climbed onto a narrow rock bank at the far end of the cavern. Emili slipped, knocking a stone from the bank into the water.

"Maybe if we could climb up these roots—" Jonathan began, and then stopped, staring at the stone that had just rolled into the water. It had broken through the pond scum. The water was a radiant blue, as though illuminated from beneath.

Jonathan stared at the water, transfixed. "Why is the water glowing?"

"What are you talking about? It can't be glo—" Emili looked down.

An incandescent blue glow emanated in the shape of the rock that had broken through the algae. It looked like an expensively lit resort pool.

Jonathan cleared more of the surface. The whole pond was a vivid, electric blue.

"Why is it that color?"

"There must be an opening under the water, allowing light to flood through." Jonathan turned to Emili. "We'll have to swim through it."

Jonathan rolled up his soaking sleeves for greater ease in the water. Emili grabbed his arm.

"Jon, we don't even know where it goes!"

There was a sudden splash behind them.

"The Waqf guards are lowering ropes," Jonathan said. The shouts in Arabic grew louder, and guns banged against the rock face.

Emili looked uneasily at the water.

"*Al tre si parte?*" she said. Count of three, then?

Jonathan nodded. "Deep breath. Follow me to the bottom."

"One."

A flashlight panned across the water and held them in its beam. They heard the triumphant shout of a Waqf guard.

"Two," Emili said, squeezing Jonathan's hand. Their gazes turned to the black water. "Three!"

They both dived in, and swam toward the light, kicking deeper into the water's enveloping peace. The sloshing of the Waqf guards above them sounded miles away. The light under the water grew brighter, moving from a purple bruise to a pastel cloud as the pressure in their ears mounted. Near the floor of the pond they could see a rock hollow, a glowing circle just large enough to swim through. Emili went first, propelling herself into the blue light. Jonathan's dress shirt floated around him as he moved through the hole after her, taking giant breast strokes upward. On all sides of them, high-tech underwater tube-lighting came into view.

72

A tour group of visiting Southern Baptists from the Valley of Souls Congregation in Hillsboro, West Virginia, stared at the peaceful subterranean pool of water before returning to their air-conditioned bus parked outside the Hezekiah Tunnel tour. After a moment of silent prayer, Pastor Josiah Briggens, the group's animated preacher, led them in a reading from Psalms in the dark tunnel by candlelight. The congregation was hushed with awe, gazing at the underground spring, where according to Gospel, Jesus cured the blind. The reverend boomed Psalm 91 in a thick West Virginia twang.

"And let us learn from these peaceful waters," he said. His congregants looked devoutly at the electric blue water, standing at the farthest point permitted for tour groups inside the ancient tunnel.

"That these waters," the reverend cried out, "should spread their calm over Israel, that their stillness will—"

As if on cue, the still surface of the water shattered like glass.

Jonathan and Emili broke through, splashing wildly, gasping for air.

The Valley of Souls members were stunned. Many screamed as others fell to their knees, crying out, "Hallelujah, father!"

Jonathan and Emili swam to the shore.

"Sweet Mary and Joseph!" the preacher screamed.

Jonathan smiled politely.

"Well, not exactly."

73

The tunnel to Gaza is still open?" Salah ad-Din asked the driver. He knew that recent Israeli incursions had discovered many of the tunnels his men had used for years to cross beneath the Gaza–Israel border.

"Yes, Sheikh," the driver, a young mullah, said. He pulled the car onto the shoulder of the road beside an abandoned roadside fruit stand. Now boarded up, the stand's faded Arabic sign for fresh pomegranates flapped in the desert wind. The driver looked at an illuminated grid of a palm-held global positioning device to confirm their location. He turned around and nodded solemnly to Salah ad-Din.

This was the location where Salah ad-Din had to cross through a system of tunnels to reach Gaza. On the other side, a plane would transport him to Rome.

The fruit stand was one hundred meters from the first of a series of triple barbed-wire fences between there and the Gaza Strip.

The mullah removed an old pistol from beneath the driver's seat. He stepped out of the car and walked toward the fruit stand. He returned a moment later and opened the sedan's rear door.

"The tunnel is secure, Sheikh," he said in Arabic.

Salah ad-Din approached the fruit stand. He pulled one of the pine-board side panels loose and stepped into the booth. Bending down, he lifted part of the floor to reveal the opening of an arms smuggler's tunnel. He slipped into the tunnel, moving the board back into place above him. The air in the tunnel was thick, smelling of wet cement.

Salah ad-Din felt his way through the tunnel's darkness. It was a good, tall tunnel, and he ducked only slightly as he walked. Arms dealers dug the best tunnels between Gaza and Israel, he knew. Passing under the high stone cement wall that separated Gaza from Israel, he could hear the Hebrew chatter of Israeli soldiers on border patrol above him.

The tunnel's exit was another two hundred meters inside the Gaza Strip.

Salah ad-Din reached the end and climbed a ladder up into another roadside shack. As he emerged, he saw an old-model BMW waiting for him, its white paint peeling, headlights dimmed by the swirling gales of sand. Salah ad-Din climbed into the backseat.

The car headed south until it reached the Gaza border with Egypt. Salah ad-Din got out of the car and slid through a sawed opening in the electrified border fence. On the other side, he walked across an abandoned stretch of broken asphalt, where he could see the tail of a midnight-blue Cessna Citation X with Egyptian military clearance.

Salah ad-Din chose this particular plane from an Iranian sheikh's wide collection, not only because its dual hydraulic engines made it the fastest civilian aircraft in the world, but because its flying altitude of 51,000 feet made it imperceptible on most radars. The Cessna had nearly turned around before landing here, because of the windstorm that now transformed the desert air into a thick orange haze in all directions.

As Salah ad-Din walked toward the plane, the wind felt solid and he covered his face with his sleeve. A man in a tightly wrapped kaffiyeh escorted him up the aluminum steps to the plane.

"Less than three hours until we arrive in Rome, Sheikh," he said loudly in the wind. "The team has already begun in Ostia."

74

Inside the Rockefeller Museum, Jonathan and Emili waited in Eilat Segev's office. They wore white jumpsuits that Segev supplied from the conservationist laboratory while their clothing machine-dried in the basement. Segev forced them to have some hot tea as she brought out an archaeological map of Ostia from the museum's library and unrolled it across her desk.

"If you're right, think of the sheer planning required for Josephus to smuggle something the menorah's size to Rome," Segev said. Ever the intelligence tactician at heart, she could not help but admire the scale of the ancient logistical effort.

"Josephus wrote in his histories that he survived a shipwreck," Jonathan said. "The cargo was supposedly lost, but—"

"—but that might have been the perfect cover to move its cargo to the port outside Rome," Segev finished.

"But if the menorah is in Rome, then why would Josephus make someone go to Jerusalem to find that out?" Emili interjected. After the second century, Jews could not even step foot in Roman-occupied Jerusalem.

"And that's the brilliance of Josephus's plan," Jonathan said. He stood up from his chair and paced, just as Emili remembered him doing in the academy library. "By revealing the menorah's final location beneath the Mount, Josephus tried to ensure that his descendants would have regained sovereignty over Jerusalem. The menorah, once discovered, could be restored immediately to its ceremonial purpose. But if his descendants discovered the menorah while still exiled in Rome, they would have no sanctuary to put it in. Remember, we're talking about eight feet of solid gold here. Greed would endanger the lamp just as much as the Roman siege did."

"And the one place Josephus knew he could get the menorah to was Ostia," Emili said. "That's the port where all the Roman ships returned after Jerusalem's conquest."

Emili tented over the map on Segev's desk. *Ostia,* she thought, *of all places*. She knew the drama of Ostia's rediscovery in the nineteenth century. Under dozens of feet of mud and silt, archaeologists found its paved streets, mosaic-tiled baths, and frescoed taverns at a level of preservation that rivaled Pompeii's.

"Have your Israeli teams done any work in Ostia?" Emili asked Segev.

Segev glanced up at a photograph of herself in army uniform that hung above her desk. "Not any archaeological work, anyway."

"What do you mean?"

"In the early 1970s, the modern city of Ostia harbored local Palestinian terrorists, because of its proximity to Fiumicino airport. In October 1973, Mossad agents arrested five Palestinians in their apartment in Ostia. Two Russian SA-7 missiles and an El Al flight schedule were in the closet."

Jonathan looked up from the map.

"You are not going to believe this," he said, angling the archaeological sketch of Ostia toward Emili and Segev. He pointed along the central line of the town. "Here is the Decumanus, or main thoroughfare. It branches off to a diagonal road, to this small building." He pointed at the words written in Italian inside it. *Sinagoga Antica*.

"That's right, I should have remembered," Segev said. "Outside of Israel, the ruins of Ostia contain the oldest standing synagogue in the world."

"That's not even the strange part. Look here, next to the synagogue, at the small neighboring structure. It's got a most unusual name."

"Domus Fulminata," Segev read haltingly.

"House of Divine Fire," Jonathan said. "*Fulmen* means 'lightning,' or any kind of fire sent by the gods."

"So it was a pagan temple, then," Emili said.

"Except that the orientation is east, and pagan temples often faced westward. And most important, a synagogue never would have been built so close unless—"

"Divine Fire had a different meaning," Emili said. "Like a place of safekeeping for a sacred vessel of fire."

Emili sat back in her chair. "It's brilliant," she said.

"Yes it was," Jonathan smiled. "What better disguise was there to keep the menorah from Titus's secret police than to give its sanctuary a pagan name?"

75

Lieutenant Brandisi cautiously stepped into Profeta's office, holding a stack of manila folders under one arm.

"*Comandante?*"

"Yes, Brandisi?" Profeta asked, not looking up.

"The staff at the Colosseum just couriered over the files we requested. They're mainly carbon copies of each *permesso* signed by the archaeological superintendent, allowing archaeologists and construction crews access to the substructure of the Colosseum."

"Construction crews?"

"The United Nations' annual World Heritage Committee meeting has scheduled its opening ceremony tomorrow inside the Colosseum."

"Yes, I saw the scaffolding for the performances."

"Scaffolding for which the crews were granted access to the *northern* end of the Colosseum," Brandisi added. "I called the International Center for Conservation. Director Olivier's office confirmed that to minimize strain on the structure, the ceremony will take place only in the northern section of the Colosseum's oval. That's the part closer to the Via del Colosseo. But it appears some personnel made repeated trips to the *southern* section of the Colosseum's oval where there was no scaffolding."

"Near the corridor we discovered this morning," Profeta said, in anticipation.

"To the exact corridor, *Comandante*," Brandisi said. "There were personnel entering the ruin through precisely the same arch that we saw Dr. Emili Travia enter on the surveillance camera."

"You're suggesting that the ceremony's preparation has provided a cover to access the illegal excavations we discovered?" Profeta put down his pen. "Have you identified any of the personnel?"

"Not yet, but we are searching."

Comandante? Lieutenant Copia said from the doorway. "We just discovered additional evidence in one of the Josephus pages from the warehouse raid."

"Something inside the text?"

"No. A word written in faded pencil on the reverse side of the parchment. According to forensics, the graphite powder is a type from sixty years ago."

"What word?"

"*Orvieti,*" Copia said. "We just discovered it's a name. We cross-referenced it with the carabinieri's parochial database for clergy and it matched the name of an elderly archivist living here in Rome."

"He works in Saint Peter's, then?"

"Not Saint Peter's, sir," Lieutenant Copia said. "Mosè Orvieti apparently has a different boss."

76

At Ben-Gurion Airport, Eilat Segev led Jonathan and Emili through restricted back corridors packed with Israeli customs officials in powder-blue shirts and navy slacks. In the accordion-walled hallways, high-level diplomatic personnel whisked past, escorting Arab sheikhs from their private planes to meet with Israeli government officials in conferences that never occurred—officially.

For appearance's sake, Jonathan tried to button his shrunken suit jacket; the sleeves had retreated to his forearms.

"I still can't believe she put *my suit* in the washing machine."

"The algae didn't match your tie," Emili said, smiling. She glanced at his shrunken sleeves. "And it's fashionable to show some cuff."

Segev abruptly clipped her mobile phone shut and turned around.

"The carabinieri in Rome have issued EU-wide rapid arrest warrants for both of you. It's going to be nearly impossible to get you back into Italy. All I can do is put you on an El Al plane to Rome. If I were so much as to help you through the doors at Fiumicino, it could strain relations between Israel and Italy for months. There are probably forty uniforms looking for you in the airport right now."

"But the carabinieri are probably monitoring only departures, not arrivals," Emili countered.

"Why?" Jonathan asked.

"Because the carabinieri officers at Fiumicino are looking for us in *outbound* traffic. The police would never imagine that either of us—even if we already left the country—are planning to *return*."

Israeli guards nodded respectfully to Segev as she walked Jonathan and Emili through the diplomatic passport check. The procedure was even more cursory than usual. Jonathan did not even remember stepping through a metal detector. A senior airport official handed them tickets. Seats had been reserved for him and Emili as visiting UN scholars of the Israel Antiquities Authority. Jonathan was surprised at how professional-looking the documents were. A door at the bottom of a metal stairwell opened and they stepped onto the tarmac.

"Once this plane touches down at Fiumicino, you are on your own. You might not even make it to Ostia!" Segev leaned in and spoke over the tarmac's din. "To give you the most lead time in deplaning, your seats are at the front of the aircraft! Remember, once at Fiumicino, you are—"

"Yes, I know!" Emili said loudly over the engines. "On our own!"

Segev nodded. Without looking back, she turned and walked away.

In the eerie quiet of the El Al first-class cabin, the tarmac's blaring noise still rang in Jonathan's ears.

"Look at the bright side"—Emili leaned over, whispering—"this takeoff ought to be smoother than the last one."

Jonathan spread the maps of Ostia over the tray table, and Emili studied them beside him. Watching her study the map, Jonathan remembered their first excavation together, along the southern Italian coast. It was the middle of summer, and he remembered them sitting after dinner, alone in the empty restaurant of their ramshackle pensione, studying aerial photographs of the village farmland where their dig team was surveying for a buried pagan temple. From the images, Jonathan had noticed that the rows of artichoke plants surrounding the pensione had grown in an irregular pattern, suggesting some large object beneath the ground that obstructed their root work. Filled with enthusiasm and too much local wine, they ran into the artichoke fields with flashlights. It wasn't long before they noticed a circular piece of white stone jutting out from the earth shining in the moonlight. They got on their knees, scraping away some of the dirt around the smooth stone, revealing a carved marble acanthus leaf.

"It's a Corinthian capital," Emili said, exhilarated, crouching in the dirt. He remembered the sudden, transcendent vision they shared of that huge marble temple slumbering beneath the moonlit artichoke field. She leaned in to brush more dirt from the exposed marble, and their faces accidentally touched. Her curtain of long blond hair enveloped them both, creating a secret moment of intimacy. She was the first to open her lips. In Emili's room back at the pensione, Jonathan lavished great attention in removing her sweat-stained blouse, her khaki shorts, her underwear, as though uncovering archaeological strata that required great study and attention. He knew it was more than the dinner's grappa that had taken them past the breaking point, it was the addiction of discovery, of unearthing the unknown. And afterward, as they lay there naked on the thin cot, her arm flung across his chest, the cool night air intruding on the warmth of their moist skin, she opened her eyes, twinkly and bright, as though remembering something.

"We found something remarkable tonight," she said, pointing through the window in the direction of the artichoke field.

"Yes," Jonathan said, not moving his eyes from her, "we have."

The El Al plane neared its approach to Fiumicino and it banked low over the Mediterranean. Small fishing boats, *gozzi*, chugged along a jagged coastline of small Italian towns rimmed with honey-colored cliffs. Flocks of migrating birds circled an abandoned tuna fishery.

The airplane taxied down the runway, and Jonathan and Emili descended the long ramp toward the gate with the rest of the commercial travelers. To their right, a group of airport security officers lounged outside the duty-free shops. A carabinieri officer flirted shamelessly with a young flight attendant.

"How are we going to get through passport control?" Jonathan said.

"With some help," Emili said.

"From whom?"

"Her." Emili pointed at the end of the Jetway, where beyond

the streams of people Jonathan made out a distinguished-looking woman.

The woman was shaking her head as Emili walked up, smiling thinly. In a formal tone, she welcomed them both, mainly for the benefit of the diplomatic-passport-check representatives who stood beside her.

"I take it neither of you has any luggage, then," Director Jacqueline Olivier said.

77

In the back of a Lancia sedan with Moroccan diplomatic plates, Salah ad-Din approached the Aurelian Wall, which surrounded downtown Rome. He knew the third-century brick fortification once defended Rome from the invading Germanic tribes from the north, and he felt the quiet victory of his own personal invasion as the car pierced the wall, through an archway now paved for a two-lane street. The sedan traveled along the Lungotevere dei Sangallo and stopped alongside the Ponte Fabricio.

Salah ad-Din stepped into the rain across the street from the Great Synagogue of Rome. He crossed the cobbles, walking leisurely past the police officers who chatted under umbrellas outside the synagogue's main gate. He turned away from the synagogue and slipped down a small side street off the Piazza delle Cinque Scole. His men, during their reconnaissance of the Ghetto the week before, had loosened a sewer grate in the cobbles. Salah ad-Din lifted it and lowered himself into the steel hull of a drainage tunnel—a point of entry to the Great Synagogue that none of the four policemen surrounding the structure knew to protect.

One line in Josephus, Salah ad-Din thought, adrenaline quickening his pace down the tunnel. *One line in Josephus will tell me where the menorah is in Ostia.*

For months, one of Salah ad-Din's local operatives had rented a flat in one of the few remaining decrepit buildings across from the synagogue. Only minutes before, he relayed to Salah ad-Din that the most valuable artifact in the Ghetto had just entered the archives: the archivist himself, Mosè Orvieti.

From the drainage tunnel, Salah ad-Din entered the synagogue's subbasement and noticed some fresh footprints in the dust near the oil tank. He followed them through a door to the spiral staircase leading up to the synagogue's cupola. He checked the clip of his gun beneath his coat.

Quietly, he moved up the staircase to the synagogue's belfry, feeling a sense of return. He had never entered this structure himself, but for him, the sense of return was more *metaphysical*. He had so fully identified himself with his grandfather's mission, so deeply internalized the stories told by the grand mufti's assistants, who had escaped the war crime trials of Nuremberg by moving to Baghdad with his grandfather, that Salah ad-Din felt it was *he* who climbed these stairs more than sixty-five years earlier and confronted Orvieti in 1943. The old men in Baghdad had often told him how much he reminded them of their deceased leader. His intensity, even his facial features, recalled the grand mufti.

Salah ad-Din reached the top of the staircase and stood in the archive's open doorway. For a moment, Salah ad-Din went unnoticed. It was then that he could truly appreciate, even respect, the sight of this old man sitting at the center table, perhaps just where his grandfather had found him a lifetime ago. Orvieti, sensing a visitor in the doorway, gestured without looking up from his text.

He would need a moment to mark his place and slowly push back his chair to stand up.

Orvieti finally lifted his head, taking in the visitor. Over the years he had visions of the grand mufti—remembering him draping his hands across the books, flanked by the Berlin professors. As a result, Orvieti's first reaction at seeing Salah ad-Din was none at all. He lived with the memory daily. But then, as though roused from a nightmare to find its monster at the foot of the bed, he wiped his eyes. The man standing before him was no trick of his mind. He was flesh and blood.

Orvieti's voice began evenly, the flat tone of a man who had prepared for this moment all his life. He finally spoke.

"Why have you not aged?"

78

Salah ad-Din took in the scope of the archives. He turned to Orvieti.

"You have something I need."

Orvieti stood up. He felt strangely unafraid, defiant, as though the sight of this ghost reversed his own aging half a century. This man wore Western clothing—black slacks, an open white shirt, and a full-length gray overcoat—not the religious garb of the mufti. But the face was unmistakably the same.

"I seek the passage in Josephus my grandfather could not find."

Your grandfather, Orvieti thought, watching the young man pace the room with the same lordly arrogance he remembered from more than half a century before.

Even the tone, the thinly veiled instability—it was all the same.

"*Signore*, do not act startled," Salah ad-Din said curtly. "You know, as well as I do, that Josephus revealed the menorah's location in a single line of his text. My grandfather believed the menorah was in Jerusalem, so he spent his life searching passages in Josephus's text that described the Temple Mount. It's why he researched all those pages describing the 'hidden gate.'"

"*Researched* those pages?" Orvieti asked. *He stole them, ripped them right out of our manuscripts, like limbs from a living animal.*

"But he had the wrong line, didn't he?" Salah ad-Din said. "The menorah is not in Jerusalem, but near Rome. And now you are going to tell me exactly where. Which line in Josephus reveals the menorah's location?"

"I don't know."

"*Signore*"—Salah ad-Din stepped toward him—"believe me, I would have preferred to find the answer in an ancient source myself. It's why you have not seen me until now. After all, Titus's mistake was in taking other people's word for it that he had captured the authentic menorah."

"Whatever information you seek about Flavius Josephus, the grand mufti stole it from this archive years ago," Orvieti said. "You know that."

"He took all the information in this archive *at the time*." Salah ad-Din stepped forward. "But you were given more information about Josephus rather recently, were you not?"

"From whom?" Orvieti asked, standing very still.

"My contacts inside the Vatican say that the previous pope, John Paul the Second, bequeathed information to the rabbi of the Ghetto."

"I know nothing of this," Orvieti said truthfully, but a sense of dread rose inside him. The depth of the friendship between the two spiritual leaders was remarkable. Orvieti knew how pained the pope had been by the Church's history of anti-Semitism, and that he often spoke with the rabbi of his own *teshuva*, or repentance, that led to his historic visit to the Great Synagogue in 1986. The rabbi of the Jewish Ghetto was one of only three people mentioned in the pope's last will and testament.

"They said the pope gave him a slip of paper with one line written on it," Salah ad-Din said. "What was the line from Josephus?"

"If it is papal information you seek," Orvieti said, "your inquiries are best taken across the river."

Salah ad-Din reached inside his overcoat, and with a single motion of his, a Beretta was touching Orvieti's face, the loose flesh of his forehead gathering around the barrel of the silencer.

"You have until the count of three to tell me the line in Josephus that reveals the location of the menorah," Salah ad-Din said. He could feel Orvieti's frail skull against the metal. "One."

Orvieti said nothing. He saw the desperation in the young man's eyes.

"Two."

Orvieti stiffened, his back straight. "I have died once before. You cannot kill me again."

"We'll see about that, won't we?" Salah ad-Din said. His finger tightened around the gun's trigger. "Thr—"

"Hello?" Lieutenant Brandisi called out, his voice echoing from the bottom of the stairwell. Salah ad-Din relaxed his finger and pulled up his gun. His eyes flashed to the stairwell.

"Don't make a sound," Salah ad-Din told Orvieti, stepping backward toward the archive's door.

"*Signore?* I need just a few moments of your time!" Brandisi called up, resting on the stairs, panting. *How does the old man do this every day?*

Salah ad-Din turned to the door and when he looked back, Orvieti was gone. The old man was halfway up the corkscrew stairwell to the archive's second story.

Salah ad-Din ran to the bottom of the stairwell. There was no clear shot. The wrought-iron bars of the stack's balcony formed a protective sheath around Orvieti.

"You cannot escape," Salah ad-Din seethed, not loud enough for his voice to travel out the door. "You expect to outrun me?" He started up the ladder rungs, taking them two at a stride, steadying his gun for aim. Salah ad-Din reached the stacks' first balcony when, beyond all expectation, a leg flew out, kicking him squarely in the face and sending him sliding down a dozen rungs. Salah ad-Din blinked, stunned, as he tasted blood from his lip. His gun spit three licks of fire into the leather-bound books inches from where Orvieti had climbed. His fury redoubled, Salah ad-Din charged upward, now only a few rungs below Orvieti.

"Hello? Signor Orvieti?"

Brandisi sounded winded as he made it up the last turn of stairs. He already had walked six blocks to reach the synagogue. Comandante Profeta instructed him to park the patrol car outside the Ghetto. *This was the Jewish Ghetto of Rome,* Profeta had told him. *Any community that watched Aurelius build his wall, Constantine build his church, and Mussolini build his empire had a good reason to be suspicious of authority.*

Orvieti made it to the top of the corkscrew staircase and opened the pane of a large stained-glass window. The rain lashed against the glass and Orvieti wondered whether his small frame could withstand the wind. He slipped through the open window and climbed onto the ledge that circled the synagogue's cupola. Salah ad-Din's desperate grasp reached through the window and missed his leg by inches.

The sky was dark gray and the swirling wind and rain hit Orvieti like a solid sheet. He leaned against the curve of the temple's dome fearing that the wind could catch his clothing and carry him off the ledge. It was as though God himself had seen the terrible storm inside the cupola and manifested it outside.

As Orvieti sidestepped along the ledge around the dome's curve, he saw Salah ad-Din lean out the window and take aim. Another bullet from Salah ad-Din's silencer whizzed past, missing him only because of the dome's curve.

"Hello?" Brandisi stood at the belfry door, breathing hard. He saw Salah ad-Din's back at the top of the bookcase's ladder, leaning out the window.

Salah ad-Din pivoted around, calculating. He slid his Beretta back inside his overcoat and padded his bleeding lip with his sleeve. He hurried down the stairs and crossed the archive toward the policeman with a large smile.

"I'm sorry, I didn't hear you. I slipped trying to close the window," Salah ad-Din said, pointing at his bleeding lip with a shrug. "In the rain, the sparrows fly through the open pane."

"I am looking for Signore Orvieti," Brandisi said with an official sense of urgency. "The security guards said he was in here."

"No, I am his assistant," Salah ad-Din said in Italian, without a trace of accent. "Is there something I can help you with, Officer?"

But the guard said he was here alone, Brandisi thought.

"We'll need to speak with Signore Orvieti personally," Brandisi said. "It pertains to an ongoing investigation."

"I see." Salah ad-Din looked concerned. "Then let me look for him right away."

"But I was just downstairs. They said he was up here."

"He could be up in the stacks."

"Up there?"

"His legs are quite strong, Officer," Salah ad-Din said, feeling his lip swell. "Trust me."

Orvieti was outside, shivering. A wet nest of huddled pigeons exploded from behind him, nearly knocking him off the ledge. His arms were shaking as he lowered himself below the travertine lip of the synagogue's cupola and tried to kick in a stained-glass pane to climb into the sanctuary. But the glass was wet, and with each attempt his feet merely glanced off the pane. He used every muscle in his thin arms to hang on to the building's cornice, but his feet were not hitting the pane with enough force to break it. Each effort was loosening his grip. Sixty feet below, the young policemen were oblivious under their umbrellas. The archivist knew he had only one more chance. At one point in his life he might have said a prayer for strength. But no longer. It had been sixty years since he had said a personal prayer of any kind. He simply closed his eyes and summoned all his remaining strength into one last kick. The stained-glass window smashed in.

"What was that sound?" Brandisi asked, peering up the stairwell. From behind, Salah ad-Din grabbed him by the neck and slammed his head against the iron railing of the staircase. Brandisi fell to the floor, unconscious. Salah ad-Din removed his Beretta and, standing over Brandisi, pulled the trigger from point-blank range. The hollow click of the hammer against the polymer frame answered. *No bullets.* Salah ad-Din never expected to waste seven rounds on that old man. He slid out the ammunition magazine to reload.

"Signore Orvieti!" another anxious voice echoed up the stairwell.

Salah ad-Din slipped behind the belfry's door. A heavyset security guard lumbered in, having heard the smashing glass. As the guard passed through the door, Salah ad-Din stepped out silently behind him, descending the spiral staircase. Reaching the basement, undetected, he slid through the heating vent in the floor and fastened the grate back into place.

79

The director nodded confidently to passing security personnel at Fiumicino airport as Jonathan and Emili followed her through a carpeted diplomatic staging area. The stacked benches on the wall were presumably for press to cover dignitary arrivals. The director spoke to Emili out of the corner of her wooden smile.

"Have you considered how you've endangered your career if you're wrong about this?" Olivier said.

"A better question, Director, is what's endangered if I'm right."

They moved past the baggage-claim area and to a separate overhead walkway for diplomats. The director showed more airport personnel her credentials and waved Jonathan and Emili through. Jonathan was again surprised at how easily he could move between two countries within the UN world, although part of him was horrified at the gap in Interpol's surveillance of international travel.

Once in the parking lot, they ducked into the director's idling UN-issued sedan, which displayed a government medallion across the license plate. Jonathan took the front seat next to the driver. Emili and the UN director sat in the back.

Once out of the public eye, the director stepped out of her professional character, becoming an irate parent. "Will someone please tell me what is going on?"

Emili turned to her. "We've done it, Jacquie."

"Done what?"

Emili spoke quickly, "We can expose the Waqf's illegal excavations beneath the Temple Mount in Jerusalem. We saw it ourselves."

"You went beneath the Temple Mount?" The director looked even more agitated. "Have you any idea how many international laws you've broken?"

"Their activity beneath the Temple Mount in Jerusalem is more destructive than we ever thought. They are trying to erase two millennia of Judeo-Christian heritage." Emili handed the director a thin blue stamp-sized piece of plastic. "The memory card from my camera. It's more than enough physical evidence to present at the plenary session of the World Heritage Committee. Just make sure this gets back to the office safely. It's footage of the Waqf's destruction fifty feet beneath Jerusalem."

The director stared at the chip. "I'll do the best I can," she said, taking it. "But, even if any of this is true, how is there a connection to the ancient port of Ostia?"

"Two thousand years ago one of the artifacts escaped," Emili said. "If it's discovered, it would unravel their campaign of historical revisionism in Jerusalem . . ."

"*Historical revisionism?*" The director shook her head, her eyes closed in disbelief. She took care to restrain her reaction as Emili spoke, appearing to remind herself that for the last two years she had trusted Dr. Travia with the most difficult missions of her organization.

"Emili," the director said, "you're saying that this man that you've told me about, Salah ad-Din—even if he exists—has followed a piece of archaeology from Jerusalem to Rome on the *theory* that it traveled here two thousand years ago?"

"That's right, to Ostia," Emili answered. "Did you bring what we discussed?"

The director reached down in the backseat and reluctantly handed Emili a plastic bag. "Two flashlights and a map of Ostia, just as you asked," Jacqueline said, "but that means you will agree to my one condition?"

"Yes," Emili said.

"What condition?" Jonathan said.

Emili turned to him. "That we call the carabinieri within the hour."

Jonathan was surprised how far the law had drifted from his mind. The American embassy or the carabinieri had not entered his thoughts since he had left Italy ten hours before. As though he were a graduate student again, Jonathan had begun to view laws as he did then: inconvenient rules that underestimated the historical significance of their chase.

"I'm already sticking my neck out a long way on this one, Emili. No more playing the outlaw, is that clear? And *please*, remember to call the carabinieri. They can protect you, do you understand?"

"Yes, and thank you, Jacqueline," she said.

The UN director said nothing, throwing a warning look to both Emili and Jonathan as she got out of the car and closed the door behind her. Her eyes sent a single message very clearly to Emili. *I hope you know what you're doing.*

80

Salah ad-Din parked a highway repair truck just outside the archaeological parts of ancient Ostia, twenty miles from Rome. He wore the orange perforated vest of a roadway repairman, pretending to supervise his team outside the ruins' wire fence. His excavations beneath the Colosseum in Rome had been extensive, but this project had already removed a three-foot section of highway asphalt to get his equipment inside. *He was here,* Salah ad-Din thought, staring at the ruins through the fence. Flavius Josephus smuggled the menorah to this coastal town rather than risk moving it deeper into Rome. Fog headlights of passing cars intermittently whizzed past. Just as the rest of Salah ad-Din's efforts, this excavation was hidden in plain view.

After five years on Ostia's police force, Officer Roberto Fiegi had never seen street repairmen work in so much as a drizzle, which was why, through the rain on his patrol car's windshield, he considered whether he was hallucinating. As he completed the first lap of his afternoon patrol around the perimeter of Ostia's ancient ruins, four men in highway construction outfits labored in the rain alongside the ancient ruins' outer fence. They were dark as Sicilians, but their work ethic could not have been further from the Sicilian lifestyle. Not only were they braving a cold drizzle that usually suspended street work, but they were working through the *riposo.* Fiegi looked at his watch. One p.m.

Officer Fiegi slowed his patrol car, a Fiat, its single blue light silently flashing as he pulled onto the road's gravel shoulder behind the municipal repair truck. Three workmen surrounded a large crater along the right edge of the highway closer to the ruins.

"Spero che vi pagano lo straordinario!" Hope they're paying you overtime! Officer Fiegi said, stepping out of his car, squinting in the rain.

The three men replied with curious stares, and their pause suddenly put Officer Fiegi on the alert. He could sense they were making calculations far more complicated than those of mere highway repairmen.

Officer Fiegi approached one of the young men, a tall horse-faced boy; he looked scarcely older than a teenager. Sicily's population is less Latin than the rest of the country, but this boy was clearly Arab. Officer Fiegi asked him a question, and he stood there frozen.

None of these men, the officer suddenly realized, spoke a word of Italian.

"Officer!" Salah ad-Din emerged through the hole in the road-way, smiling graciously in his workman's orange perforated vest. "Sometimes I think the roads were better in ancient Ostia!" He walked briskly toward the officer as though receiving visiting roy-alty. "I am glad someone finally stopped by to check up on us!" he said in fluent Italian. "Adequate drainage is of paramount impor-tance in road design, you see. The presence of any moisture within the roadway could break through the asphalt."

The officer looked at the road. Its rural paving was cracked in so many places, it was hard to believe drainage problems could dam-age it further.

"Please, allow me to show you our drainage diagrams." Salah ad-Din pointed behind the truck. Killing the officer would present practical problems. There would be a police car to dispose of, and it would burden his tight excavation schedule. But he could take no chances. Not when he was this close. *A dim-witted policeman will not come between me and the solution to a mystery two thousand years old.*

The policeman stepped around the back of the truck. Salah ad-Din followed and removed his hard hat as a sign of respect, tighten-ing his finger around the trigger of the Beretta beneath his workman's uniform.

81

I t looks abandoned," Jonathan said as the driver slowed to a stop beside the shuttered ticket gazebo outside Ostia's archaeological path.

The driver appeared to gain some satisfaction from this. He turned around, resting his chin on his arm. "I told you it was closed," he said gruffly in Italian.

"This will be fine, thank you," Emili said.

They stepped out of the car onto a long dirt path beneath a wet canopy of umbrella pines. Behind them in the distance, they could faintly see the Renaissance fortress of Pope Julius II, which was abandoned in 1567, when the Tiber River changed course in a flash flood. Alternating white and purple fields of cow parsley and lavender surrounded the ruins and stretched into the distance.

"In ancient Rome, the coast of the Mediterranean came to there." Emili pointed at the fields. "Silt pushed the water's edge four miles to the current shoreline."

"There goes the ocean view," Jonathan said.

Emili and Jonathan were greeted by a loud clap of thunder as they approached the closed front gate. Through the bars of the gate, they could see the long central stone-paved street of the ancient city lined with two-story buildings from first century A.D.

Jonathan hopped the fence, and his shoes scraped down a brick wall on the other side. He landed on a remarkably preserved mosaic of leaping dolphins that decorated an ancient communal bath. Emili followed, and Jonathan lowered her.

On a warm summer day, at the height of Ostia's tourist season, these ruins would have been full of people. But now it was closed, and Jonathan felt an acute sense of alarm in its emptiness. The rain strengthened, flooding the column-lined ancient streets and creating muddy streams that sluiced between the stones.

There was a rustling in the bushes. Both of them were silent.

"Probably an animal," Jonathan said. He reached down to pick up a thick wooden pole for protection, not sure if he believed himself.

They moved down the main thoroughfare. The remains of Ostia's ancient storefronts and apartment buildings provided a rare snapshot of ancient life. Emili and Jonathan ducked through the low brick arch of a bakery, its ancient marble counter still intact with side seats and wall paintings of bread and fruit.

"Jon, there, the synagogue is in that direction," Emili said, consulting the laminated map.

Jonathan started down a side street toward the ruins of the synagogue. Emili followed, her lighter body inclined into the wind. The gusts made a shearing whistle through the ancient brick.

At the end of a dirt path, they entered a ruin of half-stone walls surrounding four slender columns and a slab of granite open to the sky.

The floor of the ruin was a mosaic of rough tiles, and Jonathan moved his hand across them. "There are no human or animal pictures in these mosaics."

"In keeping with the Old Testament's prohibition against graven images?"

"Exactly, and look up there." Jonathan pointed below one of the columns' ionic capitals. There was the unmistakable carved rendering of a seven-branched lamp.

"This is it, Jon," Emili said. "The synagogue."

Jonathan crouched at the edge of the mosaic floor. "There is a path leading out of the sanctuary."

"It leads there." Emili pointed at a small, compact ruin of partial brick walls. She looked down at the map.

"That must be it, the House of Divine Fire, the *Domus Fulminata.*"

They walked toward the brick walls that surrounded a marble well nearly buried in long stalks of grass. The curators of Ostia's archaeological park had fastened a corrugated tin sheet on top of the wall, and the rain pelting it was deafening.

Jonathan leaned over the lip, shining his flashlight along the well shaft. He saw an inscription carved into the shaft's rock face and wiped mud from its surface.

"A Roman-era inscription," Jonathan called out, leaning over farther. "It's a mix of Latin and Hebrew. 'If I forget thee, O Jerusalem, may my right hand lose its cunning.'"

Jonathan lifted himself back out of the well, and saw Emili smiling, rain streaming down her face. "Doesn't sound pagan to me."

82

Jonathan hoisted himself over the mouth of the well and rested his legs on iron pegs that formed a crude ladder into the shimmering water below. As he descended, the inclement weather above was replaced with a warm mist and an overpowering stench of mildew and rot. Jonathan touched down at the bottom of the well. Knee deep in cold water, he tilted his head to call up to Emili that he made it safely, but she was nearly beside him, having come down the rungs in half the time it took him.

"Next time, you go first, show-off," Jonathan said at the sight of her smirk.

The well water rose above Emili's knees and she waded slowly to a wall of the shaft, where an arch gave way to a tunnel. Inside the tunnel, the earth was dry.

"There's no trace of drainage in here," Jonathan said, shining his flashlight. "No staining of the tunnel's rock that would indicate water accumulation."

Emili crouched on the ground and wiped the dust from the floor. "These stones aren't native to Roman quarries," she said. "It's Jerusalem stone."

Along the walls faded frescoes lined the tunnel, displaying an enormous artistic effort befitting a house of worship.

"A little upscale for a drainage center, don't you think?" Jonathan said.

A faded fresco on the wall depicted a bearded man on a Roman warship, amid swirling waves. Slaves pulled two stories of oars, while the bearded man stood with the Romans, holding a torch in the rain.

"That must be Josephus, traveling from Jerusalem to Rome," Jonathan said. In the last frame, the same bearded man stood on a harbor dock. The dark shading of the scene was done in charcoal and suggested it was night. In the image, the men lifted an unmistakable object from the docked warship. Staring at it, Jonathan was stunned, as though seeing indisputable evidence in court. The object was a foot-tall depiction of the Tabernacle menorah, its seven branches represented in gold stucco that dwarfed the men who carried it, preserving a sense of the enormous scale of the eight-foot-tall lamp of solid gold. The fresco's depiction of the menorah was the first patent confirmation of their search.

"It's a depiction of Josephus smuggling the menorah from the hull of a Roman warship under the cover of night," Jonathan said.

"It could really be here," Emili said, moving rapidly in front of Jonathan down the corridor.

Some rocks had fallen from the ceiling, but the tunnel widened and it was possible to squeeze through.

Their flashlights revealed a rock hollow, a small, circular room. Columns carved with images of the menorah lined the wall, and in the center of the room sat a thickly hewn rectangular stone with three steps.

"Just like we found inside the vault beneath the Temple Mount," Emili said. "The steps used by the priests to light the menorah in exile." She pointed at the darkened ceiling of the room. It was blackened from ash.

"There's an inscription on the top step," Jonathan said, his adrenaline racing. "But it's in Greek."

πρὸς δὲ τὴν πύλην αὐτὸς ἀνεχώρει

"'He retired it to the arch where the triumphal procession passed through,'" Jonathan translated. "The script looks like first century."

"It's a line from Josephus, isn't it?" Emili asked.

"Yes, and it's puzzled Josephus scholars for centuries. The pronoun 'it' has no noun to which it refers in the text."

Emili leaned closer over the inscription. "Jon," her hushed voice echoed in the chamber. "Do you think that this—"

"Yes," he answered. "I think this is the line in Josephus's text where he revealed the location of the menorah."

"But where?"

"The 'triumphal procession' clearly refers to the Roman soldiers' military parade that occurred upon their return from Jerusalem, right?"

"Of course, that was the custom. Wreathed Roman soldiers marched through the street, carrying the treasures of war."

"Which means that Josephus is referring to the Arch of Titus as the 'gate' that the triumphal procession went through." Jonathan slowly stepped away from the wall as though making a physical space for a vast realization. "I don't believe it."

"Believe what?"

"Em, it's been *right here* in the text for millennia. *He retired it to the arch.* Josephus and his men put *the menorah* inside the Arch of Titus all along."

"*Inside?*"

"That's right," Jonathan said. "Think of how Josephus would have relished the irony. The Arch of Titus was constructed to glorify Emperor Titus's conquest of Jerusalem, but secretly the arch"— Jonathan paused to digest the implication—"protected the very thing he meant to destroy."

"Jon, the menorah was *huge*. How would Josephus's network put the menorah inside the Arch of Titus?"

"It may not have been as difficult as we think. The Romans used the Hebrew slaves to build the Colosseum, the Baths of Titus, and other monuments. Where better to protect their icon than in the belly of a monument that Rome would defend for all time? It was nearly ten years after the slaves came from Rome. The arch was half constructed and the emperor was close to uncovering the spy in the imperial court. Josephus needed a place no one would ever suspect." Jonathan paused, amazed by his own suggestion.

"We can expose them here in Rome, Jon. Salah ad-Din's men could be excavating at the Arch of Titus at this very moment."

An illegal excavation in the center of the Roman Forum, Jonathan thought. A day ago, he would never have thought it possible.

They moved back through the tunnel. Emili stepped first into the well water and bumped into a large object floating on the water's surface.

From beneath the surface, as though staring up from beneath a plate of Lucite, was the lifeless gaze of a human corpse. Brown curly hair swayed back and forth in the water like a submerged plant, his palms up in a last gesture of self-defense. Beneath the water's surface, she saw the glint of his policeman's badge. With some violence, she splashed back into Jonathan. A burning tide of bile rose in her throat and she retched. By now, Jonathan saw the horror as well, and he stood there silently. Emili, still bent over and red-faced, turned up to look at Jonathan.

"It's time to notify the carabinieri," she said through shallow breaths.

Jonathan looked at his watch. "Actually, we told the director we would call by now."

Emili climbed the ladder and quickly reached the top of the well.

A silhouette of Emili's head. "There's a truck over—"

But she never finished the sentence.

From inside the well, Jonathan saw a thick arm grab Emili and whip her from his view.

"No!" he yelled.

Jonathan climbed faster, pumping his legs up the iron rungs. He could hear Emili screaming. He reached the top of the well and vaulted himself out, landing in a deep puddle of mud.

"Emili!" he yelled again.

On brute instinct he picked up the wooden pole that still lay at the foot of the well and spun around in the mist. She was gone.

83

Lieutenant Brandisi awoke on a stretcher, which tilted as the paramedics carried him above the cobbles toward an ambulance along the Via del Portico d'Ottavia. He felt an icy sensation over his heart, and for a moment feared he'd been shot in the chest. His vision was hazy, but he made out a paramedic stooped over him and realized the icy sensation was the disk of a stethoscope over his heart. He touched his forehead where he had been struck, and felt an elastic cold press.

"Brandisi?" Profeta stood over him.

"*Comandante!*" Brandisi said, startled.

"You've got quite a welt there, Lieutenant, but considering that someone was firing an automatic Beretta up there, I'd consider us pretty fortunate. Did you see who hit you?"

"A man who claimed to be Orvieti's assistant. Young and dark-skinned, might have been Middle Eastern. Silver spectacles. Black hair cropped quite short, shaved really."

Profeta turned to another officer. "Put a twenty-block-radius AP on that description."

"Did they find Orvieti?" Brandisi asked.

"You were the only one found in the archives." Profeta paused. "But there is a possibility Orvieti made it to the ledge of the cupola and smashed the stained glass of the sanctuary to escape."

"I'd like to see it," Brandisi said. Despite the paramedics' protests, Brandisi sat up and another officer helped him onto the cobble.

Profeta led him back to the synagogue and they climbed the steps to the highest of the sanctuary's velvet rows, where the air had the smell of a musty attic. Profeta stood beside a broken pane of stained glass. The shards of colored glass lay near a trail of fresh blood on the sanctuary's carpet.

"Orvieti's," Profeta said.

"Are you sure, *Comandante*?" Brandisi said, removing the cold press from the back of his head to check if the bleeding had stopped. "An eighty-eight-year-old could scale the curve of the cupola and kick in this stained glass?"

Another officer walked up the stairs. "There is no sign of the man, *Comandante*. The guards are adamant that there was no one besides Lieutenant Brandisi and Signore Orvieti admitted to the synagogue since it opened this morning."

"Well, someone was here," Profeta said. "Those three bullet holes in the archive shelving weren't fired by Orvieti or Brandisi. And Orvieti didn't climb out on that ledge and break through this stained glass simply because he wanted to. Someone was trying to kill him."

"Someone that age climbing out on the ledge in a windstorm." Brandisi shook his head, marveling. "And then lowering himself through a shattered window."

"I'm not surprised," Profeta said. "Mosè Orvieti has survived the impossible before."

84

Jonathan ran into Ostia's streets, searching behind the ruin's half-brick walls in desperation.

"Emili!" he screamed.

There was nothing but the rain and the mud. Jonathan stood motionless as the horror settled in. Although it was midday, the cloud cover was so heavy that the skies were dim as dusk. Jonathan ran at some rustling bushes, only to find a cat eating from a littered candy wrapper.

From one of the empty streets he heard sounds of struggle. He could not place its direction, and stumbled down a street at random, running into the sprawling ruins of an ancient warehouse.

A muffled yell sounded closer. It came from inside the neighboring ancient theater. The theater's stone arches were closed off by gates, and Jonathan tried each of them, rattling their bars, until he found a small rusted side gate with the lock missing. He ran into the theater, which during summer festivals was packed but now, in winter, looked as dark and abandoned as if the theater were still buried in the earth.

"Please find it."

The voice sounded harrowingly close, but Jonathan saw no one. The theater's open air acoustics made it impossible to tell from which direction it came. The words were spoken in English, but in a tone soft enough that the accent was undetectable.

"Hello?" Jonathan called out, his own echo filling the empty theater.

"Please find it," the voice said again. The tone was human. More pleading than ominous, as though asking for a favor.

"Who are you!" Jonathan yelled. He ran up the *cavea*—the theater's tiered stone seating. He saw no one.

And then, at the far end of the semicircular stone seating, a woman's figure materialized in the mist.

"Emili!" Jonathan sprinted, rounding the theater's curve.

But as he drew close, he saw it was not Emili. The woman looked just as frantic as he did. She had been standing in the rain, and neglected streaks of mascara ink-stained her face.

"He will kill you if you don't cooperate," Director Jacqueline Olivier said.

"What?" Jonathan whispered and held up his hands, as though the deception were a physical force he could somehow stop.

Slowly, the depth of betrayal registered, and Jonathan snapped his head back, angrily. "You've got to be *kidding* me! You're involved in this?"

"I didn't think it would go this far." The director's voice was unsteady.

Even in his rising fury, he could see panic in her eyes.

"Where have they taken her?" Jonathan asked, his voice tremoring with rage.

"I don't know. They contact me." She looked away. "That's how it works."

"That's how it *works*?" Jonathan asked, controlling himself. Everything became vivid, and not just the scope of Salah ad-Din's operation. The texture of the mud in the theater, the stones' sheen in the rain, the monochrome gray sky.

"You've been cooperating with Salah ad-Din since Emili and Sharif were in Jerusalem, haven't you?" Jonathan's voice strengthened. "That's how the Waqf knew about their research beneath the Old City, isn't it?"

"They agreed to *limit* their excavations beneath the Mount if I gave them information! You think I *knew* Sharif would get killed?"

She stopped. "It was supposed to be harmless." Olivier's tone shook along with the rest of her. She held the seating railing for support; her ankles buckling on the uneven stones.

"You betrayed her. . . . How could you—?"

"How could I?" the director said, her tone on the firmer ground of self-justification. "Have you any idea the influence of the twenty-one Arab nations in the UN? My organization has to work with *reality.*" Anger had rushed to her defense. "You want to protect palm leaf manuscripts in Kazakhstan, you don't just raise money for humidity controllers, you raise money to bribe the Timri rebels not to come at midnight and burn the library down. You're not going to stop the Taliban from blowing up Buddhas, but you can get their thugs to tell you where they are shipping the remains to Kabul en route to the auction markets in London. You play the game!"

"This man, Salah ad-Din, is a killer," Jonathan said plainly.

"I know," Olivier said, swallowing. "Which means you must do what he says. If you tell anyone they have taken her, he *will* kill her. Please," she said, gripping the railing as she walked down the theater's stone steps. "Just find what they want."

Jonathan watched the director hobble down the stone tiers. He knew better than to try to follow her.

"How will Salah ad-Din even know if I find it?"

"He'll know," she said, turning around. Even with the distance between them Jonathan saw the terror in her eyes. "Salah ad-Din knows more than you can possibly imagine."

She reached the bottom of the theater seats and stepped into an arch's darkness.

"What does that mean?" Jonathan called after her.

But the wet trees' unraveling branches were his only answer.

Instantly, Jonathan knew he was alone.

He sprinted up the rows of stone seating. The muscles in his legs felt stripped raw.

"What does that mean!" he screamed, standing in the highest row of the theater. From his vantage point in the ruins, ferns and vines seemed like a carpet over the ruin's labyrinth of ancient alleyways. There was no sign of life anywhere. He heard only his own winded rasp.

Jonathan ran to a pay phone outside the park's shuttered snack bar. His leather wallet was still sopping from the Temple Mount's cistern and the ink on Chandler's card had run, but it was still legible. With his hands shaking, he could barely press the numbers of the international dialing code of his credit card. He knew the transaction would reveal his location to the carabinieri, but that was the least of his concerns.

"Hello?" Chandler said. The reception crackled loudly.

"Chandler, thank God you're there," Jonathan said.

"Aurelius, where the hell have you been? They're after you!"

"Who?"

"Everyone, man!" Chandler said. "The carabinieri, the reporters—even Interpol, I'm sure!" Jonathan could barely hear him, unsure if it was because of the storm or the age of the pay phone.

"Chandler, listen to me," Jonathan said. "I'm calling you from Ostia."

"Ostia? What the hell's in Ostia?"

"Chandler, just listen. You need to meet me in the Roman Forum in twenty minutes."

The line was almost pure static and he couldn't make out Chandler's answer.

"I need to get inside the Arch of Titus!" Jonathan said.

"What?"

"I need to get inside the arch!"

"You broke up there for a sec!" Chandler spoke louder. "Sounded like you said you needed to get inside an arch?"

"Chandler, I think that's where it is, inside the arch!"

"Holy shit," Chandler said quite clearly.

"There's probably a door. I'll need your help with the lock!" Jonathan said over the rain.

"Okay, okay," Chandler said, calming himself. "I can meet you in twenty minutes. Hang on, there's someone at the door. Who is—"

Chandler cut out.

"Hello?" Jonathan said, but there was no answer. The line was dead.

85

Mosè Orvieti, his left leg bleeding beneath his torn pants, limped along the massive colonnade of Saint Peter's, moving toward the Vatican palace. He recognized the young Jewish men selling plaster sculptures and rosaries in Piazza San Pietro. Pope Paul IV may have discriminated against Jews by having them sell Catholic souvenirs in Vatican City, but now, four hundred years later, his intentions had been reversed. These young men were as proud to inherit their fathers' souvenir licenses as they would a noble title.

Orvieti remembered the last time he crossed through this piazza. It also was an unpublicized trip. A cardinal had summoned him to inquire whether a priceless Renaissance incunabulum, an illustrated Bible, had been taken from the Jewish archives during the war. Orvieti described its gilded leaf work before seeing it. The Vatican quietly returned the piece without ceremony or further questions.

At the gate to the papal apartments, a member of the Corpo

Vigilanza was advised to admit Orvieti immediately, even though the man had no appointment. The guard led Orvieti through wood-paneled doors and slowly up a grand stairway into the papal apartments. He moved slowly, leaning against the balustrade, and the guard noticed a trail of blood on the white marble behind him. Along a frescoed corridor, the guard stopped, knocked, and opened the door. Cardinal Francesco Inocenti sat in a gilt chair beside a large marble hearth. He wore his choir dress for Mass: a white lace rochet beneath a red cassock, and a pectoral cross on a cord. His white damask miter rested on a side table. A fire roared in the oversized fireplace.

"I've been expecting you, old friend," Cardinal Inocenti said, walking toward him.

Orvieti emerged from the room's shadows, a limping old man soaked from the rain. He resembled the patriarch Jacob himself after wrestling with the angel until dawn in the wilderness, Inocenti thought.

"Who has done this to you?" Inocenti said, taking his arm and guiding him to his chair by the fire.

"I have never before asked a favor of you, Francesco," Orvieti said. "But I am about to."

There was no denying the deep respect Francesco Inocenti and Mosè Orvieti had for each other. "An elder brother in faith" was how Pope John Paul II once described the Jews across the Tiber, and it was an accurate portrayal of the relationship between these two men. For all the acrimony that had transpired over the centuries between their two communities, these two men were inextricably tied together by their personal pasts.

Even so, Orvieti knew his request would strain even the tightest bonds of trust. Prime ministers, museums, and governments had asked for the Church to volunteer information about the menorah, and the Vatican had refused, preferring to remain silent. But the time had come for Mosè Orvieti to pose the question directly to one of his oldest friends. Orvieti would not have come to Cardinal Inocenti had he not remembered that day sixty years ago when the Nazis capriciously demanded that the Jews of Rome collect 110 pounds of gold within thirty-six hours, and hours before the deadline they were three pounds short. As the congregation debated what to do, there was a knock on the synagogue's back door. A slimmer version of Francesco Inocenti, then just a young priest, opened a bag that was slung over his shoulder. It contained dozens of solid gold cups with Hebrew engravings. "These belong to you, I believe," was all the young priest said to Orvieti before he slipped into the darkness.

And now here they were, old men. Francesco Inocenti, a ranking administrator of the Roman Curia, and Mosè Orvieti, the archivist, both icons in their communities.

"What is it, Mosè?"

Orvieti was firm in his purpose. Beneath his pant leg, the skin of his shins and calves were shredded from having kicked through the stained glass, but he did not mention the injury or the pain he was in.

"The menorah," Orvieti said.

"Mosè." The cardinal fell silent. He nodded to the Swiss Guard, and the sentry left the room. "You know I am not at liberty to discuss any matter related to the menorah. Not since the concordance of 1998. You were part of the meeting with—"

"The deal was not made with me," Orvieti said. "It was made with the state of Israel."

Technically, Mosè Orvieti was correct. The cardinal had been referring to a secret meeting between the state of Israel and the Vatican, stemming from a panel of Israeli archaeologists' request to investigate the whereabouts of the Tabernacle menorah. The archaeologists portrayed a convincing picture of history that led to the menorah being stored in the Vatican archives. They had prepared extensive sources from Theophanes Confessor and other monks of Constantinople to show that as late as the eleventh century, historical documents reported a massive candelabrum deep inside Byzantine palaces that corresponded to the modern location of the Hagia Sophia in Istanbul. And the Fourth Crusade's sack of Constantinople in 1204, the Israelis argued, would have brought the menorah back to Rome and into the Vatican Archives. But the spokesman for the Vatican Library was unresponsive. After the meeting, diplomats from the state of Israel who accompanied the archaeologists signed a diplomatic agreement not to pursue the matter. The agreement was reached in exchange for the permanent loan of some priceless Jewish manuscripts confiscated by the Vatican during the persecution of the Italian Jewish community in the fourteenth and the fifteenth centuries. The state of Israel returned home with enough rare manuscripts to fill a new wing in the Diaspora Museum in Tel Aviv. But they received no clear answer regarding their original request.

"They came here, Mosè, some of the most eminent biblical archaeologists in the world. The charts they brought . . ." The cardinal fell silent, staring absently at the fire. "How they competently mapped out its journey, suggesting it wound up here, as though somehow all the evidence they had gathered could magically make it so." His tone was respectful; empathetic, although with an edge of condescension. "Of course, even if those archaeologists' presumptions were correct, even if the Church took possession of the menorah from the vaults beneath the *Heptalychnos* in Constantinople in 1204 C.E."—the cardinal used the abbreviation for "common era," as a courtesy for his guest, rather than *anno Domini*—"you know I still could not possibly share that information. Mosè, more than anyone I know, you understand that an archive's greatest protection is its secrecy."

"You have the menorah taken by Titus during his sack of Jerusalem," Orvieti said evenly.

Cardinal Inocenti said nothing for a moment, taken aback by Mosè's bold assertion.

"But it is not the menorah from Herod's Temple," Orvieti continued. "It is a replica. It is a replica that has been fought and died for countless times, stolen and stolen in return throughout the Middle Ages." Orvieti pushed himself forward in the chair. "And during the early 1700s, one of the Church goldsmiths, Luigi Valadier, realized that. The artifact in the Vatican's secret archives did not match the proportions laid out in the Book of Exodus, and his exhaustive research of the Church's Josephus manuscripts suggested the true specimen was not pillaged by Roman troops at all. It was a theory so controversial that Luigi Valadier was found drowned before it could be proved. He had told only one person of his theory: his son, Giuseppe Valadier. A decade later, when Napoleon decided to rip up the Colosseum as an amateur archaeologist, Giuseppe agreed, no doubt controversially, to assist. Valadier could now explore the Colosseum in search of the truth. But what Valadier found was not the final stage of his *father's* research, but the beginning. He found Josephus's first clues leading to the original menorah, and that began his private crusade. He discovered a map of Jerusalem inside the Domus Aurea and preserved it on the wall of a synagogue in the Ghetto in Rome. Josephus's message was on the brink of extinction, and as the consummate restorer, Valadier alone kept it alive. What greater act of restoration is there than returning the sacred vessel of Jerusalem to the very people from whom it was robbed two thousand years before?" Orvieti finished speaking.

"Giuseppe Valadier was a religious man," the cardinal said. "Yes, he bequeathed his sketches to the Jews rather than to the Vatican, but you are suggesting he told the Holy See nothing of this?"

"The Jewish community in Rome was prone to pillage. Valadier knew that Josephus's final message must reside in a secure place, so he entrusted the message to the Holy See, from whom it has been passed down from one papacy to the next."

"How do you—" Cardinal Inocenti began, but gathered himself and fell silent.

"He is back in Rome," Orvieti said. "To find it."

"How is that possib—" Fear flashed in the cardinal's eyes. He rose and began to pace in front of the fire. "By now, they must have all the information they require."

"Not all the information," Orvieti said. "I believe Pope John Paul the Second signaled a message to the chief rabbi of Rome. I believe he revealed the line in Josephus that describes the menorah's location."

The cardinal's gaze fell to the floor. He knew the return of sacred relics was a private passion of Pope John Paul II. He recalled the former pontiff's controversial decision to restore the bones of two Middle Age saints, which Orthodox Christians had sought for centuries.

"I remember how moved *il papa* was when he visited the Great Synagogue in Rome. 'Open for me a pinhole of light, and I will broaden it to a sanctuary,' he said. But I don't remember him passing on any information to the chief rabbi. Even if *il papa* had information," Inocenti said, "he could not have disclosed it. Rules of the secrecy governing the Curia would—"

"Have applied only during his lifetime," Orvieti interrupted, "which is why the pope left the message posthumously. As papal chamberlain, you would have been the emissary to the chief rabbi of Rome. You would have seen any additional messages between them. The comment would have been obscure, a hint at best."

Cardinal Inocenti crossed the black-and-white marble floor, glaring at the tile as though it were about to sin.

"Before he died, His Holiness asked me to pass on a line of scripture to the rabbi of the Ghetto," Cardinal Inocenti said, picturing the pope's hand tightening around his, dictating the letter with his last breaths. "He quoted from Deuteronomy, chapter six, verses seven and nine. 'Teach these matters diligently to your children. . . . And you shall write them on your doorposts.' That is all that His Holiness said."

"A mezuzah," Orvieti said. He pushed his small frame from the chair with great effort. Orvieti knew that the Bible twice commanded to write the word of God upon the doorposts of one's house. Many of the medieval homes that still stood in the Ghetto had the ritual scrolls buried inside their stone doorframes. "The information is in a scroll parchment on a doorpost," Orvieti said. "But which doorpost?"

Orvieti closed his eyes, turning the possibilities in his mind. *Valadier excavated in the Colosseum, the Domus Aurea . . .* his eyes widened *. . . and the Arch of Titus.* "Of course," he spoke softly. "A doorpost."

"Are you all right, Mosè?"

"Francesco, do you have any drawings or photographs of the Arch of Titus?"

Within minutes, a priest returned from the adjacent Sala Consultazione Manoscritti with a book of Vatican restorations of monuments in the Roman Forum.

"Here," Cardinal Inocenti said, turning to a black-and-white photograph of the nineteenth-century inscription on the Arch of Titus.

"Giuseppe Valadier restored the Arch of Titus on behalf of Pope Pius the Seventh in 1821."

That is why he bequeathed his drawings to the synagogue. Orvieti understood at last. *Valadier discovered that Josephus's clues led to the Arch of Titus.* He leaned over, staring more closely at the photograph of the Arch of Titus's pediment, searching for anything unusual.

"There," Orvieti said, pointing at the end of the arch's dedicatory inscription.

ANNO · SACRI · PRINCIPATVS · EIVS · XXIIII

"Valadier is simply dating his completion of the arch to the twenty-fourth year of Pope Pius the Seventh's reign—" Cardinal Inocenti stopped. "It *is* curious, though," he said, pointing at the Roman numeral XXIIII. "The spelling of the Roman numeral four is, admittedly, unusual," the cardinal said. "Ancient Romans used IIII, refraining from using the IV because of the letters' pagan sanctity as the beginning of the name of the god IVPITER. So, predictably, early Church Fathers made a deliberate point of using IV in everyday usage, a statement against the pagan god for whom those letters were reserved." Francesco again pointed at the line. "But here Valadier spelled the number according to its ancient Roman style, IIII. It might have been an oversight."

Not an oversight at all, Orvieti knew, taking a step backward as he felt a sudden strength.

"Thank you, Francesco. Thank you for your help."

"But Mosè, we need to bandage that leg, you can't just—"

Orvieti barely heard him. *A mezuzah on the Arch of Titus.* The pagan monument that announced the pillage of Jerusalem's menorah actually possessed the secret of its survival.

"No," Orvieti said. "What you have just done is more than enough." He lowered his tone to a whisper as he hurried out. "You showed me where the answer has been all along."

86

Jonathan jogged into the ruins of the Roman Forum, sneaking through the northern exit gate, adjacent to the Mamertine Prison. He weaved through a tour group and walked briskly, past the rostrum and toward the Arch of Titus. His leg muscles ached as he walked up the Via Sacra's incline toward the arch's higher elevation.

The drizzle stopped and Rome's afternoon sun peeked through, brightening the air with a vividness that comes only after days of rain.

Jonathan approached the Arch of Titus. At the academy, he had studied its single-arched opening of travertine stone, which would become a model for all of Rome's subsequent triumphal arches. But the historical importance of the arch now seemed trivial compared to what may have been hidden inside for two thousand years.

Jonathan surveyed the height of the arch's attic. It was over twelve feet high—higher than necessary to hide the tabernacle's eight-foot lamp of gold. Jonathan imagined Josephus and his men hoisting the massive object into the attic in the dead of night. The millennia-old tradition among Roman Jews not to stand beneath the arch suddenly made sense. The presence of the Temple menorah resting above the arch had hallowed the ground beneath it.

But all of this was trivialized by Jonathan's dread. *Emili.*

On his way to the Forum, he must have thought a dozen times about going to the authorities. He could not go to the carabinieri without Lieutenant Rufio knowing, but he considered the American embassy, the law firm, even the New York City Police Department's international desk. But as his panic settled, he realized he could trust no one. *The UN director?* Jonathan was still bewildered. *He knows more than you can imagine,* she had said.

He circled the arch, searching for any signs of entry or recent excavation. A thin aluminum scaffolding had been constructed to clean the western façade, but the pediment was solid stone, allowing for no access to the arch.

He climbed up on the arch's ashlar base, surveying the Forum park for any signs of Chandler. He began to worry that their phone call was cut short intentionally. His eyes moved rapidly over the ruins. *No sign of Chandler.*

Jonathan stepped beneath the underside of the arch and peered up at its sculptured foliage, which descended to two bas-reliefs lining the passageway. Jonathan stood there, staring at the western interior relief, the arch's most famous element and perhaps the most famous bas-relief in all of Rome: the deeply carved depiction of a triumphal procession with the wreathed Roman soldiers carrying the menorah shoulder-high through the city. Jonathan knew the marching of Roman victory through city streets had become a frequent practice to celebrate military conquests. But his observations about this famous scene meant infinitely more now than they had in some graduate school seminar. *Emili's life could depend on them.*

Jonathan moved closer to the carved relief, so close that he could touch a stone captive of Jerusalem following behind the Roman soldier in the relief.

"Where did you put it?" Jonathan said softly to the stone. The sculpted figure on the arch seemed to march past him, ignoring his desperation. Frustrated and exhausted and standing in the cold, Jonathan stepped closer to the relief and screamed. *"Did—you—put—it—in—the—arch?"*

The sound of his voice echoed beneath the stone pillars. The

Forum was still, except for some elderly tourists who steered clear of the young madman.

"Yes," said a weak voice, and for a moment, Jonathan thought the stones had answered.

Jonathan turned around to see Mosè Orvieti. He stood very still, his pants stained dark brown with dried blood.

"Signor Orvieti," Jonathan said, "are you all right?"

But Orvieti was not concerned with himself.

"Where is she?" he asked.

Jonathan said nothing.

With an almost mystical understanding, Orvieti walked toward him. "You have to find it, don't you?"

Jonathan's fragile nod was almost imperceptible.

Orvieti walked beside him and placed his hand on his shoulder. "Okay, then. We will find it."

"Is it in the arch?" Jonathan asked hopefully.

"Yes, in the arch," Orvieti replied. "The only question is where."

"But it's right here," Jonathan said, pointing at the monument in front of them. "The Arch of Titus is right here in the Forum. The line in Josephus said, 'The gate where the triumphal procession passed through.'"

"But no triumphal procession ever passed through this Arch of Titus," Orvieti said. "That line in Josephus refers to the *original* Arch of Titus. This arch wasn't built until ten years after the conquest of Jerusalem."

"The *original* Arch of Titus," Jonathan said contemplatively. *I am rusty, aren't I?* Jonathan remembered now that the Roman practice was to build *two* triumphal arches, one for the victorious troops to march under, and after a period of time, a grander arch for ensuing generations.

"*Signore*, the location of the *first* Arch of Titus, has been lost now for at least a thousand years. The last historical record of it was the travel notes of an eighth-century monk who didn't even say where it was, only that its area had become a community for the descendants of the slaves of Titus." Jonathan pointed at the upper right-hand corner of the Arch of Titus's relief, which depicted the procession marching under the original arch.

"Even if Josephus put the menorah in the first Arch of Titus, there's no way to tell where it is."

"Unless someone has told us," Orvieti said, limping to the edge of the arch. He pointed upward. "There is a message up there."

Jonathan stepped outside the arch's shadow, shifting his attention to the weighty attic above the opening.

"In the dedicatory inscription?" Jonathan asked. The Latin inscription stenciled high above the arch appeared to use the same ingratiating language that all papal architects used to dedicate a restoration to the presiding pope.

Insigne Religionis Atque Artis Monumentum
Fulciri Servarique Iussit
Anno Sacri Principatus Eius XXIIII

"A badge of both religion and art . . . has been preserved," Jonathan translated, his head tilted upward. *Standard Vatican pomp,* he thought. But just as he was about to look away, he noticed something strange about the inscription's first word.

"*Insigne*," Jonathan said. "In Latin, the word *insigne* means 'badge' or 'emblem,' from which we get the word 'insignia.'" The full meaning of the following words began to dawn on him. "An insignia remarkable in religion and art has been preserved—" Jonathan stopped translating and turned to Orvieti.

"I don't believe it," he said, realizing the restorer's intent. "The 'insignia' is the menorah, isn't it?" *An insignia remarkable in religion and art has been preserved.*

Orvieti spoke quietly. "Pope John Paul the Second, before he died, quoted a passage from Deuteronomy to the chief rabbi of Rome. The passage referred to writing words on a doorpost."

"And you think the message refers to this inscription?"

"No, I think it refers to a scroll hidden somewhere on the arch's façade," Orvieti said. "*That* is why the pope quoted that passage of Deuteronomy to the chief rabbi of Rome. The message is written in a mezuzah. It's a clue only someone from the Ghetto would know to look for."

"The arch is huge, *Signore*," Jonathan said, turning to the monument. "He could have put it anywhere."

"Look at the date."

Jonathan studied the pediment's last line. "The papal architect used the pagan numeral for four, IIII, rather than ecclesiastical Latin, IV."

"Written on your doorposts," Orvieti repeated. "He could be drawing attention to the last 'I' for a reason."

"Because you think there is a message of some kind behind that numeral?" Jonathan asked.

Orvieti nodded.

Jonathan looked at the scaffolding. It led up to the lowest line of the pediment's inscription where the papal architect had written the date. He then looked around him. The tour groups were sparse and gathered at the other end of the Forum. Two guards sat in a sentry booth thirty feet from the other side of the arch.

I can't believe I'm about to do this.

Jonathan gripped the uprights on the scaffolding and pulled himself up. The steel frame felt rickety and he looked down to see if the scaffolding was tilting upward from his weight. The pediment was higher than he anticipated and the entablature, which consisted of huge bronze letters fastened to the marble, was much larger than anyone would imagine from the ground.

Jonathan stood on the scaffold. His shoulders reached the base of the pediment. Each bronze numeral must have been half his height.

To his surprise, the last "I" of the roman numeral XXIIII was connected to the pediment differently from the others. Along the right side of the bronze fixture, Jonathan saw hinges and, using his back muscles, he pulled at the long, rectangular numeral. He felt the fixture budge and swing outward to the side like a slender metal door. Behind the numeral, he found a rectangular compartment, a small foot-tall closet carved into the stone. A tight scroll of thick vellum had been tucked inside. *There's actually something here.*

Jonathan leaned into the bronze numeral to keep it from swinging shut, using one hand to pull the parchment from the crevice. The parchment was dry, but the bottom of the scroll adhered to the stone. Jonathan gave it a gentle tug. Now with the scroll in his hand, he stepped back and the numeral swung back into place. Focused, Jonathan walked back across the scaffolding as though unaware of its height.

"*Signore!*" he heard one of the guards shout, and startled, Jonathan nearly lost his balance. He looked down and two guards walked directly beneath the scaffolding toward Orvieti.

"The ruins are closing!" the older guard called out.

Offering apologies, Orvieti complied, careful not to draw any attention to Jonathan above him.

The older guard walked past the arch and Jonathan remained motionless. If the guard looked up, he would see Jonathan in plain view. As quietly as he could, Jonathan climbed down the scaffolding two rungs at a time.

No sooner did Jonathan's feet touch down than the guard turned back toward the arch. Looking surprised, the guard saw the young man standing at the base of the Arch of Titus. He had appeared out of nowhere.

"It's three o'clock, *Signore*! The Forum is closed," the guard said, scratching his antiquated white mustache. "I've worked here thirty years, and there is still not enough time to see these ruins!"

"Yes," Jonathan said, hurrying toward the exit. "Their importance is often over our heads, isn't it?"

87

Emili was blindfolded and seated in an aluminum folding chair. Through the small opening beneath her blindfold, she could see the glow of computer screens in a dark room. She tried to move, but polyurethane straps restrained her wrists and ankles. A cloth gag exuded a sharp chemical taste in her mouth and it burned her throat. She could hear passing buses, but the sound was faint. There was an earthen smell, suggesting they were underground. *She was beneath a bridge. Or inside a tunnel.* She remained silent, with her head still hanging to one side, pretending to still be unconscious. She used the time to gather her senses.

At the UN, she had sat through a mandatory seminar on being taken captive. Among the lifesaving imperatives were: *keep your bearings, ask questions, try to determine your location, and how much time has passed.*

She heard the clicking of a keyboard, confirming her sense that she was in a high-technology environment. In the background, she heard soft voices. *Arabic.* The dialect was the same as what was spoken in the car.

"You are trying to figure out where you are, aren't you?" said a voice, eerily close to her ear. Her captor's Italian had only a trace of an Arabic accent, detectable only by a native.

Her gag was suddenly ripped down from her mouth by a hand that seemed disembodied.

"I know who you are," Emili strained to say, her mouth and cheeks tender. "You are Salah ad-Din."

"Gather information, ask questions," Salah ad-Din said. "Is that what they taught you to do in this situation? You were mumbling in your drugged sleep. Everything is in the UN manual, isn't it?"

Emili turned her blindfolded head inches from the source of her captor's voice and spat point-blank in Salah ad-Din's face.

"That's not in the UN manual," she said.

She could hear the click of his dress shoes on the stone floor.

"You always were unpredictable, weren't you?"

Always. How would he know?

"It seems our mutual respect for history has brought us together again."

"*Respect?*" Emili could not help herself. "You are destroying thousands of years of Judeo-Christian relics. You have no respect for history."

He slammed his fist so hard on the aluminum table that it dented in. "I respect history so much that I understand the consequences of controlling it!" The echo of his outburst carried into the darkness.

He mumbled something in Arabic, and a man grabbed her head roughly and removed her blindfold. It was a dark cavern with no perceptible ceiling. Before her were two computers, both with complex subterranean maps overlaying cross-sectional views of Rome. Beside the aluminum table was a row of oxygen tanks, acetylene tanks, and underwater diving equipment.

She shifted in her seat, trying to turn around to see Salah ad-Din standing behind her.

"Ah-ah," Salah ad-Din said disapprovingly. "Keep your eyes forward."

"Emili." A different voice now, but she placed it at once. A woman stepped out of the darkness.

Director Jacqueline Olivier.

"Do as he says," Jacqueline said. "Please."

Emili stared at her for a moment, bewildered. She did not appear kidnapped. Her hands were free and she sat down in a chair across a small table. She was wearing a winter-white pantsuit and matching pearls. Despite Emili's dire circumstances, the director's polished appearance reminded Emili that the UN Colosseum ceremony was today. *She was on her way there.*

"Jacquie, what are you—"

"I can help you," Olivier said. "They are looking for the lost Arch of Titus. Not the arch in the Roman Forum, but the original one. They believe the person you were traveling with—"

"Jonathan?" Emili said.

"—yes, might have told you where it was. They need to know where it is, Emili. You must tell them."

Staring at the director, Emili suddenly felt ill. "How could you do this?"

"I would not pass judgment about the director," Salah ad-Din said, his voice still behind Emili. "She urged us to let you go. Even with the World Heritage Committee's Colosseum ceremony beginning in less than an hour, she came here to save your life." Emili heard the distinct click of a firearm loading. "And now, Dr. Travia, it is your opportunity to save hers."

"What are you talking about?" Emili said.

"Don't move, Director," said Salah ad-Din.

The look on the face of the UN director turned from despair to blind fear. She stared at Salah ad-Din above Emili's shoulder.

Salah ad-Din's voice whispered into her ear, "Tell us where the first arch is, Dr. Travia, or I will kill her."

"Wait!" the UN director said suddenly frantic. "She doesn't know!" All traces of her dignified bearing were gone.

"I would like to be certain," said Salah ad-Din coolly.

Jacqueline's eyes flickered toward Emili, registering a terror that Emili was now unsure she even could trust.

"Dr. Travia, I am going to count to three. Where is the original Arch of Titus?" Salah ah Din said. "One."

"I don't know," Emili said, her voice quivering. "We assumed it meant the arch in the Roman Forum."

"Please, Emili, for both of us." The UN director's voice was shaking uncontrollably. "Tell him what you know."

"Two."

Emili was silent. Her entire world had been upturned. Nothing was impossible.

"Three."

Jacqueline's eyes had been fixed above her shoulder. But as Salah ad-Din said three, the director's eyes lowered gracefully, locking with Emili's.

Two pops, no louder than firecracker snaps.

At first Emili was not sure what had happened. Then she saw the blood trickling from the director's forehead onto her pashmina scarf. The director appeared unsure as well. She was just conscious enough to feel the blood on her own forehead, and in a last gesture of almost farcical grace, began to wipe it away. As she stared at her own bloodstained fingers, Director Olivier's eyes glazed, and the weight of her posture caused her to collapse headfirst onto the aluminum table.

Emili stared straight ahead, frozen in terror. She could smell the smoke from the greased barrel only inches behind her head.

"Okay," Salah ad-Din said, his tone almost relieved, "she doesn't know."

Within seconds, Salah ad-Din struck Emili on the back of her head with the butt of his gun. The pain was so intense it was visual, streaks of blackness raced across her vision until they swallowed the room and everything faded to darkness. Her last horrific vision was the blush makeup on the UN director's cheek, bathing in a pool of blood on the table.

88

Jonathan hurried through the Forum's exit turnstiles and found Orvieti standing along the Via dei Fori Imperali, beside a new glass tourist center. Jonathan handed him the scroll he had just found inside the arch's pediment.

"I can't open it," Orvieti said, awestruck. "My hands are shaking."

Jonathan unrolled the vellum scroll. The leather had stiffened and it cracked in two in his hands, but the pieces easily fit together and the ink had survived remarkably well. The classicist in Jonathan appreciated that the parchment had been abraded with pumice, which kept the ink dark even after centuries. It was another architectural sketch of the Colosseum. A quotation was written above the drawing. Jonathan recognized it immediately.

Seven branches of light forge . . . on the spot where the law of Rome executes those condemned. . . .

"It's another line from Josephus," Jonathan said. He stared at the parchment, his gaze fixed on the quotation.

Orvieti looked not at the sketch, but at Jonathan, who looked whiter than a moment before.

"Do you know what it means?" Orvieti asked.

Jonathan nodded. "It looks like a location within the Colosseum: 'The spot where the law of Rome executes those condemned.'" He stared back down at the sketch. "The seven branches of light must refer to the sunlight through the arches of the Colosseum's upper tiers. They 'forge' at a place on the arena floor." Jonathan pointed at the illustration. "Look, Valadier's nineteenth-century sketch shows the light converging through the arches.

"So, Josephus's line describes a location in the arena?"

"Right, but there was a problem. The western rim of the Colosseum had eroded long before the nineteenth century, so Valadier had to *reconstruct* the western arches in 1809 to allow the light to illuminate the exact location on the arena floor that Josephus was describing." Jonathan spoke rapidly, as though hurrying to keep pace with the logical steps in his mind.

"But what could be so important about that spot in the arena?" Orvieti asked.

Jonathan fell silent and his eyes glazed.

"A trapdoor," he whispered.

"A trapdoor?"

"Yes," Jonathan said, shaking himself out of his daze. "Seven years ago, I saw an ancient fresco in a catacomb just before it collapsed. It was a painting of a man escaping from the Colosseum's arena through a trapdoor."

Jonathan took a deep breath.

He felt the *scriptio inferior* of his own past resurface again, but now old and new scripts were completing each other in a way he would rather not have seen. Seven years ago, he may have entered a tomb with a historical significance beyond his wildest imagination. *Salah ad-Din knows more than you can imagine,* Jonathan had just heard in Ostia.

"*Signore,* I think that trapdoor opens to a tunnel leading to the first Arch of Titus."

"And you think it was Josephus who escaped?"

"Yes, *Signore,* which explains why the ancient historians wrote that Titus wept so bitterly when Josephus escaped. Josephus was no ordinary traitor to Titus. He was the one priest who could still keep the flame of the hidden menorah alive. Remember how Titus and his magicians feared the flame. The only way to extinguish it was to ensure there was no priest left to tend it. That is why the ancient Romans would kill all the male priests, hoping to stomp out its patrilineal descent."

"Which has its consequences today," Orvieti said somberly. "Among all of Roman Jewry, there are still almost no *kohanim,* no priests," Orvieti said. "As a boy, I knew no others."

"Others? So you are—"

Orvieti lifted his hand, slightly, but enough for Jonathan to detect his tormented faith.

"Whatever holiness I once had," Orvieti said, "is gone."

The sun had passed over the Palatine, but its yellow stream of light flowed down Via di San Gregorio, still catching the upper lip of the Colosseum. Orvieti looked at his watch.

"It's three-fifteen," he said. "The sun will set through those arches in less than twenty minutes."

89

The evening's Colosseum ceremony was to mark the invocation of the United Nations World Heritage Committee meeting in Rome and the two hundredth anniversary of the Colosseum's first major restoration in 1809. Roman diplomats and press wearing authorization credentials on blue neck straps streamed into the Colosseum along a red carpet and through metal detectors. Parked black sedans with diplomatic plates fringed the Colosseum's outer arches. Italian soldiers mixed with plainclothes carabinieri behind white police sawhorses cordoned off the Piazza del Colosseo.

The event's corporate sponsorship had set up tables, with one national Italian bank advertising, "Like the Colosseum, Banco Roma is built to last." Local camera crews interviewed Roman celebrities. A soccer goalie from Italy's World Cup soccer team crouched between the arches, posing for the paparazzi, as though to block a kick.

Jonathan and Orvieti walked on the Via dei Fori Imperiali, along the edge of the Piazza del Colosseo. It was hard to believe he was here at the Colosseum only twenty-four hours before. *Yesterday,*

I came here as a tourist, and now I'm a fugitive. Jonathan scanned the crowd, focusing on the carabinieri officers stationed at every entrance.

"How will you get in?" Orvieti asked. "You'll have to be in the arena to see the sun's rays."

"There," Jonathan said, pointing at the far side of the plaza, where catering trucks and staging equipment were backed up against the eastern arches of the circular ruin. Just to the left of the service area, Jonathan could see a gladiatorial troupe hired for the event, practicing their choreographed fight sequences. Two of the actors worked on their thrusts and lunges. An older performer, with some apparent fencing expertise, intervened, correcting their combat theatrics. Some of the actors were already in character, fully costumed, wearing their masks.

Other members of the gladiatorial troupe exited a trailer parked beside one of the arches.

"I have an idea," Jonathan said.

Jonathan made his way through the throngs of onlookers and entered the empty trailer. Inside, the shelves were lined with classical-period swords, brass-plated breast armor, pleated leather skirts, arm guards, and gladiatorial helmets with bright red plumes made of cleaning bristles.

Jonathan quickly changed into an entire costume, complete with a sheathed dagger, which was nothing more than a cheap switch-blade glued to a costume plastic handle, and jogged over to the troupe, with his suit and shoes rolled up under his arm. He was stopped midway by an American woman with a heavy southern accent: "Darlin'," she said, "may we taykuh pichure wich'e?" A family from Texas with four different digital cameras encircled him.

Jonathan put on his tin helmet as the tourists took turns standing beside him.

In costume, Jonathan hurried past the UN security, overhearing the frantic staffers trying to locate Director Olivier to give the ceremony's opening remarks. Inside the arches, service staff, also in Roman period costume, swarmed, rolling trays of appetizers up ramps into the Colosseum. Jonathan found the acting troupe and quickly blended in with other men dressed in full gladiatorial regalia. He managed to stuff his clothing behind a rack of appetizers.

"Are you new?" one of the acting troupe members asked Jonathan in Italian. He extended a hand, and as Jonathan went to shake it the man grabbed Jonathan's forearm with a death grip. Jonathan knew this was the handshake of ancient Rome and he returned the gesture. *These guys really get into it.*

"You're the replacement," the man stated, rather than asked, in Italian. "What sort of gladiator are you?"

"Sorry?"

"Your style of combat," the man said in earnest.

"Of course," Jonathan said, remembering the different gladiator types in ancient Rome. "A *hoplomachus*," he said, naming the first kind of gladiator he could think of.

"*Salve!*" the man said. "We have needed a *hoplomachus*! You'll need a small round shield, of course, but you already knew that," the man said, motioning to the prop master. "Those two men are *retiarii*, as you've probably guessed from their tridents and armor." The two men waved lethargically. "And that man there"—he pointed to a man fastening on a visored helmet—"is a charioteer. Ah, your shield, here," he said, handing Jonathan a thin metal replica Greek hoplite shield. He explained that as an adjunct professor of classics at a local college, he insisted all the swords the men use be real, making their choreography even more important to their safety. He launched into a lecture about the different weapons gladiators used, from spiked leather arms to weighted throw nets, but Jonathan's mind was elsewhere. He looked up at the golden rays now catching the top portion of the arches.

It was only minutes until the rays would converge on a location on the arena floor.

Seven branches of light forge . . .

"You should tape up your other sword," the adjunct professor said. "Here," he said, handing Jonathan some black rubberized tape. "We use gummy tape to soften the sword's tip in case of accidental contact. You wouldn't want to hurt someone."

"No, of course not," Jonathan said. His own voice sounded tinny beneath the helmet.

But before he could apply the tape, there was sudden movement, and a dramatic solemnity overtook the troupe as the actors moved into formation.

"To battle!" the adjunct professor said in Latin as they marched in step.

The first half of the troupe ran onto the arena floor. Jonathan could hear the crowd's cheers, and through the archways he saw the actors artfully thrusting and lunging at one another in careful choreography on the arena's sand.

Discreetly, Jonathan managed to break away from the group, walking along the radial corridor. His eyes fixated on the rays of sun filtering through the seven openings along the western lip of the arena.

Amazing.

He watched as seven discrete rays of light sloped down the architecture of the western side, the rim's curvature bringing them closer together as the sun lowered with surprising speed. The rays now touched the arena floor.

"Get out there now!" one of the older actors prompted Jonathan, smacking the back of his helmet.

"I'm not part of the—" But Jonathan did not finish the sentence before he was pushed through the arch.

He stepped out into the arena and was dazzled by the ceremony's elegant atmosphere. Five hundred people in formal attire mulled around the railing: well-dressed philanthropists, corporate executives, and the beautiful women who accompanied them.

The choreographed battles swirled around Jonathan and he navigated through them, trying to stay out of their way. Their routines kicked up large amounts of sand, and suddenly he could not even see the seven rays filtering through the western rim. He ran out of the dust cloud toward the arena's center, where his view returned. The seven rays combed the floor, growing closer together.

"Watch your dramatic space!" grunted one of the gladiators as he rolled past Jonathan.

But Jonathan was too focused to respond. The rays of sunlight had forged on a single spot along the southeastern border of the arena. Mesmerized, Jonathan walked toward it, oblivious to the men somersaulting around him. Like a majestic architectural display, the seven rays formed three V's, creating the shape of the menorah itself, spanning the size of the Colosseum. *The trapdoor was here,* Jonathan thought. *Josephus escaped through the arena floor here.*

He dragged his leg across the arena's sand, marking the spot. He looked to the nearest arch that aligned with his feet. *XVIII.* The rays of light converged in front of the Colosseum's eighteenth arch.

There must have been a tunnel under here, leading out of the Colosseum.

With sudden violence, someone grabbed Jonathan from behind and threw him against the arena's railing. Jonathan's helmet smashed against the steel, and Jonathan fell to the ground. The butt of a sword landed on his head, nearly knocking him unconscious. Jonathan scrambled up and jumped back, just as the metal edge of a sword sparked against the stone behind him.

The man was dressed in gladiatorial uniform with a black breastplate and two swords, a *dimachaerius*, known as the most dangerous of gladiators. One of his swords remained sheathed at his waist; he tossed the other one side to side.

"Jesus," Jonathan said, winded. "I'm not part of the—"

Jonathan did not have time to finish the comment before the man charged, striking another blow at his chest, denting the breast-plate so deeply that the costumed aluminum nearly folded in two. The man wasn't using any rubber tape around his sword.

Something was not right.

Out of the dust, the man swung again, and Jonathan rolled off to the side of the sandy arena. He could hear exuberant screaming from the stands and he realized that the crowd was cheering him on, enjoying the performance. Jonathan was knocked down again, this time by one of the actors, who theatrically rolled away.

"I said, watch your dramatic space!" the actor reprimanded him. By the time Jonathan stood up, he could not distinguish the man who attacked him from other members of the troupe, who were swirling around him in a kaleidoscope of glinting tin and dust.

A blow landed on the back of his helmet, and Jonathan pivoted, but his helmet blocked his peripheral vision. The man struck again. His blows were different from those of the others. Trained, cutting strokes of someone who was used to wearing the plastron of fenc-ing gear, rather than the tin breastplate of gladiatorial costume.

"Who are you!" Jonathan shouted, stumbling back.

Their swords clashed, hurling Jonathan toward the arena railing. But the force of impact did not compare to the shock of glimpsing, with unnerving clarity, the familiar features between the two cheek guards of the Roman helmet.

As a reflex of rage, Jonathan unleashed his own cutting strokes. He expertly maneuvered his sword to connect first beneath the man's rib cage, sending him reeling backward in the sand, and then struck again, using the flat end of his sword to smack the man's head, knocking his helmet clean off to reveal his tousled hair and reddened face.

"Aurelius," Chandler Manning wheezed. A bitter smile twisted his lips. "I told you I'd take the match."

90

As Jonathan stood up, his mind fit the pieces together with blinding speed: Chandler finding him in the Forum, Chandler giving them maps of the Domus Aurea—all so that Jonathan and Emili could move another step in the direction in which he had been secretly steering them all along.

"You've been in on this the entire time, haven't you, Chandler?"

"That's it, now," Chandler said with a taunting smile. "That's the brilliant Marcus I remember."

"And for what?" Jonathan said, containing his rage. "To be the one who finds it? You would endanger Emili's life to find an ancient artifact?"

Chandler laughed. "Is that what you think it is, Jon? The irony, it's magnificent."

"Irony?" The shock of discovery was wearing off and a fury rose inside Jonathan.

"That you, Aurelius—you were always the first to call me gullible. You would always say that it was me who chased after alternative histories and far-fetched tales of lost treasure, and now it's you who bought it hook, line, and sinker. You really think there's some lost relic of Jerusalem, Jon?" Chandler said. "Just another example of the fantasies that kept us all busy at the academy. But now I'm finally making some money for it."

"This man Salah ad-Din is a monster," Jonathan said loudly.

"'Client' is the term I prefer," Chandler said, spreading his arms. "And with the king's ransom this guy offered me, he could have said he was looking for the goddamn sword of Excalibur and I would have said, 'Agreed.'" Chandler approached Jonathan slowly, pointing his sword straight at him.

"Fight, you two!" said the gruff voice of an acting troupe member. "You're not getting paid to talk!"

"Chandler, listen, just listen," Jonathan said, using every bit of his self-discipline to check his rage. "This is all *real*. Do you hear me? The menorah is *real*."

"Well, I know that *now*. And you're going to tell me where it is. Eight feet of solid gold has suddenly made Salah ad-Din's fee seem a bit paltry, don't you think? That's why I've got it all worked out." He patted his breastplate. "Brought my sketches of every possible escape route from the Colosseum. Only need to know which arch Josephus used to—"

"Chandler," Jonathan cut him off, "they have *taken* Emili. You don't understand—"

"I don't understand? *I don't understand!*" Chandler screamed, his eyes wilder than Jonathan had ever seen them. "No, Jon, for once *you* are the one who doesn't understand! Jonathan Marcus, *golden boy* of the American Academy in Rome when I was just the *lowly* librarian."

Only at that moment did Jonathan realize how much Chandler despised him, how easy it had been for him to pull off this deception, pretending to learn each part of the mystery along with them piece by piece.

"Where is she, Chandler?" Jonathan asked, walking toward him confrontationally. "Why do they need her?"

Chandler's eyes became slits and he began waving his sword. "Ever playing the hero, aren't you, Aurelius?"

Without another word, Jonathan lunged and caught Chandler's sword. Their metal tinged loudly. Neighboring actors looked stunned that they were not using precautionary grip tape. Chandler vanished into the swirling dust and Jonathan spun around, unable to find him among the actors. Jonathan saw a glistening sword split the air above him, and his defensive blow was so forceful it sent an actor's sword flying into the air. The man dived in theatrical slow motion to collect his sword.

"Relax, man!" the actor exclaimed from behind his mask. "My kids are here, okay?"

Jonathan limped toward the center of the arena. On all sides of him, actor pairs battled it out in a neatly choreographed mayhem. Another man came at Jonathan, but spying the rubber tape on his sword, Jonathan only ducked, letting the man harmlessly glide by. Out of the maelstrom of dust, Chandler struck again, a crushing blow, splitting Jonathan's dented tin armor in two, sending him to the ground, his rib cage pounding with pain.

"Must hand it to you, Aurelius, you aren't the same boy who left Rome seven years ago. Cast out of the Garden of Eden of academia and you didn't so much as say a word in defense of yourself. Salah ad-Din wasn't expecting a bloody hero. He was expecting a lawyer."

"Just tell me where she is." Jonathan coughed, standing up. "Why do they need her?"

"The great Jonathan Marcus," Chandler said, leering. "You still haven't figured it out, have you?" Chandler picked up his sword in an en garde position. "It's not her they need. *It's you.*"

"What?"

"You think any of this is an accident, Aurelius? Your background in Josephus. Coming to Rome to defend mysterious pieces of the

Forma Urbis? He arranged the whole damn thing. Why do you think those fragments were loaned to the museum here in Rome? Salah ad-Din knew she'd recognize them and have the Ministry of Culture bring the case. You think Salah ad-Din didn't know you'd be coming to Rome? Who do you think your client is, Jon? The one behind the shadowy Geneva corporation? *It's him.*"

"But what for! He has seen everything I have!"

"Not quite everything," Chandler said. "Seven years ago in the catacombs, Aurelius. Whose tomb do you think you stumbled into? *It was Berenice's.* And you saw information drawn on the walls that all but told you where the menorah was, *only you didn't know it.*"

"The fresco," Jonathan said.

"*Precisely,*" Chandler said tauntingly. "The fresco destroyed in the collapse."

"So I was the last person to see inside the tomb," Jonathan muttered.

"*Bravo,*" Chandler said. "Not the last technically, but Gianpaolo isn't much use to us, is he?"

"Chandler, *you idiot*, do you think he will let you live? This man killed Sharif in cold blood to protect his pursuit." Jonathan raised his arm to strike when something seized him from behind, pinning his arms to his sides.

"*We Thracians will defeat you!*" One of the large actors of the group had grabbed hold of him as part of a routine. Jonathan wrestled for a moment, the tin cheek plates of his helmet preventing him from seeing the man restraining him. Chandler walked toward him, holding his sword out. In the chaos of the arena's dust, Jonathan's writhing looked as staged as the rest of the faux combat.

"Time to stop playing the hero, Aurelius. Where is the tunnel leading to the first Arch of Titus."

The crowd roared, but Jonathan heard none of it, for at that moment something in him snapped. Without thinking, he sharply flicked his head backward, butting his helmet's plume into the actor's helmet behind him. Amid expletives, the actor promptly dropped Jonathan, who with both hands wheeled his sword around, hitting Chandler in the abdomen with the flat end of the sword's blade. Chandler stumbled backward as Jonathan swung again, harder now. Chandler fell to the sand. The crowd's cheers strengthened at the realism of it all.

"Where is she?" Jonathan raged, punching Chandler in the face with the handle of his sword. "Tell me or I swear I'll—"

"You'll what?" Chandler said as he spit up some blood. "That a threat, ol' boy? Suppose Seneca was right: *'Gladiator in arena consilium capit.'* No lawyer's advice in the arena, is there? Just brute force."

Chandler stood back up and pivoted his foot in the sand, throwing his weight into Jonathan's cracked breastplate with such force that Jonathan's sword flew out of his hand and landed ten feet away. Chandler took the advantage, charging as he rotated his sword on either side to gain torque. Jonathan then did something that no one in the acting troupe would ever forget, or be able to replicate no matter how many Saturday afternoons they tried on the blue mats of their practice studio.

Rather than retreat, Jonathan ran toward his sword, charging barehanded in Chandler's direction. Without breaking stride, Jonathan stomped his heel on the blade's tip, popping up its hilt to his hand, and in the same fluid motion swung its flat edge squarely into Chandler's kneecap, dislocating the bone with an audible pop. Chandler screamed in anguish. Jonathan used Chandler's forward motion to hurl him into the iron railings of the arena so that his body tipped over the edge. Only his right arm managed to prevent him from falling into the thirty-foot drop to the underground labyrinth below. He kicked one leg at the ancient brickwork beneath the arena, trying to find a foothold.

The guests at the event had fallen silent in shock. Jonathan got up slowly, bruised and shaky at first, hands on his knees. And then fully upright. With almost a rehearsed suddenness, the Colosseum's crowd roared. Even the actors were applauding.

"Who does their choreography?" one of the actors asked.

"We should recruit these guys," said the other.

Chandler hung on the railing with one arm, grunting. "Help me up, I can't hold on!"

Jonathan stood over Chandler. "How does Salah ad-Din know so much about me? You told him about my research seven years ago?"

"No, he told me," Chandler said, letting out a sound too painful to call a groan as he swung from the edge. "It was like . . . he *knows* you. Now help me up! My damn knee is on fire!"

Above the cheering crowd, Jonathan heard the sounds of approaching police sirens. He turned toward the arena's exit.

"How am I supposed to get up from here? The carabinieri—what the hell am I supposed to do?"

"Sorry, Chandler. *'Gladiator in arena consilium capit,'*" Jonathan said, turning to leave. "No lawyer's advice in the arena."

91

Jonathan ran out of the arena, and in one of the outer arches changed back into his suit. As instructed, Orvieti was waiting. Together they moved through the radial corridor, weaving among the guests, looking up at the numbers on the arches. Carabinieri

officers rushed past him, and no longer with the benefit of a mask's anonymity, Jonathan faced the walls as he walked past them. *We must get down to the labyrinth beneath the arena floor.*

"This is the gate," Jonathan said, pointing at the number XVIII above one of the arches.

"Of course," Orvieti said softly. *All these years, how could I not have guessed?* It now seemed obvious to him that the slaves of Jerusalem would have chosen to burrow an escape tunnel under the number eighteen, a number that in Hebrew, *chai*, had endless mystical associations with life and survival.

They ducked into the dark apse, and Jonathan held Orvieti's arm tightly as they moved down a steep stone stairwell to the maze beneath the arena. Kicked-up sand floated over the railing of the half-reconstructed arena floor above them. Orvieti struggled as his shoes sank in the labyrinth's mud with each step.

The tunnel must be here, Jonathan thought. They now stood directly beneath the eighteenth arch and Jonathan's flashlight caught a half-height archway that resembled an abandoned mine shaft, owing to the partially buried old wooden plank that boarded it up.

"This must be it," he said, pointing to a scratched inscription in the stone above the arch.

"'*Astra polumque pia cepisti mente, Rabiri,*'" Jonathan read aloud and translated, "And Rabirius used the sky in his architecture."

"Rabirius?" Orvieti said.

"One of the architects of the Colosseum," Jonathan said, managing a smile. "It was a quote from Martial, the ancient satirist, and contemporary of Josephus. It now makes perfect sense. Martial appears to be complimenting Rabirius, one of the Colosseum's architects, but really he was giving the location of a trapdoor for the prisoners."

"Are you sure he wasn't just complimenting the arches?"

"Martial was the kind of wedding guest who once stood up and toasted the groom's love for his bride, *'Quid ergo in illa petitur et placet? Tussit.'* He loves her even when she coughs."

Orvieti said nothing, but clearly did not see the insult.

"It's vintage Martial, *Signore*. Sounds romantic, but there's a darker meaning. He is warning the assembled guests that the groom loves her not because she is beautiful, but because she is suffering from consumption, which was often fatal in ancient Rome. That's why she coughs. And her imminent death means the groom gets his share of her father's fortune. It's pure Martial, throwing a right hook, and no one sees it coming. Martial's poetry was always about the darker side of Rome. Or in this case, telling prisoners where an escape path lies in a way that the Roman secret police will never pick up. Rabirius built the arches to train sunlight or allow prisoners to 'use the sky' to locate the trapdoor."

Jonathan knelt in the dirt, scraping away watery clumps of mud from the base of the plank.

"By going through here, Josephus must have made it past all of the Praetorian guards," Jonathan explained. "After he fell through the trapdoor in the arena, he went into this tunnel."

Jonathan bent down and, using the strength in his legs, tried to lift the wooden plank from the wall, but there was still too much dirt packed along its bottom. He scraped another inch and the plank came loose from the arch, nearly falling on its own weight.

Jonathan stared into the blackness.

"I'm going with you," Orvieti said. "If there are messages from the slaves of Jerusalem, they won't be in Latin. You need me." He paused. "*She* needs me."

"*Signore*, you said the air was too thin."

"That is what *my physician* said," Orvieti countered lightly. "And I'll always have this fresh supply"—he pointed at his small green oxygen tank—"should I need it."

"Need it?" Jonathan said, smiling. "From what I've seen, *Signore*, I'm not sure you've *ever* needed that."

Jonathan ducked through the opening first and guided Orvieti into the tunnel's darkness.

This may have been the corridor Josephus used to reach the Arch of Titus, Jonathan thought.

The entrance to the tunnel was low, but after a few feet Jonathan could fully stand. He noticed Orvieti breathing hard out of his nostrils. Occasional gusts of damp, fetid air made it difficult even for Jonathan to inhale. Jonathan marveled at his strength.

"Do you need the oxygen yet?" Jonathan asked.

"Not yet." He turned to Jonathan, smiling. "Do you?"

Jonathan touched the walls. "The stonework was coated to minimize absorption of water."

The ceiling of the tunnel was a high arch rather than the more common corbelled ceilings, which suggested large amounts of water moved through here at rapid speeds.

"Was this an aqueduct?" Orvieti asked.

"Perhaps," Jonathan said, "but not for drinking water, because the maintenance shafts are too far apart."

Even more strange, Jonathan thought. The floor declined as they walked away from the Colosseum. According to Vitruvius, aqueducts usually ran at a three-percent grade decline *toward* the city center to accelerate water pressure and diminish debris pickup. But this tunnel appeared built at an incline to *slow down* water moving toward the Colosseum.

"Of course," Jonathan said. "This tunnel was used to bring water into the Colosseum from the river. To fill it for naval battles."

"Naval battles?"

"When Titus inaugurated the Colosseum in A.D. 79, an elaborate system of aqueducts flooded the stadium arena for naval ship battles. These massive water channels already existed from Nero's construction of a huge lake, which sat on the spot where the Colosseum was built."

Jonathan pointed at a source of daylight a hundred feet ahead in the tunnel.

"*Signore*, if that is a manhole or a street grate, perhaps we should get you to—"

Orvieti held up his hand, anticipating the thought.

"You know I cannot turn back now."

The tunnel opened to an underground street. The asphalt of modern Rome ran ten feet above them, supported by steel pylons erected during the nineteenth-century construction of the Tiber banks. The underside of the streets stretched like a dark sky over the ravine of ancient streets between the Palatine and Capitoline hills. Compared to the tight turns of the subterranean Jewish Ghetto, this underground view provided a breathtaking vista of ancient urban planning, a ramble of half-brick walls that sprawled into darkness.

Orvieti stared up at a small hole boring through a manhole above them. He spoke softly, remembering. "'Open for me a pinhole of light, and I will broaden it to a sanctuary.'"

"You see an inscription, *Signore*?"

"No, I was just remembering something that Pope John Paul the Second said when he visited the Great Synagogue."

Jonathan crouched at the large brown cornerstone of an ancient wall. He scraped off some caked dirt to reveal carved lettering.

"*Vicus Jugaris*. It means 'Way of the Yoke,'" Jonathan said.

"Yoke?" Orvieti said.

"As in the yoke of cattle, but for the ancient author, Livy, the street's name also referred to the processions of war captives, walking under the yoke of their chains." Jonathan quickly turned to Orvieti. "Do you know what this means? It means this street was the path of the triumphal processions. It will lead us to the first Arch of Titus."

Ancient stumps of pillars and broken brick steps lined the ancient pavement, and Jonathan explained they were probably the remains of a republican-era portico, where the senators sat streetside during the triumphal procession.

Jonathan and Orvieti followed the street to its end, where they stood at the edge of a steep curved slope overlooking a huge semicircular basin that resembled a very deep, empty underground lake.

"This must have been an ancient reservoir," Jonathan said.

Orange streetlight showered through a rain grate high overhead, illuminating the enormous size of the former reservoir. At the far end of the semicircular basin stood a seventy-foot-high stone retaining wall.

"That's a dam," Jonathan said, "for the Colosseum. The wall of this basin must have served as a river intake to divert millions of gallons of water from the Tiber to flood the Colosseum for naval battles."

The dam wall was made of enormous travertine blocks fitted together without mortar, a building technique owing more to Jerusalem's Herodian construction than to local Roman brickwork. The subterranean architecture suddenly made sense to him.

"The slaves from Jerusalem must have worked for months to dam up this reservoir."

Given the subterranean dam's massive size and enormous stones, the wall bore an uncanny resemblance to the Western Wall in Jerusalem with one prominent exception: seven freestanding arches supported the wall as flying buttresses, forming seven curved staircases that rose upward from the bottom of the reservoir's basin like giant arches to converge upon a small platform high above the basin floor. The platform jutted out like a balcony from the center of the wall, and from the platform, a small door gave way to a dark corridor leading into the well. The middle staircase had partially crumbled, suggesting that someone had fallen with great violence into the deep basin below.

Orvieti walked closer to the rim of the basin, staring down at the seven arched staircases.

"It's a test," Orvieti said.

"What is?"

"The shape of the bridges," Orvieti said. "It is a *notaricon*, an ancient precaution, usually consisting of two or three possible paths. Here the builders have made seven arched staircases leading up to the platform, but most likely only one is strong enough to withstand a person's weight. The wrong ones are probably hollow and . . ." Orvieti did not finish the sentence, but his eyes fell downward to the chasm below.

92

Jonathan slid down the steep muddy slope of the basin and called back to Orvieti. "It's too steep, wait up there!" Jonathan walked to the center of the basin's floor, surveying each of the arched staircases. From the workmanship, he realized, the slaves must have stolen away as much time as they could from their construction of the Colosseum to design these intricately arched staircases.

Jonathan heard the sound of footsteps echoing in the basin.

"Hello?" Jonathan said, squinting into the darkness. In the shad-

ows there was a figure walking toward him, and moving more awkwardly, a second person beside the figure.

More silence and then a sudden voice, which through the subterranean acoustics sounded as close as his elbow.

"Remarkable work, Jonathan."

Jonathan could faintly see a man by the steep slope of the reservoir's edge. He stood in shadow just outside a natural spotlight from
the street grate above. His face was hidden but he wore an open
white shirt and dark slacks.

"How do you know who I am?" Jonathan said.

"Because . . ." the man said, swiveling the person at his side into
the spotlight in front of him. "We have friends in common." In the
harsh light, Emili stood there, her hair strewn and eyes deeply bloodshot. Her mouth was covered with gray duct tape, but Jonathan
could see her lips trembling under its surface. He could tell her wrist
restraints were pulled too tightly behind her back and her blouse
was sprayed with blood. The thin muzzle of a Beretta was pressed
against her temple.

Jonathan stared at Emili.

"Okay!" Jonathan yelled into the darkness, his arms outstretched
in a conciliatory gesture. "Okay," he repeated soothingly, "just put
the gun down."

There was silence. Emili was ripped out of the spotlight. The
man's shadow disappeared.

"I have given you all the information I have!" Jonathan pleaded
loudly. "You followed me to the Colosseum and through the tunnel
beneath the arena. I am of no more use to you. Let her go."

Jonathan heard a slow, sarcastic clap from the shadows.

"A brilliant closing argument," said the voice.

"Please," Jonathan said, "let her go."

The silence was terrifying. Jonathan feared he would never forget it, as trauma victims never forget the silence just before an event that alters their life.

In the shadow, Jonathan thought he could make out the bare teeth of a smile.

"No journey to heroism is more unlikely than yours. For all the time I knew you, I never thought I'd see the day."

"What are you talking about?"

"It's quite remarkable you are standing here, isn't it? Chalk it up to the gods of fate. Or have you wondered why it was *you* who was brought back to Rome to handle the law case for Dulling and Pierce?" The man raised his voice, as though proud of an elaborate scheme for which he had not been given full credit. He paced around the street grate's spotlight in which Jonathan now stood, his shoes kicking up dust as he circled him, dragging Emili in tow. His face was still shrouded in darkness. "Or was it just coincidence that the fresco you saw in the catacomb seven years ago described Josephus's path of escape out of the Colosseum?"

His tone sounded eerily familiar to Jonathan: the flair for narrative, the spoken italics, but Jonathan could not place it.

"How do you know of—"

"Know of? *I was there. I did it to you.* I sent you into exile, and now I have brought you back."

"That's impossible," Jonathan said softly. "Only four of us were there." *And two of them, Gianpaolo and Sharif, are dead,* Jonathan thought.

"I had been looking for that catacomb for months," said the voice in the darkness. "You had gotten too close."

"You staged that collapse," Jonathan said, nausea rising in his stomach.

"It was an event that changed your whole life." The tone coming at him in the darkness was factual, unconcerned. "It was the reason you left academics."

"Gianpaolo was killed," Jonathan said, awestruck. "And for what?"

"*For what!*" The man laughed. "How do you think I have *accomplished* this? That night changed not only your life, but mine as well. It proved to even the most skeptical imams in the Waqf that I could get closer than any other man to finding the menorah since my grandfather sixty years ago! Let other people talk nonsense about religion and mythology. My grandfather understood that who controls the past controls the future. He knew that history is written in fire."

Jonathan froze, he had heard those words before. His mind reeled back to his time at the academy, when he was sitting outside the villa with Emili. Sharif turned to both of them, holding the map of the catacombs beneath the Villa Torlonia in his hand. *"We've got to go for it. History is written in fire. Once it's extinguished, it's gone!"*

"What did you just say?" Jonathan said.

The man stepped forward into the spot of light, which illuminated his slim frame, his gray eyes, his square jaw and uneven teeth. His groomed, scholarly beard was missing and his once feathered black hair was now stubble-shaved. But the man was the same.

"No," Jonathan whispered. Salah ad-Din stood before him in the light, and Jonathan understood the whole loathsome trick.

"In ancient myth, Jon, who creates the hero?" Sharif Lebag said, leveling the gun at Emili's forehead. "The villain."

93

I've often wondered," Sharif said, "what did Titus look like at the moment he learned it was Josephus who had betrayed him?" Sharif spoke with unnerving nonchalance, raising his free arm theatrically. "There Titus was, sweating in his villa, poring over tactical routes out of the Temple Mount, to discover how the sacred relic escaped under his nose. Only his most trusted courtier sat at his side reviewing the sketches with him. Someone who was invaluable to his siege of Jerusalem. His personal *historian*, Flavius Josephus. I've imagined it over and over again. That moment Titus realized a lone historian defeated a man no army in the world could. His trusted adviser who had deceived him for years, earning greater access to the emperor with each flattering history he published.

Sharif looked only vaguely familiar to Jonathan. This man's eyes revealed something removed and cruel, a transfigured version of his former self.

"But now, Jonathan, I finally know the expression on Titus's face when the betrayal dawned on him with the force of the sun. It's the expression on your face right now," Sharif said with satisfaction.

"Jerusalem was all a setup," Jonathan said, feeling strangely little.

Jonathan looked to Sharif's side, where Emili struggled in shadow. "You monitored Emili's research, but did not count on the informer in the marketplace, did you? You had to end her research there in disgrace, just as you ended mine."

"I let her live!" Sharif said. "After she saw my research beneath Jerusalem. Have you any idea how many wanted her dead?"

"How long have you been leading this double life? How long ago did those imams at the Temple Mount brainwash you into conducting this search for the menorah?"

"Those imams understand nothing of my task! Do you know why they destroy relics under the Temple Mount? It is because they believe those Jewish and Christian relics have power. They believe in that hocus-pocus of impurity." Sharif spoke evenly, exhibiting an uncanny ease at having a gun in his hand.

"I am not so naive. The relic must be destroyed to erase the *history* of a Temple on the Mount. The al-Quds fund agreed to support my research if my first excavation seven years ago went undetected."

"You knew the truth of my Josephus thesis even before I did. It's why you convinced us to enter the catacombs in the middle of the night. . . ."

Jonathan could see the three of them, Emili, Jonathan, and Gianpaolo, being lowered into the catacomb. And who encouraged them, who volunteered to work the pulley above the manhole rather than descend into the ruin? The fourth young graduate student, Sharif Lebag. How selfless it seemed at the time, to have put in all that research, diagramming the subterranean corridors, only to sit by the manhole, like a trained astronaut remaining at ground control. But Sharif's decision was inevitable. He knew the ruin was going to crumble. He had arranged the entire thing.

"You can't win, Sharif," Jonathan said. "You cannot manipulate history."

"Do you believe that, Marcus? Or don't you lawyers manipulate history just as I do? Looking for documents to support your clients' version of the past. If you unearth a relic that supports the other side's case, what do you do? You shred it. Or you bury it in one of those document rooms where it will never see the light of day. It's rather like destroying some artifacts and not others. You think I'm driven by childish religious belief? I'm a political realist. Like Titus. Strength is the author of history, Jon, not truth."

Sharif had so completely become this persona that only small pieces of his former self were visible. His understated air and small gesticulations had vanished.

"Just let her go, and I will help you," Jonathan said.

"Let her go?" Salah ad-Din said mockingly. He pulled Emili's hair violently, burrowing the gun's barrel deeper into her temple. "Do you understand the lengths I went to bring both of you here? Orchestrating the fragment of the Forma Urbis so that she would bring this case and you would return to Rome." Sharif stepped toward Jonathan, joining him in the single shaft of light pouring down from the street drain above them.

"I knew you would unlock Josephus's messages. *I needed you to.*" He stared at Jonathan with an eerie mixture of familiarity and ruthlessness.

Salah ad-Din inched closer. "Does the shape of these arched stairways surprise you?" A ray of light glinted off the barrel of the gun in his hand. "Seven staircases in the shape of the menorah itself, each joining to reach a single platform, where an archway through the dam leads to the lost Arch of Titus. Of course, only one bridge is structurally strong enough. All you have to do is choose the correct staircase." He pulled Emili's hair, her bloodshot eyes beaded with tears, silently pleading.

"Which one is it?" Sharif asked, motioning to the stairs leading up to the wall. "You have until the count of three."

"I don't know!" Jonathan said softly, and then louder, stammering. "How— There's no way to know!"

"Then there's no sense in counting, is there?" He stood back from Emili, straightening his arm to shoot her.

"No!" a shout came out of the darkness. Salah ad-Din's flashlight beam searched the ridge of the basin, and there Mosè Orvieti stood, holding his slender green oxygen tank with both hands, his pants caked in dried blood.

Orvieti managed to slide down to the basin's floor and walked past them to the base of the seven stairwells. He turned around, glaring at Sharif, his voice fueled with disdain.

"I know which one it is," Orvieti said. He leaned over the first step of the middle staircase and rubbed its stone with the sole of his shoe. The inscribed letters revealed themselves in large block Hebrew print.

"Each staircase represents a different *sefirah*, a divine attribute through which the world was created," he said. "The branches of the menorah represent seven of them." He walked to the next staircase, knelt against the first step, and uncovered another inscription. "*Gevurah,*" Orvieti read.

"What does it mean?"

"Strength."

One by one, Orvieti cleared the first step of each stairwell, calling out each *sefirah*: "*Tipheret*, splendor. *Chesed*, kindness. *Malchut*, majesty. *Hod*, glory."

"Which is it?" Jonathan said. "What attribute would Josephus have most associated with the menorah? Splendor?"

"None of these," Orvieti said. He walked toward the one remaining arched staircase, which rose along the western wall of the basin. He rubbed the first step and there was no inscription.

Orvieti looked at Jonathan. "This is the one. The seventh branch," he said.

"There is no inscription," Jonathan said.

"The remaining *sefirah* is *netzach*, eternity. The seventh branch was the eternal light, the *ne'er tamid*," Orvieti said. "The enduring light that Josephus fought to save."

"You're sure," Jonathan asked softly.

"Not at all," Orvieti said.

"Go!" Sharif yelled, flicking his head toward the stairs. He turned to Jonathan. "And you go with him."

"Those stairs are thousands of years old," Orvieti said. "They cannot hold more than—"

"Take him!" Sharif yelled. "Perhaps you'll choose more carefully."

Jonathan walked forward, standing beside Orvieti. Both of them looked at the seven flanking arches of staircases.

Swinging his small oxygen tank in front of him, Orvieti ascended the first ancient step of the arched stairway. Jonathan followed, feeling the stones tremble beneath their weight. Orvieti walked up the arch's steps rather unceremoniously and Jonathan was surprised at his pace. His legs climbed swiftly, as though propelled by the same adrenaline that moved Jonathan rapidly behind him. Moving quickly helped them with their balance on the narrow beam of the staircase, and as they neared the apex of the arch, Jonathan tried not to look down into the blackness of the abyss below. Suddenly, the stone arch made a cracking sound beneath their feet, and Jonathan stopped.

"Keep moving," Orvieti said.

As they neared the platform at the top of the stairs, the enormous size of the retaining wall became apparent. The stones were each twenty feet in length, bearing an unmistakable similarity to the construction of Jerusalem's Temple walls. They stepped onto the platform, and noticed that the small archway leading into the wall from the platform was bricked up with smaller stones.

"The arch is bricked up!" Jonathan yelled down to Salah ad-Din.

On the platform, Orvieti stood motionless in front of the bricked-up arch. He stared at a short Hebraic inscription that had been carved above.

בְּתוֹךְ הַיָּם בַּיַּבָּשָׁה

"Dry Land in the Midst of the Sea," Orvieti translated. He looked up in Jonathan's direction. "It's a passage from Exodus. When the Red Sea split, the Israelites walked on dry land in the middle of the sea."

"What does it mean?"

As if to answer, the platform on which Jonathan and Orvieti stood began to tremble and slowly lowered a half-foot. Jonathan thought the platform could not hold them both when suddenly it stopped, as though fitted to a ratchet. A loud cracking sound reverberated throughout the cavern, and one of the arched stair-cases snapped backward, its heavy stones careening toward the basin floor. The structural instability spread like a contagion, as the wall before them began to shake.

"The stairs were not the test," Orvieti said. "This is the test."

The wall's enormous stones began to buckle outward. Jonathan watched small trickles of water bleed through the cracks, as though in slow motion, navigating the contours of the stones. The stream-ing water gathered force as boulder-sized stones shuddered and loosened. "The wall is going to burst!" Jonathan screamed. "We have to get—"

"This is the only safe place," Orvieti said.

You've gone mad, Jonathan thought. "We're right in front of the wall, Mosè! The river! This whole basin will be—"

"The Red Sea," Orvieti said calmly.

"What!" Jonathan screamed over the breaking rocks.

"You must believe in the splitting of the sea," Orvieti said.

The water began to flow into the center of the cavern. Sharif lifted his gun, preparing to fire at Jonathan and Orvieti on the platform. He cocked his elbows, using both hands to steady the pistol's aim.

He's going to shoot them both, Emili thought.

Emili slid behind Salah ad-Din and, throwing her arms over his head, yanked her wrists' plastic restraints against his throat. Unable to point his gun behind him, Salah ad-Din threw himself backward, sending them both beneath the surface of the rising waters in the cavern. Emili managed to remain fastened around Sharif's neck, keeping him underwater, but his stubble-short hair was slippery and he managed to corkscrew his head out of her grip.

Without use of her arms, Emili was unable to get up and could barely keep her mouth above the rising water.

Sharif now stood over her, aimed his black pistol at her forehead. He ripped off the duct tape from her mouth.

"Parting words?"

"You know, Sharif," Emili said, stretching her neck above the water, "you turned out to be a real asshole."

Sharif pressed the barrel below her hairline and pulled the trigger.

The pistol's hammer hit the barrel's firing contact with the deadened sound of a water-flooded gun.

Salah ad-Din appeared amused. "Luck *does* favor the brave."

At that moment, a sudden force bowled Sharif into the rising water of the cavern. Jonathan had run back down the staircase and blindsided him, tackling Sharif from the side. They landed in the churning green-gray water a foot from the reservoir's rock wall. Jonathan noticed Sharif's frame floating beneath him, lifeless, face-down. Red clouds gathered in the water, and Jonathan rolled him over to see a large jagged rock protruding from the surface of the water where his head had collided. As though moved by a force outside him, he lifted Sharif's head out of the water and let it fall again with a grotesque thud against the protruding rock. Another red cloud mushroomed in the water.

"That's for Gianpaolo."

Jonathan staggered up and waded through the water to Emili.

Emili remained kneeling in the rising water, which was already up to her waist. A bright red rectangle around her lips indicated where the duct tape had been. She blinked rapidly, her eyes moving over his face, as though inspecting an artifact.

"It's me," Jonathan said, attempting his most reassuring smile. He tried, unsuccessfully, to release the plastic restraints around her wrists.

"Where's Orvieti?"

Jonathan looked to the other side of the cavern, where Orvieti still stood on the platform, fifty feet above the basin floor. The stone retaining wall around him looked as tall as a skyscraper. The giant stones undulated; some erupted from their place, allowing huge pockets of river water to pour into the cavern.

"He says this is a test! Something about the Red Sea!" Jonathan shook his head. "We have to get out of here. There isn't time."

"The Red Sea?" Emili surveyed the collapsing basin. She saw Orvieti standing alone on the platform. She recalled her conversation with him the day before. *You must believe in the splitting of the Red Sea.* "We've got to get up there!" Emili screamed over the roar of the water.

"What?"

"That's the safest place in the cavern!" Emili said. "Trust me! I think he's right!"

The water rose past their knees, and Jonathan led Emili up the only staircase. The smooth stones were slippery from the water gushing out of the wall twenty feet in front of them. Jonathan struggled to keep his balance.

As they moved closer to the wall, jets of water burst forth on both sides of the stairs. Jonathan ducked as he climbed, lowering his center of gravity. Finally they reached the platform. Orvieti remained staring at the wall in front of him.

"The stairs were not the test!" Orvieti repeated, his eyes ablaze. *One must believe in the splitting of the Red Sea.* "Move closer to the wall!"

"Closer to the wall?" Jonathan yelled. "The whole river is going to—"

It was then that the entire wall in front of them began to shake. No longer did particular sections give way, but the entire structure of the wall seemed on the verge of collapse. The three of them stood at its center, as though seeking safety from a collapsing skyscraper by standing at its foot.

The limestone blocks, weighing hundreds of tons, burst outward on either side of the platform as two great hillsides of water—each fifty feet high—poured forth into the basin around them. Sunlight through the broken dam streamed into the basin, illuminating the fish and enormous logs of driftwood that curled over on both sides of them. The platform on which they stood had been carefully engineered to remain bone dry, lying in front of the one intact piece of wall.

Inside the archway before them, the small stones that blocked up the opening began to crumble and give way to a dark corridor that resembled a tunnel inside the curl of a towering wave.

"The Red Sea!" Emili shouted in disbelief. All three of them watched the walls of water on either side of them. "The corridor leads under the Tiber!" She shined her flashlight through the archway in front of them. They helped Orvieti step over the bricks, and the three of them entered the dark tunnel in the wall. The tunnel ceiling was high enough for them to stand, and its walls were made of very ancient brickwork made from crushed lime and sand.

94

The materials from the International Centre for Conservation in Rome had been couriered to Profeta's office. Brandisi spread them across the small conference table and studied them.

"I think you should see this, *Comandante*," Brandisi said.

Profeta looked up and noticed that the lieutenant had turned white. Brandisi pointed at one of the photographs of Dr. Emili Travia's team, standing in the Valley of Kidron adjacent to the Temple Mount, picking through huge mounds of rubble. It was a candid photograph with Drs. Emili Travia and Sharif Lebag crouching to pick up pieces of pottery. Brandisi leaned over the photograph.

"Him, without the beard."

"What about him?"

"That's who I saw in the archives of the Great Synagogue," Brandisi said.

"My God, Alessandro," Profeta said, and at first Brandisi did not look up, unsure the *comandante* even knew his Christian name.

"What is it, *Comandante*?"

Profeta remembered the director's assurance. *The DNA results confirmed Dr. Lebag's remains. I oversaw the investigation myself.* Profeta swayed for a moment, swept away by the vastness of the conspiracy. He pointed at the picture. "Lieutenant, I think you just identified Salah ad-Din."

Lieutenant Copia opened the door to Profeta's office and found the *comandante* and Brandisi standing over the photograph in a moment of apparent serenity. Although all four of Profeta's desk phone lines had lit up, ringing in an uneven chorus, neither of them seemed to notice.

"*Comandante,*" she said, "there's some kind of . . . *flood* in the Colosseum."

Profeta slowly looked up.

"What do you mean, flood?" Profeta looked out the window. "The rain has stopped."

"The entire subterranean portion of the ruin is submerged," Copia said. "That's all we've been told. In the middle of the United Nations ceremony, water began gathering beneath the arena."

"That would have to be thousands of gallons of water," Brandisi said.

Copia nodded. "A bank along the Tiber near the Piazza Bocca della Verità appears to have given way. The city engineers say a water main has burst, but investigators have not ruled out an intentional act."

"Brandisi, take three cars to the Colosseum to investigate," Profeta said. He stood up from his chair and grabbed his coat. "And send this photograph of Sharif Lebag to Interpol immediately."

Profeta turned to Copia. "Any word on the evidence found at the Villa Torlonia?"

"The results of preliminary fingerprints from the cigarette-rolling paper are almost ready. As you requested, the evidence is being processed outside our lab, so it will take another hour."

"What evidence?" Rufio said abruptly from the doorway.

"We found some rolling paper around the illegally excavated tomb," Profeta said.

"I'd be happy to pick up the lab results, *Comandante,*" Rufio said.

"I'm sure you would, Lieutenant," Profeta said. The expression on Profeta's face gave Rufio an uneasy feeling. "But I'll pick them up myself."

95

W here are we?" Emili asked, her voice echoing in the tight corridor.

"Must be the Cloaca Maxima," Jonathan said. "The sewer from republican Rome, probably dating to the third century B.C. It was probably forgotten by the time the Colosseum was built."

"Which is why the slaves of Jerusalem could have used it to reach a part of the city no longer accessible even in their own day," Orvieti said.

They waded through the dark corridor's waters, which now rose to their waists. The only sounds were the rushing current and Orvieti's oxygen tank clanking against the walls.

"How's he doing?" Jonathan said to Emili.

"His teeth are chattering," she said. "We need to move faster."

"We'll try," Jonathan said. "But the water level is rising with the evening tide." He looked at the arched ceiling. "We won't be able to breathe in here much longer."

"Seems like we are walking deeper into the Tiber," Emili said. Debris from the river around them beat hollow thumps against the outside of the tunnel wall.

She touched the stones and marveled aloud, "Two thousand years and this tunnel is still holding against the river current."

"If this was an ancient sewer," Jonathan said, "there must be an outlet to the Tiber somewhere along this passage." The tunnel's water level rose to their chests. Emili looked at Jonathan nervously.

"There!" Jonathan called out, swimming to a square of white light flooding through a barnacled steel grid above them. Jonathan could only fit his arm through the square iron bars, but he could feel the outside air and the spray of the river against the surrounding rocks.

Jonathan rubbed Emili's plastic restraints against the metal grates until they snapped.

With her arms free she lifted her head through the bars to look out.

"Which shore?" Jonathan asked. "Rome or Trastevere?"

"Neither. We're in the middle of the river," Emili said. "Look."

Jonathan moved beneath the grate and saw the underside of an ancient bridge bathed in floodlight against the dark sky.

"The Ponte Rotto," she said behind him, referring to the abandoned scenic ruin in the middle of the Tiber. The thousand-square-foot patch of overgrown river silt supported the ruins known as Ponte Rotto, Broken Bridge.

"The Ponte Rotto's base floods easily with the tide," Jonathan said. "We have to work quickly before the island is submerged. Any minute and the current will be too strong for us to climb out."

"Is there a lock?" Emili said.

Jonathan searched the grate, and lifted himself to see between the weeds lining the grate. "No, but I can see a latch."

Jonathan pressed himself against the grate, grunting as his arm scraped on the slimy plants for an object to expand his reach. He found a wet piece of driftwood and threaded the iron bars to push up the bolt of the latch.

"It's heavy," Jonathan said. "I almost have it." Jonathan used the stick to push the bolt upward. The metal groaned as the bolt gave way. "Got it," he said.

"Orvieti first," Jonathan said to Emili. "Let's go, *Signore!*"

But Orvieti did not move from the far side of the tunnel. His flashlight's beam pointed into the darkness, illuminating various tunnels branching off from the single passage where they stood.

"I can't leave," he said.

Jonathan knew time was of the essence. The tide was rising, and the island above them would not be above water for much longer.

"Emili," Jonathan said, motioning to the open grate. "You go. I'll work on him."

"Jon, I can't just—"

"*Go.* The tide is rising every second. When you get out climb to the top of the ruin and get help."

Jonathan knitted his fingers at the water's surface and Emili used them to step up through the hatch.

"*Signore*, the latch is open, your turn. Let's go!" Jonathan said.

"I will never have this opportunity again," Orvieti said. "Perhaps no one will. I know which corridor leads to the menorah." Orvieti shone his flashlight down the corridor farthest to the left. "That corridor bends back toward the Roman shore, beneath the Ghetto. You said the last known location of the first Arch of Titus was where descendants of the slaves from Jerusalem lived."

"That was written in the *eighth* century by an anonymous monk!" Jonathan said, above the rushing current. "You can come back!" The water level rose so rapidly in the corridor it was visible. He knew that even after they climbed out onto the small island, the tide would be dangerously high.

"This is my only chance," Orvieti said.

"This corridor is almost flooded," Jonathan said. "You will not . . ." He paused, looking at Orvieti with a stronger bearing, ". . . survive. You will not survive, *Signore*," he said plainly.

"It is the only way for me to survive," Orvieti answered. "This is all I have. Now go."

Orvieti turned away from him. He pushed through the corridor into the darkness.

96

Mosè Orvieti floated through the ancient sewer tunnel, his feet touching the tunnel's bottom only intermittently. His green oxygen tank bobbed beside him and the flashlight in his right hand strobed in and out of the water's surface. He was not certain how far the current had carried him. The water level had lowered, and the ceiling was completely dry. He was no longer beneath the Tiber.

The sound of rushing water grew louder, and Orvieti realized he was nearing the tunnel's outlet, not just from the noise but from a sudden, foul stench that filled the tunnel. It was almost as sour and rank as the smell of death he recalled all too clearly from more than a half-century before. For a moment he was certain the tunnel intruded upon some recent graves, until he remembered that buried Roman streets often accumulated tons of human waste and fermenting algae.

At the tunnel's outlet the water streamed down a sharp rock slope into darkness. Next to the water fall was a series of outcroppings he could use to lower himself down.

He pushed himself out of the opening, barely able to catch his breath because of the stench. He eyed his oxygen tank. He knew there was only a few minutes' worth of air in the small canister. *I must wait until I need it.* Slowly, he began to climb down the rock, the strap jangling around his shoulder. Surprised by his own agility, he carefully moved down the incline of the rock face, one foot beneath the other. But his legs shook under the strain of his weight.

The slope steepened and he slid down the moss between the foot-holds.

Catching his breath, he shone his flashlight down the rock slope and saw the ground's soft gray silt twenty feet below.

But why was the floor moving?

Beneath him, the floor seemed to be alive, writhing in some kind of rhythmic motion.

He looked at the floor more closely. He saw splashing in the water, a terrain of leathery gray ribbons arcing and slipping back into the blackness of the water, like the humps of some mythical sea beast.

"Eels," Orvieti said aloud. Thousands of them. He knew that they were the most durable of the Tiber's inhabitants, feeding off the natural minerals and algae. He remembered as a boy how the last of the Tiber's fishermen made their livelihood from eels, as the pollution had become so bad only this durable water snake could survive. He knew eels flourished beneath Rome, but he never imagined a grotto like this: an endless carpet of eels—enormous, ancient-looking things. The Tiber's native eels, Orvieti knew, were not dangerous except for their particularly keen sense of smell. Any cooked flesh and they would devour it. In his youth Orvieti watched Tiber's eel fishermen smoke their bait before setting out for the day.

His left foot slipped from the rock hold. He grabbed the rock face and his oxygen tank fell from his shoulder. He watched it descend to the gray silt below. His arms bore his entire weight as his legs clawed at the cliff face. His grip gave way and he plummeted the height of the rock face, landing on what felt like a deep cushion that moved beneath him, over him, around him, even down the back of his shirt. Orvieti rocked back and forth on the bed of eels like a man tossed about on small waves. He struggled to stand up, pulling two small eels from inside his shirt and moving his legs with great difficulty toward his oxygen tank. Each movement of his legs displaced dozens of eels. In his flashlight beam the white underbellies of the eels moved like the enormous tentacles of one seething organism. The fall of a rock outcrop had crushed hundreds of them, and their white insides coated hundreds more, giving them an even greasier feel as they slid across Orvieti. Digging through the eels, Orvieti miraculously saw a glimmer of the green metallic tank. He grabbed the mouthpiece, turned the knob a few rotations, and, panting into the plastic mask's sweet, cold air, pulled several long breaths from the tank.

Orvieti struggled through the water. He knew anyone else would not have continued, some of the smaller eels crawling up his pant leg, sliding past his calf and up his thigh. He had survived worse. The very air of this buried Roman street emitted a steam that stung his skin. Orvieti pressed forward.

Orvieti recognized the giant marble columns, rising up into the darkness. *The Portico di Ottavia.* Orvieti remembered Josephus's description of the procession. *"And Vespasian and Titus proceeded through the Octavian walks."* The base of the Portico di Octavia stood at the lowest archaeological strata beneath the Jewish Ghetto. As a child Orvieti had played among the capitals of these columns, which poked through the cobbled streets sixty feet above where he now stood. As a child, he imagined that massive pillars reached down into the center of the earth. Orvieti used the base of each column to step over the river of eels, as though using stones to cross a stream. He stepped gingerly, hoping that his frail legs would not give way. The long, dark cavern stretched beyond the columns with no end in sight. Giant stalagmites of moss and silt had grown from hundreds of years of hardening algae.

Stopping for a moment, Orvieti breathed in a snatch of air not from his oxygen tank, and he coughed violently. He dropped his flashlight, which was immediately carried away on a bed of writhing eels, its beam of light sinking and reappearing. Retrieving it was like plunging his hand into a vat of live squid.

He reached higher ground, which was not yet flooded. He pulled more small eels from inside his shirt and, unfazed, reached into his waistband to remove a large eel that had crawled up his leg nearly to his stomach. The eel fell to the ground, writhing helplessly on the dry dirt. Orvieti assisted it back into the water.

He moved between the ancient brick buildings, and his flashlight's beam illuminated narrow streets and the pink eyes of amphibious creatures that defied classification. He turned a corner. There, at the dead end of an alleyway, stood an arch. The arch looked embedded in rock, as though in the midst of being swallowed by the wall of earth behind it.

"My God." Orvieti drew close. "The Arch of Titus."

He approached slowly, almost reverently. Half buried inside the stone embankment at its back end, the arch resembled an ancient cave tomb burrowing into a hillside behind it. Orvieti knew the arch had been abandoned only a decade after its construction to shore up the Tiber's banks, which was precisely why the slaves from Jerusalem had seized their opportunity.

Orvieti waded as far beneath the arch as he could, standing in the rising water between the arch's two pilasters.

The travertine along the arch's exterior displayed rough carvings of ritual objects sacred to the Jewish slaves: ram's horns, palm fronds, and small seven-branched emblems. Orvieti stepped back outside the arch and saw the most prominent inscription of all carved above the central architrave. In his flashlight's beam, he was able to read the single line in ancient Hebraic script above him. He read it aloud, as if by hearing it he could believe what he read:

"'*Eytz chaim hee l'machaziki'im ba.*' It is a tree of life for those who grasp it."

The water's current picked up and Orvieti grabbed on to the arch's corner to prevent being washed downstream. He was now treading four feet above the ground, his fingers clutching the flutes of a column along the arch face.

Orvieti knew he didn't have much time. At high tide, the Tiber entirely submerged this lowest underworld of imperial Rome.

There must be an opening, Orvieti thought. *A door.*

With his mangled, closed fist, Orvieti banged on the arch's columns, listening for something hollow.

"Please," he whispered, searching for any seams in the stone. "Open the gate." But the water kept rising inexorably and his tears around the oxygen tank's plastic mouthpiece tasted salty. "After all you have taken from me. *Please.*"

It was the first word of prayer he had uttered in sixty years. Not since he prayed while pressing his entire body against a wooden door in the Ghetto, his arms splayed like a transom across the threshold, the Gestapo banging with the butt of their rifles. Orvieti remembered his children cowering in the corner and his wife smoothing back their hair to keep them quiet. Orvieti's strong hands gripped the door's knob—when a sudden gunshot blasted through the wood, and his right hand. Two fingers fell to the floor. That was the last thing he remembered, his fingers lying on the floor at his feet.

The water rose higher. He climbed up the volutes of the columns and then traced the travertine curve of the arch to stay under the monument.

"A tree of life for those who grasp it," he repeated like a mantra.

The water pushed him up to the arch's vaulted ceiling, the current pressing him against the carved foliage along the architrave. "A tree of life," Orvieti said, and then stopped.

It all suddenly seemed absurd, a child's tale. *The slaves from Jerusalem were defeated men, Orvieti. No different from you.* Frustrated and resigned to his own fate, Orvieti put his hands down, his head sinking beneath the surface of the water.

And that is when he realized it: *for those who grasp it.* Orvieti shot out of the water, his hands moving wildly across the arch's ceiling, searching for a marble tree carved into the stone.

He saw a carving of a marble branch and pulled it from the ceiling, summoning every ounce of withered muscle in his body. He pulled harder, his whole body shaking, reaching the peak of exertion for an old man who had withstood so much. It was just after that moment—that fraction of a second before he released an explosive exhale of failure—that he heard a sound.

The sudden, sharp sound of stone scraping against stone. A large stone block on the arch's ceiling began to move and plunged into the water next to him, leaving a black square opening in the arch's ceiling.

For a moment, Orvieti remained motionless, stunned by his success and panting from exertion. The water's surface was only inches from the opening, and Orvieti climbed up into the arch's darkness.

He collapsed on the dry stone inside, taking deep pulls from his oxygen tank. The attic was a large space, at least twenty feet high. After he caught his breath, he shined his flashlight. The dusty floor was completely dry. The water did not rise above the opening he had crawled through, even though the tide kept rising.

Orvieti realized the architectural genius. Builders from Jerusalem had secretly hollowed out this attic in accordance with an ancient architectural principle, that water will not displace air from beneath a closed container. The attic was carved from a single mass of stone to ensure it would remain dry for thousands of years.

Orvieti's oxygen tank hiccupped, signaling its last stretch of remaining oxygen. He stood up and walked within the attic: Twenty ornate stone pillars lined the walls, and the ceiling of the attic was dotted with ten bands of copper used for embroidered curtains. He recognized the room's biblical design at once.

The courtyard of the Temple in Jerusalem.

He walked past the pillars inside the attic and saw a carved rectangular doorway and a pile of wood pulp where presumably a doorway once stood. Above the transom, two lines were inscribed. One in Latin, the other in Greek.

No foreigner to pass here.

Orvieti stepped back, stunned. *The inscription from the outer courtyard of the Temple, precisely as Josephus described.*

Suddenly, a harsh beam of light flooded the attic.

Orvieti turned around. A man stood behind him, equipped with a wet suit, oxygen tank, and diving mask.

The young man's eyes were aglow with wonder as he scanned the arch's walls with an oversized lantern flashlight.

"Bloody jackpot," Chandler Manning said.

97

Jonathan pulled himself up through the grate and slammed it shut as he limped onto the Ponte Rotto's small overgrown island. The tide had already risen above the patch of grass around the ruin, and Jonathan grabbed on to the ancient bridge's plaster to anchor himself from getting swept downstream. He made a round of the entire island, which was only slightly larger than the bridge's lone remaining arch.

"Emili!" Jonathan yelled.

On either side of him, the crushing river-bend current that had washed away the bridge's other arches pounded the river-banks. Jonathan scaled up the lone arch's broken travertine, using the weeds and roots between the ancient stones to haul himself upward.

As Jonathan neared the top of the bridge, he heard a hacking cough. He reached the top of the ruin and found Emili on her knees, shuddering as she coughed up river water. She gripped the over-grown roots that strapped the stone, as though afraid her hacking would shake her off the arch. Jonathan hoisted himself up and ran toward her, ducking against the unrelenting wind.

"Are you okay?" Jonathan said soothingly, kneeling next to her, pulling her hair from her face.

She nodded as she slowly closed her eyes.

From the top of the Ponte Rotto where Jonathan and Emili stood, the double-lane highway of the modern Ponte Palatino was sepa-rated by only forty feet of turbulent water. Cars and trucks careened past in both directions.

"I'll get help," Jonathan said, rubbing his neck. He pulled to the edge of the Ponte Rotto.

"Hello!" he called out, trying to get a pedestrian's attention. The wind picked up considerably and Jonathan could not even hear his own yell. He looked down to survey the rising water on the ruin's island when he noticed something that chilled him far more than the freezing gusts of wind.

Someone had reopened the sewer grate over the tunnel they had just crawled through.

Jonathan turned around and Sharif stood behind him. He had

gripped Emili by the arm and held her over the edge of the ruin, dangling her thirty feel above the raging river current. His bloodied face held its gaze at Jonathan.

"Like Josephus," Sharif said, "it's important not only to plan a way into the emperor's court, but also a way out."

98

As one of the ranking officers at the Colosseum, Lieutenant Rufio directed other carabinieri to assist the Colosseum's evacuation of dignitaries attending the UN ceremony. The water level had reached the tourist deck and now spilled onto the *sampietrino* of the Piazza del Colosseo. A dozen municipal trucks lined the Via del Colosseo, dropping men through each manhole to find the breach in the water main. But Rufio's attention was elsewhere.

Cigarette rolling paper, he thought. *How could I have been so careless.* Rufio owed his survival to his instincts, and he already knew something was very wrong at the Command. The *comandante* sending evidence to an outside laboratory? Going to pick it up himself?

To make matters worse, he had just received an "urgent location request" from the Command, which required a carabinieri officer to respond immediately with his current position inside the city center. Rufio knew those requests were infrequent and always ominous. *Had the American lawyer spoken to the Command?* Rufio had survived internal investigations before and knew cooperation from the very start was critical. He picked up his mobile phone to respond to the Command's request when—like a prayer answered—his closed-circuit radio blared to life.

"Three unidentified persons on top of Ponte Rotto," said the young, nervous voice of an officer. "Two men and a woman near the breach in the riverbank. The woman is apparently injured."

That's them, Rufio thought, and snapped shut his phone. Rufio jogged down the Lungotevere along the river toward the Ponte Palatino. He reached the bridge and held his badge over his head, barking at the crowd now gathered on the side of the highway to move out of the way. Three young carabinieri had cordoned off the bridge, making Rufio the most senior officer on the scene. One of the officers handed him a bullhorn, happy to hand over control of the growing crowd. But Rufio just kept walking until he reached the center of the Ponte Palatino, only fifty feet from the Ponte Rotto. He could clearly see the American lawyer standing on the ruin, the river raging beneath him on all sides. Rufio prepared to issue a single warning from the bullhorn, as was standard operating procedure before firing. Within seconds after the warning he could then fire. He would say he mistook a branch for a firearm. An internal reprimand was a fair price to eliminate his larger problem.

He rested his elbow on the bridge railing and prepared to fire. He paused to regulate his breathing, but the problem was that the young man began to walk, becoming a moving target. Using a pistol in this wind, Rufio would have to wait for him to be stationary. He would only have one chance to fire.

99

Bringing me back to Rome isn't just about finding the menorah, is it?" Jonathan yelled at Sharif. He walked closer to him, crossing over some wild ferns covering the top of the bridge. "You've lured Emili and me back into your life in order to destroy the last vestiges of who you once were. This is about eradicating your own past, isn't it?"

"You think you know my past?" Sharif was unnervingly casual. "You were the lone scholar willing to suggest Josephus was not Titus's loyal historian, but a sleeper in his midst. How fitting that the same principle was at work in the very graduate student who sat beside you. Groomed for a mission beyond your wildest imagination."

"You're insane," Jonathan said.

"Am I?" Sharif tapped his bleeding forehead with his fingers and, seeing blood, wiped it on his shirt. "My grandfather believed the menorah remained aflame for two thousand years. My search has no such illusions of grandeur. I seek no mystical power from the thing. I seek power from destroying it."

"They will find you, Sharif."

"No one will believe you, Jon. Allegations against Sharif Lebag, the dead UN staffer? Do you think it is a coincidence I chose *her* to identify the fragments of the Forma Urbis? Don't come any closer," Sharif said. "Not until you tell me which corridor the old man took."

"I didn't see," Jonathan said.

"Which corridor did the old man take!" Sharif screamed, leaning

Emili farther over the edge, gripping her shirt with one hand. Jonathan saw Sharif's arm was shaking and it was not even clear he could keep holding her.

"I told you I don't know!"

"Fair enough," Sharif said, and he let go.

"No!" Jonathan screamed, watching Emili plummet over the edge. He ran across the bridge, but Sharif picked up a plank of wood and swung at Jonathan, catching him in the stomach. A searing pain shot through the center of his body, and Jonathan lost his balance and fell into the wild ferns.

"Jonathan!" he heard Emili yelling from beyond the edge. He could see she was holding on to roots along the side of the bridge. Sharif lunged again, swinging the wood plank, but Jonathan ducked and thrust his knee into Sharif's pelvic bone. Sharif fell backward and landed so close to the edge that his head hung over the side. Jonathan grabbed his throat, but as he looked over the side of the arch, the scenic floodlights below blinded him for a moment. Sharif swung his head forward into Jonathan's nose, plunging him to the edge of consciousness. Jonathan's hold on Sharif's shirt gave way, and a strange, moist heat gathered above his eyebrows. With blurred vision, he saw Salah ad-Din kneeling above him, lifting a rock the size of a volleyball.

"Beneath that corporate suit," Sharif said, smiling, "there's just not enough of a gladiator still in you, is there, Jon?"

Jonathan slowly brought up his left ankle and slipped his hand beneath his suit pant to remove the cheap switchblade from its costumed plastic gladiatorial handle, still tied to his shin. As Sharif lifted the rock, Jonathan swung the switchblade upward as hard as he could, sending it clean through the underside of Sharif's palm, ripping through the tendons between his thumb and index finger and emerging glistening pink through the back of his hand. Sharif's agony was so sudden and intense, he froze, mustering only a gasp.

His left hand fell, suddenly lifeless, and the rock dropped inches from Jonathan's head. Jonathan sliced the blade upward and turned it inside Sharif's hand, severing muscle and scratching bone. As Sharif screamed, Jonathan yanked him closer by the hair and whispered in his ear, "I suppose there is."

Jonathan pulled the blade out of Sharif's hand and held it to his neck. He dragged Sharif up to his knees and felt him shuddering in pain. He could smell the Tiber water in Sharif's hair, the smell of his Turkish cigarettes.

The sudden sound of a bullhorn came from the Ponte Palatino.

"*Riponga l'arma!*" a voice screamed at Jonathan in Italian. Lower your weapon. It was the police.

"He's right here!" Jonathan yelled, pointing at Sharif.

"*Giù a terra!*" On the ground! The officer yelled through the bullhorn, raising his gun.

"*È qui!* He is right here!"

Jonathan squinted into the wind, recognizing the officer holding the bullhorn. It was Lieutenant Rufio.

He watched Rufio put down the bullhorn and fasten both his hands on his pistol. Jonathan released Sharif, knelt on the ground beside him, and put his hands above his head. Kneeling there, his perspective sharpened. He watched Rufio lift his pistol and close one eye to mark his aim at him.

The crack of a gunshot echoed against the stone walls of the Tiber's banks. Rufio had a point-blank shot, but Jonathan found himself intact. On the bridge, he saw Rufio clutch his own shoulder and an older, bearded man in a brown overcoat run toward him from the other side of the Ponte Palatino. Two officers pinned Rufio to the sidewalk and handcuffed his hands behind his back. Jonathan realized the bearded man had intentionally shot Rufio in the shoulder before he could fire.

The man picked up Rufio's bullhorn.

"This is Comandante Jacopo Profeta," he called out. "Sharif Lebag, you are under arrest! Do not move!" Jonathan heard a boat motor beneath them. He looked down and saw two police boats fighting the currents to moor against the ruin. Countless officers screamed over one another in Italian, one louder than the next.

Sharif sat up next to Jonathan, semiconscious, his bloodied hand jammed into his shirt to stem the bleeding. Jonathan saw that his thumb was nearly severed, dangling from its fibrous sheath.

"Your days as Salah ad-Din are over, Sharif," Jonathan said, kneeling next to him. *"Done. History."*

"What'd we say at the academy?" Sharif rasped through a grisly smile. Jonathan noticed too late that he had inched toward the edge of the bridge. "History is unpredictable."

As though carried by a gust of wind, Sharif tumbled over the edge of the ruins, his body turning sideways and over itself until splashing into the raging white pleats of water thirty feet below.

100

"Who are you?" Orvieti asked.

Chandler stepped toward the center of the arch's attic. He pushed up his dive mask. "Thirty feet in length, I presume," Chandler grinned. "A precise replica of the Temple sanctuary."

"If you seek to destroy it—"

"I would hardly call melting down a few hundred pounds of solid gold *destroying* anything," Chandler said. He pointed the beam into the doorway on the far left of the attic.

"Young man, this is more powerful than you can possibly imagine," Orvieti said, inhaling from his oxygen tank. "It is protected."

"Protected? Damn right it is protected. Have you any idea what I just swam through to get to this bloody arch? The fact that you're still alive, old man, is a miracle big enough to make a believer out of me." Chandler pulled a long drag from his mouthpiece. "Air down here is nearly all methane rising from the river's silt." Chandler's flashlight traced the columns on either side of the doorway. "Two columns on either side," he said in confirmation. "It's just as Josephus said."

"It is dangerous to pass through there," Orvieti warned.

"Of course it is," Chandler said. He removed from his pocket a small Ziploc bag with an old Josephus manuscript inside it. "Which is why I've got the tricks of the priestly trade right here. It's long been a puzzle to me why Josephus describes in such detail the priestly ascent to the sanctuary. Who would have thought he was giving *instructions*?"

Chandler walked past Orvieti through the open doorway that led beyond the wall of the arch's attic. His underwater lantern revealed a long, rectangular chamber. From the doorway a thin bridge extended to a twenty-foot-square platform that was surrounded by air on all other sides. In the center of the platform was a raised stone altar, accessible by five steps from the front and a ramp leading up either side. The sloshing sounds of water echoed from the darkness below, and Chandler turned his flashlight downward to see writhing eels in an even greater concentration than he encountered before.

Chandler pointed to a square gold object glistening on the altar in the middle of the platform.

"What is that? In the center of the altar there?" Orvieti said nothing, watching from the doorway. Chandler was quick to answer his own question. "The breastplate of the high priest, isn't it?" His tone heightened with excitement. "Containing the gemstones of the twelve tribes."

"The inscription," Orvieti said, "it says you must not go or else—"

"Or else what?" Chandler said dismissively. "Some magical cherubs with flaming swords will smite me?" He smiled and walked across the bridge, hunched over, supporting the oxygen tank on his back.

Chandler reached the platform. "There are dozens of holes in the platform," he called out.

"Vents," Orvieti said softly. Already in first-century Rome, he knew, lifetimes of sewage had created dangerous levels of methane exhaust. Ancient street plans included elaborate chutes to channel flammable gases away from the streets below.

Chandler stood only feet away from the breastplate. He looked at the small open text of Josephus.

"The priests ascended by way of a ramp," Chandler said. He walked forward, avoiding the steps to walk up the ramp. He shone his flashlight on the gold rectangular breastplate, its twelve carefully arranged gemstones refracting the beam of his flashlight into hundreds of flecks of color prisming through the stones.

"Each of these gems must be nearly two dozen carats." Chandler's eyes greedily surveyed the twelve large stones, moving quickly over the deep red ruby, purple amethyst, blue sapphire, green emerald, until he found it in the second row—exactly where the chapter in Exodus described—a *yahalom:* a large rough-cut diamond. He crouched down and tried to lift the breastplate but it was fastened to the stone.

"Do not touch it," Orvieti called out, remembering the sacred object's description in Exodus: *The Breastplate of Judgment.*

Chandler leaned nearer to the rows of stones. "They seem loose in the fittings." His fingers pulled at the diamond, trying to pry it off.

"Please," Orvieti said.

"I almost have it," Chandler said. He pulled harder on the stone. He grunted, leaning back. The stone suddenly came loose from its setting.

A grayish plume emanated from the hole in the breastplate, which was still anchored to the rock.

"It's just steam!" Chandler laughed. He turned back to Orvieti exhilarated. "Where are the angels to smite me?"

That steam is heating the methane, Orvieti thought.

But Chandler was oblivious. Using both hands to hold the stone, he let the mouthpiece dangle from his oxygen tank.

A sudden odor of burning filled the attic and Orvieti noticed a small flame jumping at Chandler's feet. Chandler looked down and leaped back, but this only jerked the flame closer to him, as if it were somehow tethered to his body. Orvieti realized that the flame was emanating from the dangling mouthpiece of Chandler's oxygen tank, ignited by the heated methane vent at his feet. Chandler grabbed the hose and shook it wildly in a vain effort to extinguish the fire. But the methane traveled up the hose, and with a horrific screeching sound, the plastic tube expanded like a balloon. As Chandler scrambled desperately to get his tank off his back, the tube burst into a small fireball. Chandler began to scream and Orvieti could see him grasp at his neck where the valve of the oxygen tank was emitting a direct spray of fire onto his bare skin.

Chandler's shrieks filled the chamber as he alternated between trying to remove the flaming tank and putting out the fire that snaked along the back of his legs. Orvieti could see the bubbling

skin on Chandler's neck and back as he spasmed, a tangled mario-
nette, not yet collapsing as he spun toward the black abyss off the
sides of the platform. At that moment, the oxygen tank erupted and
the heat from the fire blew the bottom of the tank like shrapnel into
the back of his calves. Chandler screamed again and Orvieti could
see blood spurting from the back of his legs as he tumbled into the
darkness, splashing into the black water below.

Orvieti heard a sudden flurry of thrashing in the water. With a
shudder, he remembered the practice of the eel fishermen to increase their catch: *burn the flesh*. From the darkness below, the young
man's shrieks rose until there was no other sound than that of the
thrashing eels.

Orvieti closed his eyes, falling against the wall. He spoke softly
to himself, remembering the biblical warning of the horrific death
awaiting intruders who enter the sanctuary.

Consumed by fire, Orvieti thought.

Orvieti edged out of the chamber into the attic, escaping the
smell of burned flesh. The platform was an elaborate decoy, Orvieti
had known, because that chamber was beyond the western wall of
the arch not the eastern wall, which was closer to Jerusalem. Orvieti
stumbled across the attic to the eastern solid stone wall. At his feet,
beside a hatch in the floor, was another inscription. Except this one
was in ancient Aramaic.

"Only purified priests past here."

Orvieti looked into the hatch and saw a black pool of water. But
shining his flashlight into it, he realized the water was different,
purer than the raging tide outside the arch, and in Orvieti's beam
the water inside the opening emanated a crystal blue color. He saw
a set of stairs beneath the water, leading downward. *Only purified
priests past here.*

Priests, Orvieti thought, considering his own status. He recalled
his father's stories regarding papal persecution of his family on ac-

count of their priestly, kohenite lineage. *Mosè, tell no one at school you are a kohen,* his mother would say, her finger shaking with panic. Emboldened, Orvieti stepped into the cold water of the open hatch, and walked down the stairs until he was nearly submerged.

A sanctuary accessible only through water. Orvieti realized how carefully the arch's construction fit the biblical prescriptions. "And the priests shall immerse themselves to draw near the sanctuary." Holding his breath, Orvieti ducked his head under the water. He immersed himself in the darkness, realizing he would not be able to find the hatch through which he had entered. He remained completely still, but not lifeless. It occurred to Orvieti at that moment that he felt more alive than at any other time in the last sixty years. He floated in the blackness with a feeling that overpowered even the expectation of his own death, which by any rational calculation approached with every passing second, and that feeling was . . . *hope.* Nearly all of his life, he had felt abandoned, until now. This arch had waited for him. It had waited not for sixty years, but for thousands of years, and as he floated through the black space, a weightless peace warmed him. Not the weightlessness of a man on the verge of death, but of a floating unborn child on the verge of life.

Ahead in the water, he saw a faint ray of light emanating from something that appeared to be *in* the water. But as he moved closer, he realized it came from a place above the water. The current pushed Orvieti gently upward and through a square floor opening of another compartment. He hoisted himself out of the water with shaking arms into a small chamber, lit by a white light that grew softer as his eyes adjusted.

The contents of the chamber were unlike anything he could have imagined.

The walls were stucco, clearly painted at the time of the Roman conquest of Jerusalem. There was a thin layer of brown dust, but the colors of the frescoes were rich. Three of the walls were painted in a single scene, a panoramic view of a beautiful walled city beneath a blue sky along a valley dotted with olive trees.

"Jerusalem," Orvieti said, realizing that these were loving depictions by Jewish slaves of their city before the sack by the Romans in A.D. 70. In front of the wall was a low altar of rock, covered by a threadbare swatch of embroidered cloth, its motif no longer discernible. An original fabric from two thousand years before. The chamber had remained dry for thousands of years.

He looked up at the source of the chamber's light. A pinhole of light shone from the ceiling of the chamber. *Where was that light coming from?* The ground was at least forty feet above him.

Orvieti knew a chamber built with this level of technology and care must have been the final project of the master architects who constructed the Temple in Jerusalem. In this chamber they must have placed the menorah. *But where?*

The pinhole of light from the top of the chamber descended to the middle of the chamber's one unpainted wall. Orvieti moved toward it, feeling dizzy from exertion and the lack of oxygen. The wall pulsed as though it were breathing. He remembered the phrase he had heard only hours before.

"'Open for me a pinhole of light and I will broaden it to a sanctuary,'" he said.

He looked more closely where the hole of light from above hit the wall. He put his hand to the wall. He used the round end of his oxygen tank and knocked the wall. It was stucco, crumbling from the slightest force. With his own trembling hands he pulled away the stucco, revealing a gleaming yellow metal that reflected the light's ray so brightly that it burned like a growing flame, larger with each piece of wall he pulled away.

Orvieti hacked into the wall, more of it collapsing at his feet. There, behind a foot of cracked stucco, was a long branch of solid

gold four feet merely along its curve, its deeply carved floral orna-
ment in the exact biblical dimensions. "'And the workmanship shall
be beaten,'" he whispered, quoting Exodus, "'from a solid piece of
gold to its base to its flowers, beaten out from a single piece.'"

Wildly, he removed more of the wall, until nearly an entire
branch of the giant menorah was revealed, with a muted glow like
the bark of a golden trunk. Its lustrous yellow skin gleamed from
the pinhole's ray, as massive and bewildering as he had dreamed. He
realized the giant artifact was perpendicular to the wall, and the rest
of the menorah's branches spread across the room that lay beyond
the stucco. He removed enough stucco for him to stumble forward
and crawl through the wall. He was losing his breath and although
his eyelids were heavy, they flared open like a child's.

An eight-foot lamp of solid gold towered before him, and on the
westernmost branch he saw the dim red glow of a single ember
burning in the darkness.

Orvieti wiped his eyes and for a moment did not approach, as
though wanting to prolong his wonderment at the miracle.

The menorah's flame had not gone out.

Staggering closer, he realized the light above the westernmost
branch was actually a small flame, flickering inches away from the
rock wall where a small, square vent sprayed natural methane from
an adjacent cistern of river's silt and sewage. The flame hovered
over the menorah's last golden cup, the one closest to the wall. *Of
course,* Orvieti realized, *a natural, undying source kept the original flame
of the lamp's seventh light alive.*

He struggled up three stone steps that ascended to the menorah's
branches and raised his hands to the flame. But instead of seeing the
fingers of an elderly archivist, he saw those of a young man.

Liquid filled an ancient bowl of hammered copper on the stair's
top step.

Oil, Orvieti knew.

He used his remaining strength to pour it into the branch's golden cup. The oil caught instantly beneath the flame. He moved from branch to branch, and as each cup caught fire, more of him came into the light, illuminating not him but a strong, youthful version of himself.

Orvieti knew that hallucination was the last stage of oxygen deprivation, but it all seemed real: his dark, wavy hair from a half-century earlier and his broad frame shining in the lamp's refulgent gleam.

As though swallowed by the brightness, he was transported, standing no longer in a dark chamber, but in a sunlit open field in the center of the Roman Forum. He could hear children laughing. It had been sixty-six years, but he recognized the sound at once. His children. Orvieti watched his three sons dart past, their wild tufts of brown hair above tiny denim-patched overalls. His daughter trailed, wearing a small lilac-print dress. They circled around his legs, playing and laughing. Orvieti forgot how flower-filled the ruins of the Forum were before Mussolini's excavations. He used to take his children to picnic there. His wife was there, too, young and beautiful, the sun on her round shoulders and her long hair. She slipped her smooth hand into his, but his fingers were old and wrinkled. She was young, but he was old again. Orvieti not only looked old, but he felt old, too. The field was difficult for his old legs, but his wife's strides were long and graceful. He wanted so much to be with them, but he could not keep up. The children were in front, calling to him. *Try to catch me, Papa. Try to catch me.* His wife, too, had gone ahead, her expressive brown eyes looking back at him as if she had not seen him in ages.

They stood in front of him in the shade cast by a large marble arch at the end of the ruins. The Arch of Titus. His three sons and his daughter chased one another, playing under the arch. Orvieti's wife waited for him, beckoning him with her arm, and then the children waved their hands for him to follow, making playful imitations of their mother's gesture.

Orvieti stood at the base of the arch, just as he did in 1948, when the Jewish community rallied in the ruins of the Forum to walk the opposite way of the war captives depicted on the marble relief. But in 1948, Orvieti could not do it. He had walked back to the Ghetto alone.

Now Orvieti stood again at the base of the arch. His children were there, on the other side. All he had to do was walk through. His wife put down her arm, and it was the first audible thing he heard.

"*Mosè.*" The sound of her sweet voice was surprisingly close to him, although her lips did not move as she spoke.

"*It is time,*" she said, smiling.

Orvieti stepped toward the arch and took her hand. As he walked, the marble reliefs had come alive, their stone figures in motion. But they were not Roman soldiers carrying the menorah into captivity. They were young men, women, and children whom Orvieti recognized from his youth in the Ghetto. Although he last saw them huddled in cattle cars, they were now bathed and resplendent, walking in the same direction as he, carrying the menorah out of the ruins.

When he emerged from the opposite side of the arch, he looked at his wife's hand in his own. The skin on his hand was tight. He felt a strength in his legs that he could not remember. All of the fingers on his hand were there. Orvieti crouched down, his frame limber. His children ran to him, and he sobbed with a vigor that shook his wide shoulders. "*I will never let you go again,*" he said, and his daughter embraced him as a grown-up hugs a child.

"*You never did,*" she said.

101

Outside the Great Synagogue, ambulances and police cars blocked the Lungotevere Cenci. Old women leaned out their windows at the curiosity.

Emili's jacket was ripped and her face was still red from the duct tape. She wore a carabinieri blanket around her shoulders. Jonathan pressed some gauze to the side of his head; the blood trickling from his hairline had stopped.

"And all this time," Emili finally spoke. "It was him."

"Emili, don't." Jonathan shook his head. "You couldn't have known."

Profeta walked over to them.

"We still have not found Lebag. We have circulated EU-wide arrest warrant for the murders of Officer Fiegi and Jacqueline Olivier, but it doesn't mean we'll find him," Profeta said. "There are cells in the center of Rome that will give him cover."

"And Mosè Orvieti?" Emili asked.

"I'm sorry, *Dottoressa*," Profeta said somberly to Emili. "The divers will look for another half-hour before they must stop for the night. According to the experts, the entire underground street is flooded by now."

"Is there a way at least to recover his—"

"The subterranean flooding this time of year is fierce, *Dottoressa*," Profeta said. "His body could have washed anywhere beneath the miles of corridors beneath Rome." Profeta knew the Roman Mafia used the very successful strategy of dumping corpses into the Tiber, where they were often made unidentifiable by the pike, perch, and carp within hours. But this the *comandante* kept to himself.

Profeta disliked having to bring up paperwork at a time like this, but with Lebag still missing, Emili would be needed for extensive questioning to open an investigation.

"Dr. Travia, the Waqf will likely suggest that Sharif Lebag's activities were outside of their knowledge. They'll want to suppress the investigation."

"On diplomatic grounds?" The question came from Jonathan as a reflex. He was only dimly conscious that he was a lawyer at that moment.

"We'll need your statements to build a case."

Emili nodded.

"Take your time, of course," Profeta said, bowing his head deferentially. He walked toward the patrol car and turned around. "There's remarkably good American coffee across the piazza from the Command. Perhaps the three of us can talk more informally first."

"All right," Jonathan said.

Emili turned to Jonathan when they were alone.

"Do you think Mosè found the menorah?"

Jonathan shrugged. "I saw him for the last time just after you did. He disappeared into the darkness, moving in that direct—" Jonathan stopped in mid-thought, as a sudden idea took hold of him. He was looking directly in the direction of the Great Synagogue. The moonlight now coated its Assyrian dome with a white gleam.

"What is it?" Emili said. "Are you all right?"

"Emili," Jonathan said quickly. "We've got to get inside the sanctuary of the Great Synagogue."

"The synagogue?"

"I think I know where the first arch is."

"You can't be serious."

"Let's go." Jonathan grabbed Emili's hand and they moved between the police cars and through the synagogue doors.

In the sanctuary, Jonathan stared at the ceremonial ark. It was draped with a woven velvet cloth twenty feet in height.

"Did Orvieti say where Pope John Paul the Second made his silent prayer during his visit here?"

"In front of there," Emili said, pointing at the ceremonial ark.

Jonathan and Emili walked down the center aisle, up the velvet-clad steps of the bimah to the ark. Only the moonlight slanting through the double-height stained-glass windows illuminated the hundreds of pews. A carabinieri officer and a reluctant security guard were two silhouettes in one of the service doorways.

"Do you notice anything strange about this sanctuary?"

Emili looked around the dimly lit room. "Other than the fact that you told the security guard to keep the lights off? No."

Jonathan leaned in. "Look up."

Emili tilted her head backward. A massive, gilded chandelier in the Assyrian-Babylonian style dangled in the shadows above them. It was hung from a chain that attached twenty feet above, at the pediment of the ark.

"It's the eternal light," she said. "Chandler said that all synagogues have them."

"Right, but they're usually *lit*," Jonathan said. Emili followed his arm upward. "This one isn't."

"You're saying the synagogue of the Roman Jewish community doesn't have an eternal light?"

"Oh, it has one," Jonathan said. "But it's somewhere else."

"I'm not following."

"Emili, you know how close Pope John Paul the Second felt to the rabbi of this community. When he came to this synagogue in Rome, he brought a message with him. Orvieti told it to me: 'Open for me a pinhole of light, and I will broaden it to a sanctuary.'"

Emili looked down at her feet, as though steeling herself to see the impossible.

"The pope didn't come to the synagogue to return anything," Jonathan explained. "He stood here to remind the rabbi of what the Jewish community had guarded for two thousand years beneath this synagogue, without even knowing it."

Emili's gaze was now on the floor in the direction of a small inset piece of amber, a miniature representation of the menorah in its proper biblical dimensions. She suddenly realized why Jonathan asked the guard to keep the lights off.

In the glass inset, a faint spark played in its yellow translucence, as though emanating from a place somewhere beneath the synagogue.

"The triumphal procession ended *here*, along the Porticus Octaviae," Jonathan said, "and here's where the first Arch of Titus was built, directly beneath the Ghetto."

"*Quae amissa salva.*" Emili smiled. Lost things are safe.

102

The next morning, Tatton stood in the conference room of the firm's office at Piazza Navona. He put down the newspaper.

"You're a celebrity, Marcus, and you made the firm look like a bastion of goodwill."

Mildren sat next to Tatton, preparing for an upcoming meeting. He looked at Jonathan, steaming at his success.

"You managed to expose the UN director as complicit with loot-ers in Jerusalem, and the Cultural Ministry has pressured the pros-ecutor to drop the case. A gold star, Marcus. Your future here at Dulling is as bright as the Roman sun."

Jonathan stared out the window. It was late in the morning and his flight to New York wasn't for another four hours. He had tried to call Emili at the UN, but as he expected, she wasn't in her office. The media had camped out overnight at the International Centre for Conservation to feed on the tabloid-quality twist of the UN director's death.

"Excuse me," was all Jonathan said, and walked out of the office.

He left the palazzo and made his way toward Piazza Venezia, up the stairs of the Capitoline Hill, and into the Roman Forum. The day was warmer but still overcast, and the ruins in the Forum were fairly empty. A young woman in a camel-hair overcoat with a blond ponytail stood opposite the Arch of Titus, staring at its pediment.

Jonathan walked up and stood next to Emili. "I thought you'd be here."

Emili was startled, and her eyes brightened when she saw him.

"Hi," she said.

After a stretch of silence, she turned to Jonathan. "Did you know that I saw you once after you left the academy? In New York, at the Metropolitan Museum."

Jonathan laughed uneasily. "I saw you, too. It was three months after I was thrown out of the academy. All my teaching offers had been pulled."

"You were giving tours of the antiquities wing."

"And working at Sotheby's at night," Jonathan said. "I was too embarrassed to say hello to you. I hoped you wouldn't notice—"

"I watched you give that tour for nearly ten minutes before you saw me. There you were, hanging on to the subject matter you loved with every thread of your being, even though you had every reason to walk away. I never wanted to be with you more."

"Well?" Jonathan said, looking into her eyes.

"I'm afraid Sharif was right about one thing. History *is* fragile, written in fire. Once it's out . . ." she trailed off. "What we had is lost, Jon."

"But we're quite good at finding things together."

"Remember how I explained to you that in preservation circles, sometimes we oppose new excavations? We're excited about the possibility of archaeological finds like everyone else, but we also understand what it means to maintain the ruins once they are dug up. Often, they degenerate in a matter of weeks more than they did in thousands of years." She kissed him on the cheek. "Let's not disturb the past, Jon."

As Emili walked away, Jonathan realized that her feelings for him had been sewn up by the invisible layers of sediment over the last seven years. Like the ruins beneath that artichoke field in southern Italy, her emotions were now only faintly recognizable from the surface.

She turned around. "Remember, Jon, in the ground at least the ruins are safe."

103

A fter three days of heavy rain, the remains of Chandler Manning's body washed up a half-mile down the Tiber. The carabinieri gave instructions for the body to be brought immediately to Rome's municipal morgue for inspection. His corpse was to be used as evidence in the ongoing criminal investigation of Waqf Authority activity in Rome.

Inside the morgue, a man posing as a pathologist ran his hands over the body. The coolness of the river water kept Chandler's chewed flesh in better condition than it would have been had he been lost in the warmer season. Even so, the few intact portions of the body had a deep purplish hue and smelled of decay. Fungus had grown under his nails, and his ears were almost entirely eroded as a result of the aggressive pike perch that attempted to pull off what skin remained by the time the body washed into the Tiber basin. Early pathological examination could not explain the cause of the severe burns across the subject's posterior region.

The man posing as a pathologist wasn't there to inspect the body. His training was in covert operations, replete with facial prosthetics, hairpieces, and falsified documents. He was there to recover a document. The man wasn't told of its historical importance. It was not his place to ask questions.

Outside the morgue, a carabinieri car pulled up. Profeta got out, walked toward the front door, and displayed his credentials for the woman at the front desk.

"We are here to see the body," Profeta said, handing her the carabinieri's request slip. "Manning, Chandler."

"One moment, the medical examiner's office is completing their inspection."

"No one should be inspecting the body," Profeta said. "There is an ongoing investigation."

"He said it was for health reasons," the woman answered nervously, "because of the Tiber's pollution."

"Let's go!" Profeta swiveled around the desk. "I want all doors blocked!"

The man posing as the pathologist felt under what remained of Chandler Manning's wetsuit and there it was, still damp and folded in fourths. A laminated map of Rome, its edges blackened from fire and chewed by pike, still displayed Josephus's path to the original Arch of Titus as marked by Chandler's underwater pen.

The man heard doors slam and looked up through the glass walls. Three young carabinieri officers charged the examining room. The man posing as the pathologist slid the body into the iron casement and ran toward the room's other door, which led to an internal corridor ramp for loading and unloading bodies. The man was fully armed with a Bren Ten ten-millimeter automatic pistol beneath his lab coat and was carefully trained in urban chase warfare. Countless exercises, staged in corridors of abandoned buildings in the Negev, had imitated every possible surrounding, from hospitals to middle schools. But he took his hand off his pistol; his instructions were not to leave any trace of who sent him. A Bren ten-millimeter bullet was not offered on the black market; it would all but give away from which intelligence agency he came.

"He is in the building," Profeta said, "and wearing a lab coat. I repeat, he is dressed as a physician."

The door to the ramp was open and a hearse driver wearing a black cap was walking down the hallway for a pickup. The man grabbed the hearse driver, dragged him inside a utility closet, and threw his head against the metal shelving only hard enough to knock him unconscious. Within a minute, the man reappeared in the hallway, having exchanged his lab coat for the driver's uniform. Amid the officers storming down the hallway, the man walked calmly out of the hall, down the ramp, then drove the black hearse away.

In the center of Rome, the man parked the hearse outside Piazza Venezia and ducked into an anonymous alleyway. He crossed the street to a café and placed the folded map beneath a napkin holder on an outside table. Within seconds a woman wearing a broad-brimmed sun hat approached from the opposite direction, just as the intelligence handlers had planned. She took a seat, ordered an espresso, and reached for a napkin, imperceptibly moving the sketch from beneath the napkin holder. She slipped the map into a plastic protective sheathing in her inside jacket pocket.

The woman was Eilat Segev.

104

Two Months Later

The tour group was enraptured. In the antiquities wing of the Metropolitan Museum of Art in New York City, Jonathan Marcus glided backward with his tie loosened, describing a statue of Protesilaos mortally wounded on the beaches of Troy. For the Elderhostel group present, Jonathan's voice was around them like something vibrant, moisturizing. They gasped with delight, their cataract eyes ablaze.

Jonathan stopped in the hall's center and stood up on a stool. He diagrammed the breastplate of a Greek soldier on his wrinkled light blue dress shirt.

"Ah, the fierce cuirass breastplate, most useful for . . . ?" Jonathan turned to the Elderhostel crowd. "Does anyone know what?"

"Back support?" said an old man in an untucked madras shirt. The sticker across the breast pocket read PHOENIX SENIOR TOURS, and beneath that, in handwritten cursive, Mr. Feldheim.

"Fair enough, Mr. Feldheim!" Jonathan said, broadening his grin. "You, sir, are Odysseus in your cuirass, a back as strong as ten men. Your Penelope is waiting! Ready the archers with Levitra!"

The tour group laughed, swelling and stretching around Jonathan to the size of a street performer's crowd, three people deep. Jonathan pointed at various artifacts around him, translating the sarcophagi and funereal steles from Latin and Greek.

"Why aren't the gods smiling?" a child's voice asked from the crowd. Jonathan crouched to get close to the child, who looked up at the white marble gods above him. The crowd, quite large by now and spilling into the neighboring African wing, hushed at the question.

"It's a good question." Jonathan smiled. "Why aren't the gods smiling?" he repeated loudly for the crowd. "Well, in Roman art, gods don't smile because they aren't mortal," he said.

"But didn't the Romans want to be gods?" said another voice from the crowd.

"Oh, no," Jonathan said. "Without mortality, there would be no such thing as bravery or heroism. And strange as it sounds, that's why the gods don't smile in Roman statues and the mortals do." Jonathan paused, opening his arms. "Mortality means the despair of loss, but it also means the redemption of—"

"Being found," said a female voice in the middle of the gallery.

The gallery was silent. Jonathan squinted at the silhouette in the foyer's white daylight.

And there, in the center of the museum's vaulted corridor, wearing a camel-hair coat and a red scarf, was Emili Travia. Her eyes were bright and she appeared a bit jet-lagged, and it was precisely that touch of exhaustion that made her look more beautiful than ever.

Jonathan hopped off the stool, navigating the crowd as he moved toward her.

The tour group made a circle around them.

"They let tour guides stand on stools here in the Met?" Emili said. "I thought there'd be a liability issue."

Jonathan grinned. "Being the one who decides that has its privileges."

He pointed at his name tag, and Emili read aloud, "Jonathan Marcus, general counsel, Metropolitan Museum of Art."

After a moment Jonathan whispered to her, "I thought you said some things should remain in the ground. Something about lack of proper resources to sustain the excavation."

Emili straightened her back, a playful gesture of authority.

"As director of the International Centre for Conservation in Rome, I can allocate as many resources as an excavation needs." She moved her face closer.

Jonathan hesitated, unexpectedly pulling his head back. "But what about the fragility of our past? In Rome, you told me that history is written in fire. That once it's out . . ." He trailed off.

"I still do think that," Emili said. Jonathan tilted his head warily, but her smile warmed him to the core. "But to keep it aflame, we just need an ember."

Jonathan pulled her close and kissed her. With the sun pouring through the glass roof of the antiquity wing, they embraced as though in a spotlight, and struck exactly the pose of two ancient marble figures behind them, their lips pressed, limbs entwined, and the woman tilted back as though collapsing in his arms.

The crowd erupted with applause.

105

In Piazza San Pietro, General Eilat Segev stepped out of a sedan without diplomatic plates. Her visit was not on any Vatican schedule. This covert meeting reminded her of the times before the Vatican opened diplomatic relations with the state of Israel, fifteen years earlier. A Swiss Guard official escorted her into a grand hall, where Cardinal Ungero Scipiono, the Vatican undersecretary for diplomatic affairs, awaited her. Cardinal Scipiono was middle-aged, bald, and sat in a grand Renaissance chair that dwarfed his small frame.

"General Segev, it is an honor to finally meet you." As was the custom, the undersecretary did not get up. "Thank you for all the work you have done in protecting Christian sites in the Holy Land. I understand your dedication is remarkable." Undersecretary Scipiono spoke with his eyes turned toward the floor. Eilat Segev sensed his discomfort in meeting with a woman individually, but the sensitivity of the topic to be discussed precluded him from sending an administrator.

Segev nodded in gratitude. "Thank you, Your Eminence."

He motioned for Segev to sit down.

"I have sent numerous letters to your office, concerning the rampant destruction beneath the Temple Mount. They have gone unanswered."

The undersecretary was quiet. "As you know, no institution cares to intrude on the jurisdiction of another, General Segev. I'm afraid we will have to complete our own investigation regarding the alleged destruction beneath the Mount before responding."

"Your Eminence, we understand that all subterranean sites beneath the Jewish Ghetto of Rome are still within the Vatican jurisdiction, per the 1943 Concordat. Our archaeologists' permits now have been denied repeatedly to excavate beneath the Porticus Octaviae and the Great Synagogue."

"General"—the undersecretary stood up—"as you know, all subterranean religious sites in Rome are within the sole discretion of the Vatican. Is that all?"

"They are not Christian sites, Your Eminence."

"They are religious sites."

"You will not grant our researchers access beneath the Ghetto's own synagogue?"

"Such exploration would be exceedingly dangerous. Two months ago, the death of Mosè Orvieti, lost in the Tiber, tragically proved that. The subterranean corridors—even if they exist—are available for exploration at low tide only, and even then for short periods of time." Undersecretary Scipiono tugged on his robe's cincture and headed for the door. "There is unlikely anything of value beneath the Ghetto."

Segev stood up as he headed out of the room. "Then why over the last month has your security office installed high-technology surveillance over every manhole in the Ghetto, complete with motion detectors in the furnace room of the Great Synagogue to detect any unauthorized access to the subterranean passages?"

The undersecretary turned around, smiling politely. "You are a determined people, General Segev. You have excavated a national identity for yourselves buried for more than two thousand years." He stopped smiling. In his eyes flashed something dark. "But some things are meant to stay buried."

"We are merely asking for the Vatican's assistance, Your Eminence."

"General, every nation—including the Vatican—understands what it must do to protect its *own* history." With that he turned his back and stepped through a private door.

Once in the anterior room, he turned to an assistant. "Follow her."

A plainclothes Swiss Guard known as a Vatican watcher trailed Segev as she walked across the piazza and down the Via della Conciliazione toward the Tiber. Segev turned the corner into a narrow alley. A half-minute later, the watcher rounded the corner to follow when he collided with a large man carrying a stack of books. The books scattered across the cobblestones. "Oh, my apologies!" the heavyset clergyman said. "Could you give me a hand?" The watcher looked up and it was too late. Segev was gone. The clergyman, Cardinal Francesco Inocenti, walked off, the books back in his arms.

Undersecretary Scipiono flew into a rage when he heard the watcher lost Eilat Segev. A cheerful collision around a corner, a stack of books scattered on the street. It was a countersurveillance tactic older than Methuselah.

"It is a coincidence," one of his assistants said, trying to assuage him.

"It is not a coincidence!" he said. "We are dealing with the Israelis here!"

The undersecretary walked briskly across the hallway of the papal apartments to the Vatican surveillance room, where three Swiss Guard officers sat in front of their respective screens. "Were you able to pick her up on the cameras?" From the surveillance room, the undersecretary could observe every piece of cobble in Vatican City. A young guard nodded, zooming in the cameras of the quadrant, the block, and the square meter where General Segev was shown winding down the serpentine alleyways.

Segev removed a map from her pocket. The one recovered from

Chandler Manning's body. *About one thing,* Segev thought, *the undersecretary and I agree. Sometimes in protecting its own history, a nation must act alone.* It was the reason Segev's team had spent two months planning this operation.

She whispered in Hebrew into her lapel, "I am heading down the steps of the Ponte Vittorio Emanuele."

A voice echoed back, "One minute twenty seconds until you intersect with the team, General."

The undersecretary watched this on the screen. "Why is she speaking into her lapel? Zoom in."

The camera frames zoomed in on Segev. The screen captured her turning a tight corner and walking briskly down a side street. Suddenly the screen went completely black.

"What is that?" the undersecretary screamed. He wheeled around to one of his assistants. "Is that a coincidence?" The young guard frantically flipped buttons, trying to find the technological reason. Just as suddenly, the picture returned.

"It must have been litter in the wind. Perhaps a plastic bag, Your Eminence," said the young guard, his eyes returning to the screen. Eilat Segev was not there. The young guard shook his head. "Excellency, we've lost her."

High above the alleyways, where the camera mysteriously malfunctioned, the nun from the Sisters of Zion Monastery in Jerusalem moved along the roof, reentering the top-floor staff quarters for nuns who run the papal household. She had thrown her shawl over the surveillance camera for a moment, and now rewrapped it around her shoulders. Proudly, she watched Segev from the rooftop, helping her to do something the Church should have done a long time ago.

Segev approached the riverbank. An old fishing boat, a *gozzo*, slowed and an intelligence operative threw a bowline to the shore as Segev stepped on the boat. "When you have a chance, please thank Cardinal Inocenti and the sister for their help. If only all men and women of faith were such friends to us."

Traveling down the Tiber, Segev could see on her right the synagogue in the dusky light. The undersecretary was right; the tide was low enough to explore beneath the Ghetto for only a few hours a day. That was precisely why this operation required two months of preparation. Segev's team had planned to execute the extraction at high tide, rather than low tide, in order to use divers with propellered underwater platforms to move the object through the full pipes of the Cloaca Maxima directly into the river.

Segev walked toward the cabin of the boat.

"What is the progress of the Shayetet?" The Shayetet were the Israeli version of Navy SEALS, Israel's most elite commandos.

"They are through drilling, and the divers are ready to extract the artifact from the bottom of the arch."

As she spoke, Segev stepped into the boat's cabin, which had been converted into a state-of-the-art control room. Flat-screen monitors displayed the progress of three divers drilling beneath the giant underwater arch. "All the logistics are going as planned," a young technician said in Hebrew.

Another man hurried down the metal rungs leading into the control room.

"General," he said, "we have just received word that the Vatican has mobilized their Swiss Guard. They are searching the riverbanks. It will only be minutes before they discover this boat. We must go."

"We are not going anywhere," Segev said. On the screen, she could see underwater sparks from the divers sawing through the bottom of the arch.

"We're inside the arch, General. It's dry in here," said one of the divers. On the screen, Segev watched the diver's helmet light pierce the blackness.

She watched the divers lower the enormous glittering lamp from the bottom of the arch onto the propeller-driven platforms. As carefully rehearsed by these men in dive tanks on an Israeli military base, the lamp's rightmost branch had been fitted with a Lucite orb, pressure-proofed to a hundred meters and custom-fitted to create a continuous flammable atmosphere underwater for up to three minutes. With waterproof silicon, they sealed the orb to the last branch of the menorah. Inside the Lucite, the flame flickered, but continued to burn.

"The fire has been transferred successfully, General."

Within the *gozzo*'s cabin, all activity ceased and the technicians gathered behind Segev to watch history being made. Segev touched the screen. *That flame has been guarded for over two thousand years.* In the blue-black water she could see the shadowy contours of the menorah's seven golden branches being lowered onto the underwater vehicle specially crafted for this extraction, a vehicle just wide enough for its propellers to navigate the pipes leading into the Tiber.

Segev knew this was the only operation she would ever run where the commandos were selected not only for their operational skills, but their kohenite lineage.

"Is Orvieti there?" Segev said.

"His body is right here, General. It was in the chamber, lying right beside the menorah," said another diver into his headset. "We cannot put Orvieti's body on the propeller platform. It is too much weight."

But Eilat Segev was a military woman at heart and the Israeli Defense Force's reverence for the remains of the fallen was unparalleled.

"Then carry him," Segev said, "but do not leave him behind."

"General," a technician in the control room said, "we must leave the body. We have only another two minutes for the flame to survive in the Lucite case."

"Work faster," Segev said into the microphone. "Mosè Orvieti traced his lineage back to the slaves of Titus. His ancestors have been in Rome since Jerusalem was sacked two thousand years ago. We're not leaving him behind."

The loud sound of gearshifts filled the control room. A portion of the hull had been refitted with a large hatch that now opened beneath the boat, allowing the divers to enter invisibly from the depths of the Tiber. Everyone in the control room fell silent, gathering around the open hatch. The lights lining the underwater hatch reflected off the menorah's golden surface with the incandescence of a rising sun. Segev knew that no one other than she and her team would ever know of this operation.

Beneath the surface of the water lapping inside the hull, she saw the limp frame of Mosè Orvieti being carried by two divers, as well as the enormous gleaming artifact beside him.

"Two thousand years you both have been in exile," she whispered.

Segev's eyes glanced at Mosè Orvieti's body and then focused back to the menorah's last branch, its flame glowing inside the Lucite orb as it rose out of the Tiber's blackness. The menorah's sheer scale became visible as its massive golden branches broke through the water's surface.

"And it's time we brought both of you home."

ACKNOWLEDGMENTS

In antiquity, the *editor* of gladiatorial matches often decided the combatants' fates. I am grateful that my editor, Jake Morrissey at Riverhead, proved more merciful than his ancient counterparts, and assisted me in giving this project life.

And let me rush to thank my father, Dr. Sheldon Levin, for his love of history and my mother, Lynda Levin, for her love of story. Their respective passions are reflected on every page.

I am also enormously indebted to Suzanne Gluck and Erin Malone of the William Morris Agency for believing in this project from the start. Also at William Morris, thank you to Tracy Fisher and Raffaella De Angelis, Sarah Ceglarski, Eliza Chamblin, and Liz Tingue. At Riverhead a talented core group—Sarah Bowlin, David Koral, Jane Herman, Muriel Jorgensen, Nicole LaRoche, Lisa Amoroso, and designer Roberto de Vicq de Cumptich—enhanced the project at every turn.

With sadness, I also acknowledge Angelo Pavoncello, on whom the character Mosè Orvieti is—fortunately—only partly based. Angelo died during the writing of this novel, and I treasure the wisdom he imparted during our strolls through (and beneath) the Ghetto.

My gratitude also to Director Carmela Vircillo Franklin for her hospitality during my stay at the American Academy in Rome; to the Academy's assistant librarian, Denise Gavio; to David Petrain, Rome Prize winner in Ancient Studies; and to all the other fellows and staff who welcomed me as one of their own.

Thank you as well to Israeli archaeologist Eilat Mazar; Professor Elisa

Debenetti, for use of her photographs of Giuseppe Valadier's nineteenth-century sketches; fearless Domus Aurea expert Simona O'Higgins; Generale Giovanni Nisti's staff at the Comando della Tutela del Patrimonio Culturale; and a member of the Waqf Authority who guided me around the Temple Mount with integrity, despite his fear of possible consequences.

And for their inspiration and support, I would like to acknowledge Matthew Pearl; Ezra Stark; Joshua and Andrea Leibowitz; Alessandro Di Gioacchino; Sol Comet and Muriel Cohen; Ted Comet; Clement Roberts; Scott Weinger; gladiator Bob Stark; Sasson Marcus; Brett Spodak; Oshrit Raffeld; Marla Stark; Caryl Englander, for whom the impossible just takes longer; and whether he likes being mentioned or not, *mayn shver*.

And most of all, thank you to my wife, Laura Levin—painter and physician. I cannot fully express my gratitude for her tireless dedication, her keen editing eye, her courage, and most important, her faith in me. A biblical proverb says that a house rests on the wisdom of the wife. So does this novel.

Daniel Levin earned his bachelor's degree in Roman and Greek civilization from the University of Michigan and is a graduate of Harvard Law School. He was a visiting scholar at the American Academy in Rome and has practiced international law in New York. He lives in New York City.